Though Cornwell now lives in Boston, she was born in Miami and grew up in Montreat, North Carolina. After earning her degree in English from Davidson College in 1979, she began working at the *Charlotte Observer*, taking whatever stories came her way and rapidly advancing from listing television programs to covering the police beat. Cornwell received widespread attention and praise for her series of articles on prostitution and crime in downtown Charlotte. From the *Charlotte Observer*, Cornwell moved to a job with the Office of the Chief Medical Examiner of Virginia — a post she would later bestow upon the fictional Kay Scarpetta, the primary focus of many of her novels. When not writing from her Boston Home, Patricia tirelessly researches cutting-edge forensic technologies to include in her work. Her interests span outside the literary: Patricia co-founded the National Forensic Academy and created a Chair in Organic Science at Harvard. She appears as a forensic consultant on CNN and serves as a member of Harvard-affiliated McLean Hospital's National Council, where she advocates for psychiatric research.

DUST

After working on one of the worst mass killings in US history, Chief Medical Examiner Kay Scarpetta returns home to recover, only to receive an unsettling call-out. The body of a young woman has been discovered inside the sheltered gates of MIT, draped in an unusual cloth and posed in a way that is too deliberate to be the killer's first strike. A preliminary examination reveals that the corpse is covered in a fine dust that, under ultraviolet light, fluoresces blood-red, emerald-green and bluish-purple. As Scarpetta pieces together the fragments of evidence, she and her team are drawn deeper into the dark world of designer drugs, drone technology, organised crime, and shocking corruption at the highest level.

PATRICIA CORNWELL

DUST

Complete and Unabridged

CHARNWOOD
Leicester

First published in Great Britain in 2013 by
Little, Brown
an imprint of
Little, Brown Book Group
London

First Charnwood Edition
published 2014
by arrangement with
Little, Brown Book Group
An Hachette UK Company
London

A catalogue record for this book is available
from the British Library.

ISBN 978–1–4448–2100–0

AS ALWAYS — TO STACI
(you are the best of everything)

I will show you fear in a handful of dust.

T. S. ELIOT, *The Waste Land*, 1922

1

CAMBRIDGE, MASSACHUSETTS
WEDNESDAY, DECEMBER 19
4:02 A.M.

The clangor of the phone violates the relentless roll of rain beating the roof like drumsticks. I sit straight up in bed, my heart leaping in my chest like a startled squirrel as I glance at the illuminated display to see who it is.

'What's up?' There is nothing in my voice when I greet Pete Marino. 'It can't be good at this hour.'

My rescued greyhound Sock presses closer to me and I place my hand on his head to calm him. Switching on a lamp, I retrieve a pad of call sheets and a pen from a drawer as Marino starts in about a dead body discovered several miles from here at the Massachusetts Institute of Technology, MIT.

'Out in the mud at one end of the athletic fields, what's called Briggs Field. She was found about thirty minutes ago,' he says. 'I'm on my way to where she probably disappeared from, then heading to the scene. It's being secured until you get there.' Marino's big voice is the same as if nothing has happened between us.

I almost can't believe it.

'I'm not sure why you're calling me.' He shouldn't but I know his reason. 'Technically,

I'm not back to work. Technically, I'm still out sick.' I sound polite enough and calm, just a little hoarse. 'You'd be better off calling Luke or . . . '

'You're going to want to take care of this one, Doc. It's going to be a PR nightmare and you sure as hell don't need another one.'

He's wasted no time alluding to my weekend in Connecticut that was all over the news and I'm not going to discuss it with him. He's calling me because he can and he'll probe where he wants and do as he wishes to make sure I know that after a decade of taking orders from me the roles suddenly are reversed. He's in charge. I'm not. That's the world according to Pete Marino.

'Whose PR nightmare? And PR's not my job,' I add.

'A dead body on the MIT campus is everybody's nightmare. I've got a bad feeling about this. I would have gone with you if you'd asked. You shouldn't have gone by yourself.' He's talking about Connecticut again and I pretend I don't hear it. 'Really, you should have asked me.'

'You don't work for me anymore. That's why I didn't ask.' It's as much as I'm going to say to him.

'I'm sorry about what it must have put you through.'

'I'm sorry about what it put the entire world through.' I cough several times and reach for water. 'Do we have an ID?' I rearrange pillows behind me, Sock's narrow head finding my thigh.

'Possibly a twenty-two-year-old grad student named Gail Shipton.'

2

'A grad student where?'

'MIT computer engineering. Reported missing around midnight, last seen at the Psi Bar.'

My niece's favorite hangout. The thought disconcerts me. The bar is located near MIT and caters to artists, physicists, and computer wizards like Lucy. Now and then she and her partner Janet take me there for Sunday brunch.

'I'm familiar with the place' is all I offer this man who has abandoned me and I know I'm better off.

If only it felt like it.

'Apparently Gail Shipton was there late yesterday afternoon with a girlfriend who claims that at around five-thirty Gail's phone rang. She went outside so she could hear better and never came back. You shouldn't have gone to Connecticut alone. At least I could have driven you,' Marino says, and he's not going to ask how I'm doing after what he's caused by walking off the job so he could start over.

He's a cop again. He sounds happy. The hell with how I feel about the way he did it. All he wants to know about is Connecticut. It's what everyone wants to know about and I didn't give a single interview and it's not the sort of thing to talk about. I wish to hell he hadn't brought it up. It's like something hideous I'd filed in a back drawer and now it's in front of me again.

'The friend didn't think it was unusual or reason for concern that this person she was with went out to talk on the phone and never came back?' I'm on autopilot, able to do my job while I try not to care about Marino anymore.

3

'All I know is when Gail quit answering her phone or texts, the girlfriend got worried something bad happened.' Already he's on a first-name basis with this missing woman who may be dead.

Already they've bonded. He's sunk his hooks into the case and he's not about to let go.

'Then when it got to be midnight and still no word she started trying to find her,' he says. 'The friend's name is Haley Swanson.'

'What else do you know about Haley Swanson and what do you mean by *girlfriend*?'

'It was a very preliminary call.' What he's really saying is he doesn't know much at all because what Haley Swanson reported likely wasn't taken very seriously at the time.

'Does it bother you that she wasn't worried earlier?' I ask. 'If Gail was last seen at five-thirty, some six or seven hours passed before her girlfriend called the police.'

'You know how the students are around here. Drinking, they go off with someone, they don't keep track or notice shit.'

'Was Gail the type to go off with someone?'

'I got a lot of questions to ask if it turns out the way I suspect it will.'

'It sounds like we don't know a whole hell of a lot.' Even as I say it I know I shouldn't.

'I didn't talk to Haley Swanson very long.' He's starting to sound defensive. 'We don't officially take missing-person reports by phone.'

'Then how is it you talked to her?'

'First she called nine-one-one and was told to come to the department and fill out a report,

4

and that's standard. You come in and do it in person.' He's gotten loud enough that I have to turn the volume down on my phone. 'Then she calls back a little later and asks for me by name. I talked to her for a few minutes but didn't take her all that seriously. If she was so worried, come fill out the report ASAP. We're open twenty-four-seven.'

Marino's been with the Cambridge police but a few weeks and it strikes me as almost unbelievable that a stranger would request him by name. Instantly I'm suspicious of Haley Swanson but it won't do any good to say it. Marino's not going to listen if he thinks I'm trying to tell him how to do his job.

'Did she sound upset?' I ask.

'A lot of people sound upset when they call the police but it doesn't mean what they're saying is true. Ninety-nine times out of a hundred missing students aren't missing. These types of calls aren't exactly uncommon around here.'

'Do we have an address for Gail Shipton?'

'Those really nice condos near the Charles Hotel.' He gives me the details and I write them down.

'Very expensive real estate.' I envision gracious brick buildings close to the Kennedy School of Government and the Charles River, not far from my headquarters as a matter of fact.

'Probably her family's paying the bills, the usual around here in Ivy Leagueville.' Marino is typically snide about the people of Cambridge, where police will give you a ticket for being

5

stupid he likes to say.

'Has anybody checked to see if she might be home and simply isn't answering her phone?' I'm making copious notes, more focused now, distracted by a different tragedy, the latest one.

But as I sit up in bed and talk on the phone it's exactly as it happened and I can't block out what I saw. The bodies and the blood. Brass cartridge cases were bright like pennies scattered over floors inside that red brick elementary school, all of it indelibly vivid as if I'm still there.

Twenty-seven autopsies, most of them children, and when I pulled off my bloody scrubs and stepped into the shower I refused to think about what I'd just done.

I switched channels. I compartmentalized, having learned long years ago not to see destroyed human flesh after I've had my hands in it. I willed the images to stay where I left them at the scene, in the autopsy room and out of my thoughts. Obviously I failed. By the time I got home this past Saturday night I had a fever and ached all over as if something evil had infected me. My usual barriers had been breached. I'd offered my help to Connecticut's Office of the Chief Medical Examiner and no good deed goes unpunished. There's a penalty for trying to do what's right. The dark forces don't like it, and stress will make you sick.

'She claimed she went over to make sure Gail wasn't there,' Marino is saying, 'and then got security to check inside the condo but there was no sign of her or that she'd ever come home from the bar.'

I comment that she must be familiar to people who work at Gail Shipton's apartment building because security wouldn't open up a door for just anyone, and as I'm saying all this my attention drifts to the ridiculous mountain of FedEx packages still unopened by the sofa on the other side of the bedroom. I'm reminded why it's not a good thing if I'm isolated for days and too sick to work or cook or leave the house and afraid to be alone with my thoughts. I will distract myself and I did.

A vintage Harley-Davidson leather riding vest and skull belt buckle are for Marino, and there's Hermes cologne and Jeff Deegan bracelets for Lucy and Janet, and for my husband Benton a titanium watch with a carbon-fiber face that Breguet doesn't make anymore. His birthday is tomorrow, five days before Christmas, and it's very hard to shop for him and there's not much he needs or doesn't have.

There is an abundance of gifts to wrap for my mother and my sister, and for our housekeeper Rosa and members of my staff, and all sorts of things for Sock and also for Lucy's bulldog and my chief of staff's cat. I'm not sure what the hell got into me when I was sick in bed, ordering like mad off the Internet, and I'll blame it on my fever. I'm sure to hear all about the typically sensible and reserved Kay Scarpetta and her wild holiday spending spree. Lucy in particular won't let me live it down.

'Gail's not answering her cell phone, e-mails, texts,' Marino continues as rain slashes the windows, clicking loudly against glass. 'Nothing

7

posted on Facebook, Twitter, or whatever, and her physical description is consistent with the dead lady and that's the bigger point. I'm thinking she might have been abducted, was held somewhere, her body wrapped in a sheet and dumped. I wouldn't bother you under the circumstances but I know how you are.'

He does know how I am and I'm not driving myself to MIT or anywhere, not when I've been in virtual quarantine for the past five days. I tell him that. I'm stubborn and all business with my former lead investigator. Yes, *former*, I think.

'How you feeling? I told you not to get a flu shot. That's probably why you got sick,' he says.

'You can't get sick from a dead virus.'

'Well, the only two times I had a flu shot I came down with the flu, was sick as a damn dog. I'm glad you sound better.' Marino pretends to care because he has a purpose for me.

'I suppose it's all relative. I could be better. I could be worse.'

'In other words, you're pissed at me. We may as well put it on the table.'

'I was talking about my health.'

To say I'm pissed would trivialize what I feel right now. Marino hasn't seemed to consider what his walking off the job might say about me, the chief medical examiner of Massachusetts and director of the Cambridge Forensic Center, the CFC. For the past ten years he's been my head of investigations and suddenly he professionally divorces me. I can imagine what cops in particular will say or already are saying.

I anticipate being doubted at scenes, at my

8

office, in the autopsy room, and on the witness stand. I imagine being second-guessed when in fact none of this is about me. It's all about Marino and a mid-life crisis he's been afflicted with for as long as I've known him. Let's be clear, I would tell the world, if I were indiscreet, that Pete Marino has suffered poor self-esteem and identity confusion since the day he was born to an abusive alcoholic father and weak, submissive mother in a bad part of New Jersey.

I'm a woman out of his reach and the one he punishes, possibly the love of his life and for sure his best friend. His motivation is neither fair nor rational for ringing me up at this hour when he knows I've been home with the flu, so sick that at one point I worried I was dying and it began drifting through my mind, *This is it, what it's like*.

2

During a feverish epiphany I saw the meaning of everything, life the colliding of God particles that make up all matter in the universe and death the absolute reverse of it. When I spiked a tempera-ture of 103.8 it became even clearer, explained simply and eloquently by the hooded man at the foot of my bed.

If only I'd written down what he said, the elusive formula for nature giving mass and death taking it away, all of creation since the Big Bang measured by the products of decay. Rust, dirt, sickness, insanity, chaos, corruption, lies, rot, ruin, shed cells, dead cells, atrophy, stenches, sweat, waste, dust to dust, that at a subatomic level interact and create new mass, and this goes on infinitely. I couldn't see his face but I know it was compelling and kind as he spoke to me scientifically, poetically, backlit by fire that gave off no heat.

During moments of astonishing clarity I realized what we mean when we talk of forbidden fruit and original sin, and walking into the light and streets paved in gold, of extraterrestrials, auras, ghosts, and paradise and hell and reincarnation, of being healed or raised from the dead, of coming back as a raven, a cat, a hunchback, an angel. A recycling crystalline in its precision and prismatic beauty was revealed to me. The plan of God the Supreme Physicist, who is merciful, just, and funny. Who is creative. Who is all of us.

I saw and I knew. I possessed perfect Truth. Then life reasserted itself, pulled Truth right out from under me, and I'm still here, held down by gravity. An amnesiac. I can't recall or share what at last I could explain to devastated people after I've taken care of their dead. I'm clinical at best when I answer the questions they ask, always the same ones.

Why? Why? Why!

How could someone do something like this?

I've never had a good explanation. But there is one and I knew it fleetingly. What I've always wanted to say was on the tip of my tongue, then I came to and what I knew was replaced by the job I'd just done. The unthinkable images no one should ever see. Blood and brass in a hallway lined with bulletin boards decorated for the holidays. And then inside that classroom. The children I couldn't save. The parents I couldn't comfort. The reassurances I couldn't give.

Did they suffer?

How quick would it have been?

It's the flu doing this, I tell myself. There's nothing I haven't seen and can't deal with and I feel the anger stir, the sleeping dragon within.

'Trust me, you don't want anybody else taking care of this. There can't be even one damn thing that gets screwed up,' Marino perseverates and if I'm honest with myself, I'm glad to hear his voice.

I don't want to miss his company the way I just did. There was no one else I would take to a

11

frenzied media carnival on a scale that was incomprehensible, the streets overwhelmed for miles by TV vans, production trucks, and pole-mounted satellites, the thudding of helicopters incessant, as if a movie were being filmed.

Were the shots close range?

The anger again and I can't afford to rouse it, the dragon within. It was better Marino wasn't with me. I just didn't feel like it. I know what he can handle and he would have blown apart like glass shattered by vibrations too intense to hear.

'All I can tell you is I got a gut about it, Doc,' his familiar voice says but he sounds different, stronger and more sure of himself. 'Some sick fuck out there just getting started. Maybe got the idea from what just happened.'

'From what happened in Newtown, Connecticut?' I don't see how he can possibly leap to such a conclusion and he needs to stop bringing it up.

'That's the way it works,' he says. 'One sick fuck gets the idea from some other sick fuck who shoots up a movie theater or a school for attention.'

★　★　★

I imagine him driving the dark streets of Cambridge in this weather. No doubt he doesn't have his seat belt on and it will be a waste of breath for me to tell him now that he's a cop again. How quickly he returns to his old bad habits.

'She wasn't shot, was she?' I ask him pointedly to derail an inappropriate and awful subject.

12

'You're not even sure she's a homicide, isn't that right?'

'It doesn't appear she was shot,' Marino verifies.

'Let's not confuse things by comparing it to what just happened in Connecticut.'

'I'm sick and tired of assholes getting rewarded by the media.'

'Aren't we all?'

'It makes it worse and more likely to happen again. We shouldn't release their names and should bury them in a damn unmarked grave.'

'Let's stick with the case at hand. Do we know if she has obvious injuries?'

'Nothing at a glance,' he says. 'But she sure as hell didn't wrap herself up in a sheet and walk out there on her own two bare feet and lay down and die in the rain and mud.'

Marino's bypassing my deputy chief medical examiner, Luke Zenner, or any of my forensic pathologists at the CFC isn't about my being the most qualified even though I am. It's about Marino stepping back into his earlier life so he can be who he was when we first met. He no longer works for me. He gets to summon me on command. That's the way he figures things and he'll remind me as often as he can.

'I mean, if you really don't feel up to it . . . ' he starts to say and it sounds like a challenge or maybe he's goading me.

I don't know. How can I judge anything right now? I'm worn-out and famished. I can't stop thinking about boiled eggs with butter and coarsely ground peppercorns, and hot fresh baked bread and espresso. I would kill for a chilled glass of freshly squeezed blood orange juice.

'No, no, the worst is past.' I reach for the bottle of water on the nightstand. 'Let me get myself together here.' I don't move beyond taking a big swallow, the thirst no longer unquenchable, my lips and tongue no longer as dry as paper. 'I had cough syrup before I went to bed. Codeine.'

'Lucky you.'

'I'm a little groggy but fine. It's not a good idea for me to drive, certainly not in this weather. Who found her?'

Maybe he already told me that. I press the back of my hand to my forehead. No fever. I'm sure it really is gone, not just Advil suppressing it.

'A girl from MIT, a guy from Harvard, out on a date and decided to find a little privacy in her dorm room. You know Simmons Hall? That huge building that looks like it was built out of LEGOs on the other side of the MIT baseball and rugby fields,' Marino says.

I can tell he has a police scanner with the squelch turned up loud. In his element, I'm sure. Armed and dangerous with a detective's badge on his belt, driving an unmarked police vehicle equipped with lights and a siren and God knows what else. In the old days when he was a cop, he used to trick out his police vehicles like he does his Harleys.

'They noticed what they thought at first was a manikin in a toga lying in the mud at the far end of the field inside the fence that separates it from

14

a parking lot,' says the Marino from my past, Marino the detective. 'So they walked inside an open gate to get a closer look and when they realized it was a female wrapped in a sheet with nothing on under it and that she wasn't breathing they called nine-one-one.'

'The body is nude?' What I'm really asking is if it's been disturbed and by whom.

'They claim they didn't touch it. The sheet's soaking wet and I think it's pretty obvious she's naked. Machado talked to them and says he's confident they've got nothing to do with whatever happened to her but we'll swab them for DNA, do backgrounds, the whole nine yards.'

He goes on to say that Cambridge detective Sil Machado suspects the woman is a drug overdose. 'Which may be related to the weird-ass suicide from the other day,' Marino adds. 'As you know there's some bad stuff on the streets and it's causing huge problems around here.'

'Which suicide?' Unfortunately there have been a number of them while I was out of town and ill.

'The fashion-designer lady who jumped off the roof of her Cambridge apartment building and splattered the plate-glass windows of the first-floor health club while people were inside working out,' he says. 'It looked like a spaghetti bomb went off. Anyway, they're thinking it could be related.'

'I don't know why.'

'They think it could be drugs, some bad shit she got into.'

'Who's *they*?' I didn't work the suicide of course and I reach down for the stacks of cases

15

on the floor by the bed.

'Machado. Also his sergeant, his lieutenant,' Marino says. 'It's gone straight up the chain to the superintendents and the commissioner.'

I set files on the bed, what must be at least a dozen folders, printouts of death reports and photographs my chief of staff Bryce Clark has been leaving on the sunporch for me daily, along with provisions he's been kind enough to pick up.

'The concern is it could be the same really bad meth or designer-type shit — in other words, some latest version of bath salts that's been hitting the streets around here. Maybe what the suicide lady was on,' Marino tells me. 'One theory is that Gail Shipton, if it's her who's dead, was with someone doing some really bad drugs and she ODed so he dumped her body.'

'This is your theory?'

'Hell no. If you're dumping a body why do it in a damn university playing field like you're displaying it to shock people? That's my point, the biggest threat we've got to watch for these days. Do something sensational enough and it will be all over the news and get the attention of the president of the United States. I think whoever dumped her body at Briggs Field is a bird of that kind of feather. He's doing it for attention, to be headline news.'

'That could be part of it but probably not all of it.'

'I'm texting you a few photos that Machado texted me.' Marino's deep voice continues in my ear, a rough voice, a rude, pushy voice.

16

'You shouldn't text while you drive.' I reach for my iPad.

'Yeah, so I'll write myself a ticket.'

'Any drag marks or other indications of how the body ended up where it is?'

'You can see in the photos it's real muddy and unfortunately any drag marks or footprints probably got mostly washed out by the rain. But I haven't been there yet and looked for myself.'

I open the photographs he just e-mailed and note the soaked grass and red mud inside Briggs Field's fence, then I zoom in closer on the dead woman wrapped in white. Slender, flat on her back, her long wet brown hair neatly arranged around a young pretty face that is tilted slightly to the left and glazed with rain. The cloth is wound around her upper chest like a bath sheet, like the big towels people wrap up in while they're lounging at a spa.

Recognition stirs, and then I'm startled by the similarity to what Benton sent me several weeks ago when he took a considerable risk. Without authorization from the FBI he asked my opinion about the murders he's working in Washington, D.C. But those women had plastic bags over their heads and this one doesn't. They had designer duct tape around their necks and a bow attached, and that's a pattern unique to the killer and it's absent here.

We don't even know that she's a homicide, I remind myself, and I shouldn't be surprised if she died suddenly and a panicky companion wrapped her in a bedsheet, perhaps one from a dormitory, before leaving her outside, where

17

she'd be found quickly.

'I suspect someone pulled their car into the parking lot close to the fence, opened the gate, and dragged or carried her in,' Marino continues as I stare at the image on my iPad, disturbed by it on a level that's out of reach, a deeply intuitive place, and I try to reason away what I'm feeling but I can't, and I can't say a word about it to him.

Benton would be fired if the FBI knew what he's done, sharing classified information with his wife. It doesn't matter that I'm an expert whose jurisdiction includes federal cases and it would have made sense for me to be consulted anyway. Usually I am but for some reason I wasn't. His boss, Ed Granby, has little use for me and would take delight in stripping Benton of his credentials and sending him packing.

'That one gate wasn't locked,' Marino says. 'The couple that found her said it was shut when they got to it but not locked. The rest of the gates are secured with chains and padlocks so nobody can get in after hours. Whoever's responsible either knew that one wasn't locked or used bolt cutters or had a key.'

'The body's been deliberately posed.' The phantom pain of a chronic headache makes my head feel heavy. 'On her back, legs together and straight, one arm gracefully resting on her belly, the other extended, the wrist bent dramatically like a dancer or as if she passed out on a fainting couch. Nothing is disarrayed, the sheet carefully arranged around her. Actually, I'm not sure it's a sheet.'

I zoom in as close as I can before the image begins to deconstruct.

'It's a white cloth at any rate. Her positioning is ritualistic, symbolic.' I'm sure of it, and the flutter in my stomach is fear.

What if it's the same thing? What if he's here? I remind myself that the D.C. cases are fresh on my mind because they're why Benton isn't home right now and it wasn't that long ago when I went through the scene photographs and autopsy and lab reports. A body wrapped in a white cloth and positioned modestly and rather languidly by no means suggests this case is connected to the other ones, I tell myself repeatedly.

'She was left like that on purpose,' Marino is saying, 'because it means something to the sick asshole who did it.'

'How could anyone get the body out there without being seen?' I focus my attention where it belongs. 'On a playing field in the heart of MIT apartment buildings and dorms? Start with the idea that we may be dealing with someone familiar with the area, possibly another student, an employee, a person who lives or works around there.'

'Where she was dumped isn't lit up at night,' he says. 'Behind the indoor tennis courts, you know the big white bubble, then the athletic fields. I'll pick you up in thirty, forty minutes. Pulling up to the Psi Bar now. Closed of course. No sign of anyone, no lights on. I'll take a look around outside where she might have been using her phone, then head over to your house.'

'You're alone,' I assume.

'Ten-four.'

'Be careful, please.'

⋆   ⋆   ⋆

I sit up in bed and sort through files inside the master suite of our nineteenth-century home that was built by a well-known transcendentalist. I start with the suicide Marino mentioned. Three days ago, on Sunday, December 16, twenty-six-year-old Sakura Yamagata stepped off the roof of her nineteen-story Cambridge apartment building, and her cause of death is what I'd expect in such a violent event. Multiple blunt-force traumatic injuries, her brain avulsed from the cranial cavity. Her heart, liver, spleen, and lungs lacerated. The bones of her face, her ribs, arms, legs, and pelvis extensively fractured.

I sort through 8-by-10 scene photographs that include shocked people gawking, many of them in gym clothes and hugging themselves against the cold, and a distinguished gray-haired man in a suit and tie who looks defeated and dazed. In one of the photographs he's next to Marino, who's pointing and talking, and in another the gray-haired man is crouched by the body, his head bent and tragic and with the same utterly defeated look on his face.

It's obvious he had a relationship with Sakura Yamagata, and I imagine the frightened reaction of people using the fitness center on the first floor, looking out at the exact moment her body struck. It thudded hard, like a heavy sandbag, as one witness described it in a news report

20

included in the case file. Tissue and blood spattered the plate-glass windows, teeth and fragmented parts scattered as far as fifty feet from the site of impact. Her head and face were damaged beyond visual recognition.

I associate such severely mutilating deaths with psychosis or the influence of drugs, and as I skim through the pages of the detailed police report, I'm struck by how strange it feels to see Marino's name and ID number on it.

Reporting Officer, Marino, P. R. (D33).

I haven't seen a police narrative written by him since he left Richmond PD a decade ago, and I read his description of what occurred this past Sunday afternoon at a Cambridge luxury high-rise on Memorial Drive.

. . . I responded to the above address after the incident had occurred, and I interviewed Dr. Franz Schoenberg. He informed me he is a psychiatrist with a practice in Cambridge and that Sakura Yamagata, a fashion designer, was a patient of his. On the day of the incident at 1556 hours, she texted him, indicating her intention to 'fly to Paris' from the roof of her apartment building.

At approximately 1618 hours Dr. Schoenberg arrived at her address and was escorted to the roof area through a rear door. He stated to me that he observed her nude and standing on the other side of a low rail on the ledge, her back to him, her arms spread wide. He called to her once, saying, 'Suki, I'm here. Everything is going to be all right.'

21

He stated that she did not answer or make any indication she heard him. She immediately fell forward in what he described as a swan dive that was intentional . . .

Luke Zenner performed her autopsy and submitted the appropriate tissues and fluids to the toxicology lab. Heart, lung, liver, pancreas, blood . . .

I stroke Sock's lean brindle body, feeling his ribs gently rise and fall as he breathes, and I'm suddenly exhausted again as if talking to Marino took everything I've got. Struggling to stay awake, I skim through the photographs again, looking for ones with the gray-haired man who I suspect is Dr. Franz Schoenberg. That's why the police allowed him near the body. That's why he's next to Marino, and I can't imagine watching your patient jump off a roof. How does anyone ever get over that? I search my thoughts as they fade in and out, wondering if I might have met the psychiatrist somewhere.

You don't get over it, I think. *Some things you won't get over, not ever, you can't . . .*

Bad drugs, I recall what Marino just suggested to me. Designer ones, bath salts that have hit Massachusetts hard this past year, and we've had a number of bizarre suicides and accidents relating to them. There have been homicides and property crimes, an alarming increase in general, especially in the Boston area where there are Section 8 housing developments or what the police call the projects. People dealing drugs, gang members get a nice roof over their heads for a bargain, and they bring down the neighborhood and cause damage all around them. I go through my mental list of what needs to be done as I log on to my office e-mail. I notify toxicology to put a rush on the analysis in the Sakura Yamagata case and screen for designer stimulants.

Mephedrone, methylenedioxypyrovalerone or MDPV, and methylone. Luke didn't think to include hallucinogens and we should test for those, too. LSD, methylergometrine, ergotamine . . .

My thoughts drift and focus.

Ergot alkaloids can cause ergotism also known as ergotoxicosis or Saint Anthony's Fire, with symptoms resembling bewitchment that some believe may have led to the Salem witchcraft trials. Convulsions, spasms, mania, psychosis . . .

My vision blurs and clears, my head nods and jerks up as rain splashes the roof and windows. I should have told Marino to ensure someone makes a tent out of a waterproof tarp or plasticized sheets to protect the body from the weather, from the eyes of the curious. To protect me, too. I don't need to be out in the elements, getting soaked, chilled, filmed by the media . . .

Television and production trucks were everywhere, and we made sure all of the blinds were drawn. Dark brown carpet. Thick slicks of dark coagulated blood that I could smell as it began to decompose. Sticky on the bottom of my shoes as I moved around inside that room. There was so much blood and I tried so hard not to step in it, to work the crime scene properly. As if it mattered.

But there is no one to punish and no punishment would be enough. And I sit quietly

23

propped up against pillows, the anger tucked in its dark place, perfectly still, looking out with citrine eyes. I see its mighty shape and feel its weight on the foot of my bed.

Marino will have made sure the body is protected.

The anger shifts heavily. The sound and rhythm of the downpour change from fortissimo to pianissimo . . .

Marino knows what he's doing.

Fugue from adagio to furioso . . .

3

TEN YEARS EARLIER
RICHMOND, VIRGINIA

A heavy rain splashes the driveway, flooding granite pavers and thrashing trees, the summer storm beating up an angry sky over a city I'm leaving.

I cut off a strip of packing tape, sweating inside my garage, slightly disinhibited, a little weird from alcohol. Richmond Police Detective Pete Marino is trying to get me drunk, to defeat me when I'm weak.

Maybe I should have sex with you and get it over with.

Marking boxes with a Sharpie, I designate areas of my Richmond home, the one I built of reclaimed wood and stone, what was supposed to be a dream meant to last: 'living room, master bath, guestroom, kitchen, pantry, laundry room, office . . . ' Anything to make it easier on the other side, having no idea what the other side will be ultimately.

'God I hate moving.' I run the tape dispenser over a box and it sounds like cloth ripping.

'Then why the hell do it all the time?' Marino flirts aggressively, and right now I let him.

'All the time?' I laugh out loud at his ridiculousness.

'And in the same damn city. One neighborhood to the next.' He shrugs, oblivious to what's really

25

going on with both of us. 'Who can keep track?'

'I don't move without good reason.' I sound like a lawyer.

I am a lawyer. A doctor. A chief.

'Run, run as fast as you can.' Marino's bloodshot eyes pin me to his emotional board.

I'm a butterfly. A red spotted purple. A tiger swallowtail. A luna moth.

If I let you, you'll knock the color off my wings. I'll be a trophy you no longer want. Be my friend. Why isn't that enough?

I secure another lid to another box, comforted by the downpour outside my open garage door, a mist blowing in, one hundred percent humidity, steamy, dripping. Like a deep hot bath. Like being in the womb. Like a warm body folded into mine, an exchange of warm fluids over skin and deep inside sad lonely places. I need heat and moisture to hug me, to hold me close like my damp clothes clinging as Marino stares from his folding chair, in cut-off sweatpants and a tank top, his big face flushed from lust, wantonness, and beer.

I wonder about the next overbearing detective I'll have to deal with and I don't want whoever it is. Someone I have to train and put up with, and respect and loathe and get tired of and lonely for and love in my own way. It could be a woman, I remind myself. Some tough female investigator who assumes she'll be partners in crime with the new chief medical examiner, assumes who knows what.

I imagine a wolfish woman detective showing up at every death scene and autopsy, appearing in my office and roaring up in her truck or on her motorcycle the way Marino does. A big tattooed suntanned woman in sleeveless denim and a do-rag who wants to eat me to the bone.

I'm being irrational and unfair, bigoted and ignorant. Lucy isn't competitive and controlling with the women she wants. She doesn't have tattoos or a do-rag. She isn't like that. She doesn't need to be a predator to get what she wants.

I can't stand these obsessive, intrusive thoughts. What has happened?

Grief grabs the hollow organs of my belly and chest until I almost can't breathe. I'm overwhelmed by what I'm about to leave, which isn't really this house or Richmond or Virginia. Benton is gone, murdered five years ago. But as long as I stay right here I feel him in these rooms, on the roads I drive, on stultifying summer days and the raw, bleak ones of winter, as if he's watching me, is aware of me and every nuance of my being.

I sense him in shifts of air and scents and feel him in shadows that become my moods as a voice from somewhere out of reach says he isn't dead. Is returning. A nightmare that isn't real. I'll wake up and he'll be right here, his hazel eyes locked on mine, his long tapered fingers touching me. I'll feel his warmth, his skin, and the perfect shape of his muscles and bones, so recognizable as he holds me, and I'll be as alive as I've ever been.

Then I won't have to move to some existential dead place where more pieces of me will wither inch by inch, cell by cell, and I envision dense woods beyond my property and the canal and

27

railroad tracks. Down the embankment is a rocky stretch of the James River, a timeless part of the city at the back of Lockgreen, a gated enclave of contemporary homes lived in by those with money who covet privacy and security.

Neighbors I almost never see. Privileged people who never question me about the latest tragedies on my stainless-steel tables. I'm an Italian from Miami, an outsider. The old guard of Richmond's West End doesn't know what to make of me. They don't wave. They don't stop to say hello. They eye my house as if it's haunted.

I have walked my streets alone, emerging from the woods at the canal and rusty railroad tracks and wide shallow rocky water, imagining the Civil War and centuries before that the colony farther downriver in Jamestown, the first permanent English settlement. Surrounded by death, I've been soothed by the past being present, by beginnings that never end, by my belief that there are reasons and purposes for whatever happens and all of it turns out for the best.

How could everything come to this?

I tape up another box and feel Benton's death, a clammy breath at the back of my neck as humid air stirs. I'm empty, unbearably bereft by the void. I'm grateful for the rain, for the heavy full sound of it.

'You look like you're about to cry.' Marino stares at me. 'Why are you crying?'

'Sweat's stinging my eyes. It's hot as hell in here.'

'You could shut the damn door and turn on the air.'

'I want to hear the rain.'

'What for?'

'I'll never hear it again in this place like it is right now.'

'Jesus. Rain is rain.' He looks out the open garage door as if the rain might be unusual, a type of rain he's not seen before. He frowns the way he does when he's thinking hard, his tan forehead furrowed as he sucks in his lower lip and rubs his heavy jaw.

He's rugged and formidable, huge and exudes aggression, almost handsome before his bad habits got the best of him early in his hard-bitten life. His dark hair is graying and slicked to one side in a comb-over he won't acknowledge any more than he'll admit he's balding prematurely. He's over six feet tall, broad and big-boned, and when his arms and legs are bare like they are right now I'm reminded he's a former Golden Gloves boxer who doesn't need a gun to kill someone.

'I don't know why the hell you had to offer to resign.' He stares boldly at me without blinking. 'Only to hang around for the better part of a year to buy the assholes time to find your replacement. That was stupid. You shouldn't have offered a damn thing. Fuck 'em.'

'Let's be honest, I was fired. That's how it translates when you volunteer to step down because you've embarrassed the governor.' I'm calmer now, reciting the same old lines.

'It's not the first time you've pissed off the governor.'

'It probably won't be the last.'

'Because you don't know when to quit.'

'I believe I just did.'

He watches my every move as if I'm a suspect who might go for a weapon and I continue labeling boxes as if they're evidence: 'Scarpetta,' today's date, belongings destined for the 'master closet' in a South Florida rental house where I don't want to be, what feels like an apocalyptic defeat returning me to the land of my birth.

To go back to where I'm from is the ultimate failure, a judgment proving I'm no better than my upbringing, no better than my self-absorbed mother and narcissistic male-addicted only sibling Dorothy, who's guilty of criminally neglecting her only child Lucy.

'What's the longest you ever stayed anywhere?' Marino relentlessly interrogates me, his attention trespassing in places he's never been allowed to touch or enter.

He feels encouraged and it's my fault, drinking with him, saying good-bye in a way that sounds like 'Hello, don't leave me.' He senses what I'm considering.

If I let you maybe it won't be so important anymore.

'Miami, I suppose,' I answer him. 'Until I was sixteen and left for Cornell.'

'Sixteen. One of these genius types, you and Lucy cut out of the same cloth.' His bloodshot eyes are fastened to me, nothing subtle about it. 'I've been in Richmond that long and it's time to move on.'

I tape up another box, this one marked *Confidential*, packed with autopsy reports, case studies, secrets I need to keep as his imagination

30

undresses me. Or maybe he's simply assessing because he worries I'm slightly crazy, have been made a little unhinged by what's happened to my stellar career.

Dr. Kay Scarpetta, the first woman to be appointed chief medical examiner of Virginia, now has the distinction of being the first one forced out of office . . . If I hear that one more goddamned time on the goddamned news . . .

'I'm quitting the police department,' he says.

I don't act surprised. I don't act like anything at all.

'You know why, Doc. You're expecting it. This is exactly what you want. Why are you crying? It's not sweat. You're crying. What's the matter, huh? You'd be pissed if I didn't quit and head out of Dodge with you, admit it. Hey. It's okay,' he says kindly, sweetly, misinterpreting as usual, and the effect on me is a dangerous comfort. 'You're stuck with me.' He says what I want to be true but not the way he means it, and we continue our languages, neither of us speaking the same one.

He shakes two cigarettes from a pack and gets up from his chair to give me one, his arm touching me as he holds the lighter close. A spurt of flame and he moves the lighter away, the back of his hand touching me. I don't move. I take a deep drag.

'So much for quitting.' I mean smoking.

I don't mean so much for quitting the Richmond Police Department. He'll quit and I shouldn't want him to and I don't have to be a psychic to predict the outcome, the aftermath.

31

It's only a matter of time before he's angry, depressed, emasculated. He'll get increasingly frustrated, jealous, and out of control. One day he'll pay me back. He'll hurt me. There's a price for everything.

The ripping sound as I tape another box, building my white walls of cardboard that smell like stale air and dust.

'Living in Florida. Fishing, riding my Harley, no more snow. You know me and cold, crappy weather.' He blows out a stream of smoke, returning to his chair, leaning back, and the strong scent of him goes away. 'I won't miss a damn thing about this one-horse town.' He flicks an ash on the concrete floor, tucking the pack of cigarettes and lighter in the breast pocket of his sweat-stained tank top.

'You'll be unhappy if you give up policing,' I tell him the truth.

But I'm not going to stop him.

'Being a cop isn't what you do, it's who you are,' I add.

I'm honest with him.

'You need to arrest people. To kick in doors. To make good on whatever you threaten. To stare down scumbags in court and send them to jail. That's your raison d'être, Marino. Your reason for existing.'

'I know what raison d'être means. I don't need you to translate.'

'You need the power to punish people. That's what you live for.'

'*Merde de bull.* All the huge cases I've worked?' He shrugs in his chair as the noise of

32

the rain changes, smacking, then splattering, now drumming, his powerful shape backlit by the eerie gray light of the volatile afternoon. 'I can write my own ticket.'

'And what would that be exactly?' I sit down on a box, tapping an ash.

'You.'

'One person can't be your ticket and we're never getting married.' I'm that honest but it's not the whole truth.

'I didn't ask you. Did anybody hear me ask?' he announces as if there are other people inside the garage with us. 'I've never even asked you on a date.'

'It wouldn't work.'

'No shit. Who could live with you?'

I drop the cigarette into an empty beer bottle and it hisses out.

'The only thing I'm talking about is having a job with you.' He won't look at me now. 'Being your lead investigator, building a good team of them, creating a training program. The best anywhere in the world.'

'You won't respect yourself.' I'm right but he won't see it.

He smokes and drinks as rain pummels gray granite pavers beyond the wide square opening, and in the distance agitated trees, churning dark clouds, and farther off the railroad tracks, the canal, the river that runs through the city I'm leaving.

'And then you won't respect me, Marino. That's the way it will happen.'

'It's already decided.' Another swallow of beer,

the green bottle sweating, dripping condensation as he refuses to look at me. 'I got it all figured out. Lucy and me both do.'

'Remember what I just said. Every word,' I reply from the taped-up box I'm sitting on, this one labeled *Do Not Touch*.

4

CAMBRIDGE, MASSACHUSETTS
WEDNESDAY, DECEMBER 19
4:48 A.M.

An engine rumbles in front of the house, and I open my eyes expecting boxes labeled with a Sharpie and Marino sweating in the folding chair. What I see is simple cherry furniture that's been in Benton's New England family for more than a hundred years.

I recognize champagne silk drapes drawn across windows, the striped sofa and coffee table in front of them and then the brown hardwood floor becomes brown carpet. I smell the sweet putrid odor of blood. Dark red streaks and drops on tables and chairs. Pictures colored with crayons and Magic Markers, and a Peg-Board hung with children's knapsacks inside a brightly cluttered first-grade classroom where everyone is dead.

The air is permeated with the volatile molecules of blood breaking down, red cells separating from serum. Coagulation and decomposition. I smell it. Then I don't. An olfactory hallucination, the receptors of my first cranial nerve stimulated by something remembered and no longer there. I massage the back of my stiff neck and breathe deeply, the imagined stench replaced by the scent of antique wood and the

35

citrus-ginger reed diffuser on the fireplace mantel. I detect a hint of smoke and burnt split logs from the last fire I built before Benton left town, before Connecticut. Before I got sick. I look at the clock.

'Dammit,' I mutter.

It's almost five a.m. After Marino called I must have drifted back to sleep and now he's in my driveway. I text him to give me fifteen minutes and I'll be right down as I remember the Marino I was just talking to and drinking beer with in the humid heat. Every image, every word, of the dream is vivid like a movie, some of it factual shards of what really happened the summer I left Virginia for good a decade ago, some of it confabulated by my deepest disappointments and fears.

All of it is true in what it represents. What I knew and felt back then during the darkest of dark times. That Benton had been murdered. That I was being forced out of office, done in by politics, by white males in suits who didn't give a damn about the truth, didn't give a damn about what I'd lost, which felt like everything.

Lowering my feet to the floor, I find my slippers. I have a crime scene to work and Marino is picking me up like the old days, like our Richmond days. He's predicting the case is a bad one and I have no doubt that's what he wants. He wishes for some sensational homicide to reignite his lost self as he rises from the ashes of what he believes he wasted because of me.

'I'm sorry,' I tell Sock as I move him again and get up, weak, light-headed but much improved.

36

I'm fine. In fact, oddly euphoric. Benton's presence surrounds me. He isn't dead, thank God, oh thank God. His murder was faked, a brilliant contrivance by the brilliant FBI to protect him from organized criminals, from some French cartel he'd undermined. He wasn't allowed to tell me he was alive and safe in a protected witness program. There could be no contact at all, not the slightest clue as he watched me from a distance, checking on me without my knowing. I felt him. I know I did. What I dreamed about it is true and there was a better way to do what was done and I won't forgive the FBI for the years they ruined. Those years were broken and cruel as I languished miserably in the Bureau's lies, my heart, my soul, my destiny commanded by an artless ugly precast building named after J. Edgar Hoover. Now Benton and I won't allow such a thing, not ever. We're each other's first loyalty and he tells me things. He finds a way to let me know whatever he needs me to know so we never again go through such an outrageous ordeal. He's alive and well and out of town. That's all, and I try his cell phone to say I miss him and Happy Almost-Birthday. I get voice mail.

Next I try his hotel in northern Virginia, the Marriott where he always stays when he has business with his FBI colleagues at the Behavioral Analysis Unit, the BAU.

'Mr. Wesley has checked out,' the desk clerk tells me when I ask for Benton's room.

'When?' I don't understand.

'It was right as I was coming on duty around

37

midnight.' I recognize the clerk's voice, soft-spoken with a Virginia lilt. He's worked at this same Marriott for years and I've spoken to him on many occasions, especially these past few weeks after a second and third murder occurred.

'This is Kay Scarpetta — '

'Yes, ma'am, I know. How are you? This is Carl. You sound a little stopped-up. I hope you don't have the bug that's going around. I hear it's a bad one.'

'I'm just fine but thanks for asking. Did he happen to mention why he was checking out earlier than planned? He was supposed to be there until this weekend, last I heard.'

'Yes, ma'am, I'm looking. Checkout was scheduled for Saturday.'

'Yes, three more days. Well, I'm puzzled. You don't know why he suddenly left at midnight?' I'm rambling a bit, trying to work through what doesn't make sense.

'Mr. Wesley didn't say. I've been reading about the cases around here his unit's working, what little there is, the FBI being so hush-hush, which only makes it worse, you ask me, because I'd rather know what we're dealing with. You know there are those of us who don't wear guns and badges and travel in packs and we have to worry about even going to the mall or a movie. It would be nice to know what's going on around here, and I got to tell you, Dr. Scarpetta, there are a lot of nervous people, a lot of people really scared including me. If I had my way, my wife wouldn't leave the house anymore.'

I thank him and extricate myself as politely as

I can, contemplating the possibility that there's been another awful case somewhere. Perhaps Benton has been deployed to a new location. But it's not like him not to let me know. I check to see if he's e-mailed me. He hasn't.

'He probably didn't want to wake me up,' I say to my lazy old dog. 'That's one of the perks if you're sick. You already feel bad enough and then people make you feel worse because they don't want to bother you.'

I catch a glimpse of myself in the mirror I pass, pale in rumpled black silk pajamas, blond hair plastered to my head, blue eyes glassy. I've lost a few pounds and look haunted from dreams that seem a replay of a past I miss and don't. I need a shower but it will have to wait.

Opening dresser drawers, I find underwear, socks, black cargo pants, and a black long-sleeved shirt with the CFC crest embroidered in gold. I retrieve my Sig nine-millimeter from the bedside table and zip the pistol inside a quick-release fanny pack as I wonder, Why bother? Nobody cares what I wear to a muddy death scene. I don't need a concealed weapon if Marino is picking me up.

Even the smallest decision seems overwhelming, possibly because I haven't had to make any important ones over recent days. Heat up chicken broth and refill Sock's water bowl, feed him, don't forget his glucosamine chondroitin. Drink fluids, as much as you can stand. Don't touch the cases on the floor by the bed, the autopsy and lab reports awaiting your review and initialing, not when you have a fever. And of course I've done a lot of online shopping with so much time to drift in and out of thoughts and dreams and spend money on all the people I want to make happy and am grateful for, even if they disappoint me like my mother and my sister Dorothy and maybe Marino, too.

Confined to the bedroom, with Benton some 450 miles south of here, and it's a good thing I've reminded myself until I almost believe it. Most physicians really are bad patients and I might be the worst. When I got home from Connecticut he wanted to leave Washington, D.C., right then and I knew that wasn't what he should do. He was trying to be a good husband. He said he'd catch the next flight but I wouldn't hear of it. When he's in pursuit of a predator there's no room for anything else, not even me. It doesn't matter what I'm going through and I told him no.

'I'm not dying but other people are.' I was adamant on the phone with him. 'I've seen enough death. I just saw more of it than anyone ever should. I don't know what the hell is wrong with people.'

'I'm coming home. A few days early and it's not going to matter. You can trust me on that. Things are bad here, Kay.'

'A mother has a son with severe developmental problems so she teaches him how to use a damn Bushmaster assault rifle, for God's sake?'

'You need me with you and I need to come home.'

'Then maybe he can massacre an entire elementary school so he feels powerful for a

40

moment before he takes his own life.'

'I can understand how angry you must feel.'

'Anger doesn't do any damn good at all.'

'I'll catch a plane or Lucy can pick me up.'

I told him that the top priority was for him and his colleagues at the BAU to catch a killer the media has dubbed the Capital Murderer. 'Stop the *infamia bastardo* before he kills someone else,' I said. 'I'm okay. I can manage. I have the flu, Benton.' I brushed it off. 'I won't be pleasant to be around and I don't want you or anyone else catching what I've got. Don't come home.'

'It's not going well here, from bad to worse,' he said. 'I'm worried he's gone somewhere else and is killing again or will be soon, and everyone at the BAU disagrees with me about everything.'

'You're still convinced he's not local to the D.C. area.'

'I believe he's in and out, which would explain why there were no murders between April and Thanksgiving. Seven months of silence and then two in a row. This is someone intimately familiar with certain geographic areas because he has a job that requires travel.'

What he's told me makes sense but what doesn't is why he's being ignored. Benton has always gotten the respect he deserves but not now in the Washington cases, and I know he's fed up and aggravated as hell but what he can't do is worry about me. I know he's had his fill of sitting around with a group of criminal investigative analysts, what people still call profilers, and

41

listening to theories and psychological interpretations that are being run from Boston and not the BAU. Ed Granby has his fingerprints all over this case and that's the biggest problem, and Benton needs to deal with all that and not his wife.

★ ★ ★

Sock follows me into the bathroom and I squint in the overhead light, old subway tile shiny and bright. White bath sheets folded on top of a hamper near the tub remind me of the dead body wrapped in white at MIT.

Then I think again about the victims in Washington, D.C., and my review of their cases last month after two more women were murdered one week apart. I deliberate whether I should e-mail the MIT photograph to Benton but its not for me to do. It's for Marino to do and it's premature, and it's also not up to me to divulge details to him about Benton's cases. In fact, I can't possibly.

I wash my face, freshening up, as I remind myself what he said about repetitive behavior that goes beyond the killing, the bags, the duct tape, each victim wearing the previous victim's underwear except in the first case, Klara Hembree. She was originally from Cambridge and that's bothering me, too.

In the midst of an acrimonious divorce from her wealthy real estate developer husband, she moved to D.C. last spring to be near her family and barely a month later was abducted and dead. DNA on the panties she was wearing came back to an unknown female of European descent, and Benton feels strongly this indicates there are other victims.

But there's no opportunity for cases to be compared or connected because the FBI has been miserly about releasing information. Nothing about the bags or the duct tape has made it into the news. There's not even been a mention of the white cloths or sheets, certainly not about the bags, clear plastic with the hologram of an octopus, an iridescent oblong head and tentacles that shimmer in rainbow hues depending on the angle of light.

Klara Hembree was murdered last April, and then this past month before Thanksgiving there were two more — Sally Carson, a professor, and Julianne Goulet, a concert pianist. Each of the women, like the first one, is believed to have been suffocated with a plastic bag from the D.C. spa store called Octopus that was burglarized about a year ago, cases of the customized bags and other inventory stolen from the loading dock. Benton is certain the killer is escalating out of control but the FBI's not listening to him or his repeated suggestion that certain details of the crimes should be released publicly.

Maybe some police department somewhere has had a similar crime but Benton's argument continues to be overruled by his boss Ed Granby. He's ordered that there can be absolutely no sharing of investigative information about former Cambridge resident Klara Hembree and that means there can't be information released about the other two recent cases. Details will get leaked and might inspire a copycat and Granby's not going to budge from that opinion. While he's got a valid point, he's ground the investigation to a halt, according to Benton.

Since Granby took over the Boston division last summer Benton has felt increasingly ostracized and marginalized, and I've continued to remind him that some people are jealous, controlling, and competitive. It's an ugly fact of life. By now the two of them cordially despise each other and this is probably a hidden reason why my husband wanted to come home. It wasn't just about my being sick or that his birthday is tomorrow or that the holidays are here. He was extremely unhappy when I talked to him last and I've been halfway expecting him any minute, or that might be wishful thinking. He left for D.C. almost a month ago and I miss him terribly.

I walk back into the bedroom with Sock on my heels, and Marino's just going to have to wait a minute or two longer. Retrieving my iPad from the bed, I log on to my office database and find what Benton scanned to me last month, quickly scrolling through the files. The three homicides play out in my mind as if they're happening before my eyes and the details are just as perplexing as when I first looked at them. I envision what I've envisioned before, recon-structing the way I know biology works or doesn't, and I watch them die as I've watched them die before. I see it.

A woman with a clear plastic bag over her head and duct tape around her neck, a designer duct tape with a black lacy pattern, and clear plastic rapidly sucks in and out, her eyes panicked as her face turns a deep blue-red. Pressure builds, causing a light scattering of petechial hemorrhages across the cheeks and eyelids, tiny pinpricks blooming bright red as vessels rupture. Fighting to stay alive but restrained somehow and then all goes silent and still, and the final act, a bow fashioned from the same designer duct tape is attached under her chin, the killer wrapping his gift to inhumanity.

Yet the physical findings don't add up to what I would expect. They tell a truth that seems a lie. The victims would have struggled violently. They would have frantically fought to breathe when they were being suffocated but there's no evidence they did. As Benton put it, they seemed to comply as if they wanted to die and I know damn well they didn't.

These aren't suicides. They're sadistic murders and I believe the killer is restraining them, possibly with a ligature that leaves no mark. But I can't figure out what that might be. Even the softest material will leave a bruise or abrasion if someone is tightly bound with it and panics and fights. I can't fathom why the duct tape left no injury. How do you suffocate someone and leave virtually no sign of it?

Each body was found in a northern Virginia or southern Maryland public park, and I continue to quickly skim through what Benton sent to me the end of November, knowing I've got to hurry up and I can't tell Marino what's on my mind. Three different parks, two with a lake, another with a golf course, all of them very close to railroad tracks and within twenty miles of Washington, D.C. In the scene photographs the victims were clad only in panties that were identified as belonging to a previous victim except in the case of the former Cambridge resident Klara Hembree. A DNA profile recovered from the panties she had on is the unknown female of European descent — in other words, white.

I click through photographs of dead faces staring through plastic bags from the bath and body boutique called Octopus near Lafayette Square, mere blocks from the White House. There's no evidence of sexual assault, nothing significant recovered from the bodies except two types of Lycra fibers, one blue-dyed and the other white. The morphology of the fibers in each of the three cases is slightly different. It's been speculated they might be from athletic clothing the killer wears or possibly from furniture upholstery in his residence.

I sit down on the sofa to dress, conserving strength, before venturing out to MIT's playing fields where I will examine a dead human being whose truth must be coaxed and cut out of her, as I have done thousands of times in my career. Sock jumps up and rests his grizzled muzzle on my lap. I stroke his head and velvety long snout, careful with his ears, tattered and scarred from his former cruel life at the racetrack.

'You need to get up,' I tell him. 'I have to take you out, then I've got work to do. I don't want you to get into a state about it. Promise?' I reassure him our housekeeper Rosa will be here soon and will keep him company. 'Come on. Then you'll eat breakfast and take a nap. I'll be home before you know it.'

I hope dogs don't know when we lie. Rosa won't be here soon and I won't be home before Sock knows it. It's very early and will be a very long day. The message alert dings on my phone.

'You coming or what?' Marino texts me.

'Ready,' I reply.

I clip the fanny pack's nylon strap around my waist, tightening it as I move a curtain aside.

5

Veils of rain billow past streetlights in front of our Federal-style antique home in central Cambridge, close to Harvard's Divinity School and the Academy of Arts and Sciences.

I watch Marino climb out of an SUV that doesn't belong to him personally. The Ford Explorer is black or dark blue, parked in my puddled driveway, the old brick boiling with heavy rain. He opens a passenger door, unaware that I'm staring down at him from a second-floor window, oblivious to what I feel when I see him, indifferent to how anything might affect me.

He never announced his news and of course he didn't need to because I already knew. The Cambridge Police Department wouldn't have cared about his petition for exemption, and no number of glowing advisory letters was going to matter if I didn't personally recommend him for a lateral transfer into their investigative unit. I got him his damn new job. That's the truth of it and the irony.

I lobbied on his behalf to the Cambridge police commissioner and the local district attorney, telling them with authority that Marino is the perfect candidate. With his vast experience and training he shouldn't be obliged to go through the academy with rookies, and the hell with age limitations. He's gold, a treasure. I made my case for him because I want him to be happy. I don't want him to resent me anymore. I don't want him to blame me.

I feel a twinge of sadness and anger as he unlatches the dog crate in the backseat to let out his German shepherd, a rescue he named Quincy. He snaps a leash on the harness and I hear the muffled thud of the car door shutting in the hard rain. Through the bare branches of the big oak tree on the other side of the glass I watch this man I've known most of my professional life lead his dog, still a puppy, to shrubbery.

They follow the brick walk, and motion-sensor lights blink on as if saluting Cambridge police detective Pete Marino's approach. His large stature is exaggerated by the shadow he casts, on the front porch steps now in the glow of old iron gas lamps. Sock's nails click on the hardwood floor, following me to the stairs.

'My opinion is it won't work out the way he thinks,' I continue talking to a dog as silent as a mime. 'He's doing it for the wrong reason.'

Of course Marino doesn't see it. He has it in his head that he left policing ten years ago because it was my idea and completely against his will. Were he asked 'Is your every disappointment Kay Scarpetta's fault?' he'd say yes and pass a polygraph.

★ ★ ★

I turn on lights that fill the French stained-glass windows over the landings, wildlife scenes in rich, brilliant hues.

In the entryway I disarm the alarm system and

49

open the front door, and Marino looms large on the front porch mat, his dog all legs and paws tugging desperately to give Sock and me a playful, sloppy hello.

'Come in. I've got to let Sock out and feed him.' In the entry-way closet I begin collecting my gear.

'You look like hell.' Marino pushes back the hood of his dripping rain slicker, his dog wearing a working vest, IN TRAINING on one side and DO NOT PET on the other in big white letters.

I drag out my field case, a large, heavy-duty plastic toolbox I picked up for a bargain like a lot of medicolegal necessities I find at Walmart, Home Depot, wherever I can. There's no point in paying hundreds of dollars for a surgical chisel or rib cutters if I can pick up tools for a song that do the job just fine.

'I don't want to get your floor wet.' Marino watches me from the porch, staring the same unblinking stare as he did in my dream.

'Don't worry about it. Rosa's coming. The place is a mess. I haven't even gotten a tree yet.'

'Looks like Scrooge lives here.'

'Maybe he does. Come in out of the weather.'

'It's supposed to clear off pretty soon.' Marino wipes his feet on the mat, his leather boots thudding and scraping.

I sit down on the rug as he steps inside and shuts the door. Quincy pulls toward me, his tail wagging furiously, loudly thumping the umbrella stand. Marino the dog handler, or what Lucy calls 'the dog chauffeur,' chokes up on the lead and commands Quincy to sit. He doesn't.

50

'Sit,' Marino repeats firmly. 'Down,' he adds hopelessly.

'What else do we know about this case beyond what you described to me on the phone?' Sock is in my lap, trembling because he knows I'm leaving. 'Anything further about Gail Shipton, if that's who we're dealing with?'

'There's an alley in back of the bar with a small parking area, deserted, some of the lights burned out,' Marino describes. 'Obviously it's where she went to use her phone. I located it and a shoe that are hers.'

'Are we sure they're hers?' I begin putting on ankle-high boots, black nylon, insulated and waterproof.

'The phone definitely.' He digs in a pocket for a biscuit, breaks off a piece, and Quincy sits in what I call his lunging position. Ready to pounce.

'What about those treats I gave you? Sweet-potato ones, a case of them.'

'I ran out.'

'Then you're giving him too many.'

'He's still growing.'

'Well, if you keep it up he will but not the way you want.'

'Plus they clean his teeth.'

'What about the dog toothpaste I made for you?'

'He doesn't like it.'

'Her phone isn't password-protected?' I ask as I tie my laces in double bows.

'I've got my little trick for getting around that.'

Lucy, I think. Already, Marino is bringing my

51

niece's old tricks to his new trade, and all of us know that her tricks aren't necessarily legal.

'I'd be careful about what you might not want to explain in court,' I tell him.

'What people don't know they can't ask about.' It's clear from his demeanor he doesn't want my advice.

'I assume you processed the phone first for prints, for DNA.' I can't stop myself from talking to him the same way I did when he was under my supervision. Not even a month ago.

'The phone and the case it's in.'

I get up from the floor and he shows me a photograph of a smart-phone in a rugged black case on wet, cracked pavement near a dumpster. Not just a typical smartphone skin, I think. But a water-and shock-resistant hard-shell case with retractable screens, what Lucy refers to as military-grade. It's what she and I both have, and the detail might tell me something important about Gail Shipton. The average person doesn't have a smartphone skin like this.

'I got her call history.' Marino explains how he extracted the password and other data by utilizing a handheld physical analyzer he's not supposed to have.

A Lucy invention. A mobile scanner she modified to do her bidding, which in her case means hacking. Leave my niece alone with your smartphone or computer for five minutes and she'll own your life.

'The last call Gail made yesterday afternoon was at five fifty-three.' Marino's eyes are on the fanny pack strapped around my waist. 'Carin

Hegel, who'd just texted Gail to call her. When the hell did you start packing heat?'

'Carin Hegel, as in the attorney?'

'Do you know her?'

'Fortunately I've not been involved in any big lawsuits, so no. But we've met a number of times.' Most recently in Boston's federal courthouse, and I try to remember when that was.

Early this month, maybe two weeks ago. We ran into each other in the café on the second floor and she mentioned she was there for a pretrial hearing. The case involved a financial management company she described as a 'gang of thugs.'

'It's looking pretty certain that Gail left the bar, went out to the parking lot in back, pretty much what her friend Haley Swanson told me,' Marino continues. 'Gail answered a call from someone with a blocked number and must have stepped outside so she could hear. In the log it just says *unknown* and *mobile*. If you go to the corresponding info screen, it gives you the date, time, and how long the call was, which was seventeen minutes.'

He gives Quincy another piece of biscuit.

'Gail ended that call when the text from Carin Hegel landed,' he says. 'She tried to call her and that call lasted only twenty-four seconds. Which is interesting. Either she didn't get her and left a voice mail or she got interrupted.'

'We need to get hold of Carin Hegel.' Uneasiness flickers.

There was something else she told me when we were buying coffee in the courthouse café a few weeks ago. She indicated she wasn't living at home. I gathered that she'd relocated to an undisclosed place where she planned to stay until the trial was over.

It wasn't safe to have her usual routines, she confided in me. How convenient it would be if she were in a car accident right now, she joked, but it was obvious she didn't think it was a laughing matter. She was giving me fair warning in the event she showed up at my office without an appointment and horizontally, she quipped, and I didn't think that was funny. None of it was.

'I already left a message for her to call me ASAP,' Marino says.

'You mentioned that her client might be missing?'

'Yeah. Of course she doesn't know me so I don't know if she'll call me back or get her damn secretary to do it. You know how big-shot lawyers are,' Marino says as I put on my coat. 'The shoe was close to the phone, rained on but doesn't look like it was out there all that long. Hours versus days,' he adds. 'I'm thinking someone grabbed Gail and she struggled, dropped the phone, and a shoe came off. Why the hell are you wearing a gun?'

'What does the shoe look like?' I ask.

He opens another photograph on his phone to show me a green faux-crocodile leather flat upside down on dirty wet pavement.

'It would come off easily, as opposed to boots or shoes that tie on or zip up,' I observe.

'Right. Tells us she struggled as someone forced her into his car.'

'I don't know what it tells us yet. What about any other personal effects?'

'It's possible she had a brown shoulder bag with her. She carried one, and it's not inside her condo. That's what her friend Haley said.'

'Whom you've not talked to since one a.m.'

'There's only so many minutes in an hour.' Marino offers Quincy another piece of biscuit, and now we're up to three in fifteen minutes. 'Whoever got Gail must have taken her bag.'

'And nobody heard her scream? Someone grabs her or forces her into a car in a crowded area of Cambridge during happy hour and no one hears a thing?'

'The bar was loud. It also depends on how much she had to drink.'

'If she were intoxicated, it certainly would make her more vulnerable.' I've preached this for years.

Rapists, muggers, and murderers tend to prefer their victims drunk or drugged. A woman staggering out of a bar alone is a sitting duck.

'The area behind the bar was going to be pretty deserted after dark,' Marino says. 'Nothing but a cut-through to Mass Ave. In other words, real easy for a bad person to get in and out of that back area behind the bar. Stupid place for her to be talking on the phone after dark and it would have been pitch-dark by five-thirty, six p.m.'

'Let's not start by blaming the victim.' I head down the hallway with Sock, pausing to straighten Victorian etchings on the paneled wall. I feel dampness and dust everywhere, my private world in disarray and neglected, or at least it seems that way, not a single holiday light and an empty unlived-in smell, nothing cooking in the kitchen, no sounds of life. Ever since I came home from Connecticut nothing has been right.

'She shouldn't have gone back there.' Marino's voice follows me. 'She shouldn't have been on her phone, not paying attention,' he adds loudly.

6

The backyard is flooded with standing water. Trees move fitfully in gusting wind and the sound of the rain is unnaturally loud, simmering on pavers as if the back patio is hot. The air is heavy with steamy mist.

Surrounding homes are dark, their holiday decorations on timers that black out electric candles and strands of festive lights from midnight to dusk. I know the patterns by now. Every day that I've been alone since I got sick, I've done exactly this when I take Sock out. I stand sentry in the open doorway, my left hand resting on the fanny pack. I'm aware of the weight of the pistol inside it as my shy shell-shocked greyhound trots to a favorite spot, sniffing behind boxwoods, disappearing into black holes where I can't see him. He's an expert at avoiding areas of the yard that have motion-sensor lights.

I probe deep shadows and the old brick wall that separates our property from the one behind it, and maybe what Benton suggested the other day is true. I'm more vigilant than usual. He said considering everything going on it's to be expected that I might be uneasy and raw, and I didn't argue with him or elaborate. He's had enough on his mind and I didn't want him to worry, but the feeling is there as I look around at the darkness and the rain. I feel someone is watching me. I've felt it since I came home from Connecticut.

I've heard noises, subtle ones, a stick cracking, the whisper of dead leaves disturbed, and I've come to dread taking Sock out after dark and he seems to dread it too. He hates wintertime and bad weather, and I've rationalized that it's probably my unsettledness he's reacting to, and my heart sinks as he sniffs the wind just now, searching it. He stiffens, suddenly bounding back to my post at the door, his tail curled between his legs as he tries to push past me inside the house just like he's done repeatedly of late.

'Go potty,' I tell him firmly. 'Everything's fine. I'm right here.' I search for the source of whatever spooked him on the off chance it's something other than me. 'What is it? A raccoon, an owl, a squirrel somewhere?'

I listen carefully, hearing nothing but the loud splashing rain as I look around from my safe base. Light seeps through the open doorway, dimly illuminating a matted carpet of soggy brown grass and leaves and the shape of the circular low stone wall around the magnolia tree in the center of the yard. Above me, the French stained-glass window is brilliant against the back of the house, the jewel-like hues drawing attention to when I'm home or headed out with my dog.

I may as well be making an announcement to anyone with bad intentions, and it would make sense to leave the light off over the stairs. But I refuse. The vibrant colors and mythical animals give me comfort and pleasure. I won't be ruled by irrational fear. I won't allow evil people, even

58

the thought of them, to rob me of more than they already have.

'What is it? Oh for heaven's sake, come on.' I move away from the doorway, and Sock follows me into the yard, his muzzle touching the back of my knee. 'Go on.' I sound calm and unconcerned but that's not what I feel.

My conscious mind says all is fine but another part of my brain says something is off. I feel it strongly, what I've felt before. Blasts of wind-driven rain thrash the heavy branches and rubbery leaves of the magnolia tree and my pulse picks up. The storm howls around the roof and agitates the shrubbery and I physically react to something I can't identify.

A stone or a brick chinks on the other side of the back wall and my scalp prickles and my legs feel heavy, but those days of being too terrified to move or breathe were left behind in my childhood. I've been through too much and it has hardened some primal part of me that no longer panics. I peel open the fanny pack and slide out the gun as I pull up my hood and escort Sock to the stone bench around the magnolia tree. Nearby is shrubbery.

'Go on. I'm right here,' I tell him, and he ducks behind a thick cover of boxwoods, his ears back, his eyes on me.

Heavy cold raindrops tap the waterproof fabric covering my head as I stand perfectly still and scan. I watch the wall. I listen and wait. It occurs to me with dismay that I haven't chambered a round and it will be difficult to pull back the slide. The pistol is wet. It was stupid not to cock it before I came outside. Sock suddenly bolts to the open door and I follow him, not turning my back to the wall that separates the yard from the property behind it.

I feel it like a magnetic force, a malevolent presence lurking in the dark behind the wall, close enough that I can almost smell it, an acrid edge, a dirty electrical odor like something old shorting out. What people smell when they're about to have a seizure but I'm imagining it. There's no odor, only the muskiness of wet dead leaves and the ozone of rain. Water splashes steadily and the chilled wind blows humidly and whatever moved is silent and still. Physics displacing things, I think, like finding a coin on the rug and having no idea how it got there from the top of the dresser where you saw it last.

I look around and see nothing out of the ordinary, and, stepping inside the house, I shut the door and lock it. I look through the peephole at the empty rain-swept yard, then I towel Sock dry and praise him for a job well done as I wipe off the pistol and zip it back inside the fanny pack. I look through the peephole again and it's a reflex when I place my hand on the knob. I do it before I realize what I'm seeing.

The figure standing on the other side of the wall is a young male, small, maybe a boy, I'm fairly sure. Bareheaded, light skinned, and for an instant he's looking directly at the back door, directly at me looking at him through the peephole. I see the hint of pale flesh and the dark recesses of his eyes, and I swing the door open wide and he runs.

60

'Hey!' I yell.

He vanishes as suddenly as he appeared.

★ ★ ★

I walk inside my kitchen of stainless-steel commercial appliances, old wood, and antique amber alabaster chandeliers.

'What was that about?' Marino fills a glass with sparkling water, helping himself, and I can tell he assumes I was yelling at Sock, who heads to his bowls on a mat and sits expectantly.

'We had a visitor,' I reply. 'Possibly a young male, white, dark hair maybe, maybe a kid. He was behind the wall and may have been there the entire time we were in the yard. Then he ran.'

'On your property?' Marino sets down the glass and the bottle as if he's about to bolt to the back of the house.

'No.' I feel surprisingly calm — validated, in fact.

I'm not imagining things after all.

'He was on the other side of the wall in my neighbor's yard.' I drape the wet towel over a towel bar on a cabinet.

'He wasn't trespassing, then. At least not on your property.'

'I don't know what he was doing.'

'Are you sure it's not your neighbor back there?'

'At this hour and in this weather, and why would my neighbor be ducking behind the wall and then run? The person didn't seem familiar but I didn't get a good look, obviously.'

I open my pocketbook on the counter near the phone and pull out my wallet, medical examiner credentials, and keys.

'A young male who didn't look local. Are you sure?' Marino returns the bottle to a refrigerator, not the one he took it from.

'I'm not sure of anything beyond what I just said.' I find my CFC badge with its embedded radio-frequency identification chip, on a lanyard and in a plastic holder. 'But I've definitely had a weird feeling these past few days while I've been home, a sense that someone's been watching the house. And Sock's been uneasy.'

Marino thinks for a moment, weighing his options. He could go out into the rainy dark and look around for whoever it was but no crime has been committed, at least not that we know about. I'm also fairly certain my prowler is long gone and I tell Marino that. I explain that the person I saw ran off in the direction of the Academy of Arts and Sciences, which is a heavily wooded property and just north of that, across Beacon Street and railroad tracks, is Somerville. Then the jurisdiction isn't Cambridge anymore. The person could be anywhere.

'Maybe some kid looking to do a smash-and-grab,' Marino decides as I retrieve a small powerful LED flashlight from a drawer and check to make sure the batteries are good. 'Especially this time of year, there's a lot of vandalism, car breaks, windows smashed, kids stealing laptops, iPads, iPhones. You'd be amazed how many rich people in Cambridge don't have alarm systems,' he says as if I have no idea what goes on in the city where I live and work. 'Kids case a house to figure out where the electronics are, then smash out a window, grab what they want, and run like hell.'

'We're a poor candidate for a smash-and-grab. It's obvious we have an alarm system.' Inside the pantry hanging on a hook is my nylon cross-body bag, what I carry when I'm traveling light. 'There are signs in the yard, and if the person looked through a window he'd see keypads on the walls with red lights indicating the house is armed.'

'You always have it on when you're home?'

'Especially when I'm alone.' He knows that about me, for God's sake.

'And you started getting this weird feeling after Benton left for D.C.?'

'Not as long ago as that. He's been gone for about a month, right after the second and third murders happened. I don't think I noticed anything unusual as long ago as that.' He's fishing to see if Benton's cases have spooked me, abductions and murders Marino knows nothing about except what little has been reported in the news.

'Okay. When exactly did you start feeling weird?'

'Since I got back from Connecticut. Saturday night is when I first had the feeling.' My wallet, keys, credentials, badge, flashlight go inside the bag, which hugs my hip when I slip the strap over my shoulder.

Marino watches me, and I know what he's concluded. What I went through over the

63

weekend was traumatic and I'm paranoid, and, more to the point, I don't feel as safe as I did when he worked for me. He wants to believe I feel his absence deeply, that life's not as settled as it was, and it isn't. I open a cabinet above the sink.

'Well, that's understandable,' he says.

'What I've sensed has nothing to do with that, I promise.' I set a can of Sock's food and a pair of gray nitrile examination gloves on the counter.

'Really? You want to tell me why you suddenly think it's necessary to wear a gun to a crime scene? One you're going to with me?' He continues to push because he wants to believe I'm scared.

Most of all he wants to believe I need him.

'You don't even like guns,' he then says.

'It's not a matter of what I like.' I talk to the rhythm of the can opener cutting through metal. 'I also don't happen to think that guns are something one should have feelings for. Love, hate, like, or dislike should be reserved for people, pets, food. Not firearms.'

'Since when do you wear one or even bother taking the trigger lock off?'

'How would you know what I bother with? You're not around me most of the time and not at all lately.' I empty the can into Sock's bowl as he waits by his mat, his pointed face looking at me.

'Well, I don't think it's a coincidence that I don't work for you anymore and all of a sudden you arm yourself everywhere.'

'I don't arm myself everywhere but certainly

when I'm in and out of the house all hours of the night, here alone,' I reply.

Marino gulps down the last of the fizzy water and quietly belches.

'It's the oldest trick in the book to wait until someone disarms the alarm and goes out with the dog.' I feed Sock with my gloved hand, meatballs of grain-free whitefish and herring, making sure he doesn't eat too fast and aspirate food.

My rescued companion is prone to pneumonia. Eating too fast is left over from early years at the racetrack when he wasn't always fed.

'You really don't think I'd do that unarmed,' I say reasonably as I return to the entryway.

Marino places his glass in the sink and follows me, our coats dripping slowly on the floor.

'How many cases have we seen where the stalker knows his intended victim has a dog and starts watching for patterns?' I remind him, and maybe I want to make him feel bad.

He walked off the job. He didn't bother to share his news. Since I've been sick he's not called once to check on me. I set the alarm and hurry us out of the house while Sock is preoccupied with a sweet-potato treat. A second one is in my pocket and Quincy knows it, he always does. He tugs after me down the steps and along the walkway.

The rain is letting up, and it's unseasonably warm, in the low fifties, and it wouldn't seem possible that we're less than a week away from Christmas, were it not for the tasteful wreaths on doors, the red ribbons and bows on lampposts.

We've not had a hard freeze yet, the weather temperate for December and overcast, but it won't last. This weekend it's supposed to snow.

'At least I don't have to worry about you handling a gun safely.' Marino helps Quincy into his crate and latches the door. 'Since I'm the one who taught you how to shoot.'

Quincy sits on his fleece pad and stares intently at me with bright brown eyes.

'I don't want to mess up his training,' I say wryly as I produce the sweet-potato treat.

'It's a little late now,' Marino says as if his dog's complete lack of discipline must be my fault like everything else.

Quincy pokes his nose through the wire siding. I can hear him chewing as I settle into the front seat.

Marino starts the engine and reaches for his portable radio. He contacts the dispatcher and requests that any units in the area be on the lookout for a young white male who might be casing properties on the northern edge of Harvard, last seen running toward the Academy of Arts and Sciences. Car 13 immediately answers that he's a few blocks south, near the Divinity School.

'Any further description?' car 13 asks.

'Bareheaded, possibly rather slight, possibly a juvenile,' I quietly remind Marino. 'Possibly on foot.'

'No hat,' he says over the air. 'Last seen running toward the woods in the direction of Beacon.'

7

Marino's unmarked SUV is fully loaded with a scanner, radio, siren, and grille lights. Storage boxes and drawers keep equipment organized and out of sight, the dark fabric upholstery and carpet spotlessly clean. I feel his pride in his 'ride,' as he used to refer to his Crown Vic during his Richmond days.

'It looks quite new and in very good shape. And a hybrid. You've gone green. I'm impressed.' I run my finger over the Armor All-shellacked dash. 'Slick as glass. One could ice-skate on it.'

'V-four, two-liter EcoBoost, can you believe it?' he grumbles. 'The department just got brand-new twin turbo V-sixes but those are going to the brass. What happens when I'm in a pursuit?'

'You win the prize for a small carbon footprint.' I look out my window for the prowler who was on the other side of the wall behind my house.

'May as well go giddy-up to a turtle. It's like giving us water pistols so we save on ammo.'

'That's not exactly analogous.' I can't help but smile at his silliness, vintage Marino grousing.

'My last car before I left Richmond was a V-eight Interceptor. I could go a hundred and fifty friggin' miles an hour in that baby.'

'Fortunately I can't imagine ever needing to go that fast in Cambridge unless you're an aircraft.' I don't see anybody out at all.

For several minutes we don't pass a single car as I wonder why someone might be spying on me, possibly since I got home from Connecticut. I don't believe this is about a smash-and-grab. *Who is it? What does he want?*

'Benton should have come home.' Marino drives the speed limit through the Harvard campus, thirty-five miles an hour, about as fast as anyone needs to go around here. 'Sick as hell and all by yourself? Not to mention what you just went through.' He has to bring that up again, and he'll continue bringing it up.

'Benton couldn't have helped anything by coming home,' I reply, but it isn't true.

If someone is casing our house or stalking me it would have been very helpful having him around and I don't like it when he's gone. Recent weeks have been long and hard and maybe I shouldn't have told him I was fine and didn't need him because it wasn't true at all. Maybe I should have been selfish.

'You shouldn't have been left alone. I wish I'd known what was going on with you.'

Marino would have known had he bothered to ask, and I look out my window at Harvard's brick-and-glass art museum flowing past. The Harvard Faculty Club is dressed for the holidays, and the Houghton and Lamont Libraries are formidable brick shapes behind old trees inside the Harvard Yard. Tires sizzle over wet pavement. Quincy quietly snores in back, asleep in his crate, and Marino's police radio is busy.

A 911 hang-up. A domestic call. Suspicious

68

subjects in a red SUV with reflective bumpers fleeing the parking lot of a subsidized housing development on Windsor Street. He listens intently as he drives. He's content and energized, back where he belongs, and I've not had a chance to confront him about what he's done and now really isn't the best time.

'Maybe when you feel so inclined you can explain what's going on with you.' I bring it up anyway.

He doesn't answer and a few minutes later we turn onto Memorial Drive. The Charles River glints darkly on our right, gracefully curving toward Boston, the downtown skyline opaquely illuminated through clouds. The antenna on top of the Prudential Building throbs bloodred.

'We talked about it in an earlier life,' I finally say. 'I predicted it that day in Richmond right before I moved. Ten years later, here we are. I would have appreciated it if you'd talked to me about your career change.'

He cocks his head toward his radio, listening to a call about possible car break-ins at the housing development on Windsor Street referenced a few minutes earlier.

'Simply as a courtesy, if nothing else,' I add.

'Control to car thirteen,' the dispatcher repeats.

Car 13 doesn't answer.

'Shit.' Marino grabs the portable radio out of its charger and turns up the volume.

To drown me out about a subject he doesn't want to discuss, I decide, but at the same time I'm puzzled. Not even fifteen minutes ago car 13 radioed that he was near my neighborhood

69

checking for the prowler. Maybe he abandoned that call for this other one.

'Control to car thirteen. Do you copy?' the dispatcher repeats.

'Car thirteen, copy,' the officer finally comes back, his signal weak.

'Are you clear of that stop?'

'Negative. On foot approaching building three, where it appears several vehicles have been broken into. A red SUV with reflective bumpers seen driving away at a high rate of speed with several subjects inside.' He's breathing hard. 'Description fits a vehicle that's caused trouble here before. Possibly gang-related car breaks and vandalism. Request backup.'

'Dangerous as hell no matter how much they've cleaned it up.' Marino is enthralled. 'A lot of bad shit goes on there, drug dealers dropping by to visit their mothers and do a little business while they're at it. Crystal meth, heroin, bath salts. Plus car breaks, vandalism, a drive-by shooting a couple weeks back. They do shit and run like hell and then sometimes come back as soon as the police clear the scene. Like a big fucking game to them.'

I've not seen him this way in a very long time.

'That's the crazy thing around here,' he says excitedly. 'You got housing projects right next to million-dollar homes or in the middle of Tech Square with its billion-dollar business. So we're getting a lot of heat to clean things up.'

'Answering thirteen. Copy at Main,' another unit responds that he's in the area. 'Going now.'

'Copy that,' the dispatcher answers.

70

'Do you remember the day in Richmond I'm talking about?' I bring him back to that.

'What prediction?' He places his radio in his lap.

I describe the rainy afternoon in my dream, remembering the Marino from then as I look at the Marino next to me, this one older, with a deeply lined face, his balding head shaved smooth.

He's still strong and formidable, in jeans and a black Harley-Davidson slicker, and I can tell by his reaction to what I'm saying that he's feigning a bad memory. I sense it in the way he's staring straight ahead, then turning around to make sure Quincy is okay before shifting his position behind the wheel, gripping it with both of his huge hands. What he won't do is look at me. He can't because of how close we came to what neither of us will acknowledge.

Before he left my Richmond house that day he stepped inside to use the bathroom. When he emerged I was waiting for him in the kitchen. I said he needed to eat, and what he didn't need to do was drive. He'd had too much to drink and so had I.

'What is it you're offering?' He wasn't referring to food. 'We could make it together, you know.' He didn't mean a meal. 'I'm one piece and you're the other the way we fit together and it's perfect.' He wasn't thinking about cooking and he wasn't talking about work.

Marino has always believed we would be the ideal couple. Sex would be the alchemy that transforms us into what he wants, and on

71

that rainy occasion in Richmond we almost tried. I've never loved him that way. I've never wanted him that way. I was afraid of what he'd do if I didn't give in, and then I feared what would happen if I did. Marino would have been more damaged than I would have been, and I didn't want him following me anywhere, if that's what he thought was being offered.

That was what stopped me. It wasn't just about sex anymore. He was in love with me, and he told me so. He said it more than once while we ate dinner. Then he never said it again.

'I warned you. I predicted you'd want to do exactly what you've done.' I'm intentionally vague. 'I just don't know why you couldn't discuss your career plans with me instead of my suddenly getting cold calls for references and letters. The way you handled it wasn't right.'

'Maybe the way you handled things that day in Richmond wasn't right.' He knows. He remembers.

'I don't disagree.'

'I didn't want you to talk me out of it this time, okay?' he says.

'I would have tried.' I unlock my iPhone to access the Internet. 'For sure I would have tried to talk you out of quitting the CFC. You're absolutely right.'

'At least you admit it for once.' He seems pleased.

'Yes I admit it, and to talk you out of a life's decision like that would have been unfair.' I type Gail Shipton's name in a search screen. 'It was unfair the other times I did it and I'm sorry. I sincerely am. But I selfishly wouldn't have wanted to lose you, and hopefully I haven't.'

I can tell by his face in the near dark that he is moved by what I just said, and I wonder why it's so hard for me to say what I feel. But it is. It always has been.

'Now we've got a case to work,' he says. 'The way we used to.'

'Better than we used to. We have to be better. In the past ten years the world hasn't exactly become a nicer place.'

'That's one of the reasons I'm doing this,' he says. 'Law enforcement needs people with perspective who can see the way things were and where they're headed. When you and me were getting started it was all about serial killers. Then Nine-Eleven happened and we had to start worrying about terrorists, not to imply we don't have to worry about serial killers too because there's more of them than ever.'

I find a Fox streaming news feed from thirty-five minutes ago describing MIT graduate student Gail Shipton as missing, last seen late yesterday afternoon in Cambridge at the Psi Bar.

It's speculated she might be the dead woman just discovered at MIT's Briggs Field, and the accompanying video shows Cambridge and MIT police setting up auxiliary lighting in a red dirt infield near a parking lot. That scene cuts to Sil Machado giving a statement. The rain is loud in the microphone and drips off his baseball cap.

'At this time we have no formal comment about the situation.' Machado's nickname is the Portuguese Man of War but he doesn't look fierce as he stares into the camera.

A twitch of nervousness runs beneath his somber demeanor, his shoulders hunched tensely against the rain and wind. He has the stiff expression of someone who is uncomfortable and trying not to show it.

'We do have a deceased individual,' he says, 'but no confirmation of what happened or if it might be the woman reported missing.'

'I don't believe it.' Marino glances over at my phone as he listens. 'Machado and his fifteen minutes of fame.'

'Has Dr. Scarpetta been contacted?' the correspondent asks.

'As soon as we've cleared the scene the body will be transported to the medical examiner's office,' Machado states.

'Is Dr. Scarpetta on her way here?'

I scan to see what else might be on the Internet as wipers loudly drag the glass, and then Marino's cell phone rings. It sounds like a revving Harley-Davidson with Screamin' Eagle pipes. He touches a button on his earpiece and Sil Machado's voice is on speakerphone.

'Talk about the devil and look who calls,' Marino says.

'Channel Five's been showing a picture of her,' Machado starts in. 'At least we're getting a lot of tips from people who think they saw her at the Psi Bar. But nothing helpful so far.'

'How did Channel Five get her picture?' Marino's earpiece blinks bright blue.

'Turns out the girl who reported her missing posted it on their website around midnight,'

Machado says. 'Haley Swanson.'

'That's kind of weird.'

'Not necessarily. Everybody's a journalist these days. She called nine-one-one and then posted the photo and that Gail was missing. Guess she was trying to help us do our job, right? The person in the photo looks like the dead lady. Exactly like her.'

'Gail Shipton,' Marino confirms as I find a story on the Internet that grabs my attention.

'Unless she's got an identical twin.'

Gail Shipton is involved in high-stakes litigation that is about to go to trial, and I remember Carin Hegel and what she told me in the federal courthouse several weeks ago. She referenced a gang of thugs and living away from home. I scroll through the story about a lawsuit Gail filed, the details surprisingly scant for a case this big. I search some more.

'Has Haley Swanson come to the station to do a report yet?' Marino asks.

'Not that I know of.'

'That bothers me.'

'Maybe she figures there's no point, that Gail's not missing anymore, that it's a lot worse than that. How far out are you?' Machado's voice fills the car.

'ETA about five.'

'The Doc with you?'

'Ten-four.' Marino ends the call.

'Gail Shipton was in the middle of a legal battle with her former financial manager, Dominic Lombardi.' I skip through the story displayed on my phone. 'His international company, Double

S, is locally based, just west of here in Concord.'

'Never heard of it.' Marino irritably flicks his lights at an on-coming car that has its high beams on. 'Not that I give a shit about financial companies since I've never exactly needed one and think most Wall Street types are crooks.'

I search for 'Double S,' and there are plenty of stories about it, most of them puff pieces probably placed by their PR machine.

'It appears to specialize in extremely high-net-worth clients.' I dig down several pages and click on another news story, this one indicating not all has been rosy for Double S. 'They've had problems with the Securities and Exchange Commission, the SEC, investments that allegedly violated the *Know your client* rule. Plus some problems with the IRS. And this is rather interesting. They've been sued at least six different times over the past eight years. For some reason no case has ever made it to court.'

'Probably settled. Everybody settles. Litigation is the new national industry. The only thing made in America anymore,' Marino says acidly. 'Legalized extortion. I falsely accuse you of something and you give me money to shut up. And if you can't afford a hotshot lawyer you're screwed. Like what just happened to me, a class-action suit handled by a shitty little law firm and I'm out two thousand bucks in truck repairs because the dealership had the biggest law firm in Boston and a PR firm and everything. A damn design problem with the bed being out of alignment and they said it was the little guy's fault for driving it too hard over ruts.'

Marino, who is anything but little, rants on about a truck he bought in the fall, his angry story one I've heard so often I practically have it memorized. After he'd driven the brand-new pickup for less than a week he noticed the rear was *squatting*, as he put it. When he gets to the part about the bump stop being impacted by the rear axle and the frame being too weak, I cut him off.

'I can't tell if the cases were settled.' I return his attention to Gail Shipton's lawsuit against Double S and the suspicious fact that it appears she's conveniently dead less than two weeks before the trial is to start. 'But so far I don't see any mention of settlements, just that the cases were dropped. That's the word used in a story that ran in the *Financial Times* several years ago. 'Double S is a big international business run by a small company in the horse country of Massachusetts.''

I skip ahead to the most significant part. ''Claims made by former clients were frivolous and were dropped, according to CEO Dominic Lombardi. In a recent interview with *The Wall Street Journal* he explained that 'sadly, some-times clients expect miracles and then get angry when that doesn't happen.' He added that Double S continues to be a highly respected financial management company with clients all over the world.''

'A weird name for money managers. Sounds like the name of a ranch,' Marino comments as the silo-shaped silhouette of the Cambridge Forensic Center, the CFC, appears up ahead.

77

But that's not where we're going. I'm reminded of how close the death scene is to my headquarters.

'It certainly could be one of the horse farms around there.' I'm struck by another close proximity.

Double S is but a mile or two from Lucy's fifty-acre country estate, fenced in and gated, cameras everywhere, a helipad, indoor firing range, and multiple garages. She has a series of rustic buildings that belie the spartan décor and intense technology inside a main house that is sided in one-way glass with a sweeping view of the Sudbury River. I wonder if she knows her neighbor Dominic Lombardi, and I certainly hope she's not a client but I doubt she would be. My niece has been burnt before and is very careful with her money.

'Maybe he runs his financial business out of his home,' I suggest as I continue searching the Internet for details about Gail Shipton's lawsuit, what few there are.

News about her case is almost nonexistent, and I suspect Double S has made sure of that.

'It looks like she filed the suit some eighteen months ago for a hundred million dollars. I seriously doubt a jury around here would go for a number like that. Breach of fiduciary duty, breach of contract,' I read on as I explain. 'The upshot seems to be that financial management software used by Double S has rendered the accounting unreliable, and money may be missing.'

'In other words, stolen,' Marino says.

'Obviously that can't be proven or this would be a criminal matter, not civil.' I'm again reminded of the case Carin Hegel mentioned when I ran into her a few weeks ago. I wonder if it's the same one.

I have an unsettled feeling it is.

'Where the hell would a grad student get money like that?' Marino turns on the defrost.

'Technology, mobile-phone apps,' I read and again I think of Lucy, who amassed a fortune at a very young age from creating and selling search engines and software systems.

I send her a text.

'Huh.' Marino leans close to me, popping open the glove box. 'Getting filthy rich from high-tech stuff. Sounds familiar, right?' He grabs a lint-free window-cleaning paper towel. 'I sure as hell hope the two of them don't know each other.'

8

Boats moored for the winter are shrink-wrapped in white plastic on the river, the red triangle Citgo sign glowing brightly over Fenway Park on the Boston side of the Harvard Bridge.

I check my phone again but there's no word from Lucy. Fog hangs over the dark ruffled water as I ride inside Marino's SUV, an ominous feeling tightening its grip on me. I'm not sure if my unsettledness is left over from the weekend or if it's related to the prowler. I'm not sure if I'm sensing something else or am simply exhausted.

Marino is full of himself and his policing philosophies and plans. His assessments about crime trends couldn't be more depressing or bleaker. He hasn't stopped talking while I barely listen, my mind pulled into an ugly, dreadful place where I don't want to be.

Put your hands up in the air!

Don't shoot!

Words heard over a school intercom intrude upon my thoughts when I least expect it. I continue to be stunned that an exchange would be so banal between a mass murderer and his victims.

'Mimicry,' Benton offered an explanation that doesn't satisfy. 'Mimicking TV shows, movies, games. When people are reduced to their most primal impulses they talk like cartoons.'

'They cry out for their mothers. They beg. Yes, I know that and I know nothing. We know nothing, Benton,' I said to him over the phone late Saturday after I got home. 'This is a new enemy.'

'Spectacle killings.'

'That sounds trivializing.'

'A dramatic public display, Kay. The dam began to crumble with Columbine. It's not new, just the classification is. People have become addicted to attention, to fame. Profoundly disturbed individuals will kill and die for it.'

I still haven't heard from Benton. I'm beginning to worry about him, too. My worldview changed dramatically after I believed he was dead. I've lost him before. I could lose him again. Most people don't get even one miracle and I've had several. I fear I've used up my miracles and won't be granted more.

Marino turns onto Fowler Street, a hyphen that connects Memorial Drive to a narrow unlighted alley. He wipes off the inside of the windshield again with his blue lint-free paper towel. I remember I need food. I remember that tomorrow is Benton's birthday and I don't know where he is. I'm so hungry my stomach is sour. Everything will get better once I eat, and for an instant I fantasize about what I'll cook when I get home.

I will make my special stew. Veal, lean beef, asparagus, mushrooms, potatoes, onions, peppers, pureed tomatoes, heavy with fresh basil, oregano, crushed garlic, and red wine, with cayenne pepper. Simmering all day. Filling the

81

entire house with its savory aroma. Everyone will be together and we'll decorate for the holidays and eat and drink.

I text my niece a second time. 'Where are you?'

I wait ten seconds and text her partner Janet next. 'Trying to get hold of Lucy.'

Janet texts me right back. 'Will let her know.'

It seems an odd reply, as if they don't live together.

'Any area where you could possibly access the body we got a unit posted,' Marino is saying, and I tune back in. 'Nobody enters or exists without our seeing.'

A patrol officer in a Cambridge cruiser flicks his light bar at us in a quick roll of red-blue. I lower and raise my window to clear condensation off the glass.

'What I call an invisible perimeter,' Marino repeats what he's already told me. 'Uniforms on foot and tucked out of sight in cruisers, keeping a scan going.'

'That's a very good idea.'

'Yeah it's a good idea because I'm the one who thought of it,' Marino says.

He's going to be like this for a while, so grandiose it's barely tolerable and having no idea how obnoxious he sounds. But I go along with it and ask, 'Has any unusual activity been noticed so far?' I check my phone again.

When I texted Lucy the first time I asked if the names Gail Shipton and Double S meant anything to her. It's unusual that she's not gotten back to me. I have a feeling her silence spells trouble.

'Nope. Nothing out of the ordinary,' Marino answers my question. 'But the guy could be anywhere. He could be watching through one of these thousands of windows,' he adds as his phone rings again.

* * *

Carin Hegel's voice is tense and uncertain as it sounds from the SUV's speakerphone. She begins by telling Marino that she spent most of yesterday with Gail Shipton in witness preparation for the trial.

'The plaintiff's case goes on first and she's my first witness. Obviously she's my most important one and we were trying to get a good start before the holidays,' the Boston lawyer says in her distinctive alto voice with its strong Massachusetts accent that makes me think of the Kennedys.

'What time did you finish yesterday?' Marino asks.

'She left my firm around four p.m. and not long afterward something important came up that I needed to address with her. I sent her a text message asking her to call me, which she did, but we got disconnected. Is she all right?'

'When did you get disconnected?'

'Hold on and I'll check my phone so I can give you the exact time. Do we know if she's all right?'

We head deeper into a part of the MIT campus where student residential buildings and fraternity houses are brick with limestone trim.

83

They crowd the alley to our left, and to our right is the vast open area of tennis courts and playing fields behind a high chain-link fence. In the distance the luminescence of police lighting is an eerie nimbus.

'At five fifty-seven p.m. she called me.' Carin Hegel is back. 'She told me she was at the Psi Bar and had stepped outside where it was quiet. I brought up what I wanted to discuss with her — '

'And what was that?' Marino asks.

'I'm not at liberty . . . It's privileged — attorney-client privilege.'

'Maybe now's not a good time to hide behind privilege, Ms. Hegel. If you know anything that might help us — '

'What I can tell you is this,' she interrupts. 'I was talking to Gail and it took me a minute or so to realize she was gone.'

'What do you mean *gone?*' Marino drives slowly along the narrow, dark alleyway, the headlights bright on wet pavement.

'The call was lost.'

'And you didn't hear anything? Like maybe she said something to someone? Maybe someone approached her?'

A tense pause and she says, 'The call was dropped so I heard nothing at all.'

'What about right before it was dropped? You didn't hear anything?'

'Before that she was talking. Is Gail all right?' Carin Hegel's voice is demanding and as unyielding as concrete. 'What is this about her being reported missing? You left me a message that she's been reported missing and it's on the Internet. Apparently she was last seen at the very bar she called me from, a place she frequents. An MIT hangout that's not far from where the body's been found, the one on the news. Is that true?'

'It's true that a body has been found.'

'Has something happened to Gail? Do we know that for sure?'

Carin Hegel, known as a pit bull of a litigator who never loses a case, sounds terrified now.

'Is there any reason your lawsuit that's about to go to trial might be a threat to her personal safety?' Marino asks.

'Oh God. It's her.'

'That's not been confirmed yet.'

'Is Dr. Scarpetta involved in this? I need to talk to her. I need you to tell her that there are matters we need to discuss,' she says. 'Please tell her it's imperative we speak.'

'What makes you think I'd be talking to her?'

'You used to work for her.'

Marino hesitates, glancing over at me.

I shake my head. I've not said anything to her. I don't know why she would be aware that Marino used to work for me. His recent departure from the CFC hasn't been in the news. It's a detail not generally known or even of interest.

'Has Gail been threatened by anyone involved in your case?' Marino asks. 'Anyone in particular we might want to be looking at?'

'The trial starts in less than two weeks. Connect the dots, Detective Marino. This can't

85

be a coincidence. Do you think it's her? The body found at MIT? It sounds like that's what you're thinking.'

'To be honest, it's not looking good.'

'Oh God. Dear God.'

'If the worst turns out to be true, would that be enough to stop the trial?' Marino asks. 'I'm looking for a motive here if we confirm and we've definitely not done that yet.'

'It would be all the more reason to go forward. The evil bastards.' Her voice trembles. 'But the answer is yes about the motive.' She struggles to steady herself, clearing her throat. 'You have no idea what these people are like or their connections, about as far up as it goes, I suspect. That's as much as I'm saying over my phone, which is probably tapped, and not long ago someone tried to hack into my firm's computer. That's all I'm saying but it should be enough.'

'If you think of anything we need to know right away, you got my number.' Marino doesn't want to hear anything else. Not over the phone. Not when there seems to be a suggestion of organized crime or political corruption or possibly both.

9

The portable light tower I saw on the news illuminates a muddy red infield where a yellow tarp is staked down by blaze-orange crime scene flags that flutter in the wind. The body is protected from the elements and the curious, the scene secured by Sil Machado and two uniformed officers. They restlessly pace, waiting for me.

'You got any idea why she'd want to talk to you?' Marino asks me about what Carin Hegel just said.

'Probably for the same reason other people do,' I reply. 'But beyond the obvious questions I'm always asked? No, except I ran into her at the federal courthouse last month and she alluded to a case she has that involves very bad people. Thugs, she called them, and I got the impression she was worried about her safety. So I'm assuming that might be what she was just referring to. It's possible she's done a lot of digging and has discovered that Double S is involved in a number of unsavory things.'

'What does she expect you to do about it?'

'People vent. They know they can say anything to me.'

'Crooks. I pretty much can't stand rich people anymore.'

'Lucy's okay. And Benton. Not everybody who's wealthy is bad.'

'At least Lucy earned what she's got.' Marino has to get in a dig about Benton's old family money.

'I have no idea how she could have found out you don't work for me anymore.'

'Obviously someone told her.'

'I can't imagine why it would be a topic of conversation.'

'Someone with Cambridge PD might have said something to her,' Marino says. 'Or someone at the CFC.'

'I can't imagine why,' I repeat.

On the other side of the fenced-in fields and across Vassar Street, the dormitory called Simmons Hall is a massive aluminum-clad construction of cubed solids and voids that shines like a silvery space station. I note two more uniformed officers on the sidewalk in front of it, and a jogger not slowing his pace while a bicyclist in reflective clothing disappears toward the football stadium.

'Sounds to me like she's got good reason to worry Gail's been murdered,' Marino then says.

'She very well may be worrying exactly that. And she may have good reason, considering the details she'd know about Double S.'

'In other words, what Carin Hegel's really worried about is herself, worried about her case. A case she's making a fortune from,' Marino says cynically. 'Did I tell you how much I hate lawyers?'

'It will be getting light in about an hour.' I'm not interested in hearing another diatribe about litigation lawyers, or 'bottom feeders,' as Marino calls them. 'We need to get the body out of here soon.'

I watch the jogger, a distant figure in black, barely visible. For some reason he's caught my eye, graceful and lean and light on his feet in running tights, a small person, possibly a young student. MIT gets them before they're old enough to leave home, fourteen or fifteen and stunningly gifted. He jogs through a parking lot and is swallowed by the darkness in the direction of Albany Street.

'Dumping a body in the wide open for all the world to see under normal circumstances. But this isn't exactly Normalville.' Marino looks around as he drives slowly. 'He probably came down this same alley unless he accessed the area from the other side, from Vassar Street, which would have put him practically on top of the MIT Police Department in order to get back here. Those are the only two ways if you're driving. And he had to have a vehicle to transport her unless he carried her out of one of the dorms or apartment buildings. Whatever he did, he dumped her right in the middle of everything. Crazy as shit.'

'Not crazy but deliberate,' I reply. 'He was surrounded by an audience of people who don't look.'

'You got that right. And MIT's even worse than Harvard, a hundred times worse,' Marino says as if he's an expert in academia. 'They have to hand out deodorant and toothpaste in the library because the kids live in there like it's a homeless shelter, especially this time of year.

89

Final exams week. You get a B, you kill yourself.'

'Your comrades have done a good job being low-key,' I point out, figuring he'll take credit for that, too. 'It's not obvious what's going on unless you happen to see news feeds on the Internet.'

'Nothing's obvious to the Einsteins around here. I'm telling you, they're not in the same world as you and me.'

'I'm not sure I want them in the same world as you and me.'

We reach a sprawling red brick residential complex called Next House, where garden plots are dead and bare branches reach over the narrow pavement and shiver in the wind. Then the alley takes a hard right past a red steel tetrahedral sculpture, and we drive toward the parking lot, fenced-in and bordered by trees. The security arm has been raised, frozen in the open position.

The only vehicles inside are police cars and one of my CFC windowless vans, white with our crest on the doors, the caduceus and scales of justice in blue. My transport team has arrived. Rusty and Harold see us and climb out of the van's front seat.

'This is where I'd come in if it was me,' Marino summarizes as we drive in.

'Assuming you had a way to access this parking lot. It's not open to the public.'

'It is if you drive through over there.'

He indicates the far side of the lot flanking Vassar Street, where a chain-link pedestrian gate is wide open and moving in the wind. A car could fit through easily but it would require driving over the sidewalk and the curb directly across the street from the MIT red brick and blue tile police station.

'If that's what he did, it was brazen.' Everywhere I look I see fencing, gates, and parking that are off-limits to people who don't have magnetic swipes and keys.

There is nothing welcoming if you don't belong here. Like Harvard, MIT is a private, exclusive club, about as private and exclusive as it gets.

'Maybe not all that brazen at two or three o'clock in the morning when it's pouring rain,' Marino says. 'There's no other way to get in here unless you have a swipe to raise the gate.'

'Was the arm up like it is now when the police got here?'

'Nope. The lot was secure and empty except the gate for foot traffic over there. It was open like it is right now.'

'Is it possible the couple who found the body opened it?'

'I asked Machado that. He says it was already open.' Marino stops the SUV and shifts it into park. 'Apparently it's never locked. Don't ask me why because it sure as hell wouldn't stop someone unauthorized from parking in here.'

'Maybe not,' I observe. 'But most people aren't going to drive over a sidewalk and a curb in view of the campus police headquarters. I also expect that cars authorized to park here have stickers. So if you manage to get in without a swipe, you still might get towed.'

91

★ ★ ★

Marino kills the engine, switching on his high beams to annoy Rusty and Harold as they open the back of the van. They exaggerate shielding their eyes with their hands, yelling at him.

'Jesus!'

'You trying to blind us?'

'Turn those damn things off!'

'Po-lice brutality!'

'Under one of these trees in the rain and dark, and no one's going to see anything even if they're paying attention.' Marino continues telling me what his thinking would have been were he a deranged killer.

Clearly he's decided that's what we're up against and I have my own reasons to worry he might be right. I think of Benton's cases and I wonder where he is and what he's doing.

Marino lowers the windows several inches.

'Will he be okay in here?' I ask about his dog.

Quincy is awake, sitting up in his crate and making his usual crying sounds when Marino leaves him.

'I'm not sure what the utility is hauling him around everywhere if he's just going to stay in the car,' I add.

'He's in training.' Marino opens his door. 'He's got to get used to things like crime scenes and riding around in a cop car.'

'I think what he's used to is exactly that — riding around.' I climb out as Rusty and Harold clack open the folded aluminum legs of a stretcher and I'm again reminded that I've lost

92

my lead investigator.

A stretcher isn't going to work in these conditions. But it won't be Marino giving that instruction. The rain is on and off, barely spitting, the overcast ceiling lifting. I don't bother pulling up my hood or zipping my jacket as I study the fence separating the parking lot from Briggs Field. An open gate is crisscrossed with yellow ribbons of reflective scene tape.

I imagine someone parking in this lot and having a way to open a gate, perhaps by cutting off the lock. This person then moved the dead body inside the fence, transporting it some fifty yards across grass and mud, leaving it in the middle of a red infield that during baseball season might be a pitcher's mound. As I look at the scene in the context of its surroundings I think of what Marino said: *Some sick fuck out there just getting started.* Already I don't agree with the *just getting started* part of it.

My intuition picks up on a calculating intelligence, an individual with a decided purpose. He's not a novice. What he did wasn't a reaction to the unexpected. It wasn't an act of panic. He has a method that works for him. Bringing the dead woman here and leaving her the way he did has meaning. That's what I feel. I could be wrong, and I hope I am as I continue to think about the Washington, D.C., cases I've reviewed. What I'm not wrong about is whoever is responsible left evidence out here. They all do. Locard's exchange principle. You bring something to the scene and you take something away.

'The grass is soaked and the area she's in is

93

thick mud so you can forget a stretcher,' I tell Rusty and Harold, or Cheech and Chong as Marino rudely refers to them behind their backs. 'Use a spine board. You're going to have to carry her. And bring extra sheets and plenty of tape.'

'What about a body bag?' Rusty asks me.

'We're going to carefully preserve the position of the body and the way it's draped, transporting her exactly as she is. I don't want to pouch her. We'll have to be creative.'

'You got it, Chief.'

Rusty looks like a refugee from the sixties with his long graying hair and preference for baggy pants and knit beanies, what Marino calls *surfer clothes*. This early morning he's outfitted for the weather in a rain jacket with a lightning bolt on the front, faded jeans, tall rubber boots, and a tie-dyed bandanna around his head.

'I guess from now on we don't have to do what you tell us,' he zings Marino, his former supervisor.

'And I don't have to bother telling you shit or pretend I like you,' Marino retorts as if he means it.

'Do you have a gun under that jacket or are you just happy to see us?' Harold needles him back, looking like the former undertaker he is, in a suit and tie and double-breasted raincoat, the legs of his creased trousers rolled up to the top of his boots. 'I see you brought your K-nine just in case we can't find the body that's out there in plain view.'

'The only thing Quincy can find is his doggie bowl.'

'Watch out. Better not piss off De-tect-ive Marino. He'll write you a parking ticket.'

Rusty and Harold continue with the banter and snipes. They return the stretcher to the van and collect sheets, the spine board, and other equipment as I get my field case out of the backseat and Quincy cries.

'We won't be very far away. You be a good boy and take a nap.' I find myself talking to a dog again, this one vocal, unlike mine. 'We'll be right over there, just a stone's throw away.'

I stare up at lighted windows in apartments around us, counting at least twenty people watching what's going on. Most of them look young and dressed for bed or maybe they're up studying, pulling all-nighters. I don't notice anyone on foot loitering nearby, only the officers on the other side of the playing fields patrolling the sidewalk near the fence.

I imagine looking out a dormitory or apartment window at the exact moment someone was moving a dead body through the rain and mud of Briggs Field, virtually right under everybody's nose. It would have been too dark to discern what was happening except that something out of the ordinary was. But students around here don't pay attention. Marino's right about that. They don't even look when they cross a busy street, their situational awareness almost nonexistent, especially this time of year.

In several days undergraduate students will be numb with exhaustion and headed home for the holidays. The campus will be largely deserted and I can't stop thinking about the timing,

95

during final exams not even a week before Christmas. And the proximity bothers me, too. Across the street from the MIT police station and within walking distance from the CFC, not even a mile from here.

10

I dig the tactical flashlight out of my bag and shine the diamond-bright beam along the chain-link fence.

For as far as I can see, other gates are secured with padlocks and I don't know why this one wouldn't be unless it's as Marino suggested. Someone used bolt cutters or a key. I paint light over galvanized steel posts, noting multiple scratches where the fork latch would be if the gate were closed.

'Possibly from the chain and padlock.' I point out the damage to Marino. 'But this gouge right here?' I move the light closer and a deep scrape lights up like polished platinum. 'It looks recently made, possibly by whatever was used to cut off the lock, if that's what happened.'

'It's fresh.' Marino has his own flashlight out. 'MIT won't be happy but I'll make sure we dig up the fence post and get it to the labs in case anything's ever recovered for tool-marks comparison.'

'I would,' I agree.

'I'll wait until we're done out here.' His eyes haven't stopped moving, taking in everything around us, and he lifts his portable radio close to his mouth.

'Delta Thirteen,' he calls Machado and requests a backup to secure the gate and the parking lot. 'We need someone here right now so nobody else enters the scene or tampers with anything,' Marino emphasizes loudly. 'And what we don't need is cops crawling all over either. Why we got so many uniforms where you're at?'

'Just two.' Machado's radio obscures the lower part of his face.

'I can count. They the only two? Because I don't think so. We need a record of whoever accesses or attempts. Is someone keeping a log?'

'Ten-four.'

'How many reporters so far?'

'A TV crew about an hour ago, Channel Five, and they keep circling, waiting for the Doc to get here.' Machado stares at us from the muddy infield with its incongruous yellow tarp anchored by cheery orange flags. 'Then Channel Seven was here maybe twenty ago. The minute anything they're filming streams live we can expect more drop-ins.'

'It's already on the Internet,' I remind Marino.

'Too late, thanks to the little spot you did on Fox,' he says over the air for the benefit of whoever's listening. 'You trying out for a reality show?'

Marino repeats that they must keep a record of everyone who enters and leaves and to watch the area for 'nonessentials,' by which he means voyeurs, possibly whoever's involved in the body being left out here. I envision the Marino from our early years, chain-smoking, chronically in a sour mood, acting like a male chauvinist ass. But he knew what to do. He was a damn good detective and I'd almost forgotten that.

Marino squats close to the opening in the

98

fence and shines his flashlight through, the crisscrossed tape blazing neon yellow. The intense beam of light illuminates where the pavement ends at an area of soaked brown grass that is flattened and gouged as if something hard and heavy was dragged over it. Then the churned-up area recedes into the distance, to the infield, fading into a barely perceptible intermittent trail, a remnant that seems more imagined than real as if left by a phantom snail.

'She was dragged.' Marino stands up.

'I'd say so,' Harold agrees.

'He got her inside this gate,' Marino adds, 'and had to have a way to do that unless it just happened to be unlocked or the lock and chain conveniently were already cut off.'

'Unlikely,' Harold says. 'MIT campus police patrol everything around here like it's Vatican City.'

'They'd notice if one of these gates was busted into or a lock was missing,' Rusty pipes up.

'Did I hear an echo?' Marino says as if Rusty and Harold are invisible. 'Oh no. I'm sorry. It's the peanut gallery. My point being,' he says to me, 'whoever's involved had a plan for disposing of her body.' He stares at the square of bright yellow plasticized paper in a sea of red some fifty yards from us.

The wind shakes and snatches at the tarp as if what's underneath it is fighting to get out.

'Someone who knew he didn't need a swipe to get into this back lot,' Marino continues. 'Someone who knew he could drive over the curb through that pedestrian gate, that it happens to be a wide one and a vehicle could fit through it. Someone who knew that all the gates leading into the playing fields would be locked and he'd have to have a way inside the fence.'

'Unless you're talking about an individual who in fact does have a swipe, keys, access. Like a student or someone who works here,' Rusty points out and Marino ignores him.

He scans the lit-up apartment windows, a misty rain slick like sweat on his face, which is hard and angry as if whatever happened to this dead woman is personal and he might just hurt whoever's to blame. He takes his time glaring at a Channel 5 TV van with a satellite dish on the roof and a microwave antenna on the back as it pulls into the lot and stops. The front doors swing open.

'Don't even think of coming inside the fence!' Marino barks at the news correspondent stepping out, a striking-looking woman I recognize. 'Nobody beyond the tape. Stay the hell out.'

'If I wait right here and behave myself, can I get a statement, pretty please?' The correspondent's name is Barbara Fairbanks, and I've had my rounds with her, unpleasant ones.

'I got nothing to say,' Marino answers.

'I was talking to Dr. Scarpetta,' Barbara Fairbanks says as she smiles at me and moves closer with her microphone, a cameraman on her heels. 'Do you know anything yet? Can you confirm if it's the woman reported missing?'

The camera light turns on, following Barbara Fairbanks like a full moon, and I know better than to give even one simple answer. If I reply I just got here or don't know or I haven't examined the body yet, somehow it ends up an out-of-context slanted quote that goes viral on the Internet.

'Can you give me a statement about Newtown? Do you think it will do any good to study the killer's brain . . . ?'

'Let's go,' I tell Rusty and Harold.

'Stay away from the disturbed grassy area, keep way off to the side of it,' Marino says to us. 'I got to get it photographed if they haven't done it already. I'll probably get some soil samples, too. See if there's fibers from the sheet that's over her, see if we can reconstruct what the hell happened out here.'

★ ★ ★

We pick our way through sopping-wet grass and mud that sucks at our feet, headed toward Machado and the two officers, one with Cambridge, the other with MIT.

Having stood sentry over the body for more than an hour, they look wet and chilled, their boots chunked with red clay. Machado's boyish face is tired and tense, with a shadow of stubble, and I can sense his worries. He has legitimate ones.

Cambridge is a powerhouse, with Harvard and MIT and multibillion-dollar technology companies, not to mention a constant stream of visitors that includes celebrities, royalty, and sitting heads of state. The DA and the mayor will be breathing fire down the investigative unit's neck if this case isn't solved quickly and quietly.

'I don't see anybody guarding the gate,' Marino says right off. 'There's a news crew hovering like vultures. Barbara *Un*fairbanks, it just so happens. Where's the backup I asked for?'

'We've got another car coming.' Machado turns his attention to the parking lot where the news van is waiting with headlights on, engine rumbling.

For an instant I hold Barbara Fairbanks's stare. A tall lithe woman with bottomless dark eyes and short raven-black hair, she's remarkably pretty in a hard way, like a gemstone, like a perfectly shaped figure carved of Thai spinel or tourmaline. She turns away and climbs back inside the van, and she's not the sort to give up on a scoop.

'The body may have been placed on top of something and dragged,' Marino says to Machado. 'The grass just inside the gate looks disturbed and pressed down in places with divots where it got dug up in spots.'

'There are a lot of divots and churned-up areas,' Machado replies, and it doesn't seem to bother him that Marino has a way of acting as if he's in charge. 'The problem is knowing for sure when any of them happened. It's hard to tell because of the conditions.'

After setting scene cases in the mud, Harold and Rusty place the spine board and sheets on top of them, awaiting my instruction as Marino digs a pair of examination gloves out of a pocket and asks for a camera. I silently make plans, calculating how to handle what I expect will happen next as I watch the news van drive out of the parking lot. I have no doubt that Barbara Fairbanks hasn't given up. I expect she'll circle around to the other side of the field, the one nearest us, and try to film through the fence. I'm not going to examine the body until I know exactly what she intends to do.

'I'll walk around, get some photos.' Marino turns on his flashlight and is careful stepping in the muck, sweeping the beam of light over puddles and red mud.

The MIT officer says to me, 'I'm pretty sure he didn't do anything to her out here, just left her so she'd be found really fast.'

I set down my scene case as he continues to offer his opinions, and with his strong jaw and perfect build he's probably used to commanding attention. I remember him well from a case several weeks ago. An MIT freshman died suddenly and unexpectedly during wrestling practice.

'Drugs,' he adds. 'That's what I'm thinking.'

I don't recall his name but I won't forget Bryce following him and gawking when the officer appeared inside the large-scale x-ray room while I was using an embalming machine to inject contrast dye into the dead wrestler's femoral artery, a procedure that would seem bizarre to someone unfamiliar with postmortem angiography. Three-dimensional computed tomography images revealed the cause of death before I touched the body with a blade.

'We've met before,' I say to him as I crouch down by my field case. 'Earlier this month.'

'Yeah, that was pretty crazy. I thought for a minute you were a mad scientist pumping in fluids like you were trying to raise him from the dead. Andy Hunter,' he reintroduces himself, his gray eyes penetrating. 'It turns out the kid's father is a Nobel Prize winner. You'd think people that smart could have prevented their kid's death with routine tests.'

'Abdominal aortic aneurysms are called a silent killer for a reason. Often there are no warnings or symptoms.' I snap open heavy plastic clasps.

'My grandfather died from a blown aneurysm.' Hunter stares at me, and when he was at the CFC several weeks ago he openly flirted. 'Blue collar, no insurance, never went to the doctor. He had a bad headache one minute, was dead the next. I've thought about being screened but I'm phobic of radiation.'

'An MRI with contrast dye doesn't emit radiation.' I settle closer to the anchored yellow tarp with its ominous shape underneath. 'You'd be fine unless you have kidney damage.'

'Not that I know of.'

'Talk to your doctor,' Machado kids him. 'You know, the one you pay?'

'Gail Shipton was last seen possibly between five-thirty and six last night at the Psi Bar. Is that still the story?' I ask him.

'Right, and we have a preliminary ID. A visual,' Machado says. 'The photo that's all over the news, it looks like her anyway. I realize we need to verify officially but in my mind this is Gail Shipton. She left the bar to talk on her phone around five-thirty, six p.m. Supposedly. That's what we know.'

'I doubt it was raining when she stepped outside.' I tear off the perforated top from a box of exam gloves, the kind I like, latex-free, with textured fingertips. 'She was out there for a while, at least seventeen minutes, based on the duration of the first call with someone who has a blocked number.'

'It wasn't raining at the time she disappeared.' Machado's deep-set eyes are curious as if he wonders what I'm getting at with my comments about the weather. 'It didn't start raining until later.'

'Do we know exactly when? What do you mean by 'later'? I went to sleep around eleven and it wasn't raining then but it looked like it was going to any minute.'

I notice Barbara Fairbanks's crew is now in front of Simmons Hall, on Vassar Street, exactly as I expected.

'When I uncover her you're going to need to hold something up as a barrier,' I say to Rusty and Harold. 'We don't want her on TV.'

'We've got plenty of sheets.'

'We'll be ready if they head this way.'

'The storm started around midnight,' Machado answers my question. 'Rain mixed with freezing rain and then just rain. But a monsoon.'

'If we consider the possibility that she was abducted at around six p.m., then whoever's responsible knew the weather conditions or could guess what they might be by the time he disposed of her body out here.' I find two thermometers and a sterile retractable scalpel. 'It would seem bad weather didn't matter, that this person was comfortable in wet, nasty conditions.'

'When the mood strikes,' Andy Hunter says. 'People used to these parts are used to the weather.'

I watch Barbara Fairbanks as she follows the fence, her camera crew behind her. They'll have to film through chain-link but I'm not going to let them get even that. Marino's not going to allow it either. He slogs through the mud in a hurry, back in our direction, while Rusty and Harold get sheets ready for a barricade.

'Toss me one,' Marino calls out and Rusty hurls a folded disposable sheet as if it's a Frisbee.

Marino catches it in one hand. He rips off the cellophane wrapping as he sloshes through mud and puddles toward the TV crew. Shaking open the sheet, he holds it up against the fence, blocking the camera.

'Ah come on, man!' a crew member yells.

'I'm sure you already know this,' I say to Machado, 'but Gail Shipton was involved in a lawsuit that's due to go to trial in less than two weeks.'

I'm tempted to check my phone again but I don't. It continues to nag at me that Lucy might have some connection to Gail Shipton, a computer engineer with a military-grade smartphone case. The fact that Lucy isn't answering me is why I'm increasingly suspicious, and in fact I've about decided it's true. Janet said she'd tell Lucy I was trying to contact her. When my niece ignores me something is up. It's almost never good.

'I didn't know anything about a lawsuit,' Machado says.

'Are you familiar with a financial company called Double S?' I ask him as Marino moves along the fence.

He's holding up the sheet, moving as the crew moves, blocking their view.

'I can't say that I am or know anything about a trial,' Machado answers and I can tell by the look on his face that I've given him something new to think about.

Maybe he'll stop stubbornly assuming this young woman's death is an accidental drug overdose. Maybe he'll quit worrying about public relations and potentially bad press.

'Harold, if you and Rusty will stand right there,' I say to them, 'I think we'll be okay.'

Their disposable-sheet barricade goes up loudly like a sailboat tacking into the wind. Plastic rustles as I pull back the yellow tarp.

11

I'm disturbed again by the sight of her. I get the same feeling I did when I looked at the photographs Marino e-mailed to me earlier. The body is gracefully posed, draped in white in a red sea of mud.

Her eyes are barely open to the narrowest of slits as if she's drifting off to sleep, her pale lips slightly parted, exposing the white edges of her upper teeth. I study the position of her arms, the dramatically cocked wrist, the hand slightly curled and resting on her belly. Plastic rustles again as I fold the tarp and hand it to Harold, instructing him to package it as evidence. I don't want to lose any microscopic debris that might have been transferred to it.

'That's pretty wild,' Rusty observes. 'Maybe she's supposed to look like a virgin.'

'How would you know what a virgin looks like?' Harold can't resist another corny quip.

'Give me a minute.' I want them to be silent.

I'm not in the mood for sophomoric humor and I don't want to hear their opinions right now. I continue studying the body, standing back, then walking around to get perspective as my misgivings grow. I scan flawless skin that is much too clean and hands uninjured and a face too peaceful and undamaged.

There is nothing lewd or even sexual about the way she's displayed. Her legs are together, her breasts and genitals covered by the cloth carefully arranged around her from her upper chest to her lower legs. Her throat is milky smooth with no ligature mark or bruise, just a dusky redness at the back of her neck from livor mortis, the settling of blood when her heart stopped and her circulation quit. I see no injuries to her ankles or wrists. Superficially, there's no sign she struggled with anyone. At a glance there's nothing to tell me she so much as resisted her own death and I find that profoundly abnormal and odd.

I get down closer to look and I smell the earth and the rain. Decomposition isn't apparent yet but will escalate when she's transported to my office where the temperatures are considerably warmer. I detect perfume, a fruity floral fragrance with a hint of sandalwood and vanilla, more noticeable when I'm near her face and long brown hair. The ivory cloth looks like a woven synthetic and is remarkably clean. I touch a hemmed edge of fabric that has been arranged over the body in a manner that is thoughtful and deliberate, wrapped straight across her upper chest and under her arms like a bath towel.

'It's not a bedsheet,' I decide. 'A synthetic blend that's moderately stretchy, and it's been doubled over so it's quite long but not all that wide.'

'Like a curtain?' Machado asks, baffled.

'I don't think so. There's no lining or pocket for a rod and I see no evidence that rings or hooks were ever sewn on.' I check the cloth without rearranging it. 'It's smooth on one side

109

and textured on the other, similar to how tights are woven, like a low-stretch tricot.'

'I don't know what that is,' he says.

'A tricot material is used in gloves, leggings, very lightweight sweaters, for example.'

I study the position of the body and the way the cloth is draped, modestly covering her from her clavicle to several inches above her ankles.

'Evocative of ancient Rome or Jerusalem or a health spa,' I suggest as Benton's Washington, D.C., cases nag at me. 'At least that's what comes to mind.'

'Well, that's why these psychos pose their victims.' Marino has wandered back and squats close by, his feet almost slipping out from under him. 'They do it to make us think something.'

'It's been my experience that what they do isn't about us. It's about them.' I want to tell him about the Washington cases and the way those bodies were draped but I don't dare. 'It's about their own fantasies, their own emotions at the time.'

'The cloth reminds me of a shroud,' Harold says and he would know about such things. 'They're becoming popular in burials, particularly handmade shrouds that are wrapped around the body like a winding cloth. The last year or so I was in the funeral business we had a couple of what they call *green* burials. All natural and biodegradable.'

'This isn't a natural fabric and it wouldn't be biodegradable.' I sit back on my heels, surveying the body, looking carefully in detail before I touch her.

110

Pale fibers, possibly from the cloth, adhere to areas of exposed wan, wet flesh. I note that her short unpolished nails are intact and there are fibers under them, bluish ones, and I wonder what they're from. Something she may have been wrapped in while she was still alive, I consider. People no longer moving generally don't get fibers and other trace evidence under their nails all the way up to the quick. I retrieve a hand lens and small ultraviolet light from my field case.

'Is there some funeral business around here that sells cloths like this?' Machado is taking more photographs.

'Biodegradable items like urns, yes.' Harold cranes his neck, checking on the position of the TV crew as he and Rusty hold up the sheet, blocking the view. 'I'm not sure about where you'd get handmade shrouds around here. The few I saw came from out west somewhere. Maybe Oregon. You can buy them on the Internet.'

'A synthetic blend wouldn't be biodegradable,' I repeat. 'We don't know what this is.'

I switch on the UV light and the lens glows purple as it radiates black light that's not visible. A preliminary scan of the body will alert me if there's trace evidence, including biological fluids such as semen. I want to make sure I collect anything that could get dislodged or lost during transport to the CFC, and I direct the light over the body and fluorescing electric colors wink brilliantly. Bloodred, emerald green, and a deep bluish purple.

'What the hell?' Andy Hunter bends closer to

get a better look. 'Some kind of glitter, maybe Christmas glitter?'

'It's much finer than that and I doubt glitter would fluoresce like this in UV.' I move the light and every place it touches reacts in the same three brilliant colors. 'Like a very fine fluorescent powder that's all over the cloth and the body, a high concentration around her nose and lips, on her teeth and inside her nostrils.' I direct the light as I talk.

'Have you ever seen anything like this before?' Machado moves next to me, his boots sinking in red mud.

'No, not exactly, but whatever it is it's stubborn enough to survive the rain. Either that or there was a lot more of it before she was left out here.' I paint the light over the mud around her.

Sparkles light up here and there, the same three vivid colors, and I reach for a package of swabs.

'I'll collect some of it now for analysis.' I do it as I talk. 'Then I'll take her temp and we'll get her to the morgue.'

I seal the swabs inside evidence containers that I label with a Sharpie and I touch the dead woman's left outstretched arm with its dramatically bent wrist. She's cold and stiff, in full rigor mortis.

I loosen the cloth around her neck and open it. She has nothing on but panties that are several sizes too big. The hi-cut brief is peach with a lace trim around the waistband and I check the label in back, an expensive brand of lingerie called Hanro, *M* for medium, which would fit someone who generally wears size eight to ten. I note that the crotch is stained pale yellow and I'm uncomfortably reminded of what Benton said.

The three murdered women in his Washington, D.C., case were wearing each other's panties or those of someone unidentified. The panties were stained with urine. He surmises they lost control of their bladders while they were being suffocated, and there were fibers, blue and white Lycra ones that may have come from upholstery or possibly from athletic clothing the killer had on.

★   ★   ★

With the scalpel I make a small incision in her upper-right abdomen. Oozing blood is an unnaturally dull red because it's no longer oxygenated. The blood of the dead. Cold and dark like stagnant water.

I insert a long thermometer into the liver and place a second thermometer on top of my field case to record the ambient temperature.

'She's been dead for a while,' I say. 'At least six hours but I'm betting longer, depending on the conditions.'

'Maybe since early last night when she disappeared?' Machado watches me intently, a spooked look in his eyes.

No doubt he's never seen a case like this. I haven't either, not quite. But I've seen photographs that I can't share with him or Marino. Benton will have to do that.

'If she were abducted around six p.m., then that's almost twelve hours ago,' I add.

Palpating her scalp, I feel for fractures or other injuries and don't note any.

'I seriously doubt she's been dead that long. She was alive somewhere for a while,' I explain.

'Like maybe she was held hostage?' Machado asks.

'I don't know.' I check again for lesions, lifting her rigid arms and hands, examining them carefully front and back. 'So far I'm not seeing any evidence that she was tied up or struggled.' Her flesh feels cold through my gloves, almost refrigerated cold but warmer than the air. 'I don't see any defense or scrimmage injuries.'

I move down to her bare feet, shining the UV light on them and more of the same residue lights up like fairy dust. Bloodred, emerald green, and a deep bluish purple. The color combination seems to indicate a single source, a fine material comprised of three substances that fluoresce in the short wavelength of ultraviolet light. I collect more of it with adhesive stubs that sparkle electrically as I place them inside evidence bags.

'Another thought is some funky makeup she might have had on?' Andy Hunter suggests. 'These girls wear a lot of glittery stuff these days.'

'All over her and the cloth?' I reply skeptically as I pull on fresh gloves to make sure I'm not the one transferring the residue to other areas of the body. 'I'm going to speculate that her body was someplace where this residue is indigenous and it got transferred to her and the cloth she's wrapped in.'

I lift her rigorous lower legs, noting that the cloth is relatively clean underneath.

'Some kind of dirt that sparkles in UV,' Machado considers.

'I don't think it's dirt. A fine residue that consistently fluoresces the same way strikes me as manufactured, something commercially used,' I reply. 'We'll try the scanning electron microscope for a first-round screening. Hopefully, Ernie's in today.'

The bottoms of her bare feet are clean, just light spatters of mud that splashed up from the earlier heavy rain. The glittery residue is everywhere, from head to toe, as if she's been airbrushed with something that lights up in the ultraviolet range of invisible radiation. Using a hand lens and forceps, I begin collecting bluish fibers from under her nails, knocking them loose inside a small plastic evidence bag.

'She wasn't dragged out here unless there was something under her.' I turn her on her side.

'Maybe she was carried,' Andy Hunter says. 'Maybe by someone strong or more than one person.'

Her back is a deep red with areas of blanching where her shoulder blades rested against a firm surface as her uncirculating blood settled. Livor mortis is fixed. She was on her back for hours after death, possibly on a floor inside someplace warm, in the position she's in now as she got stiff, but she didn't die looking like this. She was posed postmortem, her legs straight and together, her arms arranged the way they are until she was as rigid as hard rubber.

Camera flashes strobe as Machado takes multiple photographs while Marino assists with a six-inch plastic ruler for a scale and labeling. On the other side of the fence nearest Vassar Street, the curious are gathering, cell-phone cameras small sparks of light. Several uniformed officers hover nearby.

'Maybe you should head over and help out your buddies,' Marino says to Hunter, and I know why.

Marino's had enough of Andy Hunter's extreme good looks and his habit of staring at me and hovering too close.

'Let's make sure we know who's looking and taking pictures.' Marino says it like an order.

Hunter checks his anger and smiles. 'Sure. But I don't work for your department. Not last I checked. In fact, you barely work for yours, last I checked. Hope you're enjoying the new job.'

He sets out through the mud, heading for the path of least resistance through the parking lot. I remove the thermometers and check them.

'Her body temp is fifty-eight degrees; the ambient temp is fifty-one. She's been dead eight hours, possibly longer,' I calculate. 'Much of that time she was someplace much warmer than it is out here or her rigor and livor wouldn't be this advanced. They would have formed slowly because of the cool temperature and cold rain. The conditions out here are close to refrigeration and that would have slowed everything down considerably.'

'Meaning she died several hours after she disappeared from the bar,' Machado says. 'She went somewhere with someone, maybe knew the person and ended up dead.'

'I can't tell you whether she went with someone willingly or unwillingly,' I remark. 'Not at this point.'

'But she's got no defense injuries.' Machado repeats what I said earlier. 'So it doesn't look like she struggled with whoever it was, right?'

'There are no obvious injuries but I've not thoroughly examined her in a good light,' I reply. 'She may have internal injuries. We'll see what shows up when she's scanned.'

I change gloves again, stuffing used ones in my coat pocket.

12

My purple-gloved fingers gently push open the dead woman's eyelids and the conjunctiva is florid with pinpoint hemorrhages. The whites of her eyes are almost solid red.

'She's not an accidental death.' I shine the UV light in her eyes and the same residue sparkles neon bright.

Bloodred, emerald green, bluish purple.

'Whatever this is she's got it everywhere,' I comment. 'She's a possible smothering, although petechial hemorrhages aren't always associated with that. I don't see any marks or contusions of the neck that would indicate strangulation. But something happened to cause vascular rupture.'

'What could do that besides strangulation?' Marino squats by her head to see what I'm talking about.

'An increase of intrathoracic pressure causing the Valsalva effect.' I take off my gloves, my pockets full of used ones now. 'In other words, she had a significant rise in blood pressure that resulted in minute hemorrhages.'

'And that would happen why?' Machado wants to know.

'Struggling, panicking, possibly while being smothered could be the reason. Maybe something else that caused cardiac compromise. I can't be certain at this point but preliminarily she's a homicide and we should work her as one.

Let's get her into the van and I'll meet you at the office.' I say this to Rusty and Harold as I stand up. 'Leave the cloth draped over her exactly as is and wrap her in sheets that hold her body in the position it's in now.'

'How's Anne going to scan her with the arm out like that?'

'I don't know if the bore's wide enough.'

'She'll fit,' I reply. 'I don't want her rigor broken.'

I go on to explain that I want the outstretched arm with its cocked wrist wrapped separately and secured with tape. Another sheet goes around the rest of her body except for her head. From the neck up I want her protected with a large paper evidence bag and I want smaller bags protecting her hands and feet. She will go into the CT scanner fully wrapped.

'Place the spine board on a clean sheet to protect it from mud. I want her transported exactly as I describe.' I make myself clear because the way her body was posed is evidence that I want preserved.

Evidence that might be like three other cases, and I can't say a word to Marino or Machado, and I'm feeling a sense of urgency that is building. I won't think of getting Benton into trouble for doing what was best, what was right. He wanted my help for the very reason I now fear. The Bureau has mandated an information blackout on the D.C. cases and it's possible the killer isn't in that area anymore. He might be killing someplace else and those police departments won't recognize the pattern. He might be

119

here in Cambridge, where his early victim Klara Hembree was from, and Benton doesn't know that part yet and I have to find a way to tell him.

'She goes directly to large-scale x-ray.' I continue to say what I want done. 'I'll make sure Anne is waiting for her. And we have all this photographed in situ, right?'

Machado assures me that he does as he stares across the field in the direction of Andy Hunter, who has joined other officers on the sidewalk outside the fence where the crowd is growing. Barbara Fairbanks is in front of Simmons Hall interviewing whoever will talk to her, and I detect something I can't quite hear.

A Prussian blue smudge across the horizon is the first hint of dawn, and I ask Machado to upload his photographs to me ASAP as what I detect becomes audible. We sharply turn toward the river. We look up at the same time. The rapid stuttering roar becomes louder, a helicopter flying low over the Charles to the southeast, coming closer fast.

'I hope that's not another damn TV station,' Marino says.

'I don't think so.' I look up at the dark sky. 'It's too big for that.'

'Military or the Coast Guard,' Machado speculates.

'It's not.' I recognize the high-pitched whiny roar of the turboshaft engines and the staccato thump-thump of its composite blades turning almost at the speed of sound.

'Let's cover her up until it's gone,' Harold

exclaims. 'We can't hold up the sheet with all the wind.'

'You're fine.' I indicate for them to stay put, to keep the barrier in place, shielding the body from the TV crew and spectators. I raise my voice to a yell. 'Hold your position for now. It will be all right.'

The helicopter appears in a deafening storm of strobing lights over apartment buildings, cutting across the field. It flies directly overhead at about a thousand feet, high enough to spare us its turbulent rotorwash. Lucy knows how to navigate a crime scene and she hovers high, the fifty-million-candlepower Nightsun flooding the red clay and whiting out the body, then she moves on.

We shield our eyes at the same time and turn the same way at the same time, following the ominous-looking EC145 as it circles the field. It swoops around again much lower and slower, making what Lucy calls high-and-low recons as she checks for obstructions such as antennas or power lines or light standards, any danger she might perceive. I can make out the shape of her helmet in the right pilot's seat, an amber visor lowered over her face. I can't tell who is next to her with a headset on but I know. What I'm not sure of is why. But I couldn't be more relieved.

'Stay right here!' I call out to Rusty and Harold over the deafening noise. 'Don't move yet!'

I walk swiftly through mud and the soaking grass to the empty parking lot as the snub-nosed wide-bodied helicopter lowers into a hover. It

121

hangs in the air, trees thrashing at the edge of the tarmac in the blinding glare. Then it gently sets down. Lucy doesn't cut the engines to flight idle. She's not going to stay long.

$$\star \quad \star \quad \star$$

The left front door opens and Benton plants one foot on the skid, then the other, climbing down.

His coat flaps in the violent wind as he opens the back and reaches inside for his luggage as my helmeted niece turns toward me from the right seat and nods. I raise my hand, not sure what the reason might be for what she's just done but I'm extremely glad. It's almost like a miracle, like something I would have prayed for, had I thought about praying.

Benton trots across the tarmac and I take one of his bags as he slips his arm around my waist, pulling me close, nuzzling the top of my head with his jaw. The helicopter lifts in a steep vertical ascent, nosing back to the river, and we watch it pick up speed over buildings and trees, banking around toward Boston. Its whir and winking lights recede as quickly as they appeared.

'Thank God you're here but I don't understand,' I say to him when the noise is gone.

'It was supposed to be my birthday surprise.'

'Somehow I don't believe that's the only reason.'

'It's not and I didn't plan on being here this early.'

'Saturday, I thought.'

'I mean this early today.' He kisses me and pins his attention to the scene illuminated in the middle of the mud where Rusty and Harold continue to hold up a plasticized sheet like morbid bunting. 'A present to myself, a surprise for you, and I needed to get the hell out of D.C.'

'Lucy got my text.' It begins to make sense, I think.

'Yes.' Benton scans the wet grass and soupy red mud. He stares for a long moment at the body draped in white. 'But she'd known since around midnight that Gail Shipton was missing. Her search engines found it posted on Channel Five's website.'

He explains that Lucy flew to D.C. yesterday, setting down in Dulles in the late afternoon, and the plan was to have dinner with Benton and then the two of them would fly home today. As a surprise she would deliver him to the house, where she assumed I'd still be getting over the flu. Then when she got the alert that Gail was missing, Lucy decided they needed to leave immediately.

'The first thing she said was that something had happened to her and she was probably dead,' Benton explains. 'Is the white cloth she's wrapped in yours?'

'That's the way she was found.'

He stares silently at the scene in the distance and I know he's compiling data, taking in the details. Already he is.

'The first victim was from Cambridge. Klara Hembree.' I let him know what I'm worried about. 'The cloth is unusual and the way it's wrapped around the body looks exactly the same as what I saw in Klara's case and the other most recent two. Wrapped around under the arms like a big bath sheet.'

I go on to explain that my preliminary examination of the body revealed no indication that she struggled or made any attempt to defend herself. Then I describe the way she's posed and the fluorescing residue all over her and the cloth, which I suspect is a woven synthetic blend. I tell him the low-stretch fabric is similar to Lycra and the fibers recovered in his cases are Lycra, and then I let him know about the urine-stained panties that are too big.

Benton listens carefully, compiling the information, sorting through it, and what I'm saying registers strongly but he's going to be cautious about jumping to conclusions.

'Do you know what kind of panties?' he asks. 'The label?'

'Yes.'

'Expensive ones,' I reply.

A high-quality cotton, pale peach, a Swiss designer, I explain and he says nothing at first. But I see it in his face. What I'm saying means something to him.

'The third victim in D.C.,' he then says. 'Julianne Goulet liked expensive Swiss lingerie, a brand called Hanro.'

'That's what this is. And I recall from her reports that she was about five-foot-seven, weighed around one-forty, and that could be a size medium.'

'They could be hers. He has a connection here

and I believe he stalked Klara while she still lived here and followed her to D.C. when she moved.' Benton says what is racing through his mind. 'She was a target and the most recent two were an opportunity, and now this? If so, it's at least three murders in one month. He's comfortable here — specifically, in this area of Cambridge — but he's out of control and that's why he's escalating. I need to look around, and I'm not going to suggest anything until I'm sure.'

He won't pass on this information to Marino, Machado, or any of the police working this case. Benton isn't going to tell them they're looking for a serial killer until there can be no doubt.

'And there's going to be a major problem if it's the same killer. The Bureau will deny it,' he adds stunningly. 'I'm going to need to spend some time out here.'

He's not going to explain right now. He wants to get going.

'I don't guess you have a pair of boots in your bag.' I look down at his shoes, a burnished brown leather slip-on with a double monk strap. 'Of course you don't. What am I asking?'

He wouldn't have rubber boots in his bag. In fact, he doesn't own a pair. Even when Benton is working in the yard he looks perfectly put together. He can't help it. One of these long, lean, chiseled men, he looks rich and well bred even at a crime scene in the middle of mud.

'Is her ID confirmed?' His sharply handsome face turns to me, the set of his jaw serious, his thick silver hair mussed by the wind.

'Not officially.' I walk us toward the alley so we

can leave his bags by Marino's SUV. 'But there's little doubt. We're working under the assumption that it's the woman who disappeared last night, Gail Shipton.'

'Lucy says it looks like her. Of course that was from a distance but she zoomed in.' Benton buttons his long cashmere coat with one hand. 'She caught it on film, the position of the body, the way it's draped, which is significant, very much so. You'll have an aerial if you want it. I realize there's a lot to explain but we won't get into it here. We can't.'

'At least tell me why we can't.'

'Marino picked up Gail Shipton's phone from the bar and apparently still has it.'

'I don't understand how you could know . . . ' I start to say as we near the SUV and Quincy begins to whimper.

'Not now, Kay,' Benton says calmly. 'We can't mention this in front of Marino, not the part about the phone or him finding it and that Lucy knows he did. She literally saw him do it because she'd been monitoring the phone remotely since she learned that Gail was missing. Lucy knew since midnight that Gail's phone was still at the Psi Bar outside where she'd used it last.'

'Lucy was working with her.' I'm sure of it now. 'The phone in a military-grade case, the same type of case Lucy and I have.'

'It's a problem.'

What he means is that Lucy is a problem or she's about to become one. If Gail Shipton's smartphone is of proprietary interest to my niece, then it's related to some project she's been working on. She'll interfere with the police investigation. Maybe she already has.

'You're aware of the timing. Gail Shipton was supposed to be in court in less than two weeks.' I have no doubt he knows that too and my uneasiness returns with a vengeance.

What has Lucy gotten herself into this time?

'There's a lot to talk about, Kay.' Benton strokes the back of my neck but I'm not reassured.

'Is she involved in the lawsuit?' I have to know that much. 'Is she involved in Gail Shipton's hundred-million-dollar war with Double S, a money-management firm headquartered very close to her place in Concord?'

We stop at the rear of Marino's SUV and set down his bags as Quincy begins to whine louder and bark.

'Lucy's a witness,' Benton says. 'The defendants' counsel deposed her last summer.'

'And she never told us?' I wonder if this is what Carin Hegel wants to talk to me about.

'I think you know by now that she handles things her own way.'

'What she's handled her own way now involves a homicide that could be connected to the ones you're working,' I reply. 'Maybe the timing of the trial is nothing more than a coincidence but it's troubling, extremely troubling. And I know her attorney Carin Hegel has been sufficiently worried about her safety to not live at home right now. She feels the Double S people are dangerous and hinted they may be in bed with people in high places.'

'The position of the bodies, the cloths haven't been leaked that I know of,' Benton says as Quincy's barking and crying crescendo.

'Then it's unlikely we're talking about a copycat '

'Probably not the real reason Granby's withholding every damn thing about the cases but it's a good thing in this instance,' Benton says with the hard edge his tone takes when he's talking about his boss.

I text Harold to come unlock the CFC van.

'The mud will pull your shoes right off your feet. Hopefully, we've got an extra pair of rubber boots you can wear. It's okay.' I do my best to comfort Quincy, patting the back windshield of Marino's SUV. 'Everything's fine,' I promise.

Benton stares at Marino's puppy, barking and pawing, unhappy inside his crate.

'Poor damn dog,' he says.

13

The scene is a churned-up muddy vacancy in the middle of an academic empire that has begun to stir. It is a few minutes past eight, the body transported to my office a while ago as it began to get light.

The sun is low behind brick buildings where the Charles runs languidly into the river basin and then becomes the Boston Harbor and empties into the sea. Patches of blue peek through cumulus clouds as they change shape and move and the wind has died down. There is no threat of rain as I wait in the parking lot by the open gate, waiting for Benton. I won't leave while he's here doing what he does, alone and in the place he gets, a painful place, a barely tolerable one.

I pace the wet asphalt, on and off my phone as I witness his isolation while he works, and I remember why I've always been drawn to him even when I didn't know I was. I watch him and feel how much I love him. I no longer remember not loving him, and it didn't start out like that. My dislike of him was intense at first when I was the brand-new chief medical examiner of Virginia and he was the Wizard of Odd as Marino snidely called him. I found Benton Wesley's handsomeness and acumen a little too sharp, instantly deciding he was austere like his expensive, understated suits, his demeanor lightly starched like his shirts.

At that time of my life I was into wash-and-wear men who required no effort to maintain with no harm done. I wanted men who were easy to clean up after, cheap men, simple men to have sex with, to be served and serviced by, so I could forget what I know for a while. I had no interest in a Bureau big-shot profiler, certainly not an elitist married one whose legend preceded him through the door like the earthy fragrance of his aftershave.

I'd been in Richmond but a brief time, up against odds I couldn't possibly have foreseen, when I took the job in a commonwealth overrun by men in charge. I was prepared to dislike and dismiss Benton Wesley. I'd heard about his privileged New England upbringing. He was considered gifted and glib, the gun-toting special agent with a crystal ball who was quoted in *Time* magazine as saying that violent sexual psychopaths are the Rembrandts of killers.

The analogy was offensive to me. I remember thinking *What a pedantic narcissist*, and in retrospect it surprises me we didn't become lovers sooner. It took the first time we worked a case together out of town, hundreds of miles southwest in rural Blue Ridge foothills, in a cheap motel where I would go back with him a thousand times were it still there and exactly as I remember it.

Our lying and sneaking was worthy of drug addicts and drunks. We stole any private moment we could find, shameless and bold, extremely skilled at getting away with our crime. We rendezvoused in parking lots. We used pay phones. We didn't leave voice mails or write letters. We conferred on cases we didn't need to discuss, attended the same conferences, invited each other to lecture at academies we ran, and checked into hotels under pseudonyms. We left no evidence and created no scenes, and after he was divorced and his daughters no longer spoke to him we continued our addictive relationship as if it were illegal.

On Vassar Street now, Benton disappears inside Simmons Hall, a honeycomb of cubed windows that brings to mind a metal sponge. I have no idea what he's doing or why, although I suspect he wants to get an emotional reading of the galactic-looking monolith. He wants it to tell him if it's involved in what I don't doubt is a homicide, one that could easily mislead, but I know her death wasn't quiet or gentle. I can see it in her bloodred eyes and imagine the roaring in her head and the building of pressure.

I glance down at my phone as a text lands from my technician Anne, a sensible, pleasant radiologic expert who has managed to cross-train herself in many disciplines. The body is in the CT scanner and Anne has discovered a curiosity.

'A small right-sided pneumothorax,' she explains right off when she answers my call. 'Her scan shows air trapped in the pleural space of the upper lobe, suggesting some type of trauma.'

'I didn't notice anything here at the scene, no injury to her chest,' I reply. 'But it wasn't the best conditions at the time. Basically, I had a flashlight.'

'Something caused her lung to collapse.'

'Do we have an idea what?'

'I can't examine her externally unless you want me to unwrap her, Dr. Scarpetta.'

in the stomach and lungs.'

'All I can tell you with certainty based on what I'm seeing on her scan, Dr. Scarpetta, is her collapsed lung isn't what killed her.'

'Of course,' I agree. 'But if her breathing was already compromised, then she was going to be more vulnerable to asphyxia.'

My suspicions are getting stronger that the fluorescent material all over Gail Shipton was deposited after she was dead. Why? And where was she? And is the residue an accidental transfer of evidence or did her killer want it found? The glittery substance isn't indigenous to the muddy playing field. It came from someplace else.

'For sure a collapsed lung in isolation didn't kill her,' I continue to explain. 'Right now I don't know what did but her death isn't due to natural causes. I'm working this as a homicide and provisionally that's what I'm calling it, a possible suffocation with contributing complications. I'd appreciate it if you'd pass that along to Bryce to keep him updated but please remind him we're not releasing anything to the media yet. We need to positively ID her first.'

'That reminds me, Lucy says her dentist is Barney Moore, whom we've dealt with once before. That floater from last summer, he told me. As if there was only one.'

'Gail Shipton's dentist?' I puzzle.

'Right. He's sending her charts. We should have them any minute.'

'That's probably the quickest way to confirm her ID,' I agree as I wonder why Lucy would know a detail as personal as who Gail Shipton's dentist is. 'Can you get Bryce to line up Dr. Adams ASAP?'

Ned Adams is a local dentist on call for us, a certified odontologist, an eccentric obsessed with the minutiae of teeth. There's nothing he likes better than a mouth that can't talk back, he quips every time I see him.

★ ★ ★

I search for Benton as Anne and I talk. He's still inside Simmons Hall, some of its residents emerging, slinging backpacks, grabbing bicycles or walking.

They seem oblivious or only mildly curious now that the body is gone. There is nothing left but two plainclothes cops doing battle with a fence post, a German shepherd puppy barking on and off inside a car, and a woman forensic pathologist on her phone in a parking lot.

'Do you want me to leave her in the scanner until you get here?' Anne asks me.

'No. Let's move her to my table because I'm going to need to prep her for angiography,' I explain. 'I want to see if we can figure out what might have caused her collapsed lung and also check the vessels of her heart since it's obvious she had a significant rise in her blood pressure that resulted in florid minute hemorrhages. Let's get the test contrast agent ready. Four hundred and eighty MLs of embalming fluid.'

'Plasmol twenty-five arterial? Hand injection or the machine?'

'By hand. The standard five-F angiocatheters

and an embalming trocar, plus the usual thirty MLs of Optiray three-twenty.'

'You'll be here when?'

'Within the hour, hopefully.' I watch Marino cut through chain link, the metal snapping and jingling. 'If they don't finish up here soon, Benton and I will leave without them. We'll walk back to the office. I think the two of them might be at it for a while,' I decide as an area of fencing spills loudly to the ground in a metal waterfall. 'You'd think they were archaeologists approaching King Tut's tomb the way they're deliberating.'

The gouged fence post has proven more stubborn than supposed, set in concrete and buried deep. For the past hour I've listened to Marino and Machado debate hacksawing off the area of galvanized steel tubing in question as opposed to uprooting the entire tall pole, and maybe taking the gate with its scratched fork latch while they're at it. Several times during all this, Marino has let Quincy out for walks involving mini-training sessions that are comical or pathetic, depending on one's point of view.

These exercises have been going on for weeks, ever since he decided Quincy would be a working dog. Marino hides a bit of cloth saturated with human decomposition fluids that he no doubt got from a CFC refrigerator at some point, and Quincy sniffs out this foul-smelling rag and urinates or rolls on it, a behavior not appropriate for a cadaver dog. Three times this morning I've witnessed him darting about, snuffling, digging, rolling, and peeing, while Marino the handler rewards him by blowing a whistle.

I've observed the absurd carnival of Marino tilting at a fence post and hiding bits of putrid cloth but mostly I've watched Benton wander and prowl. It's rare we're at a scene together and I'm moved and amazed in a deeply unsettled way. He seems guided by what the rest of us can't see as if he's his own divining rod, walking purposefully here and there with his suit pants tucked inside a pair of orange rubber boots several sizes too big. First he slogged out to the body before it was wrapped up like statuary and carried away on the spine board. Speaking to no one, not even to me, Benton slowly circled the dead woman like a big cat sizing up a kill.

He didn't offer opinions about the glittery residue or what it might be. He made no comment and asked no questions as he listened silently, inscrutably, to what I said about her postmortem artifacts, about her time of death, which I project was within three hours of her disappearance at most, possibly around eight or nine o'clock last night. He barely looked at the curious crowd assembling in front of Simmons Hall, dazed young students in every state of dress on the other side of the fence. It was as if he'd already made up his mind about them, as if he already knows the devil in the dance with him.

I watched in a mixture of amazement and unsettledness, mesmerized by Benton's dark theater, his behavior as ritualized as the evil people he pursues. He stalked after the body as it was carried across the field, through the open gate, and loaded into the back of the van, which he followed on rubber-booted feet to Memorial

137

Drive. From there he retraced his steps, reentering the campus alone in the gray day's first light, along the alley, back to the empty parking lot, where he stood perfectly still for a while, taking in the vista from the perspective of the 'subject,' as he calls those he hunts.

14

I watch Benton now, emerging from Simmons Hall. He strides toward us again.

He doesn't speak to Marino or Machado. He says nothing to me but sets out through the gate again, across the grass and mud again. He heads to where the body had been as if he's learned or intuited information that has caused him to return yet again to the spot where someone left the dead body of a brilliant young woman whose fatal error may be as random as stepping outside a bar after dark to hear her phone better. Except Benton doesn't think such a thing. That's not what his inner voice is telling him. I recognize that much about his behavior, which at the moment is reminiscent of a heat-seeking missile.

I'm vividly reminded of what guides him, a necessary but dangerous programming that comes from tasting the forbidden fruit of original sin. The abuse of power, Benton says. It all comes back to that. We want to be like God. If we can't create, we'll destroy, and once we've done it, once is not enough. That's the way it goes, simple and predictable, he believes. He has to understand the cravings without giving in to them. He has to make part of him what he will never allow to overtake him, and while I've known this about Benton from the beginning of our time together, when I'm face-to-face with it I'm ambivalent about what I see. I worry about poison eroding the vessel it's in.

Benton positions himself exactly where the yellow tarp was anchored by evidence flags. He crouches in the red mud and looks around, his forearms resting on his thighs. Then he gets up. He moves a short distance away, where he notices something at the edge of the infield, and he bends down. He crouches and looks. He pulls on a pair of black nitrile gloves.

He touches whatever he's found and lifts a gloved finger to his nose. Standing up, he looks across the field and meets my eyes. He nods to summon me and I know by his refusal to look at Marino and Machado that he expects me to come alone.

★   ★   ★

I carry my big case back out into the field, setting it down when I reach Benton. He shows me what looks like petroleum jelly, an irregular translucent glob about the size of a penny.

It shimmers on blades of coarse brown grass at the edge of the red mud, and he shows me a slick of what I presume is the same substance on his glove. He holds it close so I can smell the strong, penetrating odor of menthol.

'Vicks,' he says.

'Or something like it.' I open my black plastic case.

'It's not water-soluble, which is why it survived the wet conditions.' He scans the soggy playing field. 'Even so, a downpour would have pushed it deeper into the grass. We probably wouldn't have found it.'

I get out a photographic scale and my camera. 'You're concluding it was deposited here after the rain stopped.'

'Or when it had let up considerably. What was it doing around two or three a.m.?'

'Pouring, at least at our house.' I have no idea what he's getting at.

'Do any of the cops put Vicks up their nose?' Benton watches me take photographs. 'Are any of them still into that numbskull trick?' He glances in the direction of Marino and Machado.

The body isn't decomposing. There was no stench at all, I remind him, and I would have smelled Vicks or some other mentholated ointment. I would detect it a mile away, I add. Certainly Marino didn't swipe Vicks up his nose. He knows better by now. I corrected him of that bad habit after the first time I saw him do it in the morgue. Now you've just trapped all those molecules of putrefaction inside your nose like flies on flypaper, I remember saying to him, and then he didn't do it anymore.

'I was with Marino from the moment he first got here,' I explain to Benton. 'I've been in close range of him the entire time and I haven't seen him carrying Vicks around in twenty years.' I pull on fresh gloves. 'And Machado wouldn't. There's no way he would. With rare exception, this generation of cops knows better than to do things like that. They're trained that odors give us information and using any substance at a crime scene, whether it's petroleum jelly or smoking a cigarette, can introduce contamination.'

141

'And there was nothing like this on the body.' Benton wants to make sure.

'I noticed a faint scent of perfume and that's it. I certainly would have smelled Vicks.'

'He didn't use it on her,' Benton decides as if it might be reasonable to wonder if a killer smeared vapor rub on his victim.

'I didn't smell menthol and I would have. It's an overpowering odor pretty hard to miss.'

'Then how the hell did it get here?' He asks a question that sounds ominously rhetorical.

'The police have been on the scene since around four a.m.,' I remind him. 'If somebody suspicious was out here in this spot, he would have been very close to the body and certainly would have been seen.'

'What was it doing around that time? The weather?' Benton stares off, deep in thought.

I call Marino. I watch him answer his phone and turn in my direction as I ask him what time it was when the police responded to the scene this morning. He talks to Machado and then gets back to me.

'It was close to four,' he says. 'Maybe ten of four when the first cruiser rolled up.'

'How hard was it raining out here in this exact location? I know it was heavy on the other side of Cambridge about the time you came to the house. It was pouring when I took Sock out,' I recall, and he turns to Machado again.

'It was raining on and off, not too bad here on this side of town,' Marino lets me know. 'Just the conditions were bad by then. You see how much mud there is.'

I thank him and end the call. I relay to Benton what I was told.

'It probably was left not long before the police got here, could be minutes before they got here,' he deduces, 'by which time the rain was light and not a factor.'

'What about the couple, the two students who found the body and called the police?' I point out. 'Wouldn't they have noticed someone hanging around?'

'That's a good question. But if they did, they wouldn't have had cause for concern.'

Benton is implying that he knows this killer and it's someone who blends in or can make himself disappear. He's suggesting that this person left a mentholated ointment in the grass close to where the body was discovered.

'You're thinking it was left on purpose?' I return the camera and scale to my field case.

'I'm not sure,' he says.

'This person digs into a jar of a mentholated ointment or squeezes it from a tube and some of it falls off his finger? Or he wipes excess in the grass?' I'm aware of an undercurrent of uneasiness and doubt.

'I don't know. What's important is it may have been left by him because using it is part of his MO.'

'You're considering this because of what you've observed in this one case, at this one scene?' I ask because it's not possible to reach such a conclusion based on so little data. 'Or is it because of the other ones?'

'I haven't seen this in the other ones. But he

may have left it this time without knowing he did. I believe he's losing control.' He repeats what he has said several times now. 'Something rather catastrophic is going on with him,' he says as if he knows who and what this killer is, and my misgivings grow.

I fear Benton has gotten too close to the killer and I've feared this before. I hope there's not a legitimate reason his colleagues at the BAU aren't listening to him.

'He could have gotten the idea about a mentholated vapor rub. It's not new under the sun,' Benton says.

I bag and label his smeared glove. Separately, I collect the menthol gel and the blades of grass it adheres to as he mentions that horse trainers smear Vicks under the nostrils of their racehorses to keep them focused.

'It's used on stallions, mainly,' he explains in the same reasonable tone.

He may as well be talking about a movie we just saw or what we should have for dinner. The abnormal has to be normal to him or he'll never figure it out. He can't be repelled and repulsed by the demons or they won't talk. He has to accept them to conjure them up, and witnessing the mode he goes into bothers me again. It bothers me more than it ever has before.

'The odor distracts them from distractions,' he explains. 'All they can focus on is running because they can't smell anything but menthol.'

'In other words, they can't smell mares.' I snap shut the heavy plastic clasps of my field case.

'They can't smell anything that would tempt

them. But, yes, mostly mares,' he replies. 'There's also the added benefit that the menthol helps the horse's breathing. Any way you look at it we're talking about the same thing.'

'Which is what exactly?'

'Performance,' he says. 'Winning. Outsmarting everyone and the thrill of it for him.'

★ ★ ★

I think about it, examining what he said as best I can, trying to figure it out as I return to the parking lot. Racehorses and Vicks.

Such an abstruse bit of trivia in the context of a homicide would seem crazy if it came from anyone else, but Benton has a reason for knowing what he told me. It wasn't a detail out of the blue. It came from somewhere that's no place good.

'What did you find?' Machado asks me between loud stabs of the shovel into hard, rocky dirt, what sounds like a grave being dug.

'Is anybody using Vicks out here?' I return my field case to an area of pavement near Marino's SUV. 'I assume not but let's make sure.'

'Shit no.' Marino rubs the small of his back, scowling as if I accused him of a sin he hasn't committed since our early years.

'Somebody used it and most likely quite recently,' I reply. 'Somebody used Vicks or a similar mentholated ointment.'

'Not that I'm aware of.' Machado looks across the field at Benton stepping through the mud in his big bright rubber boots, headed toward us again. 'You're saying he found Vicks? It was in the grass?'

'Something like it,' I reply.

'Maybe it's a heat balm, a muscle rub. After all, this is an athletic field.' Machado has stopped shoveling.

He stares at Benton as if he's unusual, maybe a little unglued. The two of them have worked together before, but as I watch the young detective watching my husband I feel a chill run through my blood. I feel unnerved.

'You got any idea what he's thinking?' Machado asks me skeptically as if he really does suspect Benton is a human Ouija board and not to be trusted.

'He pretends he's the one who did it,' Marino says before I have the chance, not that I would have answered the question, certainly not the way he did.

I don't offer what I imagine Benton is thinking. If I knew, I wouldn't tell. It's not my place to say. Often I don't have a clue and it doesn't surprise me that he doesn't belong to a fraternity of male friends, not FBI buddies, cops, other federal agents, or attorneys. He doesn't hang out with professional peers at local watering holes like Tommy Doyle's, Grafton Street, or Marino's favorite, Paddy's.

Benton is an enigma. Maybe he was born one, a contradiction of soft interiors and hard surfaces perfectly packaged in a tall, lean body and neatly cut hair that has been silver for as long as I've known him, and tailored suits, matched socks, and shoes that always look new.

He is handsome in a clean angled way that seems a metaphor for the precision of his perceptions, and his aloofness is an air lock that controls his vulnerability to people who pass in and out of his spaces.

'You know he's got to get into their mind.' Marino flings a shovel full of rocky soil to one side, barely missing Benton as he passes through the gate saying nothing to us.

He is silent. At times like this he seems a peculiar savant, one who is antisocial and off-putting. It's not uncommon for him to wander about a scene for hours and speak to no one. While he's always been well respected, he isn't necessarily liked. He's often misunderstood. Most people read him completely wrong. They call him cold and odd. They assume someone so contained and controlled has no emotional reaction to the evil he sees. They assume he gives me nothing I need.

I watch him stride out of the parking lot back in the direction of Vassar Street and its silvery dorm.

'He's got to look through their eyes and pretend he's the one doing it.' Marino has a smirk on his face, his tone derisive as he continues to describe what he truly knows very little about.

Benton doesn't simply get inside a violent offender's mind. It's much worse than that. He gets in touch with the midnight of his soul, a wretched darkness that allows him to connect with his prey and beat them at their hideous game. Often when he comes home after weeks of working some nightmarish case he's so spent he's psychically ill. He takes multiple showers a day. He hardly eats or drinks. He doesn't touch me.

After several restless sleep-disturbed nights the spell breaks like a fever, and I cook a hearty dish, maybe Sicilian, one of his favorites, like *Campanelle Pasta con Salsiccia e Fagioli* with a Barolo or a red burgundy, a lot of all of it, and then we go to bed. He drives the monsters out, desperately, aggressively, exorcizing what he had to invite into his mind, into his flesh, and the life force fights hard and I give it back. It goes on until we're done, and that is what it's like with us. We aren't what anyone would think, not reserved and proper the way we appear to be, and we never tire of each other.

I watch my husband now walking along the sidewalk in front of Simmons Hall. He enters its parking lot, where he wanders through a scattering of student cars, taking photographs with his phone. Behind the dorm, he looks up and down railroad tracks before crossing them to an open area of raw dirt and broken concrete crowded with semi-trailers, earth-moving machines, and temporary fabric shelters.

He heads toward a black pickup truck parked near a dumpster filled with construction debris. He peers through the truck's windows and into the open-top bed as if he's been given information, and he has. He's directed by his own mind, by the currents of subconscious thoughts that like computer subroutines move him effortlessly.

He walks over to a bright yellow bulldozer, its

148

blade locked in the raised position like a pugilistic crab. Crouching near the rear claw, the ripper, he looks in my direction at the same time my phone rings.

15

'One of them needs to come over here.' Benton's voice is in my earpiece. 'And I need you to listen to me first and listen carefully, Kay.'

I look at him standing up, then moving around in the construction site while he looks at me in the parking lot. I keep an eye on Marino and Machado, making sure they have no idea what's going on over the phone.

'What I'm about to say must stay with us right now. I can give them guidance but I can't elaborate. We need to be absolutely sure.' But I can tell he is. 'And we don't know who to trust. That's the bigger point. One slipup and it's everything Granby's been looking for to get me the hell off this case.'

'This case or the others?' I ask.

'All of them. I can't say for a fact how many, but now there are at least four.'

'There's an inconsistency, a significant one.' I'm referring to the plastic bags that the three D.C. victims had over their heads.

'Something threw him off this time, that's the only thing I can think, unless he's trying to disguise that this one is connected to the others. But I don't believe that's it. Cambridge is a familiar hunting ground for him. He's stalked here before, and I'm not surprised he's stalking here again, but this victim isn't random. The first one, Klara Hembree, wasn't random either. The second and third might have been.'

Benton doesn't sound excited or frazzled because that's not who he is. But I know him. I'm sensitive to his every shading, and when he's getting close to his quarry, his voice is taut as if he's hooked something big and it's fighting him. I listen and know what's coming but there's something else, the same threat that's chilling. I feel it with increasing intensity as we talk on the phone a muddy field apart.

Over recent weeks Benton has continued to mention this problem with trust. It's come up repeatedly since he left for D.C. and he was adamant several nights ago when he'd had a few too many Scotches and said the Capital Murderer case would never be solved. Someone doesn't want it solved, he said, and I didn't believe him.

How could I possibly believe such a thing? Three women were brutally slain, and Benton is the FBI and he was implying the FBI didn't want the killer caught. And now it seems he's murdered again and Benton has the same worry as with the other ones. Maybe my husband has gotten too close: it enters my mind again. As bad as that would be, what he's suggesting couldn't be worse. It's finally gotten to him. I've always worried it could happen.

'The storage locker in the back of a truck has been broken into,' he tells me over the phone. 'There's a tool in the dirt. It's been rained on but doesn't appear to have been out here long. It stopped raining completely several hours ago so it was left here before that.'

'What kind of tool?' I inquire.

'A ratcheting cutter of some type, possibly for cutting metal tubing or pipes. It was deliberately left where it is with a rock placed on top of it.'

'A rock?'

'A decent-sized rock that was picked up and placed on top of it.'

'For what reason?'

'Paper, rock, scissors.'

I wait to see if he's joking. But he's not.

'Something from a sick, childish mind that was stunted and got even sicker, and now he's extremely sick and rapidly decompensating, and it seems early for that and I can't tell you why. But something's happening to him,' Benton says. 'The rock and the tool are an atavistic throwback to a game from his past. It's a feeling I've felt since the first time I saw what he left some distance from the body. You have to think to look for what isn't obvious and the police usually don't.'

'But you do.'

'I'm the one who's found it in each homicide, even as long as two days after the fact, by the time I got there,' he says. 'A rock trumps scissors and scissors trump paper and cops are nothing but paper — they're officials who fill out paperwork, adults who make up rules and are a joke to him. Police aren't a worthy audience and he places a rock on top of a tool he used to commit his crime, like a rock on top of scissors, to remind the police how unworthy they are compared to him. It's a rush to him. It's thrilling and fun.'

'The police are unworthy but not you.'

'He wouldn't consider me unworthy. He would know I understand what he's doing as much as it can be understood, far more than he understands himself, which is limited. It always is with offenders like this. They're morally insane and insanity has very little insight. Maybe none.'

I glance back at Marino digging around the pole, starkly alone with its attached fencing cut free. Already I can foresee him getting very defensive with Benton. Marino has a hair trigger when it comes to him and they will have a real war now that Marino has power again. This will get ugly before it gets easier, and as I stand out here I can't imagine this getting any better.

I can't stop thinking about the timing. Benton flies home three days early and the Capital Murderer has struck again here where we live like a tornado suddenly veering off track and slamming right into our house. I continue to think of the person behind the wall, bareheaded in the rain and staring at my back door, and all morning I've continued to glance around as if someone is watching.

'Do you think the killer somehow knew you'd be here?' I ask what I don't want to consider.

'Frankly, it worries me,' Benton says.

Certainly it's happened before. Violent offenders have left him notes, letters, body parts, photographs, video and audio recordings of their victims being tortured and killed. Vicious reminders, gruesome ones, cooked human flesh, a murdered child's teddy bear. I've seen the grisly threats and heartbreaking taunts and nothing would surprise me anymore except this. I don't want to believe what Benton is contemplating for a simple reason I can't get past, maybe because I refuse.

He's supposed to be in Washington, D.C. until Saturday. Had he not decided to return home early, he wouldn't be here right now saying these things and finding a tool and a rock.

'How could he possibly know you'd be here, Benton?'

'He's probably seen me, seen all of us,' he says and I look around at buildings in the sun, at students walking and on bicycles, at light bright on cars in parking lots. 'It's inevitable I'd be here. Maybe not right this minute but as soon as I knew. Hours, a day later, but I'd be here doing what I'm doing right now.'

'Watching is one thing. Knowing you were coming home today is another.'

'He might not have known I was coming home today but he would figure I'd show up soon. I don't have an answer but I have to consider the possibility, any possibility. What I know for a fact is this scene is like the other three. The tool and the rock are an obvious red flag and the BAU assumes it's staged, it's faked. They say it's like the Beltway Sniper and the tarot card found near a cartridge case where a thirteen-year-old was shot. Ten people killed, a number of the shootings in Virginia around the time you moved from there.'

Around the time I thought you were dead. It enters my mind weirdly, painfully, and for a flash I think of my dream. Then I don't. Benton begins stalking the construction site near the bright yellow bulldozer. He's talking uncharacteristically fast and fluently now.

''Call me God, do not release to the press' was written on the tarot card,' he says. 'Staged to screw with police, to lead them down the wrong track, to make them think the killer had something to do with magic shops or the occult. It was bullshit, the FBI said, and in those cases maybe it really was bullshit. This is what I've been hearing for weeks about the tools and the rocks and the white cloths, the bags from Octopus, all of it, that they're bullshit. But they aren't. I promise you they're not. They mean something to him. A game. He's showing off. I worry he's driven by delusions.'

'Including ones about you?'

'He might delude himself into believing he impresses me.' Benton says it easily, the way zookeepers speak of their most dangerous animals. 'I can't possibly know for sure but I believe he's familiar with my work. He's narcissistic enough to fantasize that I would admire him.'

'Maybe he struck now for another reason,' I say calmly, sensibly, 'and it has nothing to do with you happening to be here. It has nothing to do with you at all.'

'It worries me,' he repeats. 'He might have heard something, I don't know but he has a connection to this area, a powerful one. He left her body here because the location means something to him and I'm not ready to mention this to anyone, not specifically or directly,' he emphasizes. 'I will but not yet. There are phone calls I have to make first. The decision isn't up to me — that's the way they think — it's not about the case. It's about some agenda that is extremely troubling. I have to notify Granby. That's the protocol and it will be a problem.'

He will brief his boss, the special agent in charge, Ed Granby, who is an obstructionist and can't stand him, and I know how that will go. As poorly as anything can go.

'I presume Granby will take over this investigation,' I reply.

'We can't let him, Kay.'

'How could the killer have heard something that might lead him into believing you were coming back to Cambridge now?'

'Exactly. If he did, how could he? It's possible he's connected to someone close to the investigation.'

I remember what Carin Hegel said about corruption that reaches into high places, as high up as it gets, and I think of the Department of Justice, the FBI, and then I don't want to think any of it at all. My thoughts retreat to the safer ground of what Benton told me after climbing out of Lucy's helicopter several hours ago. He said his coming home a few days early for his birthday was her suggestion.

'Exactly when was the idea of your coming home today first discussed?' I retrieve my field case again.

I move farther away from Marino and Machado so they can't hear what I'm saying.

★   ★   ★

'Three days ago,' Benton tells me. 'Sunday morning was when the subject first came up. Lucy knew what you'd been through over the weekend in Connecticut. She worried that's what made you sick.'

'A virus made me sick.'

'She wanted me to come home and I did too and had basically threatened I was going to, but you said it wouldn't work. I was certain if you knew, you'd say no as you already had — to me at least.'

To hear it stated so starkly reminds me unhappily of other revelations of late. I don't always show what I feel or say what I want and that's not fair. It's hurtful.

'We agreed it had to be a surprise,' he adds.

'Who else knew?'

'Internally it was known.'

He tells me that on Sunday the FBI was aware that he was leaving Washington, D.C., earlier than planned. In fact, his Boston division had to approve his return to Cambridge and Ed Granby was more than happy for Benton to do just that, to get out of Washington. He encouraged it, Benton says, and next I think of the hotel where he was staying.

People working there also would have been aware of what Benton was doing. I imagine he changed his reservation in advance, possibly as early as this past Sunday, the minute he knew. Of course Lucy was in the loop and my thoughts continue drifting back to her. I wonder if she happened to mention the birthday surprise to Gail Shipton and, if so, why and what that might mean.

Lucy had to file a flight plan before she flew out of Massachusetts with the destination of Dulles International Airport. For security reasons, private aircraft aren't allowed to land in the D.C. area without permission and a filed Federal Aviation Administration flight plan. Hotel and FBI personnel, flight service and air traffic controllers, I ponder those who would have had reason to know details such as times, locations, aircraft type, and even Lucy's helicopter's tail number and what equipment she has on board. Who had access to information about what she and Benton were doing and where and when?

It's possible someone might know personal minutiae about our lives and perhaps passed information on to the wrong person. I can't rule out that there could be a deranged, cunning killer fixated on Benton and committing deviant, violent acts for his benefit or to best him. Such a thing rarely happens. I'm not sure I know of any instance when a serial killer has developed an erotomaniacal obsession with a forensic psychologist or profiler. But that doesn't mean it hasn't occurred somewhere. It probably has.

With human behavior anything is possible, and I've been witness to sadistic violent gestures that I couldn't have imagined in a vacuum. There is no outrageous crime I can invent that's original, nothing new that hasn't been done, and Benton isn't just anyone. He's published books and papers and often is in the news and has been linked publicly to the Capital Murderer cases, with great frequency after the most recent two. If the killer has been following the media, he knows

Benton's been in D.C., that the search there has been intense even as the details of the crimes remain out of sight, tightly wrapped in the FBI's cloak of secrecy.

It would have been a very good time for the killer to do what Benton has suggested, to move on, and maybe this cunning, cruel individual anticipates what Benton might deduce and intuit next. My husband has believed from the start the Capital Murderer is connected to Cambridge, that it's a location he knows and a safe harbor for him.

That's what Benton has said and he's been saying it since April when Klara Hembree was murdered not even a month after she moved from here. He said she was stalked in Cambridge for a while and her stalker followed her to D.C. and he wouldn't have done that if he wasn't comfortable with Cambridge and familiar with the Washington area. He knows his turf, that's what Benton has continued to believe. The killer is on a whistle-stop murder tour, jumping off where he's in control, hitting in places we might not know about, and that's what I've been hearing since my husband left before Thanksgiving.

I could understand it if Benton worries he's being targeted by this killer or any killer he pursues even if it isn't true. How much can he subject himself to before his barriers begin to break down, before what he does gets under his skin like a parasite, like an infection? The question has lingered for as long as I've loved him.

'Obviously I would look over here,' Benton says on his phone a muddy field away from me. 'Maybe the police would have gotten around to it. They probably would have even though it's remote from where her body was.'

'Why would you look?' I ask.

'Because of the truck.'

'The one broken into.' I fix my attention on the black pickup he's slowly circling as he talks.

'It's out of place here,' he says. 'It's not related to the construction going on. It's someone's personal truck improperly parked here so of course that would get my attention instantly.'

He stands still and stares across the field at me.

'That's assuming the tool was used on the gate's lock and chain.' I watch Marino and Machado give up with the shovel and decide on the hacksaw.

'He used this tool,' Benton says. 'And he wanted us to find it, and when the labs examine it you're going to see I'm right. We're his audience and he wants us to know everything he's gone to the trouble to do. That's part of the thrill — '

''Gone to the trouble'?' I interrupt him, getting angry because he's scaring me and for an instant I feel the flare of heated fury that I work so hard to bury.

Then I will myself to feel nothing at all. It's not helpful to react the way a normal person would. I banish what will interfere with my clinical discipline and reason, I run it off and far away from me. After all these years I'm good at

160

emptying myself out.

I watch Marino rummaging inside his big scene case, what's actually a portable tool chest. I take a deep breath. Calmer now, Gail Shipton enters my mind again. It would make sense if she's the link. If so, it would mean she had some connection with her killer even if she didn't know him, even if they'd never met, as Benton has said.

16

The tool has a red fiberglass handle and a metal blade. It looks similar to a wrench and is capable of cutting through hard metals like brass, copper, and steel.

Marino is able to tell us that at a glance. He takes photographs of the tool with the rock on top of it, a chunk of native stone about the size of a softball. Then he moves the rock out of the way. He picks up the tool.

'Okay, so where's the lock and chain?' The tool is overwhelmed by Marino's big gloved hands.

He turns it, studying it, careful not to destroy evidence like fingerprints, which I suspect aren't there.

'If he wanted us to find the damn tool he used, you might think he'd leave the lock and chain, too, right?'

Marino places the tool in an evidence bag.

'You know, if he's going to jerk us around, the more the merrier, right?' Marino's mood has gone from somber to sour and sarcastic.

The first death scene he's worked as a cop in a decade and he's feeling lost and pushed around. Benton is making him feel small and Marino is spoiling for a fight.

'My point is we shouldn't assume this was used by him.' He loudly tears off a strip of evidence tape. 'Maybe it wasn't. Maybe you strayed off the beaten path and found something unrelated.' He directs this at Benton, staring at him with an open challenge mixed with something else. Doubt.

Then Marino looks at me as if expecting I'll take his side. Or maybe he's trying to figure me out, figure Benton out, because Marino doesn't know what to think. It's just the three of us standing near a bulldozer on a construction site and I wonder how Benton is going to communicate what Marino needs to know. Benton can't be forthright and Marino won't make it easy even if he believes him. And I anticipate he won't, not at first.

'Maybe somebody broke into a truck, which wouldn't be unusual,' Marino goes on in the same snide tone. 'Vehicles get broken into all the time. Maybe that's all there is to it, plain and simple.'

'I suggest you also collect the rock,' Benton says. 'He touched it. Most likely he had gloves on but he might not have, depending on his mindset at this point.'

'Who the hell are you talking about?'

'The person you're looking for. What's not a question is he handled the rock. He picked it up and placed it where it was. We should check it for DNA, for any residue, that might have been transferred on it.'

'Jesus friggin' Christ. You got to be kidding me.'

'He drove the body here,' Benton says as if there can be no question. 'He parked in this lot first.' He points to the parking lot next to the dorm. 'He got out of his vehicle, walked into this

163

construction site, broke into the truck's storage box and took the tool. After that he drove the body to the lot over there.' He points again, this time to the parking lot where I was on the phone for the past hour or so.

The pedestrian gate is still wide open, stirred by the wind, and I remind Benton of the risk. That parking lot is across the street from the MIT police station. The killer — and I'm openly calling him that without reservation — would have had to drive over the curb and the sidewalk.

'There was a chance the police might see him,' I conclude.

'There was no chance of that,' Benton says flatly. 'This person is calculating and he watches. He spies. He thrives on risk, on the thrill of taking a chance, and he manages to look like he belongs wherever he is, assuming you see him at all. He pulled into that lot, cut off the lock and chain from the gate. He placed the body on a sled of some sort that flattened the grass, gouging out clumps of it, as he dragged it to the infield and posed it.'

'Why?' Marino stares hard at him, then looks at me, almost rolling his eyes.

'Because it aroused him and is symbolic. We don't know exactly why. We never do but what you're seeing are the hieroglyphics on the wall of his deviant psyche.'

'Now I'm thinking total crap.' Marino defiantly places his hands on his hips. 'Whatever happened to her isn't the fucking *Da Vinci Code*. She's as dead as hamburger and I don't give a shit about his psyche.'

'You need to pay attention,' Benton says to him. 'He spent time posing the body, walking around, looking at it from different angles. This is what gets him high, a game that gets more daring and out of control. He has his methods and everything he does has meaning to him, but he's like a top spinning toward the edge of the table. Close to spinning off, a crash waiting to happen.'

'How the hell can you know that based on what's out here?'

'I know his type and what I'm seeing tells me he's killed before and will again.'

As Benton describes all this I think of the Vicks-like ointment we recovered from blades of grass not far from where the body was found. I imagine the killer looking at the posed body from different angles, admiring his work, as Benton just described. The final act, a murderous triumph out on a soggy playing field in the dark, and he applies more of the vapor rub, breathing in its sharp, penetrating odor so he doesn't forget his purpose or make mistakes, or maybe he's already making them. Like a racehorse running powerfully, single-mindedly, but on the brink of stumbling or striking a hurdle or flying over a cliff.

'When he was done he returned to this spot, cleaned off the tool, and left it,' Benton says. 'He left it for us.'

'It might not have been noticed over here,' Marino continues to argue. 'This construction site's not all that convenient to where the body was left.'

'He knew we'd find it eventually.'

'Why would he give a shit?' Marino angrily yanks off his gloves. 'And how the hell could he know what was in the truck's storage box? We're supposed to believe the pipe cutter came from there? How does that make any sense at all? It wouldn't be smart. Start with that. What if it hadn't been in there? What if he's parked out here with a dead body in his car and then doesn't have a tool to cut the chain off the gate?'

'He gathers intelligence,' Benton says patiently. 'This isn't an impulse crime, Pete. It was premeditated carefully, with a motive he had in mind that's not his real reason for killing her. He did it because he wanted to, because he's driven by an overwhelming compulsion. That's not the way he sees it but it's the reality we're dealing with.'

'You're talking like you know who it is.'

'I know the type,' Benton says and that's all he's going to say.

He's not going to explain the rest of it. Not right now.

'You know something you're sure as hell not saying,' Marino accuses angrily and uneasily.

'He's the type to target his victims, to gather detailed information about them,' Benton explains. 'He's the type to access their residences, wander into their private spaces, surf the Internet for information, find whatever he can. That's part of his arousal pattern.'

'We've checked out Gail Shipton,' Marino counters. 'No police reports filed. No house break, nothing at all to suggest a possible B-and-E.'

'You should talk to people and find out if at

any time, especially of late, she's felt someone is watching her.'

'Good thing you told me. I wouldn't have thought of it.' A flush creeps up Marino's neck. 'And there's nothing to say he's not some local fruitcake and maybe this dead lady is a stand-alone case. How come you haven't bothered considering that?' Marino stares off at Simmons Hall with its thousands of cubed windows and silvery skin. 'Maybe he knows certain details because he's operating in his own neighborhood. Maybe we'll get lucky and this is his damn truck. Maybe he left the tool accidentally. Maybe he meant to put it back inside his truck and forgot.'

'He watches,' Benton again says as if Marino had said nothing. 'He knew this pickup truck would be here. You'll likely find out from the owner that he's left it here overnight on more than one occasion. Possibly he leaves it here overnight often because he likes to drink after work.'

'That's just pure guessing,' Marino snaps as if he's a defense attorney objecting, 'based on nothing.'

'You're probably going to find he's had a DUI in the past and isn't going to take the chance of getting another one.' Benton is relentless and unflappable. 'You'll likely discover he has some special status with MIT, maybe works here, and he can leave his truck and no one gives him a problem. He uses his own tools for whatever his job requires and anybody interested might know what he keeps locked up in his truck.'

167

'What's the point?' Marino retorts as he glances at me repeatedly.

'What I can tell you is he has one that means something to him. His behavior is calculated and it all starts with what he sees and fantasizes about.' Benton predicts and projects, offering details that might sound ludicrous if they came from someone else.

But Benton is right most of the time no matter how much I might wish otherwise. It's not because he's lucky. It's not because he's clairvoyant. His conclusions are drawn from an unfathomable database built over decades of every conceivable atrocity he's seen. He's paid a high price to be good at what he does.

'Keep what I've said in mind as you work this scene and investigate this case. You're hurting yourself if you don't.' Benton nods at the pickup truck. 'I'd check the storage box if I were you. Chances are you're going to find something in it besides tools.'

Marino radios Machado that they need to process a vehicle in the lot over here, that some-one pried open a storage locker.

'Have you looked inside it?' Machado's voice is loud over the air as he and Marino face each other from opposite sides of Briggs Field.

'Not yet.'

'You're thinking it's related?'

'We need to work it like it is,' Marino says with a bored shrug in his voice for Benton's benefit. 'I'll radio control, see what we can track down.'

Machado stops working on the fence post, which is dug up now and partially wrapped in heavy brown paper. He heads in our direction as Marino radios the dispatcher to run the truck's tag for him.

'Once the owner's located,' Marino lets us know, 'I can figure out how long the truck's been parked in this location and get an idea of when it was broken into.'

'I think we already have an idea.' Benton's attention is fixed on the railroad tracks that run between the construction site and the back of Simmons Hall. 'The body was discovered around three-thirty a.m.'

'We got the call at exactly three thirty-nine.' Marino can't resist correcting him.

★   ★   ★

Grand Junction Corridor cuts through the MIT campus and runs in a straight line from east Cambridge, passing very close behind the CFC before crossing the Mystic River and into Boston. I'm reminded that whenever a circus comes to neighboring cities and towns, the train parks on the Grand Junction branch very close to where we're standing.

Beyond that conspicuous and highly publicized use of the nearly defunct rail line, only an occasional freight train clatters through, usually on the weekend. I've had my share of getting stuck after work, waiting for a train carrying fresh fruits and vegetables to the Chelsea Produce Market. A few weeks ago I waited for a circus train that was a mile long, red with gold lettering, the Cirque d'Orleans out of South Florida, where

I'm originally from.

'He wanted the body found quickly and likely watched it found, watched the scene being worked, possibly from right here in this construction site.' Benton continues to describe what he thinks the killer did. 'Once it was daylight, he was long gone.'

Machado has reached us now and he looks curiously at the black pickup truck. Then he looks at Benton.

'You're saying he was hanging around the whole time we've been here?' Machado asks dubiously.

'Not the entire time but long enough to watch Kay work the scene, to watch Lucy land.'

'And to watch you?'

'Possibly,' Benton says. 'By the time he left it was still dark and he was on foot. Most likely he followed the train tracks out of the campus, which would have enabled him to avoid car traffic, campus security, students. No one was going to see him back here where the tracks are. They're not lighted and there's no pedestrian path alongside them. They're a very effective and efficient way to get in and out. Unless a train is coming,' he adds. 'He had to know about the tracks back here. He had to be familiar and comfortable with them.'

'You're suspicious maybe he's a student who knows the area inside out,' Machado supposes.

'I'm not suspicious of that.'

'Then how come you were photographing cars in the dorm parking lot?' Marino digs his big hands into a new pair of gloves, splaying his thick fingers, stretching and flexing them out.

'Because they're here and somebody should for exclusionary purposes, mainly. They're not going to be helpful for any reason other than that.'

'I get it. You drop out of the sky so you can tell us how to do our job.' Marino retrieves a dusting kit from his scene case.

'I dropped out of the sky because Lucy gave me a ride home,' Benton says without a trace of defensiveness and again that's all he's going to say.

Marino leans over the side of the black pickup truck, which I note is dirty and scuffed, a Toyota several years old that hasn't seen a coat of wax in recent memory.

'Just so you know,' he says, 'we wrote down every tag in every lot around here. Any place someone may have stopped to dump a dead body.'

'Great,' Benton says blandly.

Marino inspects the damaged area of the storage locker's diamond-steel plate lid, an area of metal sharply bent near the lock's keyhole. He opens the lid, propping it against the back windshield of the truck.

'Shit,' he mutters.

17

Marino reaches inside and lifts out a handbag, brown leather with a double handle, an unassuming, moderately pricey satchel. He unzips it.

'Bingo,' he says sarcastically. 'One more present to piss us off.'

'That's not why he left it.' Benton is matter-of-fact.

He doesn't look surprised or particularly interested as Marino pulls out a wallet. He opens it and produces Gail Shipton's driver's license.

'If he took her someplace first, explaining why her clothes are gone, then why leave this here?' Marino studies the license, his jaw muscles clenched. 'Why not throw it in a dumpster somewhere?'

In the photograph she's in her late teens or early twenties when her hair was much shorter and she had bangs. She's wearing heavy framed glasses that mask her prettiness, and her expression is self-conscious, her smile frozen, her eyes askance. She doesn't have the open, friendly face of someone who is accessible or warm, but perhaps the camera made her shy.

'His motivation isn't about pissing us off,' Benton says as Marino goes through the wallet's compartments. 'It's about showing off, and what he does is deeply personal. It's about what he feels and not about us.'

'How is leaving her pocketbook showing off?' Marino asks.

'It's brazen. He's assisting with the ID. He's helping us because that gives him a rush.' Benton says and it tells me he's found the victims' IDs in the other cases.

'I don't see it,' Marino says.

'It sounds like you're talking about some sort of psychopath, like a serial killer.' Machado looks impressed and at the same time incredulous. 'I'm sure as hell not passing that up the chain unless we're sure.'

'I wouldn't suggest you pass anything up the chain or anywhere else right now,' Benton replies.

'The trial that's about to start is what we should be considering, you ask me,' Machado says in a tone meant to remind us that his police department is in charge. 'You know, maybe someone wanted her dead. I don't know why you'd be thinking some sort of deranged psychopath. I sure don't want a rumor like that getting out. If we're going to involve the FBI, there need to be some ground rules.'

He stares at Benton and I can imagine Machado's unspoken thought. The FBI hasn't formally been invited into this investigation. Benton is being given free rein as a courtesy simply because he showed up. He's my husband and they know him and I sense doubt again. I have a feeling Marino has been badmouthing him to Machado, flaunting himself, by disparaging Benton.

'Credit cards.' Marino leaves them in their slots. 'AmEx, Visa, ATM, maybe she had others. No cash. We'll process this for DNA, for prints.'

'Then if she had cash, he took it, which seems

173

to argue against someone killing her because of the trial coming up,' Machado considers. 'Not that I'm an expert in professional hits but taking her money doesn't fit with what I know. Usually you don't want any connection with the victim, am I correct?' He directs this at Benton. 'Just offering that thought as a possibility since Gail Shipton was involved in a hundred-million-dollar lawsuit.'

'Hit men usually don't steal.' Benton watches Marino go through the handbag, his gloved fingers lightly touching items by the tips and edges, impacting as little surface area as possible.

A compact. Lipstick. Mascara. Black ballpoint pens. A pack of tissues. Throat lozenges. A round hairbrush.

'I'm just putting it out there,' Machado says. 'It sure as hell is convenient for the defendants that she's suddenly dead.'

'Usually contract killers have as little physical contact with their targets as possible,' Benton replies. 'They don't conspicuously leave evidence such as a tool or a pocketbook for the police to find. They have no interest in showing off or attempting to impress those working the case. Quite the contrary. Typically, they don't want to draw attention to themselves and they're not delusional.'

'This guy's delusional?'

'I'm saying successful contract killers aren't.'

Marino lifts out a black notebook, pocket-sized, with a green elastic band around it that he slips off.

'So that brings us back to the possibility that what happened to her could be random,'

174

Machado says. 'A motive that involves robbery.'

Marino flips through pages that look like graph paper, white with a fine grid, as if intended for math or diagrams. The notebook is filled with small, neat handwriting and precise columns of dates and numbers that seem coded and mysterious. The writing ends midway through the notebook with an entry made in black ink:

61: INC 12/18 1733–1752 (<18m)
REC 20-8-18-5-1-20

'If you don't mind?' I take a picture of it with my phone in its military-grade case that is similar to Gail Shipton's phone and similar to Lucy's.

'Looks like a log of some sort. Maybe something the lawyers were making her keep track of.' Marino tucks the notebook back inside the handbag and next produces a small sheet of stickers, each one red with a white X in the center. 'Got no idea.' He tucks the stickers back inside.

I think of the last telephone call Gail Shipton received, the one from a blocked number.

* * *

I interpret the note as meaning the call was INC, or incoming, yesterday at 5:33 p.m., ending slightly less than eighteen minutes later, which was when Gail would have been behind the Psi Bar, standing near a dumpster in the dark.

While I can't be certain how to interpret the rest of the entry, *REC* may indicate the call was recorded, and it's possible the string of numbers is an encryption, and I imagine Gail Shipton ending the call and pausing long enough to make the entry in her notebook. Maybe she used a flashlight app on her smartphone so she could see what she was doing, and I continue forming an impression of her. Possibly introverted and insecure. Precise, deliberate, possibly rigid and obsessive-compulsive.

I imagine her preoccupied with her niggling, coded recordkeeping and not necessarily aware of what was going on around her. Was a car parked back there? Did someone pull up and she paid no attention? What I do know is that she called Carin Hegel next and the connection was quickly lost. At around six p.m. Gail must have encountered her killer.

'When you looked at Gail's phone,' I say to Marino, 'did you notice if there were any recordings on it? Video or audio, for example?'

'Nothing like that. Just incoming and outgoing calls, e-mails, text messages,' he replies distractedly as he listens to Machado and Benton go at it with each other politely but stubbornly.

'She was in the wrong place at the wrong time,' Machado asserts. 'She ducked out of the bar to make a phone call and there he was, sitting in his car.'

'That part I don't accept,' Benton replies.

'And he saw her, an easy target, a victim of opportunity.'

'She was exactly where he knew she'd be.'

'How do you know robbery wasn't a motive?' Machado is getting testy.

'I'm not saying he didn't take money or souvenirs.' Benton repeats what he's said several times now. 'Human behavior isn't just one thing. There can be a mixture of traits and inconsistencies.'

'He may have taken her jewelry,' I point out. 'Unless she wasn't wearing any, not even earrings. Of course we don't know what she had on when she was abducted.' I don't hesitate to use that word now.

'So he took her money and possibly her jewelry. Probably kept her clothing, too,' Marino says as the dispatcher comes back over the air. 'Maybe we'll get lucky and he left his DNA on her wallet, maybe on her purse. And the pipe cutter,' he adds sarcastically.

'Thirty-three,' Marino answers his radio.

The dispatcher informs him that the owner of the pickup truck is a fifty-one-year-old male named Enrique Sanchez. He works maintenance for MIT. He has no outstanding warrants and no prior arrests except for a DUI reckless-driving charge in 2008. He's been contacted and is en route. Benton doesn't say I told you so. He says nothing.

'I need to head to my office,' I let everyone know as I walk over to my field case.

I open it and begin gathering the packaged fluorescent residue I collected with stubs and the fibers and Vicks-like ointment. I seal the evidence in envelopes that I label and tuck inside my bag as a car engine sounds nearby. I glance up as a black-and-white Cambridge cruiser appears on the street behind us.

'I'll get the evidence to the labs expeditiously but if you don't mind I'll leave my case here,' I say to Marino. 'We're going to walk back to the office and I'd rather not carry it. I figure you can bring it when you come by during the autopsy. Benton's shoes and luggage are in your SUV and those will need to be dropped off, please.' I'm careful not to sound like I'm giving him orders.

The cruiser stops behind the black pickup truck and a uniformed officer climbs out. He has a notepad in hand and the name on his shiny steel nameplate is G. B. Rooney.

'I didn't want any of this going out over the air,' he says to Marino and Machado. 'The call I responded to earlier? The one on Windsor?'

'Man, you got to be more specific than that,' Machado says.

G. B. Rooney pauses with uncertainty, his eyes cutting to Benton and me.

'They're okay. Benton Wesley with the FBI. Dr. Scarpetta, the chief medical examiner,' Marino introduces us in a blasé way as I realize that G. B. Rooney is car 13.

Earlier this morning he responded to the call about my prowler and then he wasn't answering his radio for a while.

18

Tall and thin, somewhere in his early forties, he sounded out of breath when he finally resumed contact with the dispatcher at around five forty-five a.m.

I remember my surprise that car 13 would be in Tech Square when moments earlier it had been several miles away on the Harvard campus, in my neighborhood. I figured the officer had abandoned that call when the possible car break-ins were reported, but G. B. Rooney offers a different story.

'I hadn't gone two blocks when I noticed a subject inside a parked vehicle behind the Academy of Arts and Sciences on Beacon Street,' he explains. 'It's the area where the prowler was spotted running and he fit the description, at least close enough that I figured I'd better check him out.'

The way he says it piques my curiosity. Already I can tell that Rooney thought there was something unusual about this person and I can sense Benton's quiet attention. The area Rooney described is very close to our house.

'Tall, slender, young, white. Dark pants and sneakers, a black hoodie with Marilyn Monroe on it,' Rooney recites like a police report. 'I waited until he drove off and then I tailed him but not conspicuously. He headed directly to the projects on Windsor, which is why I happened to be in that location where the car breaks occurred, possibly gang-related. A lot of them in that area, kids going through parking lots and stealing what they can, plus vandalism. I'm in one parking lot and they're in another one, smashing out windows or coming back for more. Unbelievable.'

'I'm assuming you ran the guy's plate,' Marino says.

'A 2012 Audi SUV, blue, registered to a twenty-eight-year-old male with a Somerville address near the hockey rink at Conway Park — Haley Davis Swanson,' G. B. Rooney says.

'What?' Marino looks sucker punched. 'Haley Swanson?'

'He has an uncle that lives in building two of the projects there on Windsor.'

'Haley Swanson is a man?' Marino's eyes are bugging out of his head.

'I agree it's an unusual name for a male. A family name, he told me. He goes by the nickname Swan.'

'This isn't making a damn bit of sense.' Marino is thoroughly frustrated now.

He looks angry enough to have a stroke.

'Did you talk to this guy?' It's Machado who asks. 'Did you find out why he was parked behind the Academy of Arts and Sciences at the back of the woods there?'

'He told me he'd picked up coffees at Dunkin' Donuts, the one on Somerville Ave, and one of them spilled so he pulled over to clean it up. There were two coffees in the front seat and one of them had spilled so he wasn't making it up.'

'Did you ask what he was doing in the projects at the exact same time we're working a death scene over here?'

Rooney looks confused. 'I didn't mention the death scene over here.'

Machado asks nothing further and I suspect I know why. He's waiting to see if the officer volunteers that Haley Swanson was a friend of Gail Shipton's. Machado wants to know if Rooney is aware that Haley 'Swan' Swanson is the person who reported her missing and posted her disappearance and photograph on the Channel 5 website.

'What else do you know about him?' Machado then asks.

'He works for a local PR firm.' Rooney flips another page of his notepad.

It doesn't appear he's aware of the connection. It would seem that Haley Swanson didn't mention Gail Shipton to Officer Rooney and that's more than a little suspicious. Swanson had reported her missing and now it seems he might have been hiding behind my wall, watching my house? It seems illogical. Why would he have coffees? It doesn't add up that he stopped for coffees and then decided to leave his car on Beacon Street and travel on foot through the rainy dark to spy on me.

'Was he wet when you talked to him? Did it look like he'd been out in the rain?' I ask Rooney, and Benton watches us with no expression but he's listening carefully.

'He didn't appear to be wet,' Rooney says. 'I got the name of where he works.' He flips back several pages. 'Lambant and Associates in Boston.'

'They specialize in crisis management.' Benton is scrolling through e-mails on his cell phone. 'What in the legal world is known as spin doctoring in the court of public opinion.'

'I wonder if Gail Shipton retained them,' I suggest. 'Maybe that's how she became acquainted with Haley Swanson.'

'The firm's well known to our Boston field office.' Benton doesn't directly answer me. 'They represent wealthy high-profile defendants, white-collar mainly, corrupt politicians, organized crime figures, an occasional celebrity athlete who gets involved in a scandal.'

He looks long and hard at Marino, then Benton says, 'Recently Lambant and Associates handled the class-action suit relating to the pickup truck you had problems with, Pete. The case was thrown out of court. No damaging press, no harm done. In fact, the plaintiffs ended up looking like the bad guys for driving irresponsibly off-road in extreme conditions, souping up the rear axle, the frame, et cetera.'

'Total bullshit.' Marino's face turns bright red. 'Like your average person can afford a spin-doctoring firm. As usual, the little guy gets screwed.'

I'm afraid he's going to launch into his truck tirade again. But he manages to control himself.

'I'm simply suggesting Swanson might know who you are,' Benton adds. 'If he worked on that case for his firm, he would have come across your name since you were one of the plaintiffs.'

'It looks like we got a lot to check out here.' Machado is making notes. 'Starting with the exact nature of Swanson's relationship with Gail Shipton. And where he was around the time she went out to make her phone call last night and disappeared. And why he reported her missing and hasn't bothered to show up at the department and give us whatever information he's got. I'd say we might have a suspect.'

Benton doesn't comment. His attention drifts back to the railroad tracks.

'We'll check with the Psi and find out if anyone remembers who she was with and if it was Swanson and do they know him,' Marino says.

'You want my personal opinion?' Rooney leans against the hood of his cruiser and digs his hands into the pockets of his jacket. 'It's not politically correct but I feel I should say it. I'm not sure he's a male. I don't know the extent of it but if you heard him talk you might think he's a female. He could pass for one anyway. It wasn't something I could question him about, obviously. If he had gender reassignment or is taking hormones, I couldn't exactly ask and it doesn't have anything to do with anything, I guess.'

'Does he present himself as a female?' Machado inquires.

'All I can tell you is at first I thought he was one. When I questioned him in the projects, I said, 'What's a nice young lady like you doing here at this hour?' He didn't correct me, and I'm pretty sure he had a bra on. He definitely has breasts. He claimed he has an uncle who lives over there, a Vietnam vet, disabled, right there in the middle of all the drug-related crime we know goes on. And that was my other suspicion. Maybe Swanson's got a side business going, maybe that's why he can afford an expensive, brand-new SUV. I pushed him pretty hard about what he was doing there and he said he sometimes drops by to see his uncle before heading into Boston to work and he brings coffee. His story checked out. He does have a disabled uncle who lives there. I got his name, and all of it will be in my report.'

'Get it to me ASAP,' Marino snaps, and he feels foolish.

He talked to Haley Swanson around one a.m. and had no idea about any of this.

'That's it?' Machado asks Rooney. 'He offered no clue why he was driving around Cambridge? Or why he was parked near Harvard on Beacon Street? You sure it's because he spilled coffee as opposed to him maybe casing the neighborhood? He mention Dr. Scarpetta's house or knowing where it is?'

'Why would he care about where we live?' Benton asks.

Rooney gives both of us a blank look as he shifts his position on the cruiser's hood, careful his duty belt doesn't scratch the paint.

'Someone was prowling around your house this morning and I had units looking, that's why,' Marino answers before I can, and Benton stares at me and then he stares at the railroad tracks again. 'Like maybe this guy's been spying on the Doc,' Marino adds with satisfaction, pleased he might know something about me that Benton doesn't.

184

'It's not a PR guy who's possibly dealing drugs in the projects,' Benton says as if there can be no debating it. 'That's not who you need to be worried about. The type of person you're looking for doesn't kill people and then report them missing and give his damn name to a detective he asks for by name.'

'And you can't possibly know that,' Marino replies. 'We're going to find Swanson and he's got some talking to do.'

'He said he'd had a bad night, was upset and driving around, went home to shower and change clothes, then picked up coffees before heading into Boston,' Rooney summarizes.

'He was upset?' Machado says. 'Did he look upset?'

'I thought he seemed nervous and upset. He seemed scared. But then a lot of people do when they're being questioned by the police.' Rooney turns around as an old white Chevy panel van with ladders on top veers off Vassar Street, heading toward us. 'There are no outstanding warrants on him. There was no reason to hold him.'

'Yeah, well now there is,' Marino retorts.

A heavyset man's tense face stares out at us from the van's front passenger seat and his door flies open before the van is completely stopped. He trots to the black pickup truck and it's obvious he's the owner, Enrique Sanchez, and that he's frightened. In jeans, a wind-breaker, and scarred work boots, he has the red nose and puffiness, the big gut, of a heavy drinker.

'I leave it here when I ride with friends. If we

have a beer,' he says loudly in a heavy Spanish accent, his wide eyes darting at each of us.

Benton gives me a signal and we start walking toward the railroad tracks.

'You left here when and had a beer where?' Marino asks Enrique Sanchez, stepping closer to him.

'Yesterday at five o'clock in the afternoon. We go to the Plough. I was there no more than two hours and then my friend drop me at my house and pick me up this morning.'

'The Plough on Mass Ave?' Marino says. 'They got a pretty good Cuban sandwich. How often do you leave your truck here overnight, buddy?'

19

We follow railroad tracks past a generator shelter, then a plasma science and fusion center. Next is a sprawling magnet lab. Between chain-link fencing, through parking decks and dumpsters, over broken concrete and dead weeds, we walk. We take our time, looking for any sign of him.

Benton is sure this is the way the killer escaped before dawn. I don't sense the slightest hesitation or misgiving and it's difficult for me to imagine someone taking this route in the dark. I can't envision stepping around mud and glass-slick wet iron and wood and winding past the backs of buildings that would have been deserted with lights out. One could get hurt. How could someone fleeing a crime scene see where he was going?

'You should have told me,' Benton says, not accusingly but quietly and with concern. 'If you felt someone was watching you, why wouldn't you say something?'

'I thought it was my imagination. Then I saw someone this morning and he ran off. Marino assumed at first it was a kid who intended to do a smash-and-grab.'

'It wasn't.'

'Now he believes it was Haley Swanson.'

'It isn't, and I think you know the bigger worry. But I'm home and if he didn't know it before, he knows it now.' Benton says it as if he's referring to a malevolent old friend.

'Because he's watching,' I reply.

'That's what he does. He watches and fantasizes, and of late you've been all over the news. This is someone who follows other cases.'

'You're saying he intended to do something to me.'

'I'll never give him that chance,' Benton says.

We reach massive HVACs and generators and liquid-nitrogen containers connected to stainless-steel transfer lines wearing thick icy sleeves. Tall light standards on cracked concrete tarmacs look like windmills, and smokestacks rise above flat roofs, tall and conical like missile silos and organ pipes. We give a wide berth to a helium truck as sadness wells up inside me. I don't know where it's from.

Benton has been away from home for not quite a month but it seems forever. He's not the same or maybe it's me who's changed and I'm seeing him in a way I haven't before. I feel shaken to my core. I'm afraid to trust his perceptions. I worry he's personalizing and paranoid. I think of how many times I've warned him about getting too close to what he chases. When you dine with the devil use a long spoon, and I've repeatedly preached that to him, too.

I glance over at him and can't read what might be wrong as he's careful how he picks his way along in dirty orange rubber boots, his cashmere coat neatly folded over an arm. His suit is charcoal, his shirt deep blue, and his purple silk twill tie has a digital pattern of tiny computer on/off switches, a playful gift from Lucy.

Slanted sunlight on his face shows the smile lines at the corners of his eyes and the folds along the sides of his proud straight nose. The bright morning accentuates the finely etched wear and tear of time and his tall frame looks thinner than it did when I saw him last. He never eats enough when I'm not around.

'Did you do this with the others?' I'm going to dig it out of him.

This morning I've been witness to what I usually don't watch and I insist on knowing all of it. Did he retrace the killer's steps in the Washington, D.C., cases? Did he do exactly what he's doing now?

'We're talking very different settings.' His voice is more subdued than it was earlier. 'In the first one, Klara Hembree, he pulled off a major road and cut through a security chain.' Benton keeps looking at his phone, a part of him in some other place that's not a happy one.

'And he left a tool with a rock on top of it.'

'Yes.'

'Stolen?'

'A golf course shed was broken into.' He types a reply to someone as he walks, his expression vaguely angry. 'A small metal shed where maintenance and landscaping equipment are kept. That's where he got the tool, a cable cutter, meaning he knew what was inside the shed.'

'What's the matter?' Something is.

'I'm not dropping everything and heading back into *work* right now. As if what I'm doing isn't work.'

Ed Granby must be e-mailing him or someone on his behalf is.

'The killer knew his way around.' Benton glances at his phone again, irritably, then with no expression on his face. 'He cut the security chain and drove along a cart path to the edge of the wooded picnic area where he posed her body. When I visited the scene several days later I found the tool with a rock on top of it behind the picnic area near railroad tracks.'

'He drove his vehicle through a golf course? That seems beyond risky. It strikes me as reckless.'

'There are security cameras in the parking lots of each location he picked and he would have been aware of that.' Benton bends down to pull up his socks inside the boots. 'He thinks the way the police do. He knows what to look for and avoid. He does exactly what the police assume he won't, such as breaking into a tool shed and driving through a golf course after dark because, as you put it, that would be interpreted as reckless. The police wouldn't anticipate it or think to look.'

'But you would.' I watch him fuss with his pants cuffs, tucking them in.

'What I'm describing is exactly what I believe he did.' Benton straightens up and glances at his phone again and a spark of anger glints, then is gone. 'I could see where his tires went over the path and into the grass. Goodyear mud tires associated with trucks and off-road sporting and that told me something about him.'

'Which is?'

'Late twenties, early thirties. White,' Benton says. 'Engages in high-risk activities, possibly extreme sports, has a career that isn't regimented so he can come and go at irregular hours without attracting notice. He lives alone, has an IQ in the superior range but didn't finish school. Charming, attractive, entertaining but easily offended if he thinks you've slighted him. In summary, a violent sexual psychopath with narcissistic and borderline traits. The ritualistic way he captures, controls, and kills his victims takes the place of sex with them. But the last two a week apart and now this one? He's losing it, Kay.'

'And your colleagues don't concur with you.'

'That's putting it mildly.'

'You found the tire tracks because you looked for the unexpected, because you're not the police.'

'I think differently from them,' he says, and his pants are bunching up again. 'Christ, I can't believe I'm walking around in these.' He bends down and tucks his cuffs back in.

'You think differently from the police, differently from your colleagues. But you can think like this killer.'

'Someone has to.' He resumes walking. 'Someone has to honestly.'

'You sound awfully sure.'

'I am.'

'Does he do what you assume he won't?'

'Not anymore.'

'You know what he'll do. Like the Vicks.'

'That's a hypothesis. It hasn't been found at the other scenes but I can imagine the utility of him using it and I know where he could have gotten the idea.' Benton is having a hard time in the boots or maybe his aggravation has to do with me as I continue to question, digging deeper relentlessly.

'You can imagine it why?' I have to know how far down he's sunk into his dark ugly hole.

'You've read the journal articles I've written about Albert Fish and before that my master's thesis. Pain is ecstasy. A perfume that burns. Rubbing a mentholated vapor rub on your genitals so you don't rape anyone. He prided himself on his self-control. All he did was strangle her and cook her into a stew with vegetables and potatoes but he didn't sexually molest her and he made sure he told her mother that. The buttocks were the tastiest part but at least he didn't rape her.'

'You're entertaining the possibility the killer used a vapor rub on his genitals.'

'It's a reference I made to Baudelaire's *Les Fleurs du Mal*, the flowers of evil, specifically to menthyl salicylate used in perfume, a fragrance of pain, which was what Albert Fish craved. Pain was his evil perfume. It gave him sexual pleasure to insert needles into his groin and rose stems into his penis. He loved being beaten with a nail-studded paddle. Why? Because at the age of five he was placed in an orphanage in Washington, D.C., stripped naked, and whipped in front of the other boys who bullied and teased him because the beatings gave him an erection. He rewired himself to enjoy pain. It was erotic to him.'

'Washington, D.C.' I point out the connection. 'Are you considering that the Capital Murderer may be influenced by one of the most notorious killers in history?'

'We don't know who's read what I've published about a psychiatric phenomenon the likes of which no one had ever seen. He got away with his crimes for decades, was married the entire time with six kids. It's suspected he enjoyed his own execution.' Benton recites all this as if it's normal.

'I hope we're not dealing with someone like that.'

'He would crave being that infamous. It would make sense he reads about notorious killers and vicariously lives the violent atrocities they've committed,' Benton says. 'This is someone who spends most of his time in a deviant and violent fantasy world that's rooted in events from his past. He's wired to enjoy and be aroused by what most people would find appalling. Maybe he was born that way or maybe something happened in his childhood or more likely it's both.'

'And you've told your colleagues what you've just told me.'

'They think I should quit while I'm ahead. I'm rich enough to do whatever the hell I want. That's what they tell me. Enjoy your hard-earned family money is what they say. Spend more time in Aspen. Get a place in Hawaii.'

'They know about your concern that the killer might be reading what you've published and getting ideas from it.' I can't imagine the reaction Benton would have gotten to such a suspicion.

'It didn't start out my concern. Granby suggested it first, which makes matters worse,' Benton says to my surprise.

'That's a terrible thing to accuse you of,' I reply.

'It feeds right into what he preaches, that the Bureau no longer should be involved in the, quote, profiling of the eighties and nineties, and the BAU should be absorbed into the Joint Terrorism Task Force,' Benton says. 'Everything should be about combating terrorism and the types of mindless mass murders we're seeing and not individual serial offenders. I'm obsolete and maybe I'm compounding the problem. People get my publications off the Internet. There's no telling who sees them and we shouldn't be in the business of dispensing provocative information that could inspire copycats.'

'He's such a petty bureaucrat.' I try to be reassuring as we walk in the sun and the wind. 'He resents the way you dress. He resents your car and your house and is none too fond of me no matter what he pretends about any of it. He resents that you basically started profiling, are a trendsetter and authority in the field, and he has no legacy. Granby will never be known for anything except that people like us talk badly about him.'

'Eventually he'll force me out, and Marino didn't help matters by alerting my office that I'm assisting in an investigation they know nothing about.' Benton stares down at his big orange feet as they slap against mud. 'I've not talked to Granby, obviously. I've been a little busy.'

'What did Marino say?' I feel a rush of annoyance.

'Suggesting we find a time to have a meeting about the case. He wasn't thinking.'

'Dammit. That's unfortunate. It was stupid. He was flaunting himself and whenever he does that he has terrible judgment. And he has to pick on you, Benton. Especially right now because he's not feeling much confidence.'

'It doesn't matter why. But I wish he hadn't done it.'

'Besides, they've asked you to retire before. They always change their minds because the people with good sense realize your value.'

'This case may be what finally does me in.' He tucks his phone into his pants pocket. 'Especially if there's a perception that I've helped someone become a better murderer.'

'That's preposterous, and it may not be true he's read anything you've written.'

'It could have given him ideas. But it didn't make him kill anyone. It doesn't work like that. Granby's changed who and what I am to everyone and I can't stop it.'

'What you're describing is disturbing.' I'm more direct. 'I'll just say it. I'm worried about you and your state of mind.'

He gently grips my elbow as we maneuver around thick mud. He touches the small of my back the way he does when he's letting me know he's here. Then he watches where he's stepping, not close anymore, and I feel the distance between us, a cool emptiness. I feel unsettled and anxious. Nothing feels safe, and I find myself looking around, wondering if we're being watched or followed.

'Tell me how you're doing, Kay.' He glances at me and he continues his sweep, looking around and straight ahead, his profile keen.

'I'm fine. How about you? Besides not eating or sleeping enough. Who's chasing who?' I go ahead and say it.

'You're probably not fine. In fact, I know you're not. When what we believe we've mastered is no longer predictable we're not fine. The world suddenly is a very scary place. It loses its charm.'

'Charm,' I repeat ironically, stonily. 'The world lost its charm when I first met death. We were unhappily introduced when I was twelve and have been together ever since.'

'And now you've met something you can't dissect. No matter how many times you take it apart you won't figure it out.'

He's not talking about Washington or Cambridge. He's talking about Connecticut. I don't answer right away as we walk. I pause to put my coat back on as the wind picks up sharply. I dig my hands into my pockets and they're stuffed with dirty gloves. I look for a trash can but there isn't one.

★ ★ ★

'Let's be honest, the world's always been a scary place with very little charm.' I try to brush it off as I've brushed off the flu, as I brushed off the death of my father when I was young, as I've

196

brushed off so much since Benton has known me.

'You've been drawing from a well that you never knew was bottomless and you just found out the unlimited depth of inhumanity,' he says. 'A type of senseless slaughter you can't solve because it's already over by the time you get there, decimating a shopping mall, a church, a school. And I can't profile who will do it next, what demented empty person will strike out of nowhere. Granby's right about that much at least.'

'Don't give him any credit.'

'All I can do is predict the aftermath because such a person does it only once. Then he's dead and we're looking for the next one.'

'How many next ones?' The anger raises its head again. I feel the hot breath on my neck and don't want anything to do with it.

'The more it happens, the more it will,' Benton says. 'The lowest common denominator used to be what's primal no matter how perverted. Murder, rape, torture, cannibalism, even the public executions the Romans orchestrated to entertain Colosseum crowds. But nothing in history is like this. Committing mass murder as if it's a video game. Killing children, babies, unloading high-capacity magazines into crowds of strangers, creating a gruesome spectacle for fame. No, you're not fine, Kay. Neither of us is.'

'A lot of the first responders will quit.' I look down where I walk. 'It was too much for even the experienced ones, the EMTs and police I met. Those who got there first were like zombies, doing everything they were supposed to do but nobody was home. It was as if a light had gone out inside of them forever.'

'You won't quit.'

'I wasn't first, Benton.' I step around bent rebar and a railroad spike half buried in the rocks.

'You saw the same thing they did.'

I slip my arm around him and feel the slimness of his waist as I lean my head against his shoulder and breathe in the subtle smell of him, his skin, his cologne, the wool of his jacket warming in the sun.

'You're projecting about me,' he says into my hair. 'I'm not straying out of bounds but you're worried you are. You're projecting your fears about yourself onto me. That's what happens when something really gets to you. No matter what we see, we're never ready for the next thing that's inconceivably awful.'

'Well, that sounds grim. With all you and I have dedicated ourselves to? And the world is more screwed up than it's ever been. Sometimes I wonder why we bother.'

'No you don't.'

'You're right,' I reply. 'I don't wonder. I don't know any better and maybe that's worse.'

'Do you have that little flashlight you usually carry?' he asks.

We've reached an institute for brain research where the train tracks bore through the building, literally through the middle of it, a tunnel maybe half a block long. It's semi-dark inside and at least ten degrees cooler and I get out the flashlight and turn it on. I illuminate our way as pebbles we dislodge click against one another and chink against iron rails, reminding me of the sounds behind the wall at the back of our yard. Leaves and sticks disturbed, a rock or piece of brick dislodged, and then the young male running.

Reemerging into the bright, rain-scrubbed morning, I return the flashlight to my bag and we step over puddles in gravel, reaching a stretch of mud that has washed over the tracks in a thin gray slick. Both of us see the impression at the same time, what looks like a bare footprint.

20

My first thought is *Gail Shipton*. Her feet were bare but that's ridiculous. She didn't wrap herself in a white cloth and walk along these tracks in the pouring rain to die in the middle of Briggs Field as if she willed it. More important, the footprint is pointed the wrong way, headed out of the campus and not in.

We stop beyond the tunnel where rusty iron rails are missing crossties, a toothless stretch of railroad tracks spanning six or seven feet. Then the crossties resume and on the first one is the footprint left in a dirty patina coating the old creosote-treated wood. I crouch to take a closer look at the distinct shape of an insole and five toes with odd scoring at the ball of the foot and the back of the heel. The footprint is anatomically perfect. Too symmetrical and too perfect. It looks fake for a reason.

Three crossties away I find another identical impression, then one more, and in the dirt nearby on the other side of the tracks there are several partial ones spattered by rain that oddly point the opposite way, toward the campus, as if the person were heading into it. The impressions were left at different times, the partial ones earlier while it was still raining lightly, I decide, and the others later when it had stopped. Each footprint is slightly smeared as if the person was jumping from tie to tie or running or both.

Sure-footed, strong, and agile, he wasn't slipping or stumbling in conditions that most of us couldn't navigate at a rapid pace.

The footprints look inhuman as if made by a superhero in a rubber suit who vanished along the railroad tracks as abruptly as he appeared. A Batman, a Superman, setting down before springing into flight again. Only this character isn't dedicated to fighting threats against humanity, and I envision the figure in black tights I noticed jogging when I arrived at the scene while it was still dark. Agile and fast, and for some reason he caught my eye as he headed toward the very area of the campus where the railroad tracks run behind Simmons Hall.

★ ★ ★

'A shoe glove.' That much is obvious to me. 'Lucy wears them sometimes, five-fingered running shoes, as they're called, for minimalist jogging or sprinting.'

'Minimalist like a white cloth. Like simple clear plastic bags adorned with simple bows made out of decorative duct tape. Minimal injuries. A minimal struggle if there was one at all.' Benton says all this as if he's computing out loud. 'Killing minimally but with great fanfare and mockery. He knows how to get attention.'

'Have you seen a footprint like this before?'

He shakes his head, his jaw hard set. Benton hates whoever it is.

'No footwear patterns have been found at any of the other scenes,' he says. 'He drove and then

201

was on foot through woods. It doesn't mean he didn't have something like this on. I don't know.'

'Supposedly running gloves are the closest thing to being barefoot, what Lucy calls running naked,' I tell him. 'They're certainly not what you would expect anyone to be wearing out here, especially in these wet, muddy conditions. They have protective soles but you can feel the terrain through them, every rock, stick, or crack in the sidewalk. Or so I'm told. Lucy usually wears hers on the street, on the beach, but not off road.'

Within a space of ten crossties the shoulders of the tracks are gravel again. The dark hardwood is wet but relatively clean and I wonder if the footprints are another premeditated surprise. I wonder if we're supposed to find them like the tool, like Gail Shipton's handbag and wallet. Or did her minimalist, attention-seeking killer finally slip up and was the bead of mentholated ointment adhering to grass also an error? I can get DNA from Vicks. All I need is a few skin cells.

I dig my phone out of my jacket pocket and use it to take several photos of a footprint and when I stand up my vision goes black. For an instant I feel faint. My blood sugar is low. I look up at the bare tops of trees against the bright sky, at clawlike branches swaying in wind that is shifting, and the air is brisk against my skin. I look around for him, for whoever is stalking women and murdering them and very likely stalking me. I need to get to my office.

I need the body to talk to me because it will tell me the truth in a language that makes sense and can be trusted. The dead aren't capricious with me. They don't lie. They don't create spectacles and they don't prey on anyone. I don't want to be inside the killer's mind. I don't want to witness what Benton does. I'm reminded how it feels to watch him bond the way he must with a person who brings the dead to my door.

'I'll get hold of Marino,' I decide. 'He needs to come here now so I can get to the office and start on the autopsy.' I text the photos to him.

I include the message that we've found unusual footprints left on the railroad tracks on the other side of the tunnel that cuts through a brain research institute, maybe a quarter of a mile from the tennis bubble.

Not a minute after I've pressed *Send*, Marino calls me.

'You got any good reason to think they're his?' he asks right off.

'They were left in the past few hours as the rain was light and then later when it stopped,' I reply. 'Some impressions are partially washed away and heading into the campus while others are intact and heading out. Therefore, I think we can safely conclude these were left by someone walking, possibly running, back here recently, headed into the campus and then away from it while it was still dark and we were still working the scene.'

'He wouldn't be heading toward the scene on foot if he had the body with him,' Marino says, his voice heavy with doubt.

'No he wouldn't.'

'Then what the hell was he doing going in and out?'

'I don't know but you should check to see if you find other footprints, ones I might have missed.'

'I don't know why he'd go in and out on foot. Maybe different people left what you're looking at.'

'Are you familiar with shoe gloves?' I ask.

'The freaky shoes Lucy wears. She got me a pair a couple of Christmases ago, remember? They got no arch support. I looked like a frog in them and kept stubbing my damn rubber toes.'

'I'm estimating they're twenty-six, possibly twenty-seven, centimeters in length.'

'How about inches. I live in America.'

'Approximately ten inches, which would be the equivalent of a size eight in men's shoes or a size ten in women's.'

'Size eight?' Marino's voice is loud in my ear. 'That's pretty damn small for a man. Could be a kid playing around back there along the railroad tracks. Not to mention the weird-ass shit MIT students are into, and some of their nerdy little genius-types are like fourteen years old, right? Wouldn't surprise me if one of them would wear shoes with toes in them.'

'We need these footprints photographed to scale.' I hear myself telling Marino what to do as if he still works for me.

No matter my intentions I can't seem to resist supervising him. I can feel him bristle over the phone. Or I imagine I do.

'It may be that they turn out not to be relevant,' I add diplomatically as I hear the background sounds of metal jingling and a car door thudding.

I hear Marino getting Quincy out of the SUV and on leash.

'But let's play it safe. Photos and measurements, please,' I add. 'I don't think you'll be able to cast the impressions but you might want to collect the soil for trace. We'll get Ernie to take a look at that, too.' Ernie Koppel is my most senior microscopist and trace evidence examiner. 'It's a long shot, I realize, but if it's not necessary or possible to preserve the footprints intact you may as well get whatever you want while you can.'

'I'm coming,' Marino says. 'Heading toward you even as we speak. Hold on a few minutes and I'll grab the photos, whatever's needed. It doesn't make sense wearing shoe gloves but I guess if they're rubber you can wash them off easy enough like flip-flops. What a whack job. Certifiable. We should check area mental hospitals to see who's gotten out recently.'

'I wouldn't make that the first thing on your list.' I hear myself telling him what to do again.

'How 'bout you let me do my job?'

'That's what I want you to do.'

'Is he right there?' Marino lowers his voice.

I look at Benton waiting restlessly, walking along one side of the fence, stooping over again to tuck his pants legs in.

'That's correct,' I reply.

I can't tell if Benton is listening but it doesn't matter if he is. He doesn't have to work hard to figure out what Marino might be thinking. Benton doesn't have to guess at what Marino might say or wish were true.

'He mention anything about Lucy?' Marino asks. 'Whether she knew her?'

He wants to know the details of Lucy's relationship with Gail Shipton and I can't talk about it.

'Not really,' I answer as I watch Benton move around, not looking at me, but suddenly I have his attention, I can tell.

'Not really that she knew her or that you don't know the details?' Marino says.

'I don't.'

'Huh,' he replies. 'But they knew each other somehow.'

'It would seem so.' I'm not going to lie. 'I don't know to what degree.'

'Something's going on with Gail's phone. When I first got into it early this morning there were text messages, which is how I knew Carin Hegel wanted her to call. There were e-mails. Now they're gone.'

'Are you sure they were there in the first place?' I ask and Benton is listening.

He looks at me.

'Hell yes,' Marino says. 'And every text message and e-mail's gone, and before that all the photographs were gone. I don't believe there weren't any. Who doesn't have a single photo on their phone? I think when I was picking it up off the pavement somebody had already started deleting shit.'

'You're looking at her phone again right now?' I puzzle and I can tell by Benton's reaction that this has his attention in a powerful way.

'Why the hell do you think?' Marino asks.

'It needs to go to the labs.'

'It's not that simple. I was just showing the phone to Machado because we're trying to figure out what to do with it,' Marino says. 'Suddenly all that's left on it are incoming and outgoing calls. No voice mails, no apps, no e-mails, fucking nothing.'

'You need to get it to the labs,' I repeat.

'How the hell am I supposed to do that? Considering who would be the one examining it? That's what Machado and me were talking about. It's a serious conflict.'

It would be Lucy who examines it. She's the CFC's forensic computer and technology expert, and she analyzes any evidence relating to cybercrime. I understand what Marino's getting at and why he was having a conversation with Machado. I imagine her deleting certain information from the phone when she discovered it was on the pavement near the Psi Bar around midnight.

After that she was flying her helicopter, flying Benton home, while she remotely monitored what was going on with Gail's phone. I suspect when Lucy realized Marino had found it in the parking lot behind the bar she quickly deleted more and by now may have deleted almost everything, and he's onto her. He's certain she's scrubbed the device of any information she doesn't want the police or anyone else to see.

'Then I suggest you submit it to the FBI,' I answer him and Benton holds my stare and begins to shake his head. 'Let their labs handle it,' I add and Benton startles me by shaking his head *No, absolutely not.*

'I do that I lose any control,' Marino says.

'It sounds to me that you feel you have anyway.' I can tell by Benton's face that he doesn't want me to mention the FBI again and I won't but I don't understand it and I feel slightly shocked.

'I'll never know what they find out either,' Marino says. 'They don't exactly work and play well with others.'

'You'll lose control,' I reinforce his misgivings, trying to take back what I suggested that has created such resistance in Benton.

'And to be fair, I've got to talk to her first,' Marino decides.

Not before I do, I think and I move closer to Benton, both of us watching each other, and I can tell he's angry and going to do something about it.

'Maybe there's an explanation, right?' Marino says conspiratorially. 'You'd tell me if you knew, right?'

'Be careful out here. There's a lot of slippery mud and rusty metal. We're just on the other side of the tunnel.'

'Okay, you can't talk. But this is exactly what I don't need right now. A problem with her, and you and me both know what the hell she's like. Right now I fucking don't need this,' Marino declares. 'One month on the job, not even.'

★ ★ ★

'Don't encourage Marino to turn over the phone to the FBI,' Benton says and he's adamant about

208

it, referencing the FBI as if it's separate and apart from him.

'I already did and you heard me. It made sense to suggest it.'

'It doesn't.'

'What on earth is going on?'

'Don't suggest it again.'

'If you say so I won't.'

'I mean it, Kay. Goddamn it, I don't want Granby to know about the phone. I hope to hell Marino stops shooting his mouth off. He has no idea what he's dealing with.'

Our eyes are locked as we wait near footprints in a section of muddy tracks, MIT's nuclear reactor just up ahead, what looks like a big white fuel tank with a tall brick smokestack painted red. For weeks Benton has been talking about a problem with trust and now it's coming out. He's not just having personnel disputes, something is terribly wrong and his reaction is unnerving.

'Is Lucy going to be all right?' I ask. 'What's happening, Benton?'

'I don't want some case made about obstruction of justice. She could go to prison and he would do that.'

'Marino would?' I can't believe it.

'Not him, not intentionally. You don't want my division involved. Cambridge PD can analyze the phone.' His rubber-soled feet crunch on gravel as he moves around, the wind in his hair. 'One of their detectives is assigned to the Secret Service and they can do the forensic analysis at their field office in Boston.'

'How is that better than your office doing it?

Your office, where people know us.'

'Knowing us is worse. And I don't work for the Secret Service.' Benton steps on a railroad tie, testing how slippery it is. 'That's why it's better.'

'What are you saying?'

'You can't trust them, Kay. That's what I'm saying. Do you have any idea how much fun Granby would have if he knew anything about the phone? Marino needs to keep his damn mouth shut.'

It alarms me to think that Benton's boss would relish going after my niece. I've always found him boring and a lightweight, a typical example of what rises to the top, but it's becoming quite clear that Benton is suggesting Ed Granby is more than an irritant and an obstruction, and not just to him but possibly to all of us.

'The phone has nothing to do with Gail Shipton's murder anyway,' Benton says in a steely tone. 'Lucy will tell you what she's done and what she's trying to prevent. It should come from her. I have to be careful what I say and I've already said too much.'

'I don't think you've said nearly enough and now's not the time to be careful,' I reply. 'We've been down this road before when you've been so damn loyal to the Bureau and so damn careful and look what happens? All of us get torn apart.' I'm feeling upset and I don't want to feel like this. 'I'm sorry. I'm tired and I haven't eaten and this is unnerving.'

He's silent and I can see his conflict, which is

like a war inside him, then he says, 'I won't let that happen ever again.'

'You've said you wouldn't.'

'You know what the FBI expects. It not only comes first, it owns you, and then when it's done with you it exiles you into oblivion or worse.'

'It doesn't own either of us,' I reply. 'It did once and it won't again and your people won't touch Lucy.'

'They're not my people.' His anger flashes again.

'You own yourself, Benton.'

'I know that, Kay. I promise I do. I wouldn't be here right now if I didn't own myself.'

'What is it I can't trust exactly?' I look at him. 'I think it's time you spell it out.'

'I'm not sure I can spell it out. But I can tell you what worries me and that I'm alone in it.' Sticks break as he steps farther from the tracks. 'I don't want you hurt and I don't want Lucy hurt. Granby will hurt you if he can. He'll hurt all of us and I hope to hell Marino doesn't say anything about the phone to him or to anyone at my office. Dammit. Why does he have to stick his nose in it? He shouldn't have called my office and there will be hell to pay if he turns over the phone to them.'

'He won't. Marino hates the FBI.'

'Maybe he should.'

'I need to know what you're alone in.' I will make him tell me. 'Whatever you're up against, I'm up against. All of us are.'

'Now that he's murdered here, you're up against it, that's for sure.'

211

'There can't be any secrets, Benton. The hell with the FBI. This is us. This is people who are dying. Fuck the FBI.' I can't believe I said it but I did.

'Marino probably just got me fired but I don't give a shit. We can't let Granby get away with this.'

'We won't, whatever it is, but you have to talk to me.'

Benton sits on his heels, his back against the fence, about to tell me what he believes he shouldn't.

'They think they know who it is and I'm going to give you the information because anything you hear from them you can't trust. It's probably a lie.' He continues to refer to the FBI as if he isn't the FBI. 'These cases now involve you directly and I'm not going to let the Bureau do this to you. You're right. I promised that would never happen again and it won't.'

'Do what?'

'They've done enough to you, to both of us.'

'What's happened, Benton?'

He goes on to explain that his colleagues at the BAU are certain they know who the Capital Murderer is and Benton is just as certain that they're badly mistaken. Or, as he puts it, *dead wrong*, because the theory is more wrong than mistaken, that's what he's getting at, and the implication is what he's been alluding to for weeks. It's about trust. It's about a possibility that couldn't be more shocking or disheartening.

'It's too damn obvious, too good to be true,' he says. 'Someone this calculating wouldn't leave his DNA, leave it so conspicuously you could see it. You didn't need any special lights or presumptive tests to find it right away. It doesn't feel right and it's been my experience that when something doesn't feel right almost always it isn't.'

'Who does the FBI think it is?'

'Martin Lagos,' Benton replies, and hearing the name gives me a strange feeling at first. 'He disappeared seventeen years ago after murdering his mother, I should say 'allegedly.' He was fifteen at the time. The Bureau has his name but not him because nobody can find him. I'm the only one who's not convinced, not even slightly. Warren, Stewart, Butler, Weir, all of them think I'm nuts,' he says, referring to colleagues at the BAU.

I feel astonished and I feel something else. I realize the name Lagos is familiar. I don't know why. I can't conjure it up.

'How could the FBI know his identity and not release it to the public?' I ask. 'If the public is informed about who you're looking for, someone might come forward and tell you where he is.'

'He can't be tipped off that he's been connected to the D.C. murders. That's the reasoning, not mine but Granby's. Martin Lagos has no clue the FBI knows it's him; that's the operational theory. When the timing is right Granby will hold a press conference, a big one.'

'Why Ed Granby and what will make the timing right?' I stare down the long stretch of empty railroad tracks, looking for Marino.

'His reasoning is the first victim was from Cambridge so there's a strong local interest and our division has been involved from the beginning. When enough time has passed and no one else is caught and he doesn't strike again information will be released to the public.'

'It appears he's already struck again.'

'That's the problem Granby faces. Assuming I'm right, the evidence won't point to Martin Lagos because it can't,' Benton says. 'Not in this case or any other, if there are more.'

'I have no idea what you mean by that.'

'Nothing else will come up to divert attention away from Martin, not now or down the road or even in the past. His DNA won't be found again but nobody else's will either. That's what I'm afraid of. The three D.C. cases will be exceptionally cleared and closed and certain parties can move on to what's next because I believe that's what Granby wants for reasons I don't understand. But I sense it. And I've been looking into it on my own while I've been gone these past three weeks.'

'And what have you discovered?' I ask.

'There's no record of Martin Lagos, not a trace of him.' Benton picks up a stick and starts breaking it into pieces. 'He's a Red Notice and has been since he disappeared. For seventeen years Interpol has circulated information about him and not one sighting or lead has turned out to be legitimate.'

'Then it's been considered from the start that he might be living in another country.' I can't imagine any other reason for Interpol to be involved.

'It's supposed he was well equipped to manage

abroad in Europe or South America,' Benton replies. 'A substantial amount of money was missing from the house, and Martin spoke French, Spanish, and Italian in addition to English.'

'By the time he was fifteen?' *Lagos*. I know the name but am drawing a blank.

'It's how his mother raised him. They spoke several languages at home and he was an experienced traveler. Extremely bright but troubled. Isolated, bullied at school, didn't participate in group sports or anything social. Straight A's, a computer nerd until his freshman year of high school when his grades began to suffer. He became more withdrawn, depressed, got into alcohol, and then his mother was murdered.'

'He's believed to have killed her where and when?'

'Fairfax, Virginia, in July of 1996.' Benton flicks pieces of wood, kicks them with his finger like tiny footballs.

'His mother had something to do with rare art and the White House.' It comes back to me and I'm confronted with images of her suddenly vivid in my memory.

Bloated and discolored by decomposition, her skin and hair slipping off her body. Her teeth bared in a face that was blackish red and grotesquely swollen. Nude and partially submerged in scummy water.

'Gabriela Lagos was your case,' Benton says.

21

I was the chief medical examiner of Virginia then but I didn't do her autopsy. My northern district office took care of Gabriela Lagos and I didn't realize there was a significant problem until her body had been autopsied and released.

I remember driving to a Fairfax, Virginia, funeral home and the displeasure of the people who worked there when I showed up with a crime scene case. The body wasn't viewable but that didn't mean I should further mutilate it by incising reddish areas that I suspected were bruises.

I spent long hours with Gabriela Lagos, looking at her body after reviewing the reports and photographs of what was a sensational death, an incredibly troubling one, and I felt the way Benton does right now. I was the odd person out. I was convinced she was a homicide disguised to look like a natural death or an accident.

'She was a Washington insider, divorced from a former minister of culture at the Argentinian embassy, an art historian who was vibrant and quite beautiful,' Benton says. 'A curator at the National Gallery, and she also oversaw exhibits at the White House, authenticating new acquisitions for the First Family, which at the time was the Clintons.'

'I recall a suggestion of scandal that never

surfaced publicly.' I sensed someone was trying to manipulate my office from the moment I informed the police that Gabriela Lagos was a homicidal drowning and the focus became her only child, the son she was raising alone.

The fifteen-year-old boy had vanished. When a warrant was issued for his arrest I got aggressive phone calls from the mayor's office and my longtime friend Senator Frank Lord warned me to watch my back.

'Clearly she'd been dead for three or four days in the middle of summer, the air-conditioning turned off, possibly deliberately to escalate decomposition,' I tell Benton. 'Suffice it to say she was in very grim shape. Fresh contusions weren't readily apparent but they were there, and the typical fingermark pattern I expect in homicidal bathtub drownings when victims are lifted by the ankles, causing their heads to submerge. Almost always there's significant bruising around the lower legs and also over the hands and arms from violently striking the sides of the tub as the victim flails helplessly.'

'Christ, remind me not to go that way,' Benton says from his position against the fence, sitting on his heels, his forearms on his knees, while we wait for Marino.

'The pattern was harder to see because of the advanced decomposition.' The details rush back at me like remembered bad dreams. 'And my deputy chief had neglected to incise those areas of discoloration to look for hemorrhage and he misinterpreted contusions as postmortem artifacts.'

'I know all about his negligence.' Benton flicks more bits of broken stick.

'Jerry Geist.' My tone turns disparaging.

'It's hard to forget a pompous old fart like that.'

'For a number of reasons she easily could have been signed out as an accident.'

'If you hadn't been involved, she would have been.' Benton reminds me I had quite a fight on my hands.

The prosecutor was adamant that a jury would never convict Martin Lagos, a juvenile, assuming he was ever found and taken into custody. The physical evidence wasn't strong and I disagreed. It was plenty strong. A healthy young woman who wasn't impaired with drugs or alcohol didn't accidentally drown in a tub filled with water so hot that her entire body was scalded. There was no sign of a seizure, stroke, aneurysm, or myocardial infarct, and she shouldn't have had fresh bruises. She was murdered and it was my belief that whoever was involved had attempted to obscure the crime.

'Dr. Geist wanted the death signed out as an accidental drowning and I wouldn't let him.' I haven't thought of him in years.

He was in his sixties at the time, an old-school pathologist, blatantly misogynistic and quite happy when I resigned and he didn't have to answer to me anymore. I remember feeling he was inappropriately influenced by anyone who was powerfully connected and I strongly suspected he maneuvered behind the scenes to force me out of office.

'He maintained the skin slippage and blistering were due solely to the bad condition she was in when in fact her entire body was covered with full-thickness burns,' I explain. 'It was apparent to me that after she was dead someone refilled the tub with scalding tap water, probably to hasten decomposition and obscure injuries. That and turning off the air-conditioning in July made for a tough case that Dr. Geist debated with me disrespectfully and inappropriately.'

'He was an arrogant little bastard.' Benton runs his fingers through his unruly hair as the wind kicks up.

A high-pressure front has followed the retreating storm and sharp gusts blast along miles of tracks stretching out like sutures. In the distance I make out the figure of Marino walking his dog.

'Why would Martin Lagos's name come up now?' I ask.

'His DNA was supposedly recovered in the third case, Julianne Goulet, on the panties the killer dressed her in, which were identified as belonging to the victim from the week before, Sally Carson.' Benton gets to his feet, shaking out his legs the way he does when his knees are bothering him.

'Identified how?'

'Visually. Her husband recognized them, lingerie he'd bought for her that he recalled she had on when she left the house, when he saw her last. We never got her DNA from them.'

'That's unusual if she had them on when she was abducted and murdered.'

'Maybe you're beginning to see it from my point of view. We didn't get Sally Carson's DNA but we got Martin Lagos's. Supposedly.'

'Yes, you've said that twice now. *Supposedly.*'

'The killer dresses his most recent victim in the panties of the last one,' Benton says. 'Totally textbook. I've written about it.'

'And for some reason in the third case, Julianne Goulet, he left his DNA.'

'That's the way it's supposed to look.'

'Are you thinking it was left deliberately?'

'I'm thinking someone did,' he says.

★   ★   ★

Benton puts his coat on as he stares off in the direction of Marino, whose advance is in fits and starts. Quincy tugs him like a sled dog, following the scents of God knows what, finding clumps of weeds to mark.

'We can't locate Martin Lagos,' Benton continues to explain. 'The theory is he created a new identity, possibly as long ago as when he vanished. He had one close friend who I strongly feel helped him disappear or was involved in Gabriela's murder and we don't know where this friend is either. But nobody's listening to me.'

'What about forensic age progression to predict what Martin might look like now?'

'Believe me, I've tried.'

'You have? By yourself?' I continue to be dismayed by the way he refers to himself now as if he's completely alone in this investigation.

'We've searched mug shots that include police departments, prisons, plus the Bureau's national repository of surveillance, passports, driver's license photos, you name it, and also whatever else Interpol might have. Black notices, for example, the unidentified dead,' he says. 'Nothing, not even remotely.'

'Who is 'we'?'

Benton doesn't answer me, and Marino is nearing the other side of the tunnel now.

'You don't think he's alive,' I say in a quieter voice because I don't want Marino to overhear a word.

'I don't,' Benton replies. 'No matter what name Martin Lagos might go by or how he might have tried to alter his appearance, his facial landmarks should be the same. The spacing between his mouth and nose, the width of his eyes, measurements like that.'

It sounds like something Lucy would say.

'Everything makes me suspect he's not been around for the past seventeen years, which is why we can't find him,' Benton adds. 'It's possible he's dead. He may have committed suicide or he may have been murdered.'

'Maybe Lucy can help.' I suggest what I'm beginning to suspect has happened already. 'The computer programs she's created using neural networking recognize objects and images much the way the brain does. I know that she's been doing research with irises, facial features, and other biometric technology. Of course I'm sure you know what she's been doing; maybe know more than I do,' I add pointedly.

'A forensic app.' He stares down the tracks, watching Marino get closer. 'With a potential of being used in vehicles manned and unmanned.

In other words, possibly drones targeting people of interest, a handheld way of searching almost anything you can think of, assuming you have access to databases that are off-limits to most people.'

'If you can give Lucy the most recent photograph. Or a video or a recording of his, whatever you've got.' The forensic app may have been on Gail Shipton's phone.

It may be a project the two of them were working on and Benton may be suggesting that Lucy has been helping him by searching databases she isn't legally allowed to access. Government databases, for example.

'The most recent photo is when he was fifteen, his birthday,' Benton says. 'Just four days before his mother died. Age progression, facial recognition, came up with nothing. There's no match to be made because he's dead. That's what I believe even if I can't prove it yet.'

If Lucy has been helping him, it not only would be in direct violation of FBI regulations but it would be a violation far more serious. She's not supposed to know what Benton is doing, much less assist, unless it's been approved by his division, specifically by Granby, but then I'm not supposed to know about the Capital Murderer cases either.

Lucy conducting clandestine data searches for Benton reinforces just how much he doesn't trust those around him. It would explain why she scrubbed Gail Shipton's phone. If this forensic app he just mentioned was discovered, someone might question what it was being used for. Any hint that it was capable of searching classified law enforcement repositories could lead right to Lucy and also to Benton and to very big trouble. Both of them could face criminal prosecution. Benton would never encourage such a thing with her unless he was certain he had no choice.

'Do we have a clue about why Martin Lagos might have killed his mother?' I don't recall being told a motive at the time and I don't want to ask him for further details about what he and Lucy have done.

'We have a purported one. Supposedly she began sexually abusing him when he was six.' The sun is directly in Benton's face as he turns toward the river, which we can't see from here, then his eyes are back on Marino, who's entering the tunnel now.

'Where did the information come from if she's dead and he's vanished?'

'A computer disk. At the time of his mother's murder we got information off a disk the police discovered hidden in his bedroom. His computer's hard drive was missing. Presumably removed by him,' Benton says. 'A spy video camera may also have been missing, used to film his mother bathing, based on what Martin wrote in his diary.'

'Wasn't Granby in Washington back then?' I have an instinct, an unpleasant one of how this is looping around.

Granby can't resist reminding anyone who will listen that he was an assistant special agent in charge in D.C. and what an exciting time it was when everything wasn't about 9/11 and the war in the Middle East. During a dinner not long after he moved here he asked what I remembered about him from when I was the chief of Virginia and I told him I was sorry if we'd met then and I didn't recall it. I could tell I offended him. Then he seemed relieved.

'He was an inspector in place and on the White House's National Security Staff,' Benton says. 'The details about Martin Lagos's abuse were never in your office records.' He changes the subject back to that. 'There was never anything in the police report. The medical examiner didn't need to know and it would have served no useful purpose for the media to get its hands on such an accusation. That was the decision.' Not Benton's decision but someone else's.

'Do you believe the abuse happened?'

'From what I've read in the diary, yes.'

Marino is midway in the shadowy tunnel now, Quincy straining toward us with his tongue hanging out. It looks like he's grinning.

'I'd like to review the Gabriela Lagos case to refresh my memory,' I say to Benton. 'Everything you have on it. I'd rather not go through Virginia. Nobody wants a former chief meddling. My input wouldn't be welcome.' I have more than one reason.

If there's a problem with Martin Lagos's DNA, I'm certainly not tipping my hand by calling the office that handled the original analysis even though I was in charge of it at the time, in 1996. If something has happened, it's happened since I was chief, possibly very recently, as recently as the third victim's murder, which wasn't even a month ago.

'I can get you a lot more than your former office can as long as I don't clear it with Granby,' Benton says. 'He won't say no. It just won't happen and then other things will.'

'As soon as I can get anything that might relate to what's going on,' I reply. 'You think my case here is connected to the ones in D.C., so let me look at the evidence. I have that right and jurisdiction. Let's compare the DNA, let's compare the fibers to what I've recovered from this morning. Give me everything you've got as quickly as you can.'

'Leave it!' Marino orders his dog.

'The DNA is harder,' Benton says.

'Heel!' Marino's voice echoes inside the tunnel, where Quincy is pulling him around. 'Shit!'

'I can e-mail the microscopic images of the fibers,' Benton says. 'But the DNA profiles have to come from CODIS and I can't access that directly. I'd have to put in a formal request.'

'Who did the original analysis in Julianne Goulet's case?'

'The Maryland medical examiner's office. Baltimore.'

'I know the chief very well.'

'You can trust him without reservation?'

'Absolutely.'

Quincy sloshes into a puddle and drinks from it and Marino yells, 'No! Leave it! Dammit!'

'About the time it's believed Gabriela Lagos died an anonymous caller reported witnessing a young male jumping from the Fourteenth Street

225

Bridge into the Potomac at night,' Benton tells me. 'The body was never found.'

'Never?' I question. 'That strikes me as strange.'

'No drinking puddles!' Marino is the one barking.

'Were you the profiler on her case?' I don't remember Benton ever telling me at the time that he was involved in Gabriela Lagos's homicide.

'I was consulted, yes. Not about her but about Martin and what was in his diary' is all Benton says, and Marino has reached us.

Benton holds out his hand to encourage Quincy to come. 'That's a good boy.' He ruffles the German shepherd's neck. 'I can see you're very well trained,' he says with quiet sarcasm.

'He's sure as hell not being good,' Marino is grumpy and out of breath. 'Don't be a bad boy.' He pats his dog, thumping him on the sides. 'You know what to do. Now, sit.'

Quincy doesn't.

22

Not far up ahead but out of sight from where we wait is a Bank of America kiosk.

'At Mass Ave and Albany. It would have been an ideal place for the killer to leave his car,' Benton describes the very intersection where I get stopped on occasion when the circus train lumbers through.

The last time wasn't that long ago, the first of December, when the long candy-apple-red train with gold lettering on the sides took forever to clatter past, headed into the MIT campus to park at the Grand Junction branch. I sat and imagined the exotic animals inside those cars, remembering when this same Florida-based circus performed in Miami several times a year during my childhood. The Cirque d'Orleans casts a shadow over my mood every time it sets up in an arena around here, reminding me of my past, of my father who used to take me to see the elephants walking trunk to tail along Biscayne Boulevard.

'He could have left his car there in the public lot.' Benton continues talking about where the killer may have parked as I hold Quincy by his leash and pet him. 'And nobody would have paid attention. Cars are in and out of that lot at all hours because of the ATM. He left his vehicle and returned on foot probably right along these tracks. It would have been raining when he did.

The footprints he left when he returned to the scene would be gone for the most part, just the partials we've noticed. The intact ones are from when he left the final time, possibly right before dawn when the rain had stopped.'

'If they're his, he must be a pipsqueak,' Marino says. 'Size-eight feet? What would that make him, maybe five feet? I'm betting it was a kid goofing around back here.'

'We can't say with any degree of certainty how tall,' I reply. 'The correlation of foot size and height isn't an exact science. While we can estimate based on statistical data, it's not possible to be precise.'

Marino repositions the scale, the same six-inch yellow plastic ruler he was using earlier only with a different label. 'How about for once not talking like a nerd on *The Big Bang Theory* and just give me a garden-variety guess,' he picks on me.

'On average a male with a size-eight shoe is around five-foot-five. But that doesn't mean the person who left these footprints is that height. There are short people with large feet and tall people with small ones.' I ignore his rude aside, which I suspect is more for Benton's benefit than mine.

Marino can't stop asserting himself because for one thing he's stung by what Benton has predicted so far. The MIT maintenance worker Enrique Sanchez routinely leaves his truck overnight at the construction site. The pipe cutter is his and he uses his own tools on the job. He has a DUI. A second offense and he could lose his license so he never drinks and drives.

Benton hasn't been proven wrong about anything so far and Marino has shown his gratitude by causing trouble with his office in Boston, unwittingly adding more grist to Granby's treacherous mill.

'Five-foot-five for the sake of argument?' Marino says to me. 'A kid, someone short, whatever. Pretty damn stupid if he did what you think,' he fires at Benton. 'It would have been a lot smarter to leave the body and then get the hell out. You return to the scene you could get caught.'

'It's not possible for him to resist watching.' Benton is back to checking e-mails on his phone. 'He has to witness the spectacle he creates.'

That word again. *Spectacle.*

'He's been back here before. He knew where to go and what to do. He was comfortable.' Benton continues looking through the eyes of the monster he's after.

Through the eyes of Martin Lagos, I think.

Or someone who had access to his DNA.

Specifically, someone who had access to his profile in the FBI's Combined DNA Index System known as CODIS, and I indulge in imagining worse-case scenarios. I think it through, what I would do if I were a bad person skilled in computers or, more disturbing still, if I worked in a DNA lab and had evil intentions or did the bidding of someone corrupt who is powerful.

A DNA profile doesn't look like a biological sample on a microscopic slide or the barcode on an autoradiograph. It's not visual like a blood-spatter pattern or the loops and whorls of a fingerprint. In a database a profile is a series of numbers that are manually entered and assigned an identifier generated by the crime lab that conducted the analysis. It's these numbers that are compared to an unknown profile run against a database like CODIS and when there's a hit the numerical identifier is the link that leads to the name and personal information of who it is.

The growing reservoir of information found in DNA databanks has been controversial since the testing was first introduced in the late 1980s. People worry about privacy. They worry about genetic discrimination and a violation of their Fourth Amendment rights, which protect against search and seizure without probable cause. There's a growing concern about DNA dragnets or trolling for suspects by taking samples from people within the geographic proximity of a crime.

I've heard the objections and fears for years and I don't disagree with some of them. Even the most perfect scientific procedures can be misused and abused by imperfect human beings and it's within the realm of possibility that a DNA profile could be deliberately altered. Numbers entered into a computer by an overworked lab technician can be accidentally corrupted. They can be tampered with. While I'm not aware of this happening, that doesn't mean it hasn't. There's no guarantee that such a mistake or misdeed would be publicized, certainly not voluntarily.

If Martin Lagos's identification number were substituted for another person's in every database, we'd have no way of knowing the DNA profile wasn't really his. It would be the ultimate identity theft and I can't mention this now in front of Marino.

★ ★ ★

I watch him return the camera and scale to his scene case. Quincy is sitting on my foot and licking my hand.

'Let's go,' Marino commands his dog who isn't interested in going anywhere. 'I'll catch you at your office in a while,' he says to me, ignoring Benton. 'Machado and I've got a few things to finish up such as finding Haley Swanson who's ducking us now. Later I plan to drop by Gail Shipton's condo, if you want to come.'

'You know what to do' is my response. 'Make sure you get everything out of her medicine cabinet. I want to know what meds she might have been on. Let me know what's inside her refrigerator and in her trash.'

'Jesus Christ,' he complains. 'Am I wearing a T-shirt that says *Stupid*?'

I wait until he and Quincy are through the tunnel, headed back to Briggs Field. Then I suggest to Benton that he should consider possibilities that might explain the DNA recovered from the panties Julianne Goulet had on when her body was found.

'If one wanted to be one hundred percent certain the DNA is Martin Lagos's,' I elaborate as we begin walking again, 'the FBI should have checked it against the original analysis done by the Virginia labs in 1996. The profile also should

231

have been compared to his mother's. Her blood card from the autopsy my former northern district office did should still be in her file.'

'As I understand it, all of the appropriate steps have been taken,' Benton says with no inflection in his voice as if he's parroting what he's been told. 'The DNA's been verified as Martin Lagos's. Nothing in the CODIS database has been entered in error or altered, I'm assured.'

'You actually asked the question?'

'I presented the possibility to Granby. It would have to be someone at his level to discreetly question the lab director in Quantico.'

'If you didn't have people gunning for you before, now you certainly will.'

'Nothing is out of line. The DNA recovered from the panties shows a direct maternal relationship to Gabriela Lagos.'

'New analysis of her blood card was done?' I push him on this.

'I'm telling you what I was told,' he says in a way that continues to concern me.

'If it really is Martin Lagos's DNA, that argues against him being dead,' I say to him. 'The test results seem to support that he murdered Julianne Goulet unless his DNA got on the panties in some way other than his depositing it on them.'

'I'm thinking that's the only other explanation.'

'What you're suggesting would be rare if not impossible. Laboratory contamination after seventeen years wouldn't make any sense.'

'I don't think it would.'

'Semen, skin cells?' I suppose one or the other

232

was what was recovered and tested.

'Blood,' Benton says.

'Visible blood. You're right. That seems too obvious. Why would the killer leave his blood on a pair of panties? How could that happen and he didn't notice and realize what it would mean when the panties were analyzed?'

'What if someone kept a sample of Martin's blood all these years?' Benton asks.

'It would have had to be preserved properly. Frozen, in other words,' I say dubiously. 'You're talking about something planned well in advance by someone who knew what he was doing. And you have to ask why a blood sample of his would be stored to begin with. By whom and for what purpose?'

'What about people who exchange blood-vial jewelry? They wear it around their necks.' Benton is looking for any possible explanation because he has misgivings, sinister ones that he's not going to verbalize.

He doesn't want to openly accuse. He wants me to figure it out.

'What if he'd exchanged something like that with someone?' he asks.

'And seventeen years later this person uses it to frame him in multiple homicides?'

'I just know DNA from a blood sample was identified as Martin Lagos's and I'm coming up with anything I can think of to explain how that could have happened, Kay. Besides the obvious.'

'The obvious being a problem with CODIS and your fear that people like Granby are lying to you.'

'I wish I'd never mentioned it to him.'

'Who else could you mention it to?'

'To you, to someone I trust with my life.' He doesn't mention Lucy because he won't. 'I'm going around him every chance I get.'

Ahead of us a dark brick warehouse looms, its hundreds of windows blanked out by the sun.

'Saying someone was wearing Martin Lagos's blood in a vial on a necklace and then decided to use it to frame him?' I play it out. 'Days, not to mention years, without being air-dried or properly stored and you can forget it. The blood would have decomposed, the DNA destroyed by bacteria or UV light if it was exposed to the sun.'

'What if it had been kept in a lab for some reason?'

'Not our labs in Virginia or Washington either,' I remind him. 'There would have been no blood drawn, obviously, because there was no case, no autopsy, not if Martin Lagos jumped off the Fourteenth Street Bridge and his body was never found. When the police worked his mother's murder and realized he was missing, I assume they got his DNA profile from a toothbrush, his hairbrush, something like that.'

'Yes,' Benton answers. 'I'm not saying it isn't his blood. I'm saying I don't understand how it got there and I don't trust it worth a damn. It's what someone wants us to think.'

'What does the BAU say about what you're suggesting?' I can only imagine the reaction.

'They think I've been doing this too long.'

'You won't retire. That's not you.'

He's not going to teach somewhere or be one

more former FBI profiler out there who's a hired gun or on TV whenever there's a big crime or a big trial.

'I'm pissing everybody off and talking to you without authorization. I've talked to Lucy and you know that without my saying it,' Benton says. 'If they find out, well why should I even care anymore? As far off course as this has gotten and what it very likely means . . . Christ, Granby and all of them can go to hell.'

23

It's almost eleven a.m. when we reach the back parking lot of my seven-story, titanium-skinned building that is shaped like a bullet with a geodesic glass roof.

The anti-climb fence is tall and PVC-coated black, and above it satellite dishes and antennas bloom silvery white from the rooftops of MIT labs that back up to the CFC on three sides. Transmissions travel invisibly nearly at the speed of light, many of them classified, a lot of them military and related to secret government projects.

My phone rings and I look up at Bryce's window bright with sunlight as if I might spot him, which isn't possible. But old habits don't die easily. The glass in my building is one-way. We can see out but no one can see in. My chief of staff may have us in his sights but I can't tell.

'The Tooth Whisperer left about twenty minutes ago,' he says of Dr. Adams. 'It's Gail Shipton, all right. One of these people with a great mouth because there's so much wrong with it? I guarantee she was picked on in school just like me.'

I enter my code at the electric gate. It beeps and for a moment nothing happens. I've been out five days and Marino no longer works here and I'm reminded that it took the two of us to run this place. I try my code again.

'Possibly an exposure to tetracycline as a child, causing tooth discoloration. You know those ugly spotted and pitted teeth that make you hate school because kids are so mean?' Bryce says as the gate shivers to life.

It begins to slide open on its track slowly, shakily, still not working properly since the last time it was repaired several weeks ago. There's no one to supervise the security engineer now that Marino isn't here. He used to hover over whoever answered the service call but those days are gone. I'm having a hard time believing it.

'I had a tooth like that because of a fever. Of course it was a front tooth and my nickname was chalk tooth. 'Bryce can write on the blackboard with his tooth.' I didn't smile the entire time I was growing up.'

On the other side of the limping-open gate our white vans and crime scene trucks are parked haphazardly and I notice they're dirty. The mobile mass casualty trailer is grimy, too. Marino would throw a fit if he hadn't quit and I suppose we'll have to find an affordable washing and detailing company that can be trusted and is willing to service our equipment on-site. It's just one more housekeeping concern to take up with Bryce, who'd rather talk than breathe.

'Plenty of restorations, all of it costing a pretty penny. But then again she was rich enough to sue someone for a hundred mil, according to what's all over the news,' he's saying. 'I don't mean it disrespectfully.'

'Benton and I are here,' I remind Bryce, who manages to find something in common with almost every dead body passing through. 'Why don't we have this conversation inside, preferably a little later? I have evidence rounds to make, then I need to get started on her and check on everybody else.'

I unbutton my coat and remember I'm carrying a gun. Only law enforcement can be armed inside my building. All CFC personnel, including me, are supposed to leave firearms at the security desk, where they're locked inside a ten-gauge steel pistol cabinet. Not that everybody complies. Marino never did. I have no doubt Lucy doesn't. I release the fanny pack's clip in back.

'Of course you're here. I can see you on closed-circuit camera and out the window, take your pick. The gate is alllll-mossst opppen' — he exaggerates how slow it is — 'and there you and Benton are, the happy couple walking through, and you're pushing the button to close it behind you, which will take an hour. Get a load of those big, bad blaze-orange boots. Let me guess. He's got nothing to change into because his luggage is in Marino's car, am I right? Benton flew in with Lucy and landed at the scene and you asked Marino to hang on to his belongings, which are now held hostage. Meaning he'll be in those awful boots all day. Tell him to come upstairs and see me.'

I switch my phone to speaker so Benton can hear.

'I've got extra sneakers he can borrow. Black leather that won't look too terrible,' Bryce's voice sounds in the parking lot and I wonder who else knew about Benton's flight home.

I'm not surprised Bryce was informed. The question is when did he find out and from whom?

'I think we wear the same size or close enough,' he says.

'You knew he was coming home today?' I look at Benton busy e-mailing with his phone.

He's preoccupied with conveying information that his colleagues may disagree with or ignore and he's being extremely careful, more so than he's ever had to be. Agents, most of them young, who started out regarding him as a legend and now want to take his place, want to show they're more fit for the job he does, and that's to be expected. But the other isn't. Benton suspects conspiracy and sabotage and it very well may not be his imagination.

'Well, of course I had an inkling. I did have errands to run,' Bryce says mysteriously. 'Tomorrow's his birthday and I wasn't sure if you'd remember, as sick as you've been. Not to mention decorating for Christmas, so he walks into a happy, festive house?'

'You found out when, and who did you tell?'

'Lucy and I had conversations. I mean, you don't have a tree or a single light, not one candle in a window,' he lectures me. 'That was painfully loud and clear every time I dropped things off, such a dark, unfriendly house, with no fire on the hearth not even a week before Christmas? Could it be more depressing? I imagined poor Benton coming home. He can't hear me, can he? And, yes, the gate needs to be adjusted again. I'm watching it *not* shut, stammering like it's having a seizure or trying to say something. I'll try to do it from in here.'

'The problem is it wasn't properly adjusted the last time it was supposedly serviced.' I tuck the fanny pack under my arm, feeling the weight and shape of what's inside it.

'You're telling me? This morning cars were backed up onto the street, it's so damn slow, and I almost got smacked by a Honda Element and guess who would have paid the piper even though it wasn't my fault? A tin lizzie like that hitting my big bad X-Six, can you imagine? Well, I should say Ethan's. I can't exactly afford a BMW on my salary. Speaking of — what the hell is Lucy driving and what is that you just took off? Are you wearing a gun? Since when?'

'I don't want any information about the ID or anything else released yet,' I tell him as we walk past Marino's empty spot where he won't be parking his design-flawed pickup truck anymore. 'Who else knows that Benton was coming home?'

'If I'm not mistaken, you're packing a pistol. Sexy, but how come? And why such an ugly accessory, that big black bulky thing? Don't they make them in leather or cheerful colors? I could tell Cambridge PD to release the information. Then it's their discretion and not our problem.'

'That's probably best as long as we're absolutely positive — '

'It took Dr. Adams all of half an hour,' Bryce interrupts again. 'Apparently in addition to everything else she had a recent extraction of

240

number twenty — '

'Bryce, who did you tell that Benton was coming home and when? It's important I know — '

'A healing socket with a titanium post for an implant yet to be *installed*. I know that's not the right word for it.'

'Bryce . . . ?'

'I realize crowns aren't installed like crown molding, excuse the pun.' He drops his voice for emphasis. 'Well, it's not exactly a pun except the *crown* part of it.'

★ ★ ★

I lift the box cover of the jackshaft operator next to the bay and scan my thumb into the biometric lock.

'Not that I'm sure what a number twenty is,' Bryce continues talking nonstop. 'But I think it's a molar.'

'Did Lucy tell you Benton was flying in today?' I press a button and the torque motor starts. The massive metal shutter door lurches up loudly.

'Of course. I encouraged her to fly her big bird to D.C. and airlift him out. Did someone ruin your surprise? I promise it wasn't me.'

If Bryce knew, there's no telling who else did, not that I'm sure it explains anything. In fact, I don't see how it does. Even if he were indiscreet, how would the killer have found out such a detail, assuming Benton's suspicions are valid? Why would it matter when he was flying home?

Maybe the killer can't resist watching the spectacle he creates but that doesn't mean the victim selection or the timing has anything to do with Benton. It's more likely that Granby is capitalizing on Benton's deepest fears, wearing him down and upsetting him, knowing full well what it would do to him if he thought anything he's published might influence a violent predator. Benton very well may be paranoid by now, and based on what he's just told me I wouldn't blame him.

'Is Ernie in today?' I ask. 'I've got trace evidence to drop off to him and we've got a fence post and bolt cutter coming in for tool marks. Plus DNA. So if you'll alert Gloria, and while you're at it also check on the tox lab, the additional screens I want in the suicide from last week, Sakura Yamagata, I want a rush on everything as quickly as humanly possible.'

'Tell me something new.'

'This is new. I'm very concerned about what we might be dealing with around here.'

'You're not going to give me a clue?'

'I'm not,' I reply. 'I also need you to find out when Dr. Venter, the chief in Baltimore, could have a word with me.'

'I'll get right on it,' Bryce says. 'And Ernie's in the evidence bay, working on the totaled car from that drunk driver Anne's this minute scanning. Plus we got a possible OD on the way, probably a suicide, a woman whose husband got killed in a motorcycle crash exactly one year ago to the day. One Happy Holidays deserves another, as they say. An average of ten suicides per week since Thanksgiving. Has it gotten worse?'

'More than twenty-five percent worse.'

'Well, now my day is totally ruined.'

Through the widening space beneath the door I see Lucy's huge SUV inside where it really shouldn't be. But she parks where she wants whether she's driving one of her supercars or roaring up on a motorcycle, rules meaning nothing to her. I note the two gurneys haphazardly abandoned against a wall, a body pouch wadded up on top of one of them. A hose is sloppily coiled near a floor drain, the spray nozzle leaking.

'Why are we working up a car from a motor-vehicle fatality?' I ask Bryce.

'Because lawyers are calling.'

'Lawyers are always calling. That's not a reason.'

'Not just any. Carin Hegel.'

'What exactly does she want?' I ask.

'She wouldn't say.'

Benton and I duck under the door rolling up as he communicates with someone, typing with his thumbs. I press the *Stop* button just inside, then I press *Close*. I turn on lights. All of the storage cabinets are locked at least and the floor is clean. I don't smell any bad odors.

'I think it's something to do with the blood alcohol so maybe you should talk to Luke. Lawsuits and more lawsuits,' Bryce says as the heavy door rolls back down, clanking and humming. 'Would it be okay with you if I have pizzas sent in from Armando's? By early afternoon we're going to have a full house and I don't mean dead people. You need to eat, for once, and I have a change of clothing for you all laid out. The usual navy blue suit fresh from the dry cleaner and sensible low-heeled pumps plus brand-new stockings with no picks or runs.'

'Where am I going? I'm not even supposed to be in today.' I stop by the hose and turn off the water all the way.

'I'm interviewing Marino's replacement, remember?' Bryce says. 'Jennifer Garate, rhymes with *karate*. She's worked in New York City as a death investigator for the past five years and was a physician's assistant before that? We went over her application some weeks ago, but of course we went through a lot of them. She was very pleasant on the phone and Luke seems to like her photograph a little too much. I admit I thought it a bit odd that she had it taken on a beach wearing what I call *bootyfits*, hot yoga shorts or whatever to show off what she's got, which is quite something I guess. You're here, thank God, and can weigh in. Maybe Benton would since he's in the neighborhood?'

'No,' I answer. 'Benton wouldn't.' I turn off speakerphone because Benton isn't listening.

I imagine he's dealing with his field office or the BAU and politics are kicking into a higher gear. I wonder if the FBI will begin looking for Martin Lagos around here, looking for someone Benton is convinced is dead. Already I'm calculating what to do about any DNA results we may get from the panties on Gail Shipton's body or from the mentholated ointment recovered from the grass. For the first time in my career I don't trust what might happen to any profiles my DNA lab uploads into CODIS.

'Well, it's only the most important position in terms of how it affects absolutely everything.' Bryce is back in my earpiece. 'You end up with a shitty lead investigator and you know what they say? Garbage in, garbage out.'

We walk through the bay as big as a hangar. Parked off to one side is my niece's two-ton black SUV built of ballistic hardened steel, according to her, with an explosives protection system, surveillance cameras, searchlights, a survival kit, a siren, and strobes. It has a black box like an aircraft and a PA system with loudspeakers, among other things. I've not had a chance to ask her what such an ominous-looking vehicle costs or why she suddenly feels the need for one.

'Who wants to spend the rest of our lives with a bully who crashes on an inflatable bed when he's drunk, picks up women on Twitter, and lives in a house that's become a stop on the tacky tour?' Bryce exclaims. 'I won't forgive Marino for using e-mail to walk off the job. Not even the decency to tell me to my face. Anyway, what's your answer about Armando's and can I rob petty cash?'

At the top of a ramp the door that leads into the lower level opens. Lucy is dressed in a black flight suit that accentuates her slender, strong build, her bright green eyes, and her rose-gold hair that she's cut boyishly short.

' . . . Dr. Scarpetta? I think I'm losing you

245

inside the bay. Hello, hello . . . ?' Bryce says, and I end the call as I realize how intolerant I've become of chatter after days of being alone and quiet.

Lucy holds the door open, leans against it to avoid a hug, and I can feel her mood like a blast of hot air. I wrap my arms around her whether she likes it or not.

'Don't tell me something I shouldn't hear,' I say quietly.

'I don't care what you hear. I'm sure Benton gave you the important points anyway.'

My open affection for my niece usually is reserved for outside the office and a shadow of annoyance crosses her pretty face as she pulls away. Then she looks tense, a glint of aggression showing.

'I'm sorry,' I tell her and her reaction is stoical and steely as if she has no feelings at all about what happened to Gail Shipton.

What I sense is a resolve that always goes the same way, in a direction that's predictable and troubling. My niece is gifted at vengeful anger and bad with sad.

'I'm taking Bryce up on his offer and borrowing a pair of shoes.' Benton steadies himself with the doorframe, struggling with the boots one at a time, tugging them off.

He parks them at the top of the ramp, where they flop over like wilted traffic cones, and he walks past us in his stocking feet. Inside the building he turns left toward the elevator, busy on his phone again, his expression unreadable, the way it is when he's met with resistance and ignorance and maybe something far worse than that.

'We need to talk.' I take Lucy by the arm. I steer her away from the door she holds.

24

Alone inside the bay, we head to the small round plastic table and two chairs that Rusty and Harold have christened La Morte Café. On temperate days they drink coffee and smoke cigars with the door rolled up, waiting for the dead to arrive and be taken away.

I set my fanny pack on the table and Lucy picks it up. She unzips it to check what's inside. Then she zips it back up and returns it to the table.

'Why?' she asks.

'It probably was my fever and having too much time to think.'

'It probably wasn't.'

'Something didn't seem right. I assumed it had to do with my bout of bad health and taking Sock out.' I don't want to get sidetracked right now by talking about the person who may have been spying on me because it will send Lucy on the warpath.

I don't want her looking for Haley Swanson or someone else. She already has enough trouble with Marino.

'You should come over and go on the range with me at least.' She watches me carefully. 'When's the last time you practiced?'

'We will. I promise.'

I place a pod in the Keurig set up on a spraddle-legged surgical cart with rusted seams and bent wheels. Its decrepit condition has been draped with a French country vinyl cloth, red and yellow *vent du sud* and there's an arrangement of plastic sunflowers and a Bruins ashtray on it.

'I'm sure you must feel slammed. Out of the office since Friday and returning to this.' Lucy stands behind a chair with her arms crossed. 'You look pale and tired. You should have let me come over.'

'And catch the flu?' I open a pack of cheap paper towels, the type found in public restrooms.

'That could happen anywhere, and I'd never leave you alone because I'm afraid of what might happen to me. Janet and I would have brought you to the house and taken care of you. I should have come and gotten you.'

'I wouldn't wish that on anyone.'

'It's not a chore like with my mother.'

'*Chore* isn't the word that comes to mind with Dorothy.'

'I'm just saying.' Her green eyes are intense on me.

'I know and I'm sorry if I didn't seem grateful.'

She doesn't make an insincere effort to reassure me. I'm not good at seeming a lot of things and both of us know it, and I'm reminded again of what I don't like about myself.

'It's not about being grateful,' Lucy then says. 'You wouldn't let me stay alone if the situations were reversed, if I'd just been through what you had and then got sick. Especially if I were scared enough to carry a gun everywhere.'

'You're never scared and you do carry a gun everywhere.'

'You'd be camped out and showing up every other second with the thermometer.'

'I admit I have ways of doing things that aren't easy for others.'

Brewing coffee spews into a brown paper cup with a fish icon, Navy surplus that Bryce orders by the pallet.

'Creamer, sugar? Or the usual black?' I ask.

'The usual. Nothing's changed.' She looks at me with a face I love, angular and strong, more striking than beautiful.

I remember when she was a pudgy little know-it-all too smart for anyone's damn good and missing the genetic piece responsible for boundaries and rules. As soon as she could walk she followed me from room to room, and when I sat she was in my lap. It would infuriate her mother, my selfish, miserable sister who writes children's books and has no use for her own flesh and blood or for anyone, really, only characters she invents and can control and kill off. I haven't talked to my family in Miami for a while and for a second I feel guilty about that, too.

'Bryce is ordering pizza. I might eat an entire pie by myself.' I set a coffee and a paper towel in front of Lucy.

'These cups suck.'

'They're biodegradable.'

'Yes. They fall apart while you're still drinking out of them.'

'They don't damage marine life and are

invisible to spy satellites.' I smile at her.

'You need to eat an entire pizza and then some.' Lucy scrutinizes me, arms crossed stubbornly. 'Bryce is telling everyone you've turned into a skeleton.'

'The first time he's seen me was five minutes ago on a security monitor. Please sit down, Lucy. We're going to talk.'

I start a second cup, the aroma overpowering. My stomach feels inside out it's so empty and Marino's calling me at four a.m. seems a year ago. It doesn't seem like it happened.

'The pizza's not here yet and she can wait.' Gail Shipton can. 'What I'm most concerned about at the moment is you,' I say to Lucy, 'and I do care what I hear even if you don't. I don't want either of us compromised. Or anyone else.'

She stares at me and I can tell she knows I'm referring to Benton.

'Compromised?' She pulls out a plastic chair.

'I don't want to know anything illegal.' I'm that blunt.

'There's nothing to know.'

'By whose definition?' I carry my coffee to the table and sit across from her. 'I have some idea what you've been doing. Marino is aware that whatever was on Gail Shipton's phone isn't on it now. He's told me that and maybe told other people.'

'It's not her phone.' Lucy props an elbow on the table and rests her chin in her hand and the table rocks because the plastic legs aren't even. 'I should say it *wasn't*. And what happened to her has nothing to do with what in fact is an

251

extremely unique device and Marino has no right to it because it wasn't hers,' she repeats.

'Then whose?'

'The technology's mine but I'd gotten to the point I didn't care anymore.' She wraps her hands around the coffee.

'You don't sound like someone who doesn't care.'

'I didn't care about what the technology should be worth because I wanted to end the partnership and it was one of the things Gail and I talked about yesterday, not that it was the first time or all that friendly. She wins her lawsuit and buys me out.'

'There's never a certainty anyone will win a lawsuit.' It surprises me Lucy would be that naïve. 'Juries can be unpredictable. Mistrials happen. Anything can.'

'She felt sure it would settle at the last minute.'

'I can't imagine Carin Hegel would assure her of such a thing.'

'She didn't. She was ready for court and still is. But there won't be a trial.'

'It would be difficult with the plaintiff dead.'

'There's no case and there hasn't been one for a while. That's why there won't be a trial.'

'Does Carin Hegel know she doesn't have a case?' I'm baffled and disconcerted by what Lucy is saying.

'I was going to tell her when I could prove it, which would have been soon. Gail was sure she'd get money from Double S and her mistake was telling me that and promising to buy me out.

I wasn't asking for much but I had to ask something or it would have looked suspicious,' Lucy says dispassionately, coldly. 'It was important to extricate myself from her with surgical precision in a way that didn't draw attention. I was almost ready and now she's dead.'

'It's a good thing you were out of town when she disappeared.'

'I'm sure they'd say I had something to do with it.'

'With the way you're talking right now I'm sure they would.'

Lucy has a reputation and Marino knows it all too well. He knows her history and capabilities in exquisite detail. While I've never known her to hurt someone gratuitously or because she has a grudge, she'll do things other people won't.

'The fact is I wasn't here when she disappeared. I wasn't here when she was killed,' Lucy says. 'I'd just landed at Dulles and then was at a hotel and that can be proven.'

'You certainly don't have to prove it to me.'

'You worry too much,' Lucy says. 'I didn't like Gail and ultimately had no respect for her but I certainly didn't hurt her. But I would have eventually.'

'At the very least you sound more like a witness for the defense.'

'I didn't want to be a witness for anyone but in a case like this it's all about manipulation and big money. They found out we'd started working on a project together and next thing I was subpoenaed to be deposed.'

'That's interesting. What you do isn't exactly

public information. Even I didn't know about your relationship with Gail, professional or otherwise. So how did Double S's attorneys find out?'

'That's what lawyers do. They find things out.'

'Someone had to have given them information,' I reply. 'Is it possible Gail did without intending to?'

'No. She didn't do it without intending to. It was deliberate,' Lucy says.

'What did Double S want from you?'

'To be my friend.'

'I'm serious.'

'So am I.' Rage makes her hard and Lucy has no trouble hating if she decides it's earned.

When she trusts there's no limit to what she'll do for someone, but once crossed she won't stop until she's annihilated whoever it is. She has to because she can't go after the worst offender in her life, her mother, who has sovereign immunity. Lucy would never harm the person who has damaged her the most, my ungrateful, loveless sister who sinks her teeth into the hand that feeds her and does so without warning or provocation. I've watched the syndrome for years and it makes me rather crazy. Dorothy commits her petty acts of cruelty because it gives her pleasure.

'When I was deposed I was asked a lot of personal questions about my work in computers and my law enforcement background, why I left the FBI and ATF and what I wanted in life,' Lucy is saying. 'Their attorneys were kidding around with me, being nice. I played into it

254

because I had a sense about what was really going on.'

'Does Carin have this same sense?'

'She thought they were being manipulative assholes.'

'Maybe they were hoping you'd take their side against Gail.'

'That's what Carin said.'

I ask Lucy why she ever trusted Gail Shipton. 'Because it doesn't sound like it lasted long,' I add.

'In the beginning I thought she was one of these smart people who's stupid in business and got screwed because she got tangled up with the wrong people, which I didn't completely understand,' she says. 'But I figured she was a techie with poor judgment, someone naïve as hell about the real world. If you really dig, the stories about Double S should give you pause although someone must be full-time PR for them, making sure anything negative is buried, and I suspect they pay freelancers to write fluff and spin whatever comes out.'

'You suspect it or you know?'

'It's obvious they do. I don't know it for a fact.'

I'm reminded of Lambant and Associates, of Haley Swanson.

'She didn't check them out before she turned over everything, some fifty million, and then they supposedly lost all of it on bad investments,' Lucy says. 'Unlike their other former clients, Gail decided to fight. She wasn't a brave person or remotely confrontational, yet she didn't back

255

down when everybody else had in the past. You have to ask why.'

Lucy has gotten more animated as she talks, gesturing with her hands, light winking from the rose-gold signet ring she wears on her left index finger. Oversized, with a flying eagle and nature scenes, the vintage heirloom has been in her partner Janet's family for more than a century, from what I understand.

'How long was Gail with Double S?' I ask.

'About the time she started grad school. She's always worked since she was a kid, not just R-and-D but basic programming, engineering, and database design. Double S hired her two and a half years ago to build a new database management system for them and that's how it started. During the course of things they convinced her to let them take care of her money, and in hardly any time at all?' She wiggles the table, testing which leg is the problem. 'She fired them and hired Carin Hegel.'

'They lost fifty million dollars that fast?'

'Yes, almost all of it, and Carin didn't take the case on contingency. So you also have to ask how someone who's lost almost everything could afford the legal fees. Maybe at first but not for long. By now the fees are well into the millions.' Lucy folds her paper towel into a small square, leans down and wedges it under the offending table leg. 'Did it ever occur to you that in the world of white-collar crime technology is a valuable commodity? Take drones, for example. Imagine sophisticated surveillance devices in the wrong hands.'

'I can't verify it yet but I believe Gail was murdered. You've probably already figured that out but I want to make sure you understand she likely was targeted and abducted.'

Lucy wiggles the table and it's more stable.

'I wish I'd activated the video camera when it would have mattered,' she says as if that's what bothers her most about what I just said.

Beneath her flat calm she's agitated. She's upset. I can tell.

'You had a way to control her phone remotely.' I remember to take off my coat and I place it in my lap.

'Her phone?' Lucy's green eyes flash. 'The chip stacking, the camera capabilities, the connectivity, the range of operating bands, everything's mine and I have the tech specs, invoices, and copyrights to prove it.'

'Then what was it Gail had to offer?' I realize how badly I need coffee. It warms my throat and gets my blood flowing.

'Multimedia subsystems, packet data, fiberoptics with upstream speeds about ten times what can be done today, and search engines that match intent not just keywords. All the same stuff I've been really interested in and working on. Her promises sounded good over a couple of drinks.'

'I see. It sounds like at the end of the day she proved totally useless.'

'Not useless but weak, and then she turned. I didn't let on that I was aware of it. I had one particular app and to give her credit she had some pretty ingenious ideas about it. Then she got other ideas that were fucking scary,' she says as I think of Benton's remark about biometric software and its potential use with drones.

'You met her casually. Since when do you trust strangers?' I ask.

'About eight months ago.' Lucy sips her coffee and makes a face. 'Generic Kenya that tastes like Kmart. Why the hell does Bryce have to be so cheap? Janet and I ran into her at the Psi Bar and we started talking. We run into a lot of MIT people and talk. They're the kind of people I'm most comfortable with.'

'And you decided to work on a project together just like that.' Caffeine dulls the edges of a headache that's lingered since Marino woke me up. I realize I need a lot of coffee badly and I push my chair back.

'I don't know why.' She toys with her cheap cup, turning it in slow circles on the table. 'Sometimes I'm stupid, Aunt Kay.'

'You're never stupid but all of us have trusted people we shouldn't.'

'I felt bad for her at first because it was a terrible story she told, growing up poor in California, her father an alcoholic who killed himself when she was ten. Her mother has early Alzheimer's and is taken care of by a sister who's mentally challenged. Then Gail trusted people to manage everything she has and next thing it's gone.'

I get up to start a refill of generic stuff that right now tastes wonderful.

'I thought her areas of expertise could be helpful,' Lucy says. 'Unfortunately I was basing my assessment on her having made a lot of money from really cool phone apps when she was a teenager.'

'You related because it sounded like you. A kid, a prodigy, who's suddenly incredibly wealthy with everyone trying to take advantage including your own mother who was never there until you had money. You support her, and the more you do, the worse she is.'

'Who? My mother?' Lucy says sarcastically.

'That's a lonely place to be.'

'She's dating some rich Venezuelan twice her age. Did I mention that? Lucio something or other, owns a lot of Miami real estate, South Beach, Golden Beach, Bal Harbour, hosted some TV show when he was young, recently got a Lap-Band so he'll look good for his new *mujer fatal*. It's confusing. She calls both of us *Luce*.'

'The misfortune of having my sister as your mother.' It has left Lucy with a vulnerability that I don't think will ever heal. She trusts completely, and when she's hurt she goes after the enemy with an energy that's dazzling.

'She's not making much of a living anymore after putting a vampire in the children's book before last and more recently a kid with magical powers who constantly recites these clunky rhyming spells,' Lucy says.

'I haven't read them.'

'I do out of self-defense. She should write her autobiography. *Fifty Shades of Dorothy*. That would sell.'

'One of these days you're going to give up hating her.'

'I think Grans is really getting old.'

'My mother's been old for quite a while.'

'Seriously. She shouldn't be driving. She goes to Publix with that huge white Chanel pocket-book that's a hand-me-down from Mom and then can't find her car so she walks around pushing her grocery cart and clicking her key until headlights go on. It's a miracle she hasn't been mugged.'

'I need to call her.'

'The word *need* is never good. I hope you never use it when you're talking about me,' Lucy says.

25

'I'll call her and she'll tell me how bad she feels and what a terrible daughter I am.' I fill the water filter pitcher at the stainless-steel sink. 'That's what it was like over the weekend right after I got back.'

'Did she know what you were doing in Connecticut?'

'She saw it on the news.' I'm not going to get into what my mother said about it, almost blaming me while bemoaning the fact that I never save anybody's life. I should work in a funeral home. She said what she's said before.

'Tell me more about your work with Gail.' I pour water into the Keurig's reservoir.

'All she was supposed to be doing at this stage was bench-testing, which has dragged on for a reason,' Lucy explains. 'Months and months of troubleshooting while she's secretly worked on copies of my apps, adding features and edits that I would never permit. She assumed I wouldn't find out.' She takes a swallow of coffee and leans back in her chair. 'Her programming is now nonexistent. Nobody should have it.'

'They will anyway. If you're talking about bio-metric technology, specifically facial-recognition software that's used by domestic drones, it won't be you who stops that sort of scary progress.'

'And it won't be me who puts digital eyes in the sky to target our own citizens or law enforcement or politicians. The problem is it won't just be our government doing it. Imagine criminals having access to drone surveillance technology.' She brings that up again. 'Something small enough to fly through an open window and hover at a thousand feet if you want to scout out where a target lives or follow people in their car or orchestrate a huge heist or a home invasion or assassinate someone. I'd rather be figuring out ways to combat nightmares like that. Which reminds me. The missing guy Benton's told you about? The kid who disappeared seventeen years ago?'

I don't respond one way or another.

'You don't have to answer,' she says. 'I know Benton would tell you because he has to tell someone he can trust besides me. Things aren't good for him at the Bureau.'

'Yes, I know.'

'Age progression, facial recognition. Put it this way: Martin Lagos isn't in any database anywhere on the damn planet. So the idea that he's suddenly a serial killer leaving his DNA? Forget it. I can run a search like that from my phone.'

'Is yours identical to the one Gail was carrying? The one Marino has in his possession?'

Lucy unclips it from her flight suit's waist belt and places it on the table. It looks like an everyday smartphone except for the black rubbery military case it's in.

'Perfectly normal,' Lucy says. 'It's just a phone with the usual apps on the home screen.'

'So it appears.' I remove my second cup of

262

coffee as the Keurig stops sputtering.

'You can't see what's running in the background. The good stuff.'

'Dangerous stuff?'

'As is true of everything, it's all about how it's used. I have the IP of the phone Gail had in her possession and would maneuver around her lame attempts at security. Everything on it also ended up on my phone, my tablet, my computer, so when she altered something I was developing with her I could see every keystroke.'

'You didn't trust her in the least.' I return to my chair.

'Hell no. That ended about the time I got deposed.'

From where I'm seated I'm staring dead-on at Lucy's massive matte black SUV, a stealth bomber on wheels with the ultra-luxury of a private jet.

'Did she trust you?' There's so much I want to ask.

'I never gave her a reason not to.'

'You stopped trusting her last summer and obviously didn't end the relationship then because you decided against it.'

'I was going to do it very soon.'

'Is what was going on with her why you're driving an armored vehicle these days?'

She looks at her SUV as if it's a child or a pet she loves. 'I didn't get it for any particular reason.'

'Who else have you pissed off besides pig farmers, Lucy?'

'Al-Qaeda doesn't like me. The Aryans don't.

Gay bashers, male chauvinists, supporters of the Defense of Marriage Act, Jihadists, and pretty soon Double S wasn't going to want to be my friend anymore,' she says and the thought seems to please her. 'And, yes, there's a long list of pig farmers and most recently a foie gras farm in New York State. That hellhole should have been burned to the ground as long as the geese got out first. Marino's probably not happy with me now that we're going down the list. SUV envy. His new police vehicle is a V-six, mostly plastic.' She says it cynically, angrily.

'Exactly what does he know?'

'Exactly nothing and I don't intend to explain a damn thing. He has no idea I watched him in real time when he picked up her phone behind the Psi. He hasn't got a clue and he never will, right?' Lucy looks at me.

'It won't come from me. It should come from you.'

'It shouldn't come from anyone,' she says with a bite. 'This is Marino playing cops and robbers after years of feeling like a lackey.'

'I hope you never put it that way to him.'

'When I realized Gail was missing — '

'When was that? I didn't text you until about five-thirty while Marino was driving me to Briggs Field. When did it occur to you to access her phone?' I sound like I'm interrogating her. I don't try to disguise it.

'Midnight,' she confirms what Benton told me, 'when my search engines were alerted about a posting on the Channel Five website. I immediately locked in the GPS location of her phone, which was the Psi, which I called and was told she'd left at least six hours ago. Right off I knew it was bad and I activated the video camera and left it in an auto mode. It has a motion-detection zooming lens with a speed dome pan that could pick up whatever was going on until I got here.'

'You were going to retrieve the phone as soon as you flew back.'

'Yes.'

'But Marino got there first.'

'I watched him.' Lucy seems angry with herself more than anything else. 'I wish I'd thought to turn the video camera on when I was talking to her late yesterday afternoon but I had no reason to suspect anything was wrong.'

She gets up and pours her coffee into the sink.

'If I'd had even the slightest reason to be concerned, I would have looked.' She leans her back against the sink. 'I could have seen her and whatever happened when she was outside the bar. It was a blitz attack, I'm sure of that. Had she even a second or two warning, she could have activated the camera herself and whatever was going on would have live streamed on my phone instantly. An In Case of Emergency or ICE one-touch app was all she had to press but she didn't. It was right there on her home screen and it didn't enter her mind.'

'After your conversation with her she called Carin Hegel and the connection was lost,' I encourage her to tell me what she knows about it.

'Within twenty-four seconds.' Lucy drops her

cup into the trash and sits back down.

'That's the part I don't understand,' I reply. 'One might have expected Gail would have said something, indicated someone came up to her, that perhaps she was interrupted or startled. According to Carin, the call was dropped. She continued talking and didn't realize Gail wasn't there.'

'It wasn't dropped.' Lucy picks up her phone from the table. 'The call wasn't ended until Carin did it and by then Gail had been separated from her phone.' She enters a password on the touch screen.

'How could that happen without Carin hearing something? A protest, a scream, people talking or arguing?'

Lucy clicks on an audio file.

★　★　★

'Carin Hegel,' the lawyer's familiar voice answers on a recording Lucy must have made secretly.

'Hey. Anything new since I just saw you? Let me guess. They've filed another twenty motions to waste our time and run up my bills.' Gail Shipton's voice is softly modulated, high-pitched, and girlish.

I don't detect the anger running deep that I would expect to be there. She should have despised Double S and been chronically resentful and stressed, especially when she's referencing the expenses they've been deliberately causing.

'Replay that, please,' I say to Lucy and she does.

266

Gail Shipton sounds too calm. I detect a note of artificiality, like a pedestrian actor reciting a line woodenly. I notice because I'm listening for anything off. Lucy starts the recording again.

'Carin Hegel.'

'Hey. Anything new since I just saw you? Let me guess. They've filed another twenty motions to waste our time and run up my bills.'

'Unfortunately you're not completely wrong,' Hegel says.

'I'm at the Psi Bar and stepped outside but it's still kind of loud,' Gail Shipton says. 'I'm sorry? What can I help you with?'

'I wanted to give you a heads-up about your latest bill that just crossed my desk,' Hegel's recorded voice continues.

A pause and there's no response.

'It's considerable, as you might expect this close to trial.'

Another pause.

'Gail? Are you there? Damn,' Hegel sounds impatient. 'I'm going to hang up and try you back.'

'And she did,' Lucy says to me. 'But Gail didn't answer.'

She replays the first part of the recording.

'I'm sorry?' Gail's voice says. 'What can I help you with?'

'She's not talking to Carin.' Lucy replays the same sound byte, turning up the volume.

'*I'm sorry? Can I help you?*'

I listen for background noise and can hear the distant rhythm of music from inside the bar. If Gail was talking to someone in the parking lot, I can't tell. I don't hear anything except the faint music, New Age, which is what the Psi Bar typically plays when I've been there.

'How long have you been recording Gail's phone conversations?' I ask.

'Easy to do when it's my device she's talking on. Now listen,' Lucy says. 'I've cleaned it up, separated any background noise from the music in the bar and enhanced what's there, pinpointing the timing and sequence of precisely when it was introduced. Which was before she called Carin.'

She plays the enhanced recording, an earlier one, and I hear the distinct noise of a car engine idling. Then I hear something else. I hear my niece.

' . . . We'll get something drafted when I get back from D.C.,' Lucy's recorded voice says. 'Now's not the time to start a problem, in light of the trial, even if you don't think it's going to happen. You don't need even the appearance of a problem with me.'

'Why would there be? They'll settle. Don't you worry and everything will be fair,' Gail says sweetly, what sounds insincere to me, and I hear what else is there.

The rumble of an engine. A car idling nearby in the dark behind the bar and if Gail notices, she doesn't seem concerned, not even slightly nervous.

26

'A V-eight,' Lucy says to me. 'Decent horse-power, four hundred maybe, a sizable sedan or SUV.'

SUV mud tires for off-roading, I remember Benton said. Someone involved in high-risk activities and sports who doesn't hesitate to break into a pickup truck or drive through a golf course.

'Not a performance car, definitely not that kind of high-rev sound,' Lucy says. 'It was there the entire time she was talking to me which means it was out back when she left the bar to take my call. She has no interest, possibly little or no awareness until this.'

Lucy clicks on a file, playing the same sound byte I've heard before.

'*I'm sorry? Can I help you?*'

'She's not saying this to Carin. She's saying it to someone else,' Lucy explains decisively. 'You can tell. Her tone changes. It's very subtle as if someone has walked up to her, someone who intends to speak to her, someone doing so comfortably, calmly.'

'This person is approaching her even though she's on the phone. He doesn't hesitate to interrupt her,' I consider. 'And she doesn't sound alarmed or guarded.'

'She doesn't sound friendly either,' Lucy replies. 'I don't think the person was familiar to her but she's not afraid of whoever it is. She sounds polite but not threatened. And here's the other thing, if I enhance the background noise at the beginning of the conversation with Carin? I've separated everything out except the car.'

She plays a clip and I hear the rumble of an engine. That's all I hear, just that low steady noise of a large gas-powered engine idling.

'Then she speaks to someone,' Lucy says.

'*I'm sorry? Can I help you?*'

'But what you didn't hear is a car door shutting,' Lucy explains. 'Whoever was back there must have gotten out of his vehicle and approached her but he left his car door open or at least didn't shut it all the way or we'd pick it up as an audio event. There's absolutely no fluctuation in the sound measurement. Whoever he is he's quiet as hell and she doesn't seem the least bit startled, just politely curious but cool.'

Lucy plays the sound byte again.

'*I'm sorry? Can I help you?*'

'He masquerades as something that causes no suspicion at first.' I can see it.

Dressed a certain way with an impeccable rehearsed approach that's worked for him on at least three other murderous occasions, and also many more times than that when someone stalked had no clue what a close call it was. Offenders like this thrive on dry runs. They encounter potential victims and get off on the fantasy until they finally consummate the act by abducting and killing someone.

'You're thinking her death isn't isolated.' Lucy watches me intensely. 'Is that what Benton thinks after prowling around Briggs Field? You examined her at the scene. She was murdered, not just possibly but definitely? Is what happened to her something you recognize? Or Benton does?'

'Who else might have known about these capabilities, about the technology you and Gail had been working on?'

'Whoever attacked her didn't have the slightest idea.' Lucy stares intensely at me. 'It's got nothing to do with what happened to her and I repeat that emphatically. Would you grab somebody carrying a device like this? If you knew?' She indicates her phone on the table.

'If I knew, I'd be wary,' I agree. 'I'd worry about being recorded.'

'And if the point was to steal the technology, the phone wouldn't have been left on the pavement,' Lucy says. 'Whoever grabbed her wasn't interested in it, didn't have a clue about a drone phone.'

'I have no idea what that is.'

'It's basically a handheld robotic device and not evidence in this case.'

'Marino has decided it is.'

'He's full of shit.'

'It appears you surreptitiously made recordings — '

'Because I couldn't trust Gail and was trying to get to the bottom of it. I was almost there.'

'And now Marino doesn't trust you and you don't trust him. I don't want you having a problem with him,' I say it again.

'He can't prove a damn thing. I saw everything he did. By the time he so cleverly bypassed the

271

password with the analyzer I programmed and taught him how to use, I was ten steps ahead of him. I was seeing him and he wasn't seeing a damn thing I didn't want him to.'

'He says apps, e-mails, voice mails that were on the phone earlier are gone.'

'Once he picked it up, there were certain precautions to take.'

'I don't believe he'll cut you any slack, Lucy. It might be the opposite, in fact. He'll want to show everyone he doesn't have favorites and the past is past.'

'The phone can go to the CIA, I don't care. No one can prove anything. And I don't have to worry about her sick shit or anything else getting into the wrong hands. It won't now.'

'Sick shit that could be motive for murder?' I ask.

'No way. Whoever killed her didn't realize the importance of the device she was talking on when he approached her. It was just a phone.'

Lucy looks at me and beneath her indignation I detect disappointment and hurt.

'She wasn't a good person, Aunt Kay. She tried to screw me. She tried to screw Carin. At the end of the day Gail didn't care about anybody but herself and she had even less than she did before. I don't mean money.'

'What exactly is a drone phone?' I ask.

The bay's buzzer sounds and its intrusion is loud and grating.

'My idea was domestic usage that actually could help people,' Lucy explains. 'It could save lives. Imagine controlling drones with your phone, not military unmanned aircraft but smaller ones. For aerial filming of real estate, sports events, highway and weather monitoring, wildlife research, activities that aren't safe for pilots.'

She becomes animated as she talks about what gives her joy and it is always inventions and machines that she finds more compelling than a sunset or a storm.

'That was the point and then she headed off in a bad direction or maybe that was her intention all along.' Her mood goes back to dark. 'Paparazzi photos, violating privacy in the worst way. Hunting animals. Hunting people. Spying. Acts of aggression committed by civilians for the worst of reasons.'

I watch the bay door begin to crank up and the narrow bar of daylight in the opening space beneath it isn't as bright as it was earlier.

'Something happened to her.' Lucy sounds hard and unforgiving. 'It may have happened to her before we met but eventually it owned her. That I know for a fact. I would have helped her if she'd asked but instead she tried to hurt me.'

I feel the damp chill of the late-morning air seeping in as my phone rings and I look to see who it is. The Maryland Office of the Chief Medical Examiner, Dr. Henri Venter, and I answer.

'It's not a great signal in here,' I say to him right off. 'Let me call you back on a landline.' I get up and go to a phone on the wall next to the coffee cart.

* * *

273

I dial his number. 'How are you, Henri?'

'Fighting over grant money, short half my staff it seems because of the flu and the holidays, and they sent us the wrong HEPA filters in this big order that just came in. I'm fine. What can I do for you, Kay?'

I start by telling him there is a sensitive situation with the DNA in the three D.C. cases and that we have what appears to be a related homicide in Cambridge. The Capital Murderer may now be in Massachusetts.

'This is extremely confidential on multiple fronts. And there may be a problem at the federal level,' I add in a way that conveys my meaning.

'I saw on the news there was a body at MIT,' Dr. Venter says. 'No details other than that. A bag from that spa shop was over her head, I presume? And fancy duct tape?'

'No bag or duct tape but she was wrapped in an unusual white cloth and asphyxia is in my differential.'

'That's interesting,' he replies. 'Because in the case here, Julianne Goulet, I believe she was suffocated but not necessarily with the plastic bag that was taped around her neck. Her postmortem artifacts were perplexing and I found bluish fibers in her airway, her lungs. What I'm wondering is if he had some sort of cloth over her.'

'Lycra.'

'Yes.'

'And while she violently struggled to breathe, she inhaled fibers and clawed and these same fibers ended up under her nails,' I suggest.

'Precisely. I believe the bag and fancy tape were added as some sort of creepy adornment after the fact. Just like the white cloth and the way the body was posed. That's just my opinion of course.'

'Henri, when our DNA analysis is done I'd like to compare it with your initial results in the Goulet case and not with what's in CODIS.' I get to the most important point. 'Or maybe a better way to put it is I don't want to compare any DNA profile we get with what's in CODIS now.'

'In it *now*?'

'I'm not questioning the integrity of CODIS overall, just this one sample in the case your office handled, Julianne Goulet and the DNA profile your labs recovered from panties she had on. I'm wondering if there was some sort of entry error when the profile was uploaded into CODIS,' I explain, and Lucy's eyes are riveted to me.

'My Lord.' He understands what I'm implying. 'This is quite disturbing.'

The bay door is annoyingly loud, and in the widening space I see the hearse rumbling on the other side, a Cadillac with a Christmas wreath attached to the front grille.

'As I understand it this DNA profile from the panties on Goulet's body has been matched with a suspect, someone who's been missing for seventeen years and is believed at least by some to have been dead that long.' I continue to give him enough to illustrate the ugly picture of tampering.

'I know nothing about a suspect,' Dr. Venter says.

'The FBI has one.'

'No one has told me that or attempted verification with our records. And that would be mandatory when there's a match in CODIS. The lab that did the original analysis has to confirm and what you're suggesting is outrageous.'

'I understand the stain in question was blood?' I inquire.

'That's not exactly right. We analyzed a mixture of fluids comprising a stain on the panties Julianne Goulet had on,' he recalls. 'These panties are believed to have come from the previous victim, a woman whose body was found in Virginia a week earlier. I'm trying to think of the name.'

'Sally Carson.'

'Yes.'

'But the profile on the panties didn't turn out to be hers,' I inform him, 'which is odd since they were identified as having been worn by her when she left the house before she vanished. Apparently her DNA wasn't recovered at all.'

'I don't know anything about the Carson case. It was Virginia's and nobody's talking.'

'For a reason that's not a good one, I fear.'

'I'm pulling up the actual report from the Goulet case but I'm quite sure the DNA wasn't hers either because of course we have her blood card, her profile. So we'd know if it was her DNA on the panties she was dressed in, probably postmortem. As you're aware, we routinely use certain biospectroscopic methods for different body fluids, mainly looking for ribonucleic acid markers, the same techniques you use. So I can tell you exactly what those fluids were and if there was more than one profile mixed in but I'm fairly sure there wasn't. What I remember is it all came from a single source, the same person.'

I wait as he finds what he needs in his database and the motor of the bay door completely stops. In the big square opening I see feathering clouds and farther-off ones that are building. The long black hearse noses forward slowly, propelled by its quiet engine, new and sleek, what funeral workers proudly call a landau coach.

'I have the report in front of me.' Dr. Venter is back. 'Vaginal fluid, urine, and menstrual blood all from the same individual. We have only the identifier we assigned when we uploaded the profile into CODIS. As you would expect, we don't know who it is.'

I'm surprised by the information and unfortunately I'm not. I inform him that Sally Carson's autopsy report indicates that she was having her period when she was abducted and murdered. It's possible if not probable that the stain on the panties Julianne Goulet's body had on should have matched Carson's DNA. But it didn't, most likely because somebody tampered with a profile in the FBI's database CODIS. I suspect but don't say it openly that Carson's profile was substituted for Martin Lagos's, which would explain why it appears he left 'blood,' as Benton referred to it, on the panties Julianne Goulet's dead body had on.

'I'm looking at what we have and we definitely

weren't notified about a DNA match,' Dr. Venter says darkly. 'We should have been sent the suspect's profile to compare with our records and we weren't.'

'A suspect's profile from DNA analysis that I have reason to suspect was originally done in Virginia seventeen years ago,' I say. 'A male who hasn't been seen since, I'm told.'

'A male?' he exclaims. 'A male certainly didn't leave vaginal fluid and menstrual blood.'

'Exactly. Now you see the problem.'

'Virginia also should have been notified for a verification,' Dr. Venter says.

'I'm not checking with Virginia. Last summer their former lab director was hired as the new director of the FBI's national labs. She got quite a promotion. I don't know her personally.'

'This is extraordinarily disturbing,' Dr. Venter says. 'I did the Goulet autopsy myself and frankly have had some concerns about the way it's being handled even before knowing any of this. The one who used to be with the D.C. division back in your Virginia days and now is in Boston . . . Well, you might not have encountered him back then.'

'Ed Granby.'

Lucy hasn't taken her eyes off me.

'In not so uncertain terms he threatened me,' Dr. Venter replies. 'He said I didn't want to be on the wrong side of the DOJ and I would be if I leaked a word about the Goulet case, that he was taking extreme measures to prevent copycat crimes.'

'So he continues to say.' Then I bring up the

fluorescing residue in Gail Shipton's case that doesn't seem to have been found in the others. 'I'm just making certain you didn't see anything like that,' I add.

'A grayish viscous material I found in her mouth and nose.' He opens that report next. 'A mineral fingerprint on SEM, halite, calcite, and argonite that lit up a rather spectacular vivid red, a deep bluish purple, and emerald green when exposed to ultraviolet light.'

'I remember a mention of this viscous material in records I've reviewed. Something grayish in Goulet's teeth and on her tongue.' I don't go into more detail than that.

But he knows who I'm married to and can well imagine where I got the information. Lucy gets up from her chair and stands closer to me, staring, making no attempt to hide what she's overhearing.

'There was no mention of these minerals fluorescing in UV. But that wouldn't necessarily be included in the elemental report,' I add.

'It wouldn't be.'

'I found a residue that lights up like that all over the body in my case from this morning.' I watch the two funeral home attendants in formal suits open the tailgate of the hearse.

They smile and wave as if their business is happy.

'It showed up fairly dense on CT,' Dr. Venter says. 'But there was no evidence she aspirated whatever it is. I didn't find this material in her sinuses, airway or lungs.'

'In the Virginia case, Sally Carson, there's no

reference to a material like this. But they don't have a CT scanner.'

'Few facilities do. So it wouldn't have been seen readily and very well may have been over-looked during the autopsy,' Dr. Venter says.

'If you can send me whatever you can electronically. Time is of the essence.'

'I'm doing it as we speak.'

I thank him and end the call.

'Is everything all right?' Based on what Lucy listened to she knows it couldn't possibly be.

'Reports will be coming in from the chief in Maryland, Dr. Venter,' I say to her. 'Maybe you can help by checking my e-mail and making sure they get routed to the proper labs as quickly as possible. And I'm expecting a case from Benton.' I don't mention the name Gabriela Lagos in front of the two funeral home attendants. I'm not going to say another word and Lucy knows not to either.

She's already checking e-mails with her phone to see if any reports are landing as we head up a ramp to the door leading inside. I scan my thumb in the lock and the attendants roll the stretcher up to us, small wheels clattering.

'How you doing, Chief? I heard you had the weekend from hell.'

'Doing fine.' I hold the door for them.

'The world's gone to hell in a handbasket.'

'You might be right.' I shut the door behind us.

'That was quite a storm we had. We may get snow in another day or two.'

They push the stretcher inside the receiving

area, where massive shiny steel walk-in refrigerators and freezers fill the far wall.

'The temperature's dropped ten degrees in the past hour. Blowing off the water on the South Shore, it was pretty frigid but not so bad here, sort of in between needing a winter coat and not. A sad one we got. It seems like a lot of people kill themselves this time of year.'

'It seems that way because nobody should.' I check the tag attached to the outer body bag, fake blue leather with the name of the funeral home embroidered on it. 'You can have this back.' I unzip it, revealing the flimsy white pouch underneath, the dead woman's rigorous arms pushing against it, raised and bent at the elbows like a pugilistic boxer.

'Only thirty-two years old,' an attendant tells me as we remove the pleather-like outer bag. 'Dressed for church with makeup on and dead in bed. Empty pill bottles on the table. Ativan and Zoloft. No note.'

'Often they don't,' I reply. 'Their actions speak louder.'

27

At the security desk Ron is seated amid flat-paneled security displays, his office behind bulletproof glass. He slides open his window as I pick up the big black case log to sign in the latest. I copy what's written on the body bag's tag.

Heather Woodworth, F 32, Scituate, MA. Unresponsive in bed. Poss OD suicide.

An old South Shore name scribbled in ball-point pen, a young woman who decided to end her life in her quaint seaside town, and I check the log for what else has come in. Five other cases in the CT scanner and on steel tables, in different stages of undress and dissection. Poly-substance abuse, an accidental shooting, a jump from the Zakim Bridge, an elderly woman who died alone in her house a hoarder, and the motor vehicle fatality I've heard about and I pause at the name.

Franz Schoenberg, M 63, Cambridge, MA. MVA.

The psychiatrist I noticed in the photographs I reviewed earlier this morning, I recall, slightly startled. His patient committed suicide days ago, jumped off a building right in front of him. Maybe that's why he was out drinking and driving. More senseless tragedies. Most people dying the way they lived.

'What about her meds?' I ask the attendants.

'In a bag inside the pouch,' one of them says. 'The empty bottles that were on the bedside table. Her kids had spent the night at her mother's, thank God. Little ones, the oldest only five, the father killed exactly a year ago on his motorcycle. A neighbor she was supposed to give a music lesson to found her. She didn't answer the door and it was unlocked. This was at exactly ten a.m.'

'She planned it, thought it out.' I slide the log through the window so Ron can enter the information into his computer and program the RFID bracelet that will go around the dead woman's wrist.

'She didn't want anyone home when she did it. She didn't want to hurt anyone,' an attendant offers.

'Think again,' I reply. 'Now the kids have no parents and will probably hate Christmas for the rest of their lives.'

'Apparently she'd been depressed.'

'I'm sure she was and now a lot of people will be, too. If you'll lock this up for me . . . ' I hand Ron my fanny pack.

'Yes, ma'am, Chief.' He bends down to enter the combination and gives me an update without my asking. 'All is quiet, pretty much. A news van drove real slow past the front of the building several times.'

'Just leave her over there on the floor scale,' I tell the attendants. 'Ron, can you let Harold or Rusty know a case just came in? She needs to be weighed and measured and gotten into the cooler until Anne can scan her. I'm not sure which doc. Whoever's the least busy.'

'Yes, ma'am, Chief.' Ron tucks the fanny pack inside the safe and slams shut the heavy steel door. 'That anchor lady you don't like was here.'

'Barbara Fairbanks,' Lucy says. 'She was filming the front of the building when I pulled in. She may have gotten footage of my SUV while I was waiting for the gate to open.'

'And she was hanging around out back after that, too, probably hoping to sneak in again while the gate is shutting,' Ron says. 'She did that a few weeks ago and I threatened to have her arrested for trespassing.'

Former military police, he's built like a granite wall, with dark eyes that are always moving. He walks out of his office and waits for the attendants to leave.

'We'll need the stretcher back . . . ?' one of them says.

'Yes, sir. When you pick her up.'

'Later today,' I promise them.

★   ★   ★

Through another door and down a ramp is the evidence bay, a windowless open space where scientists are covered from head to toe in white Tyvek protective clothing.

They're setting up cyanoacrylate fuming equipment around a vintage green Jaguar that is under a blue tent. The roadster is twisted and smashed in, the roof peeled off, the long hood buckled, the shattered driver's-side window streaked and spattered with dried blood, the trunk and bashed-in doors open wide. Trace evidence examiner Ernie Koppel is leaning in the driver's side.

He looks up at me, his eyes masked by orange goggles, an alternate light source set up on a nearby cart. He holds the wand in his gloved hand, processing the car as if it's connected to a homicide.

'Good morning, glad to see you back. One nasty bug. My wife had it.' His cheeks are rosy and round, tightly framed by white polyethylene, the same flashspun material used to wrap buildings, boats, and cars.

'Don't catch it.'

'I've been spared so far, thank you, God. I saw what's parked in the bay. That's some ride you've got,' he says to Lucy. 'I was looking for the gun turret.'

'You have to order it special,' she says.

'When you get a minute?' I grab disposable gowns and shoe covers off a cart. 'Obviously this isn't a routine motor vehicle fatality. It's quite the workup.'

'One more pass of the driver's seat and you can fume it for prints,' he calls out to other scientists as he dims the lights.

'Did he have his seat belt on?' I tie my gown in back.

'Side impact — being belted wasn't going to help him. Take a look at the left rear tire,' Ernie says.

I slip on shoe covers that make papery sounds as I move close to the car to see what he's talking about. The tire is flat. That's as much as I can tell.

'It was punctured with some type of sharp tool,' he explains.

'Are we sure it didn't happen during the accident? For example, if he ran over a sharp piece of metal? Tires often are flat in bad accidents.'

'It's too clean a puncture for that and it's in the sidewall, not the tread,' Ernie says. 'I'm thinking something like an ice pick that caused a slow leak and he lost control of his car. There's a transfer of paint on the rear bumper, which I also find interesting. Unless the damage was already there? And I doubt that as meticulous as this car was.'

I see what he's talking about, a small dent with a transfer of what looks like a reflective red paint.

'He may have had a flat tire and been swiped by someone,' I suggest.

'I don't think so, not as low to the ground as this car is.' Lucy pulls shoe covers on. 'If it was hit, it was by something else low to the ground or maybe a larger vehicle with a bumper guard. Some of them are reflective.' She takes a closer look. 'Especially with gangs who trick their cars out like crazy, usually SUVs.'

'Give me one sec.' Ernie bends back inside the car, moving the wand, and I resume talking to Lucy about Gail Shipton.

It's a subject I'm not finished with yet.

'A notebook was recovered from her purse,' I begin.

'Which was where?'

'The killer left it near the scene. Obviously he wanted it to be found. There was no money in her wallet but it's hard to know if anything else was missing. Apparently he wasn't interested in her notebook.'

I open the photograph I took at the construction site and show her the page with the odd encryption.

61: INC 12/18 1733 (<18m)
REC 20-8-18-5-1-20.

'The last entry she made in it,' I explain. 'Apparently right after she got off the phone with you, possibly moments before she was abducted. A small black notebook with pages that look like graph paper and there were stickers, red ones with an *X* in the middle. Do you have any ideas?'

'Sure.' Lucy works her arms into the sleeves of the gown, the synthetic material making slippery, crinkly sounds. 'It's a note in her rudimentary code that a first grader could break.'

'Sixty-one?' I start at the beginning of the encrypted string, standing shoulder to shoulder with Lucy, both of us looking at the picture on my phone.

'It's her code for me,' she says as if it's perfectly reasonable that Gail would have assigned a code to her. 'The letters in my name correspond to numbers. *L-U-C-Y* is twelve, twenty-one, three, and twenty-five. If you add them up it equals sixty-one.'

'Did she inform you she had a code for you?'

'Nope.'

'INC is an incoming call,' I assume, 'and twelve-eighteen is the date, which was yesterday, and the military time of seventeen-thirty-three.'

'Correct,' Lucy answers. 'We talked for less than eighteen minutes, and REC means received, and in this case the rest of the numbers are the code for *Threat*. Same thing, the numbers correspond to letters of the alphabet. In summary I called her and she recorded the conversation as a threat. I threatened her. That's the takeaway message, which of course is a lie.'

'Who was supposed to get this takeaway message?'

'It's intended for whoever she might sic on me eventually. Her encryption isn't meant to be secure,' Lucy says as if it's nothing, as if Gail Shipton was a simpleton. 'In fact, just the opposite. She wanted someone to find this and figure it out. She wanted it to be evidence at some point. She was cutting pages out of the notebook in case I ever got my hands on it. I wouldn't find the incriminating entries, so she assumed. I wouldn't know she was making false entries about me in a record she was keeping.'

'The notebook entries were meant to be evidence in her lawsuit or a different one?' I don't understand.

'She probably wanted to intimidate me eventually and I just sat back and watched. She'd get a settlement from Double S and then she'd want what's next. She'd make the claim she'd invented every aspect of the drone phone. She wouldn't have to pay a dime, would simply own all of it.' Lucy speaks calmly, matter-of-factly. 'And she'd claim credit for work she could never do on her own. That would have been almost as valuable as the money. She wasn't exactly feeling great about herself. The whole thing's pathetic.'

'If she was cutting out the negative entries about you,' I reply, 'then what was the evidence she intended to intimidate you with?'

'First of all, it's a joke.'

'I fail to see anything funny about it.'

'It's no damn wonder she got taken advantage of,' Lucy says. 'The reason the pages look like graph paper is because they're from a smart notebook. What she would do is photograph every page, digitizing her entries, including her fraudulent ones, so they could be searched by keywords or tags like the sticker with the X. Then she'd remove the paper and ink false entries about me by cutting out the pages she'd photographed so that the only record to turn up would be the electronic one.'

'Which you were aware of.' I know what that means.

It's exactly as I suspect. Whatever Gail was up to, no matter how clever she believed she was, Lucy was onto all of it. She wouldn't hesitate to search Gail's pocketbook or her car or apartment for that matter. It would be business as usual for her to hack into whatever she wanted, and I recall what Marino said about there being not a single photograph on Gail's phone. Lucy had deleted them, including ones Gail had taken of the lies she recorded in her notebook.

'She was building a case against me and had been for months. Pretty soon she would have what she wanted and I needed to be out of her way, or at least that was what she'd fooled herself into believing,' Lucy says in a measured way that is meant to hide what hurt must be buried somewhere. 'You know what Nietzsche said. Be careful who you pick as an enemy because that's who you become most like.'

'I'm sorry she became your enemy.'

'I'm not talking about me. I'm talking about Gail and Double S. She was well on her way to becoming just as bad as they are.'

I watch a fingerprint examiner work dials on a distribution box connected to thick bright red power cords snaking over the epoxy-painted floor. Cyanoacrylate humidifiers, evaporators, and fans begin to whir as Ernie heads in our direction, pulling off his gloves and dropping them into the trash. I hand him packaged evidence and a pen.

'I can see you're up to your ears today,' I say as he initials what I'm receipting to his lab. 'I apologize for adding to it.'

'Another unfortunate story that may get even more unfortunate.' Ernie indicates the mangled Jaguar as he takes off his goggles. 'A psychiatrist has a fight with his wife and heads to the pub, which is about to get sued for serving him alcohol when he was impaired. Supposedly. Luke says his STAT alcohol is below the legal limit. What killed this man is somebody punctured his tire and he swerved out of control into a guardrail and an autopsy's not going to tell you that. The skid marks do. And the hole in the tire. Question is, did the damage occur while he was parked at the pub or while his car was at his house? Who had access? Or did someone puncture his tire and then follow him to add an extra shove, explaining the paint transfer?'

'Juveniles, typically gangs,' Lucy says. 'There have been a number of tire slashings in the Cambridge area of late. Kids stab the tires of half a dozen cars in a lot and hide out and watch the fun. Then they tailgate one of their victims to have the extra fun of watching the tire go flat and rob the person when he finally pulls over. A car like this would cost you more than a hundred grand if it's in mint condition. The assumption would be if they caused him to crash he might be worth robbing.'

'Well, now their little prank may have just killed someone.' Ernie mops his forehead with his Tyvek sleeve.

'Why do you think I have run-flat tires?' Lucy walks around the wreckage, peering inside at what looks like the original saddle leather interior, the rosewood gearshift and steering wheel, blood and gray hair everywhere. 'The question's going to be whether other cars parked at the pub last night were similarly damaged.'

'I'll pass it along because it's a very good point,' Ernie says. 'What else can I do for you?' he asks me.

I tell him about the fibers and fluorescing residue and the ointment that smells like a mentholated vapor rub.

'If you could check the residue in SEM because I have a hunch about the elemental composition. It may be something that's showed up in an earlier case in Maryland. There's also a fence post that might have been damaged by a tool coming in,' I add.

291

'Who's doing what?' He wants to know the order of examination.

'You're the first stop for everything except DNA. I'm hoping to get lucky with the vapor rub and then it will be your turn,' I answer. 'Possibly we'll be able to tell by the chemical composition exactly what it is.'

'Maybe not the brand,' he considers dubiously, 'but menthol for sure. An alcohol found naturally in mint oils, plus eucalyptus, cedar leaf, camphor, turpentine, to mention a few. A home remedy that's been around forever and people can be extremely creative what they use it for.'

'Have you ever had it show up in a case?' I ask.

'Well, let's see. Anal swabs were positive for it in a possible sex crime, this was years ago. It turned out the victim was using a vapor rub to treat hemorrhoids. We recovered it from someone's scalp, which the police thought might be part of some kinky ritual or maybe the decedent was demented. A treatment for dandruff, we found out. I once had a case of a homemade vaporizing lamp with an open flame. Unfortunately it exploded and a toddler was killed. And then there are people who apply the stuff on open wounds and to chapped lips, and camphor can be toxic.'

I explain the petroleum-based ointment was found in the grass of an athletic field and that one theory is it could be a muscle rub and unrelated to Gail Shipton's death.

'Certainly it would be a similar composition,' Ernie ponders. 'Although pain-relieving ointments tend to be more potent with higher levels of certain oils. I'm not sure we'll be able to tell.'

'It might not matter. Maybe we'll get lucky with DNA,' I reply. 'But I'm having a hard time envisioning why someone would be digging into a jar of a vapor rub outside in the rain.'

'It depends on what he was using it for,' Ernie explains. 'He might not have been wiping it on himself or on his skin.'

'Then on what?' I ask.

'Some people saturate nasal strips with Vicks to help their breathing, snoring, sleep apnea.'

'That would be a weird thing to do outside in the middle of the night,' Lucy comments as I recall Benton's dark ramblings, what struck me as a disturbing non sequitur about the depraved killer Albert Fish.

Inhaling a sharp odor to block out distractions, to focus. Pleasure laced with pain, a fragrance that contains methyl salicylate, and Benton worries about the influence he's had. He fears that the Capital Murderer may have read journal articles that reference *Les Fleurs du Mal*, the flowers of evil. What I remember about Baudelaire's poetry from my college years is its cruel sensuousness and his view that human beings are slaves toiling through their uncertain, fleeting lives. I found him as depressing as Edgar Allan Poe at a time when I still held the belief that people were inherently good.

I peel off my gloves and ask Ernie to let me know when he has anything and then my phone rings.

'Nothing for you to do about right now,' Bryce tells me as Lucy and I leave the evidence bay.

'Just a heads-up. Marino overheard a call on that channel he loves to monitor constantly on his radio? When he scans for other area frequencies — you know, like he's always done? What I call snooping?'

'What kind of call?' I ask.

'Apparently a Concord PD dispatcher mentioned NEMLEC. It sounds very secretive, whatever it is, nothing on the news so far. I've been checking every other second. Marino asked if I knew *if anybody's dead* and I said *only everybody in this place*. Beyond that, he wouldn't give me any information, but I'm assuming it's probably something big if the local troops are being called out.'

'Is he responding?'

'Well, you know he will now that's he's *Sherlock*. Maybe they need a K-nine, one that rides around in the car all day.'

Marino must have volunteered his services to the North Eastern Massachusetts Law Enforcement Council, comprised of more than fifty police departments that share equipment and special expertise such as motorcycle units, SWAT, bomb techs, and crime scene investigation. If NEMLEC mobilizes, the situation is serious.

'Make sure one of the scene vehicles is gassed up and ready to go just in case,' I tell Bryce.

'No offense but who's supposed to do that these days? Harold and Rusty are busy with autopsies, I can't ask the scientists or the docs, and I wouldn't think of asking Lucy. Is she standing right there? I hope she hears me. Until we hire Marino's replacement, and even then there's no guarantee . . . Wait. Are you asking me to play gas station attendant?'

'No worries. I'll take care of it myself.' I don't need another reminder that Marino's quitting has changed everything for me. 'I'm off to find Anne. See if Gloria can drop by x-ray so I can turn over DNA evidence to her.'

28

Through a cloud of soft lighting we follow gray walls and recycled glass tile glazed a grayish-brown called truffle. The acoustical ceiling conceals RFID trackers and miles of wiring while hushing our progress as we bend around a floor that eventually will run into itself. Every corridor in my building is a circle.

Life stops where it starts and what is straight becomes round and I define my facility as a port not a terminal. I illustrate the work in this place as part of a journey that redefines and re-creates and not the endpoint or final destination. The dead help the living and the living help the dead and I find the seven round corridors inside my round building to be a metaphor for hope or at least a springboard for a less morbid conversation.

Long past are days when I didn't think twice about referring to the Office of the Chief Medical Examiner as the morgue or a hospital for the dead. It's part of my employee handbook and a priority in our training that we are appropriate and professional in all we do and say. One never knows who's listening, and those we serve aren't stiffs, corpses, crispy critters, roadkill, or floaters. They're patients or cases. They're someone's family, lovers, friends, and I encourage the perception that the CFC isn't a dead house but a lab where medical examinations are conducted and evidence is scientifically analyzed and those left behind are welcome to learn as much as they can tolerate.

I've instituted a spirit of transparency that allows visitors to watch us work through observation windows and the one Lucy and I walk past now is the evidence room where bloody clothing is air-drying from hanging bars inside HEPA-filtered cabinets. Spread out on a white paper — covered table are a pair of broken eyeglasses, a hearing aid, shoes, a wallet, cash, credit cards, and a wristwatch with a shattered crystal. The personal effects of the man whose wrecked car we just saw, I suspect, and next is ID. I nod a good morning at forensic technicians processing fingerprints on a pistol inside a downdraft powder station and at other stations are other weapons. A barbell, a knife, a mop handle, a brass art sculpture, all bloody and being fumed with superglue.

'The Medflight chopper just radioed Logan requesting clearance to the southwest at one thousand feet.' Lucy is monitoring an app on her phone. 'Their BK117 took off from a location in Concord, headed back to Plymouth.'

'If it's not headed to a hospital then it's either nothing or someone's dead.' I open the door to large-scale x-ray.

Lucy scrolls down on her phone, checking air traffic control live streams. 'It landed in Concord exactly fifty-five minutes ago. Obviously it responded to something there. It could be unrelated. I'll keep listening.'

★　★　★

I take a seat at Anne's console. On the other side of a leaded window is the large-bore CT scanner and she's sliding the table in.

From my perspective I can see a deformed head and gray hair matted with brain tissue and blood. I see a bloody lacerated ear. The sixty-three-year-old psychiatrist who crashed into a guardrail, a possible homicide by kids who thought it was entertaining to puncture a stranger's tire and possibly rob him. Or alcohol really could be to blame. You don't have to be legally drunk to fall asleep at the wheel or lose control of your car.

I push the intercom button to talk to Anne on the other side of the glass.

'Who's posting him?' I ask.

'When Luke finishes the fire death,' her voice sounds from a speaker on her desk. 'He already did a blood draw for a STAT alcohol.'

'I heard.'

'Point-oh-four. Barely a decent buzz and not worth dying for.' Anne continues talking as she opens the door connecting her work area to the scanner room. 'Anyway, his super-lawyer's already called.'

'I heard that, too,' I reply.

'And how's Lucy today?' she asks me as if Lucy isn't here.

Shy-Anne, as Lucy calls my gifted radiology tech, who couldn't be more pleasant but talks about people disconnectedly and often won't look them in the eye. She's the sort I imagine as the class brain in high school who got the attention of cheerleaders and football players only if they needed help with their homework.

'Life sucks,' Lucy says to Anne. 'And you?'

'By the way,' I add, 'we don't talk to lawyers who call about our cases unless they're prosecutors or defense attorneys, preferably with subpoenas in hand.'

'Bryce didn't tell her anything that matters but was on the phone long enough to get an earful and then he gave me one,' Anne says as I spot Benton through the observation glass, walking briskly along the corridor, headed toward us in a pair of borrowed black leather sneakers.

'Carin Hegel,' I assume, and Lucy is next to me, looking at what's on the flat screen, postmortem images of the man whose car we just saw.

Dr. Franz Schoenberg, with a home and office address in Cambridge near Longfellow Park, and I keep seeing him in the photographs I looked at hours ago. Gray-haired with a kindly, pleasant face that couldn't have looked more stunned or distraught as he stared at his dead patient who had texted him she planned to fly to Paris from her roof. Maybe she was out of her mind on drugs. But it seems what she did was for his benefit, what I call taking someone out with you, and so many suicides are more angry and vindictive than just plain sad.

'We had his patient through here a few days ago,' I comment. 'The young fashion designer who committed suicide. She jumped off the roof of her building right in front of him.'

'Maybe that's why he was fighting with his wife and went out drinking.' Anne sits down beside me and I notice she's wearing purple scrubs with lace trim, pockets, and pleats, what I call her *Grey's Anatomy* attire.

'It didn't help matters, that's for sure.' I study Dr. Franz Schoenberg's scans.

Open comminuted fractures of the left temporal and parietal bones, axons and blood vessels sheared due to extreme rotational forces. His head accelerated and decelerated violently on impact and probably struck the side window, not the windshield. I wonder how fast he was going. The skid marks should tell us. I note very little cerebral edema. His survival time was minimal.

'Carin Hegel was trying to reach me earlier,' I tell Anne. 'At around five-thirty this morning as I was headed to the scene at MIT. She told Marino she wanted to talk to me. I assumed it was about Gail Shipton.'

'Business is booming for ambulance chasers,' Anne says.

'She isn't exactly an ambulance chaser.' I'm amused but puzzled.

Hegel and I usually don't have cases in common for the simple reason that most of my patients and their families can't afford an attorney like her. Most of what I deal with is on the criminal side and the super-lawyers of the super-rich very rarely appear on my radar and yet she has twice today.

Anne slides out a call sheet and other paperwork from a file holder on her desk as Benton walks in. Not far behind him is Bryce, with big sunglasses parked on top of his head, in extra-slim jeans, a chunky cable-knit sweater, and red suede loafers. He's carrying a pizza box, napkins, and paper plates, and Lucy steps into the doorway to intercept him, making sure he doesn't escape until we're fed.

'Are you aware of anything going on in Concord?' I ask Benton and the way he looks at me conveys that something is.

'Approximately an hour ago.' He positions himself behind my chair. 'A call for an active shooter that turned out to be false.'

'Explaining why Medflight was deployed and then turned back,' I suggest.

'I assume so.'

But the way he says it makes me think there's more.

'What else do we know about this case?' I then ask Anne for more details about the patient in her scanner, Dr. Schoenberg.

'DOA at Cambridge Hospital at around four a.m.' She shuffles through paperwork. 'Apparently he left the pub around two but it took a while to get him out of his car. If you look at it in the evidence bay, you can see why. One of these classic old Jags, a real beaut before hydraulic tools opened it up like a can of soup.'

'A Jag E, early 1960s.' Lucy is standing back from us, in the doorway. 'It was probably what he envied when he was old enough to drive and didn't have the money. The problem is these antiques don't have air bags.'

'Which pub?' I ask Anne.

'The Irish one Marino likes so much. He's taken me there a few times pretending it's not a date. I admit their lager mac and cheese is to die for — and I didn't just say that, sorry, Fado's. They've got a killer slow-roasted pork belly in a cider-reduction sauce ... I'm going to stop talking now because my Tourette's is acting up.'

'Fado's isn't in the best part of town,' Benton says. 'Not far from the projects in West Cambridge.'

'He left the pub and do we know where he was headed?' I inquire as I remember the police call earlier, suspicious youths in a red SUV who may have just broken into a number of vehicles in the parking lots of the subsidized housing development on Windsor Street.

'According to his paperwork, he was on Memorial Drive near the Mass Ave Bridge. It may be he was headed home,' Anne says.

I imagine gang members in a red SUV following the Jaguar, waiting for the tire to go flat, maybe planning to rob the driver, but things turned out a lot worse than that. Possibly they nudged the car, sending it out of control into a guardrail.

'If they get the kids seen fleeing the projects on Windsor, we need to compare the paint of their red SUV to the paint transferred to the Jaguar,' I decide. 'Let's make sure the Cambridge police know.'

'Well, if Carin Hegel was trying to find you as early as five-thirty, she sure as hell didn't waste any time.' Anne stops talking about food and quits the bad puns. 'She called here about an hour ago, at almost eleven. You know it's got to be the pub's fault. The pub shouldn't have kept serving him. And of course we couldn't offer what his blood alcohol is, that he wasn't intoxicated, because we can't release his information before the investigation is completed, et cetera, et cetera. The usual, from what I gathered from Bryce, who told me the same story in fifty different ways of course.'

'I heard my name and it better not have been in vain,' he says.

'Apparently Hegel doesn't know a tire was slashed and that he may be a homicide,' I say to Anne as Lucy holds out her hands to make Bryce surrender what promises to be a large pie with beef, sausage, pepperoni, peppers, fresh tomato, onions, garlic, extra mozzarella, and Asiago. The usual I order.

My mouth waters and hunger stabs my empty stomach. It feels constricted, practically tubular, and if aromas were audible, the volume would be as high up as it could go. It would be deafening.

'Not so fast.' Bryce pulls the box away from Lucy. 'Not even if you tell me to put my hands up or you'll shoot.'

'Don't dare me.'

'Oh I'm scared. You're not even armed.'

'How do you know?'

'You're such a monster even when you're sweet.'

'Looking for someone to sue,' Anne is saying to me. 'Let me guess. The wife wants money from her husband's death and we've not even autopsied the poor guy yet.'

'I guess Carin Hegel doesn't discuss her other clients.' I look at Lucy.

'She has a lot of rich ones but how do we know he was a client?' She directs this at Bryce.

'Well, I assumed,' he says. 'She was asking questions about how drunk he was and if that's why he crashed his car. She sounded upset and sensitive for a lawyer and kept saying what a bad day it's been. Maybe she knew him.'

He's typing something on his phone.

'He had a fight with his wife?' I repeat this to Bryce. 'Do we know where that detail came from?'

'It's on the call sheet,' he says. 'When he didn't come home his wife called nine-one-one all teary and described his car. She said they'd had a disagreement and he left the house angry. And, well, look at this. Dr. Schoenberg was an expert witness in several lawsuits with big verdicts over the past few years and guess who the trial lawyer was? So maybe Carin Hegel was calling because it's personal. She just lost a friend and a consultant who helps her make a lot of money.'

'We don't take personal calls from lawyers,' I reply. 'No information goes to her or anyone else about this case or any of our cases. We don't do those types of favors.'

'Granby wants to meet at three.' Benton places his hands on my shoulders from where he stands behind my chair.

'I'm sure he does.'

'What should I tell him?'

'With the way my day is looking, it will have to be here.' I turn around to answer him. 'I'll reserve the war room or the PIT, depending on what we'll be looking at.'

304

The PIT is our Progressive Immersion Theater, where we review cases in three-dimension or virtual reality. One of Lucy's latest innovations as she continues her efforts to rid the world of paper, it features a HAPTIC and a Lidar data tunnel among other far-flung things.

'I need to replace a projector in the multi-touch table,' she lets me know as DNA scientist Gloria walks in.

I hand over evidence to her.

'After you it goes to Ernie,' I say as she initials the package. 'As fast as you can.'

In her thirties, with spiky black hair and a pierced left nostril, she specializes in low copy number DNA and is used to my wanting everything yesterday.

'I'll move it to the head of the line,' she says to me.

'You may be getting lab reports from Dr. Venter's office in Baltimore,' I say next.

'I've already forwarded them,' Lucy informs me.

Gloria gives me a lingering, curious look as she heads to the door. A DNA profile from one of the Capital Murderer cases and my top molecular biologist isn't ignorant or out of touch. Something big and bad is going on and she knows it.

'Needless to say . . . ' I meet her eyes.

'Of course, and I'll have something by tomorrow morning but will shoot for sooner.' And then she's gone, out the door, on the other side of the window, walking fast down the corridor toward the elevator, like everybody else glued to her phone.

'When did Benton get back from Washington?' Anne asks me. 'Is he doing okay because he looks like he could use a little meat on his bones. Did you get a load of that tank Lucy drove up in? When she pulled into the bay it sounded like she flew her helicopter in.'

'I'm standing right here.' Lucy sets the pizza box on a desk. 'There'd better be vegan or I really will kill you, Bryce.'

'Wish Anne a good morning for Benton, who's standing right behind you,' Bryce says to me. 'I mean, really?' He directs this at Anne. 'Sauce, mushrooms, broccoli, spinach, eggplant.' He counts on his fingers for Lucy's benefit. 'And let's see. Presto!' He opens the lid. 'Two boring slices just for you.' He hands her a paper plate, making sure he flaunts his leather bracelets. 'Do you like?' He holds up his wrist. 'Totally made by hand with a dragon clasp. In brown and royal blue because, what can I say? Ethan is way generous. And Anne? Lucy says good morning to you through me and I'm wishing you a good morning through her. *Point taken?*'

Anne is unable to refrain from talking about people as if they're not in the room but it's hard to take offense. She's one of the least provocative people I've ever met, with her gentle face and demeanor and her plain-speaking and practical manner. No amount of ragging by Marino has ever gotten a rise out of her and even Bryce's silly compulsive blather doesn't pluck at her nerves.

She opens Gail Shipton's scan for me, 3-D

images of the head and thorax appearing on a flat screen.

'J.Crew,' Bryce shows off more bling. 'And this one is almost over the top, but far be it from me to look a gift horse in the mouth.' He plucks at a black leather cuff with a stainless-steel chain. 'To go with . . . ' He pulls a necklace out of his sweater, black leather with some sort of tribal metalwork, and then he places a slice of pizza on a plate and presents it to me.

The first bite is an explosion of pleasure. My God, I'm starved. I've eaten half the slice before I can talk.

'This is what's significant.' I wipe my fingers on a napkin. 'Starting with a fairly dense material that fluoresces in UV. Some kind of dust that was all over her.'

I point out intense white areas on Gail Shipton's scan, the residue in her nostrils and mouth. The vague, dark, air-filled space in the pleural cavity is the small pneumothorax in the upper lobe of the right lung, I go on to explain. Clicking on a different image, a cross section of the thorax and a coronal section, I can see the problem more clearly.

'The buildup of air in the closed space would have put pressure on the lung, making it impossible to expand,' I explain to Benton and Lucy.

'Making it harder to breathe,' she says.

'Even I know that,' Bryce exclaims.

'She already had some problems breathing,' Lucy informs me. 'She would get winded. She sighed a lot as if it were hard to catch her breath.'

307

'I'm not sure I see what you're talking about.' Benton puts on his reading glasses. 'And would a pneumothorax kill someone?'

'If left untreated, it would have caused her severe respiratory distress,' I reply. 'It would have put pressure on her heart and other major vessels.'

'I'm still trying to see it.' Benton leans over me, peering at the flat screen, and I feel his breath in my hair.

'This black area here,' Anne helps him out. 'That's air density. See? It's the same inside and outside the chest. And it's not supposed to be like that.'

'There should be no black area at all in the pleural space,' I add. 'This lighter area here in the soft tissue of the chest is hemorrhage. She suffered some type of trauma that collapsed her lung. The first order of business is to find out how she got that.'

29

Inside the anteroom I grab protective clothing from shelves. It's half past noon.

I put on booties, a face shield, and gloves. Lucy and Benton do the same but I know when he doesn't plan to stay long. He'll learn what he can from Gail Shipton's body and then he's got Bureau swords to clash with and maybe something more. I can always sense when a dark front has rolled through him. It's as if the air has shifted the way it does before a storm, and I think about the DNA and what Dr. Venter told me.

'Is there anything on the news?' I ask Lucy.

'Just what he mentioned.' She looks at Benton to see if he has anything to add. 'About an hour and a half ago nine-one-one got a call about an active shooter in Concord. Police responded and said there's no gunman and nothing further.'

'Where in Concord?'

'Minute Man Park, where there were a bunch of schoolkids.'

'And Medflight responded?'

'That's pretty much all there is to it,' Benton speaks up. 'A suspicious person in dark clothing was spotted running through the park. Supposedly a car backfire on Liberty Street was mistaken for gunshots. Kids were screaming, teachers panicking, thinking it was another Newtown.'

'Did they catch the person?' I ask.

'They didn't.'

'And that's the whole story.' I look at him.

'I doubt it. Area-wide emergency radio communications between departments tell me NEMLEC is responding to something but the FBI hasn't been called. I don't know what it is. They might not know what it is at this point. Granby's being pushy about meeting with you,'

'Why is he going through you?' I feel myself getting stubborn. 'He needs to call my office.'

'He's decided I shouldn't be there,' Benton says. 'That's the latest.'

'You schedule a meeting and then aren't invited,' I reply. 'That's choice.'

'He should work on not being so subtle,' Lucy says. 'What a tool.'

I push a hands-free button with my elbow and steel doors automatically swing open to the sounds of running water and steel instruments clicking and clacking against cutting boards. An oscillating saw whines, then grinds loudly through bone. Voices of doctors and autopsy technicians blend in a low murmur and I detect decomposing blood and fermentation. I smell burnt flesh.

Natural light filters through one-way glass windows and banks of high-intensity lamps in the thirty-two-foot ceilings blaze as my staff works at stainless-steel sinks and portable tables along a wall. Luke Zenner is finishing an autopsy at his station, number 2, next to mine, where Gail Shipton's body holds its rigid pose still wrapped in plasticized sheets. The bag was removed from her head, probably by Dr. Adams when he charted her teeth.

She's not looking quite as pristine now that she's in a warmer place and tampered with by a forensic dentist who had to break the rigor in her jaw to force open her mouth. Her lips are drying, beginning a slow retraction as if she's snarling at the violation, what couldn't be a more necessary or degrading one.

'Glad to see you're still in the land of the living,' Luke's vivid blue eyes look at me through large safety glasses, his blond hair covered with a colorful surgical cap.

'It's not exactly the land of the living in here,' Lucy says. ''Tis the season.' She stares at the charred body on Luke's table, the chest cavity empty and bright cherry red, the ribs showing through curved and white.

'What about a CO level?' I ask him.

'Sixty percent. *Ja, in der Tat, meine Freundin,*' says Luke, whose first language is German. 'He was still breathing when he caught his house on fire. Smoking and drinking, his STAT alcohol point-two-nine.'

'That will do it.'

'The thought is he passed out and the cigarette started smoldering on the couch.' Luke wipes his bloody gloved hands on a bloody towel and calls out to Rusty on the other side of the room, asking him to close up for him. 'One big drunk tank in here today, what I've come to expect right before the holidays.' Luke pulls off his bloody apron and drops it in the biohazard trash. 'Dr. Schoenberg is up next. How's that for

311

a twist of fate? A shrink with poor coping skills.'

I signal Harold that I need some help.

'I'm not sure there isn't some cause and effect at work.' Moving a surgical cart close, I retrieve a pair of scissors and begin cutting through tape. 'You took care of one of his patients last week, Sakura Yamagata, the woman who jumped off the roof of her apartment building.'

'Good Lord.' Luke's eyes widen. 'The twenty-two-year-old so-called fashion designer, thanks to her biopreneur molecular millionaire daddy who basically bought a career for her? Most recently he paid half a million dollars to some reality star to make a personal appearance at a fashion show and endorse his daughter's label, which is a horror. In the inimitable words of Bryce, all high-tech drama and no story, or the Jetsons meet Snooki.'

'How do we know all this?' I ask.

'Googled it,' Luke says. 'Amazing what's out there about our patients.'

'I've notified tox to check for hallucinogens such as mephedrone, methylone, MDPV in her case.'

'Good idea, and we're going to need to talk when you've got a minute. I fear this Dr. Schoenberg's going to be high-maintenance.'

'Vitreous, blood, urine, liver, no stone unturned.' I fold the sheets and hand them to Harold. 'Not to mention his gastric. Had he eaten recently? Did he order food at the pub? Maybe he didn't go there to drink but to eat alone and calm down before he went back home to patch things up with his wife. Maybe he was trying to sort through why it wasn't his fault that a patient killed herself right in front of him.'

I remove the ivory cloth from Gail Shipton's body, nude except for the pale peach panties she has on, an expensive, high-thread-count cotton, Swiss-made. The wound on her left upper chest is so faint it easily could have been missed.

★   ★   ★

The circular skin discoloration is a very faint pink and no bigger than a dime. Under a hand lens I can see the puncture in the middle of it made by a barbed shank that penetrated her right lung, collapsing it.

'Have you come across this before?' I ask Benton as if my question is hypothetical, a teaching exercise, nothing more than a quiz.

What I can't allude to is the D.C. murders. I don't want to alert any members of my staff that Gail Shipton likely is the victim of a serial killer who has terrorized our nation's capital for the past eight months. It will be up to Benton to open that door.

'It looks like an insect bite.' He studies the magnified wound, his disposable gown rustling against me. I feel his warmth. I sense his intensity.

Then his hazel eyes peer at me above his surgical mask and I see what's in them. He hasn't encountered this before. The injury is new to him.

'I don't know what it is, not firsthand,' he says. 'Obviously an insect couldn't penetrate her lung.

Do you think it could be an injection site?' he asks and I don't think that.

We may have discovered how the killer controls his victims. It's possible this attention-seeking psychopath has inadvertently left a peephole into his modus operandi. I see what the bastard did. I have a better idea what kind of cowardly brute he is.

'It's not an injection site.' I hold Benton's gaze and it's my way of communicating that I'm not going to tell him what caused the wound. Not in front of an audience.

Gail Shipton was shot with an electrical weapon, a stun gun, and not the type the average person can buy on the Internet for home protection. She may have been shot more than once but this wound to her chest is where one of the probes struck her bare skin and the dart penetrated her chest wall and lung. If other probes struck clothed areas of her body, I might not see any injury. Since we don't have what she was wearing at the bar last night I can't look for tears.

Stun-gun shocks are silent. The victim is completely incapacitated while wire-attached darts deliver 50,000 volts. It's like going into a cadaveric spasm or instant rigor mortis while you're alive, if such a gruesome thing were possible. You can't speak and you can't stand up. The most threatening injury can come from dropping like a falling tree and striking your head.

'Do you mind if I borrow your office?' Benton holds my stare. 'I've got some calls I need to

314

make and then maybe Bryce could drop me by the house so I can get my car.'

'Harold?' I push up my face shield. 'If you'll get Anne in here, please? I'll be right back and we'll get started.'

'Sure thing, Chief.'

30

I escort Benton back to the anteroom as if he needs to be shown the way or maybe people assume I want a moment alone with my husband. He removes his protective clothing, pulling apart the papery tie of his white gown, heaping it into a bright red biohazard trash can.

I tell him the truth, a cruel one with even cruder implications.

'If she was killed by the Capital Murderer, then he's using an electrical weapon, a type of stun gun, on his victims. At least he did on this latest one,' I explain. 'And not just any model. The type used on her fires cartridges with wires and weighted probes that anchor into flesh like fishhooks. In other words, he has the sort of weapon I associate with law enforcement.'

'Unless he bought it on the street.' Benton sits down on a bench and pulls off his shoe covers. 'Which wouldn't be hard. And, for that matter, there's not much you can't get online.'

'Certainly that's possible. But he knew what to get and what it does.'

Benton takes off his gloves and surgical mask, reaching for the trash. 'Sadism and control,' he says as he folds his safety glasses and gives them to me. 'Just the anticipation of being shocked would be terrifying.'

'It would be.' I return his glasses to a shelf lined with different sizes of glasses and a spray

316

bottle of disinfectant.

'That's why they don't fight him.' He stares off as if seeing a vision, a horrible one.

'Paralysis lasted only as long as he squeezed the trigger unless you're as unlucky as I suspect she was. Or maybe what happened to her was unintentionally merciful. Maybe he used an electroshock weapon and her premature death spared her from a tortured one. Maybe that's why there's no bag, no frilly tape or bow.'

'He didn't get to the best part and his ritual was aborted.' Benton rests his arms on his knees and stares at his bare hands, tapered and graceful like a musician's and pale because of where we live. He fingers his simple platinum wedding band, turning it slowly.

'We'll see what the autopsy says but if he shot her with a stun gun while she was in the dark parking lot it might be why she suddenly got quiet when she was talking to Carin Hegel,' I add and I tell him about the recorded telephone conversation Lucy played for me.

I describe the sound of a car engine behind the Psi Bar and Gail Shipton saying *'I'm sorry? Can I help you?'* And then nothing. I sit down next to Benton shoulder to shoulder, knee to knee, my papery cocooned feet next to his borrowed black sneakers.

'It would explain Gail not talking anymore,' I suggest. 'She would have dropped her phone and been unable to say a word. But she didn't collapse to the ground or she'd have scrapes, contusions, possibly serious injuries if she struck her head. Something prevented her from falling

317

when her muscles locked up.'

'He may have caught her and maneuvered her into his car.' Benton plays it out, staring down at his hands solemnly as if he's just discovered he's been missing something important all along. 'She was going to be disoriented and she wasn't likely to struggle if it meant being shocked again. Obviously she didn't scream or that would have been on the recording Lucy's not supposed to have and hasn't turned over to the police.'

'Not everybody screams and some people black out. If she had underlying cardiac disease or damage, she may have gone into arrest.' I'm not going to get into what Lucy has or hasn't done.

At the moment I'm not interested in her usual violations of protocols and splintering of rules. I'm more worried about Benton's FBI boss doing that and then some.

'If she died of a heart attack, that would be a major cheat for whoever this is,' Benton says as we get up and I know what he's feeling.

I can see it in the tightness in his face and the haunted shadows in his eyes that are the ghosts of every savaged person whose case he's worked. He has to bring them back from the dead to be their champion. He has to know what they were like before some predator ripped their souls from them. He can't let the victims go. They are a crowd inside him, a disembodied population that by now is vast.

'Don't be so hard on yourself. Please try not to be.' I look at him and touch his hand. 'You can't know something if it hasn't presented

318

itself. You can't conjure it up from thin air.'

'There must be some trace of what he's been doing to them and I missed it.'

'If anybody missed it, the medical examiners did. Maybe he didn't use a stun gun on the others.'

'Their lack of injuries make me think he subdued them in a similar way.' He collects his blazer and coat from a hook on the wall.

'If they were shocked through clothing, especially layers of it, there's a good chance the darts wouldn't have left a mark or at least not one that would have been noticed.'

'Witnessing a victim's panicky death as she's suffocating is part of the thrill,' he says. 'It would suck for him if she had a heart attack. That would be his coitus interruptus and would frustrate and infuriate him. He was interrupted and his compulsion wasn't satisfied. Dressed up with no place to go and she cheated him. He'd studied her and yet she did the unexpected. She had the gall to die before he could finish killing her. He'll do something again. He'll do it soon. I didn't calculate this.'

'Why would you?'

'It's really important.' He works his arms into the sleeves of his blazer. 'It might explain a lot of things. He goes through only part of the ritual because the fantasy isn't there. It was ruined by her when she behaved in a way he didn't expect and then had the audacity to die on him.'

'I'm going to do my best to find that out.'

'Maybe that's why he dug into the Vicks while he was out there with her body. He was having a harder time than usual, was thrown off his game by what he didn't anticipate. He was angry and distracted, trying to regain his focus. She didn't let him finish. She robbed him. That's the way he looks at it. The flower of evil never bloomed and he's an enraged bull.'

'We have to see what her body says.'

'He's losing his way and his control,' he says as if Armageddon is about to start. 'It always happens. I didn't think it would happen this fast with him when in fact it was already in the works, which is why he came back here. Christ. He's here because he's straying out of bounds and he has no insight, guided by a force he doesn't understand, the malignant one that owns him, and this is home. This is where it started and will end. Something will.'

What Benton is seeing he can't stop. He's tense all over as if he's the one being shocked.

'Decompensating, getting more caught up in his deviant violent fantasies, ones he doesn't even know are sick and unjustified. He doesn't see himself as cruel. It's everybody else's fault.' He stares off without blinking. 'He thinks he's as normal as you and me. He thinks what he does makes sense,' he says as Anne walks in to suit up. 'I'm going to get my car. I'll tell Granby if he wants to meet with you at three it has to be here at the CFC.'

'Yes, with me,' I repeat because Benton has been uninvited. 'What time is Bryce interviewing the candidate for Marino's job?' I ask Anne.

'Three of course.' She eyes Benton curiously. 'I could tell him to push it back to five.'

'If there's even the slightest chance I can stop by,' I reply. 'Is this a necessary case discussion or politics?' I ask Benton as he opens the door. 'And maybe I'm not inclined to meet since he doesn't want you to attend,' I add and I go cold inside.

The hell with Ed Granby.

'I'm not interested in his damn politics and agendas,' I add, feeling more offended by the minute. 'FBI jurisdiction and all that goes with it has nothing to do with the CFC.'

I can't stand the idea of Granby wasting my time and I won't be able to look at him without thinking of vaginal fluids and menstrual blood that couldn't possibly have been left by Martin Lagos. I've never been fond of Benton's boss and now I want nothing to do with him until I discover the truth of what happened in CODIS. If Granby instructed someone to alter a DNA profile, I want to know why and I want him to get the trouble he deserves.

'Well, that's the problem as I understand it.' Benton stands in the doorway, looking at me. 'Marino basically indicated I worked the MIT scene when we hadn't officially been invited in by Cambridge. And next the Cambridge superintendent called with his tail feathers ruffled. So Granby's trying to sort it out. That's what he says. And I can't be there since I'm the problem.'

'And it's not his real reason,' I reply.

'I can see Marino's social skills haven't gotten any better,' Anne remarks. 'Why does he have to be such a jerk?'

321

'It's always sensitive,' Benton adds because it takes nothing to get local police pissed off at the almighty Bureau. 'Granby wants to know what you know,' he says to me and that's really what the meeting is about.

'Know what I know?' I'd be amused if it were anybody else. 'In general? That could take a while.'

'Like the rest of his life if he wants to know what you know,' Anne says.

'He says it's to clear things up about why I was with you at Briggs Field when no one has officially asked for our help.' Benton tells me more of Granby's mendacious blather.

'Did you happen to pass on your theory about our case from this morning, the one that's caused ruffled feathers?'

'I do my job and report to my supervisor,' Benton says with a straight face that doesn't hide what he really feels.

Granby has been alerted that Gail Shipton's murder may be connected to the ones in D.C. and if he tampered with evidence he's got to be paranoid and know he has a problem. Of course he'd like to meet with me and hear all the details and of course he doesn't want Benton present.

'I have a feeling I'm going to be busy at three,' I decide. 'I just realized I will be. You know what? It just isn't possible to meet today or tomorrow either. I'll get Bryce to look at my calendar when I have a chance.'

Benton meets my eyes and smiles and then he leaves.

'Well, you're back with a vengeance.' Anne

plucks protective clothing off shelves.

'Not because of anything I did,' I reply. 'This party wasn't thrown in my honor. I just happened to wander in.'

'Did I hear something about a stun gun?'

'You didn't hear anything at all.'

'Harold says you need me,' Anne says. 'What exactly would you like me to do?'

'Assist. He can help Luke while you help me. We've got to do an angiography and scan her again to see if my suspicion is right and she has an underlying cardiac problem that made her susceptible to sudden death. I'd like whatever is said about this case to stay between us for now. I'd like whatever you just heard to stay in this room, please.'

'Loose lips.' She zips hers and throws away the imaginary key. 'Not from me. What are you thinking?'

'We may be dealing with a killer who has some connection to law enforcement or has access and an interest,' I answer.

'A killer cop?'

'I don't know and not necessarily. But not just anyone can acquire the type of stun gun used on her. Either he got one illegally or has law enforcement ties or someone close to him does.'

'That's what caused her pneumothorax? I almost said *I'm shocked*. I don't think we've ever had a stun-gun injury before.'

'That's because most people don't die from them.'

'I dated this guy for a while, a rookie cop. Part of their training is they have to be shot with one.'

323

She puts a gown on over her purple scrubs. 'He told me it doesn't hurt as much as it scares the shit out of you.'

'You know what it feels like when you whack your funny bone? Imagine that times a thousand all through your body for five seconds or longer. It's about as painless as having a grand mal seizure.'

'So my guess is if you do that to someone once, they're not going to resist you and risk a second dose.'

'Unless they're high on coke or PCP. Were you aware that Lucy was picking up Benton in Washington and bringing him home a few days early as a surprise?' I can ask Anne anything and she won't repeat it or make judgments.

'Bryce told me. I think a lot of people knew and were really pleased,' she says. 'We felt bad about what you'd been through in Connecticut and then you got the flu. It's almost Christmas and Benton was gone and tomorrow's his birthday. It may surprise you but people here think all you do is work and we want you to have a little ease now and then and be happy.'

I realize how much I need to talk. I can't stop thinking about Granby's outrageous suggestion that the Capital Murderer is influenced by what Benton has published and therefore these sadistic deaths are partly Benton's fault. So he should retire and the Bureau shouldn't be involved in profiling anymore; it's outdated and dangerous. Granby is trying to poison him and he knows how to do it, and I'm trying to be my objective, calm self but I'm seething inside.

'People here knew Lucy was flying Benton home today,' I say to Anne. 'His FBI colleagues knew, his damn boss knew, and his hotel in northern Virginia and whoever saw the flight plan Lucy filed also knew.'

I try to work through it, any possibility of how the killer might have been aware that Benton was flying home today, but I'm as unconvinced as I was when he first suggested it. He's upset and bruised. He's blaming himself. I have to understand but I can't listen to it. And it doesn't matter anyway. Whatever the killer knew doesn't make any of this Benton's fault. How dare Granby suggest anything to the contrary? How dare he invalidate Benton's accomplishments and real sacrifices?

'Why?' Anne asks.

'Lucy knew Gail Shipton.'

'I've gathered that.'

'Benton is concerned that whoever killed her may have had some idea he would be here when her body was found, that maybe he timed it with Benton in mind.'

'That's creepy.' I can tell she doesn't buy it, not even slightly.

'I'm wondering if Lucy may have said something to Gail.'

'And then Gail told the person who intended to murder her? Said hey, Benton's coming home, why don't you do it now? And is this Benton's theory?'

'Obviously it sounds silly when you put it like that.' I press the wall button with my elbow and the steel doors swing open wide. 'It may be one of those questions that's never answered but I can't stand what it's doing to him.'

'You know what I have no doubt about?' Anne follows me inside. 'He looks stressed. He looks tired and strung-out and a little bit down. Sometimes when I get that way I think everything's my fault. I worry something's hiding in my closet and under my bed. I get weird, to be honest.'

'Yes, well, Granby's certainly doing his best to make Benton feel that way.'

'You need to sort it out for him, Dr. Scarpetta. Or he'll torture himself.'

'I'm trying to figure out how to do that.'

'Ask Lucy,' she says. 'Just ask her who she may have told and then you'll know for sure.'

'I don't want her to feel I'm blaming her.'

'You're not blaming her or anyone and you need to stop being responsible for everybody's feelings.'

'That will never happen,' I reply.

★ ★ ★

I excise the puncture wound and wait for Lucy to respond to a question that's uncomfortable for her. It's a question I didn't ask earlier because there was so much to ask and now priorities have shifted and I also know how she'll react.

Lucy hesitates before deciding, 'In passing, I think I did. I wouldn't have supposed it mattered.'

My brilliant, clever niece is obvious when she

326

perceives that I think she screwed up. It's as if she suddenly has on wooden shoes. I pick up forceps from the surgical cart.

'Vaguely I remember saying something,' she adds, not defensively but indifferently, and she doesn't like what I'm asking and I knew she wouldn't.

So she rationalizes out loud that it would make sense if she referenced Benton's birthday surprise during the telephone conversation with Gail when she was behind the Psi Bar. Lucy had just flown into Dulles when she made that call. She was there to pick up Benton and bring him home the next day.

'I said where I was and why,' she adds from the other side of the steel table, talking to me while she stares at her dead former friend, someone she once trusted, someone who was lying to her and robbing her, someone she won't miss.

'You're sure it didn't come up before.' I drop the sectioned wound into a bottle of formalin.

'It probably did,' Lucy admits and that doesn't bother her but she resents the question.

The helicopter flight to pick up Benton was a subject that could have been introduced earlier. In fact, she's fairly certain it did. Lucy does her best not to show what she feels. Anger, embarrassment, picked on, and hurt that I don't trust her. If I did, I wouldn't ask questions like this. That's how it goes through her mind, the way she thinks and reacts as if I'm her mother belittling her and I'm certainly not. A circle of emotions as old as her history, one causing the next one and the next. A circle I know like the circles in my building, like the corridors that begin where they end in this place of life and death.

What she doesn't feel is responsible. Whatever I'm implying isn't something she caused and she's not going to pretend to care that this woman who intended to screw her isn't around anymore. Lucy doesn't give a damn about what she might have said to her and I'd always rather that Lucy be honest, but when I witness her most basic programming it's sobering. It's close to unbearable. I call her a little sociopathic and Benton never fails to remind me you can't be a little of that. Like a little pregnant or a little raped or a little dead.

She goes on to mention that Gail visited her this past Sunday, the day the birthday surprise was decided. Gail, Lucy, and Carin Hegel met that late morning at Lucy's Concord home to discuss the upcoming trial and review depositions and other documents. It's possible that during this visit she mentioned Benton's birthday and her concern about me being home alone after returning from Connecticut.

'I just think it's significant she was killed soon after that.' Lucy shrewdly makes what she believes is the most important point and one I've completely missed. 'It was all over the news that you helped out the ME's office in Connecticut.'

'Bryce and his big mouth,' Anne says.

He had to mention it to the Armed Forces chief medical examiner, my ultimate boss, and then the public information officer decided it would be good PR. The CFC is subsidized by the Commonwealth of Massachusetts and the Department of Defense and I get reminded from time to time that the buck doesn't stop with me unless something goes wrong.

'It went viral on the Internet last Friday that you responded to the school and assisted with the autopsies.' Lucy doesn't take her eyes off the wan dead face, lips drying, eyes duller.

Gail Shipton's rigor is beginning to relax. Soon it will pass like a fist too tired to clench anymore.

'I don't believe this is about me,' I reply.

'And I don't believe we should assume it's about Benton,' Lucy says. 'Or if it is, maybe that's just part of it. Maybe your role in Connecticut is the rest of it.'

'I see what she's getting at.' Anne agrees with a theory that is new and not what I expected. 'Benton's worried the timing is about him when it may very well be about you.'

Creating a spectacle, Benton keeps saying. A violent drama that I don't want to imagine for a moment could include me.

'Anybody keeping up with the news would have known when you were in Connecticut and when you came back,' Lucy points out. 'The second-worst school shooting in U.S. history, second only to Virginia Tech. That would turn the head of some psycho who craves attention.'

A narcissist with borderline traits, Benton said. The killer has to watch the drama he creates.

'All of the publicity might have lit his powder keg,' Lucy adds.

'Gail Shipton wasn't murdered because I helped out in Connecticut,' I state flatly. 'That makes no sense at all.'

'Would you rather blame it on Benton?' She looks coolly at me.

'I'd rather blame it on the person who did it.'

'I didn't say it's why.' Lucy's face is bright as if she's found an answer. 'I said the mass murder and your part in it — '

'My part in it?'

'Try not to be defensive, please,' Lucy says very calmly. 'I'm saying it could have exacerbated what was already going to happen. That's what I mean. I think Gail was targeted but maybe he decided to kill her now because what's been all over the news excited him and fed into his sick shit.'

'I saw it on CNN that you were there and then it was mentioned that you'd returned to Cambridge.' Anne agrees and I don't want to hear it. 'The killer could be interested in you. It's not your fault if it influenced him.'

'Are we about ready?' I say to her as I envision the young man behind my wall in the rainy dark. 'We need to move quickly.'

31

For the next half hour we take photographs.

We fill in anatomical diagrams and recover trace evidence from the body's surfaces and orifices, and I find more bluish-colored fibers. They're inside her nose and mouth and in her hair. They're on her tongue and caught between her teeth and inside her nostrils as far up as I can reach. I puzzle over how they got there.

They didn't come from the white stretchy cloth she was wrapped in and it would make no sense that they're from whatever clothing she had on when she was abducted and killed. Dr. Venter's comments resurface as I work. He suspects Julianne Goulet inhaled fibers from a Lycra material that might be a blue, and I very well may be looking at something similar.

'On autopsy we need to check her airway and lungs for these,' I say to Anne, and I use forceps to lift a fiber as delicate as gossamer.

I place it on a slide, protecting it with a cover slip.

'She might have aspirated fibers? That would seem unusual unless it was something that shed like crazy.' Anne opens a Physical Evidence Recovery Kit, a PERK.

'I doubt it,' I reply. 'If it shed like crazy, they'd be everywhere. But if a blue fabric covered her face while she was violently gasping for breath, that could be an explanation.'

'Like when people are smothered with a pillow,' she considers. 'I've seen tiny particles of feathers and fibers in their airways and lungs.'

'But usually there's no significant injury because a pillow is soft.'

'I've always thought it's an explanation for some cases of SIDS. Postpartum depression, and Mama uses a soft baby blanket or a baby pillow.'

'Jesus, the two of you are depressing,' Lucy says.

I carry the slide to a counter where there's a polarizing light microscope, and, turning the objective lens to 100x, I adjust the focus and peer through the binocular eyepiece. The fiber is actually a group of them fused together, multicolored, like bundles of electrical wiring, pale green and peach but predominantly blue.

'Synthetic.' I return to the table. 'Beyond that, Ernie will have to figure it out,' I add as I continue to think of the bluish Lycra fibers recovered in Dr. Venter's case. 'In her hair, in her teeth, up into her sinuses.' I remove a plastic speculum from its sterile wrapper. 'That makes me strongly suspect she was suffocated with a fabric that's stretchy and a multifilament synthetic weave is going to have some flexibility.'

'Like the polyester pants I used to wear as a kid.' Anne clips fingernails, collecting them in an envelope. 'Just stretchy enough to show every roll of flab, and, yes, as hard as it is to believe, I was a bit of a butterball and never went to the prom. So the fibers aren't from the cloth she was wrapped in because it's white.'

'No, they're definitely not from that,' I answer.

'The white cloth was the finishing touch after she was dead. He kept her someplace where he could pose her body, leaving her in the position she's in now until rigor was fixed enough to move her.'

'You can tell that how?' Lucy stands back from the table, watching us.

'Her postmortem artifacts,' I reply. 'The position she's in now was the one she was in as she cooled and began to stiffen as her livor and rigor formed.'

'He positioned her arm out like that deliberately.' Lucy holds hers out and drops her wrist.

'Yes.'

'Like a clay sculpture hardening,' Anne says.

'That's bizarre.' Lucy ponders such a detail. 'Why?'

'Why do any of these people do what they do?' Anne replies.

'It must mean something.'

'I think for people like this they don't even know what it means.' Anne hands me an envelope to initial. 'They do these awful things but if you asked them why, they have no idea.'

'That's probably true,' I agree.

'It may go back to when they were a baby or too young to remember,' Anne says. 'You know, like the time when I slammed this door and didn't know a cat was back there and broke its tail. I never got over it, but what if that was my signature if I were a criminal? I was traumatized when I was ten and always do something to cats. I break their tails.'

'You know what?' Lucy says. 'You're sick.'

'Tell her I'm not,' Anne says to me.

We begin to swab orifices, all of them.

'She was wrapped in something else while she was alive,' Lucy returns her attention to what's on my table.

'It would explain the fibers under her nails, in her hair and mouth,' I reply as my mind sorts through possibilities.

A way to restrain his victims without leaving a mark, I recall thinking as I reviewed the D.C. case reports.

I remember sitting up in bed and envisioning each excruciating death, a transparent plastic bag from a spa store called Octopus taped over a victim's head, her face turning a dusky bluish red, her eyes wide and terrified as arterial blood pumps and veins are obstructed by duct tape around her neck, a shower of pinpoint hemorrhages appearing on her lids and conjunctiva. It's like attaching a balloon to the end of a hose. Water gushes in and has no place to go and pressure builds and the balloon ruptures, and I imagine the roaring in the victim's head and her desperation to breathe. But Gail Shipton had no bag over her head and maybe he didn't use the plastic bags to kill any of his victims.

Maybe Dr. Venter's hypothesis is correct. The bags are a morbid ornament the killer incorporates into the way he symbolically poses the bodies when he leaves them displayed and he didn't bother with that finishing touch in Gail Shipton's case because she interrupted his ritual and fantasy by dying prematurely. It could be he actually suffocates his victims with a soft, stretchy fabric, possibly one made of Lycra, and this could explain their lack of defense injuries. It could explain the fibers deep in Gail Shipton's nasal cavities and in Julianne Goulet's airway and lungs.

People being smothered fight like hell and there's no evidence these women did. As Benton says, it's as if they died willingly, and that just isn't possible. People don't. In suicidal asphyxiations, biology has the final say after they have decided their lives away and set the plan into motion. They claw at the noose around their neck as they dangle and flail after they've kicked over what they were standing on. They rip at the bag over their head and they fight until the end when they drown. Pain and panic change their minds as every cell screams to stay alive and I imagine wrapping someone from head to toe in a synthetic fabric that has some give. Something stretchy.

The pelvic exam reveals no evidence of sexual assault, no semen, no contusions or inflammation, and I work swiftly. I have a mission in mind, an additional scientific step before the autopsy, and snapping a new blade into the scalpel I make the Y incision, running down the length of torso, detouring around the navel. I reflect back tissue but don't remove the breastplate of ribs just yet. I find the bifurcation of the aorta in front of the sacroiliac joints at the pelvic brim. Using angio-catheters, I cannulate the left external iliac artery and begin pumping in large syringes of pink embalming fluid laced with a non-ionic contrast agent that will light up neon white on CT.

It fills out arteries and veins, and they expand visibly beneath the surface of the skin as if Gail Shipton's blood is circulating again. She almost looks alive and yet my station in the autopsy room smells like a funeral home.

'Let's get her back into the scanner.' I take off my gloves and face shield. 'We'll see if something was going on with her vascular structures. Let's see if she went into cardiac arrest before he had the chance to murder her.'

'What are you thinking killed her exactly?' Lucy asks.

'This likely is going to be a diagnosis of exclusion,' I reply. 'Determining what didn't kill her might help us figure out what did. I know, for example, that at some point her blood pressure went through the roof, causing petechial hemorrhages in the conjunctiva of her eyes.'

I detach the autopsy table from the sink and release the brakes on the swivel caster wheels.

'I'm entertaining the possibility that she died of cardiac arrest while being shocked with a stun gun,' I explain, 'or perhaps while he was attempting to smother her with something that left fibers in her nose and mouth. She may have been struggling to breathe but I don't think she struggled long, not as long as it usually would take to smother someone, especially if the killer does it slowly, sadistically, enjoys drawing it out.'

'Like he waits until they pass out, then loosens the cloth so they can breathe, and does it over and over again,' Anne suggests.

'Possibly, but not with Gail. Not with a pneumothorax. Did she ever complain to you about chest pain, about any cardiac problems?' I ask Lucy.

'Not specifically. I know she complained of being really stressed. As I mentioned, sometimes she said she felt short of breath. She sighed a lot, was tired a lot, but that could have been from anxiety, and she didn't exercise. The most she'd do was walk on a treadmill.' She stares at Gail Shipton's face, her own a hard mask that gets more rigid with each minute that passes.

'Are you hanging in there?' I ask her.

'What do you expect?'

'You don't have to be here.'

'Yes I do. It doesn't bother me the way you think it would.'

We wheel Gail Shipton across the autopsy room.

'She did this to herself,' Lucy says. 'That's what bothers me.'

'She didn't do it,' I reply. 'Someone else did.'

'I'm not blaming her for what he did. But I'm blaming her for what she set into motion.'

'Let's not blame her,' I say to my niece. 'No one ever deserves to be murdered, I don't give a damn what they do.'

Back inside large-scale x-ray, we cover the scanner's table with clean sheets and position the body on its back. I push more embalming fluid through the iliac artery and Anne presses a button and the table slides in with a quiet hum. She angles the gantry, pressing a red button to landmark where the laser lines intersect at the head.

'We'll start the scan at the carina, the lowest tracheal cartilage, and scan to the top of the orbit,' I instruct.

We retreat to Anne's console behind glass and turn on the bright red *X-Ray in Use* warning sign and shut the door. The level of radiation in that room is safe only if you're dead.

'Virtual 3-D volume rendering from inside out,' I decide. 'Thin, thin cuts, one-millimeter, with an increment between them. What do you think?'

'Point-seventy-five by point-five will do.' Anne uses her computer to turn on the scanner.

It begins to pulse. *Buzz-buzz-bloop-bloop* — warming up. We hear the sounds of the x-ray tube rotating, and she selects *Chest* on the menu, opening a box on the area of interest, which is the structures of the heart. That's what we'll start with. I want to know if Gail Shipton suffered from some vascular defect that might have made her vulnerable to a sudden death that, as Benton suggests, cheated the Capital Murderer.

When he shot her with a stun gun did she go into an arrhythmia and die before he could suffocate her? Did her heart quit while she was struggling violently to breathe and he didn't get to finish torturing her? I have a suspicion that the pinpoint hemorrhages in the conjunctiva of her eyes might be related to a blood flow constriction, possibly a problem with one or more of her valves. The Washington, D.C., victims had a light scattering of petechiae across the cheeks and eyelids but Gail Shipton's ruptured capillary vessels are profoundly florid.

What happened to you?

'If you follow the contrast agent through her vessels,' I explain to Lucy, 'you can see the structures in exquisite detail, nice and bright like well-lit roads. And here's the problem. Right here.' I point at the computer display. 'In real time we're seeing a defect she likely had no idea about.'

'Wow, that's too bad.' Anne moves the cursor, opening a new box and grabbing the image. 'It's always scary to think what might be inside us just waiting to ruin our day.'

I show Lucy the narrowing of a coronary artery that caused an insufficient blood flow to the heart.

'Aortic valvular stenosis, which has caused thickening of the muscle wall of the left pumping chamber,' I note. 'Possibly this is a congenital condition or maybe as a child she suffered a bacterial infection that caused inflammation and scarring. Strep throat, for example, that turned into rheumatic fever.' I recall what Bryce said about Gail Shipton's teeth. 'That might be why she had enamel malformation, if she was on an antibiotic such as tetracycline.'

'What would this valve problem do to her?' Lucy asks.

'Over time her heart would have continued to lose its ability to efficiently pump blood, eventually reaching a point when the muscle would no longer expand.'

'Meaning she was a candidate for heart failure. In other words, she wasn't looking at a healthy long life,' Lucy says as if that's what she wants to believe.

'Who knows what anybody has to look forward to?' Anne says. 'Remember Jim Fixx, the running guru? He goes out for his daily jog and drops dead of a heart attack. Rich people on the golf course get struck by lightning. Patsy Cline went down in a plane crash. Elvis died on the toilet and that sure as hell wasn't what he had in mind when he got up that morning at Graceland.'

'She would have had fatigue, shortness of breath, heart palpitations. She might have felt faint during exertion, which is consistent with what you've described to me,' I say to Lucy as I study the scan. 'She may have had swollen ankles and feet.'

'Sometimes she complained about her shoes being tight.' Lucy sounds more entranced than somber or sad. 'She liked slip-ons, sandals.'

I envision the green faux-crocodile leather flat Marino found behind the Psi Bar.

'Sounds like she was already decompensating. Did she have routine physicals?' I ask.

'I don't know except she hated doctors.'

'Her heart had to pump harder than it should have,' I continue to explain.

'She hated people, really,' Lucy says. 'She was introverted and antisocial and I should have known better when she tried to pick us up.'

'Pick you up?' Anne turns in her chair, her mouth agape. 'She tried to pick you and Janet up in a bar? Well, that's living dangerously.'

'At the Psi one night last spring,' she says and

I recall that in the spring I didn't yet know Janet was back in Lucy's life.

I don't like to be reminded of what my niece doesn't tell me. By now I should be callous to her secrets and deceptions or at least no longer give that part of her nature a second thought. Why should I care in the least when so much of what she withholds I'm better off not knowing? I've asked myself that for the better part of thirty years, since Lucy was an enfant terrible getting into my computer, my desk, my personal life, into every facet of my being. She knew Gail Shipton and isn't bothered to see her dead, to see her internal organs, to smell death and feel how cold it is.

'She sent drinks over. Then she pulled out a chair at our table and we started talking. Initially I thought there was something off about her, but around MIT?' Lucy shrugs. 'People are a little different. That night was the friendliest I ever saw her for a reason. It was an act.'

'The act of someone who was a walking heart attack,' Anne says. 'If you think of the valves as doors, hers didn't open and close properly. It's hard to imagine she didn't feel a fluttering in her chest or maybe angina.'

'She would have just thought it was stress,' Lucy says. 'Which is part of Carin's case against Double S. The stress of what they did to Gail was affecting her health, causing shortness of breath, tightness of the chest, acute anxiety that was crippling her ability to work.'

'If you're going to make a case about it, then why not get a physical?' Anne asks.

'Gail didn't want it disproven. She didn't want a clean bill of health.'

'The irony is she wouldn't have gotten one. See the narrowing of the mitral valve?' I point it out on the scan. 'It may also have been leaky.'

'You get what you get when you pick your victim,' Anne remarks. 'Acute physical distress and she probably died on the f'ing bastard.'

'We know she died on him one way or other.' Lucy stares at the 3-D image of Gail Shipton's damaged heart as if it's a metaphor for who she really was. 'Flawed,' she adds. 'Too damn bad you can't see it in everyone,' she says with a trace of frost.

'Her cause of death is going to be cardiac arrest due to valvular stenosis with contributing factors of a left pneumothorax and acute physical distress due to being shot by a stun gun,' I conclude.

'A homicide by heart disease,' Anne says cynically. 'Defense attorneys will have a field day with that one. They'll say she was ripped off by Double S and died of a broken heart,' she adds as the door suddenly flies open.

Bryce rushes into the room like a turbulent wind, a call sheet in hand that's filled with his carefully formed, copious script.

'Holy shit, holy shit, holy shit!' he exclaims as he hands the sheet of paper to me, what I can tell at a glance is information about a case just called in by Marino. 'They've had a horrible massacre in Concord!'

342

32

The V-10 sound of Lucy's SUV is a cross between a Humvee and a Ferrari, a chugging and growling with an underlying two-beat rhythm of thick rubber tread on asphalt, a combination of thrumming and clop-clopping. The massive wheels seem to float over the roughest pavement as if my cognac leather seat is a cloud.

My niece calls her latest acquisition a land crusher with air suspension and I accepted her offer of transportation, having no intention of riding with Rusty and Harold in the large-capacity removal vehicle we refer to as a bread truck. I won't be ready for them for quite a while and I also wasn't about to stop somewhere to gas up whatever Bryce found for me in the lot. My docs are overwhelmed with autopsies stacked up and more on the way and I didn't want to bring one of them to the scene or borrow Anne. Lucy can help me and Marino will be there.

I feel better inside an armored vehicle that brings to mind Darth Vader or Middle Eastern potentates who have galactic wars and bombs and bullets to worry about. I'm relieved to be in Lucy's SUV. I'm relieved to be with her. The information Marino relayed to me over the phone as we were pulling out of the bay is scant. But it's ghastly, almost unbelievably so. The 911 call this morning about an active shooter wasn't completely wrong in its implications that a

343

madman in Concord may have just gone on a killing spree.

But the suspicious person seen running through Minute Man Park late this morning wasn't there to spray bullets at schoolchildren on an outing. It's unlikely he knew the children would be there when he fled through acres of forest separating the Revolutionary War battleground from the rolling pastureland, outbuildings and main office and house of Double S, a horse farm and financial firm where at least three people are dead in what Marino described to me as a 'Jack the Ripper bloodbath.'

The victims didn't know what hit them, Marino said, their throats cut while they were getting something to eat or sitting in their chairs. The suspect, who witnesses describe as a young male dressed in jeans and a dark hoodie with an Andy Warhol-like image of Marilyn Monroe on it, burst out of the woods and flew over a wooden footbridge. He leapt through a swarm of fourth graders on a path 'scattering them like bowling pins,' in Marino's words. The man raced across Liberty Street and into a public parking lot thick with cars.

There was so much panic and confusion, no one seemed to know what happened to him after backfires that sounded like gunshots, with children and teachers grabbing one another and running and diving to the ground. When police units and SWAT showed up the man wasn't to be found. No one recalled a vehicle speeding away or even noticing one shortly after the incident. The Medflight helicopter was turned

344

around and the police probably would have assumed the entire incident was a false alarm were it not for one important detail.

Concord detectives searching the park in the area where the man had been spotted discovered a thick envelope with blood on it and the printed return address of Double S Financial Management. Inside it was ten thousand dollars in hundred-dollar bills. The envelope was below the footbridge the man had sprinted across and it's conjectured he was startled by the crowd of children and teachers blocking the path and in his alarmed confusion dropped what Marino calls getaway cash.

'Three people so far died for ten measly grand, a little over three thousand bucks per, a cheap price for your life but I've seen cheaper,' Marino said to me over the phone. 'A hoodie with Marilyn Monroe on it and, bingo, Haley Swanson, who's vanished into thin air, and now he's been spotted and we know what he is. Jesus, it's just a damn good thing I was at your house when he was spying behind your wall. Imagine? He kills Gail Shipton and then comes back for more, stalking you, about to grab you from your damn yard. He would have seen me and Quincy getting out of my car.'

Marino wants to believe he's saved me, and I don't argue. It doesn't matter.

'He wouldn't have had a way to know I was going to show up as opposed to you driving yourself to the scene,' he said, 'so that screwed it up for him.'

I didn't tell him it doesn't feel right. Marino

has his mind made up and he wasn't going to listen. But I don't believe the person I saw early this morning intended to harm me while I was outside with my dog. I don't know what he wanted but he'd had plenty of opportunities during the days and nights I was home alone sick with the flu. And as I think of my feverish dreams and the hooded man in them I wonder if I was having moments of clairvoyance. I was under intense scrutiny. I was obsessively on the mind of a stranger and a part of me knew it.

For sure I'd had the sensation of being watched when I was taking Sock out into the backyard after dark. And if it's true that Haley Swanson was stalking me or casing my house because he wanted to rob me or worse, why didn't he? Possibly because he saw I had a gun, I suppose. But I don't think that's it either. It may be what Lucy has suggested, that the Capital Murderer had gotten interested in me because of what's been all over the news, and, yes, one thing could lead to another. Sexual violence begins with fantasy, and what a demented killer might imagine would be fueled by what he sees.

I envision the footprints along the railroad tracks, leading into the MIT campus while it was still raining and away from campus some time later. Our house is barely two miles from where Gail Shipton's body was left and if her killer is even mildly well informed, he would have known there was a good chance I would respond to the scene. He may have been watching. He may have been behind the wall, observing lights go on inside my house, and he may have seen Marino pull up, and then he would have seen me taking Sock out.

I felt the presence of what very well may be the killer. I heard him back there, and then I saw him and he ran. Fleet of foot, with running gloves on, he returned to MIT to watch the rest of it. My arrival, the helicopter landing, his spectacle being worked, and as Benton has suggested, the killer left a final time before dawn along the train tracks to retrieve his car.

'The simplest of motives, the oldest on the planet. Money,' Marino said to me moments ago. 'We know who it is and he's probably not gotten far, maybe is hiding out on someone's farm in a shed or a barn, and we're calling out cops from area departments and will do door-to-door searches until we find him.'

When he said *we* he meant NEMLEC.

'Haley Swanson robbed Double S and something got out of hand and he killed everyone,' Marino said and I know damn well that's not the whole story or even part of it, maybe not any of it.

This isn't a robbery gone as badly as one could. I'm convinced the police are wrong about what they suspect very early into an investigation that will be taken over by the FBI if it hasn't been already. Minute Man is a national park and therefore the jurisdiction of the Feds, who will use that one location as justification for horning in, and it's hard for me to imagine that Benton isn't mobilizing. He won't wait for an invitation by Concord PD or Marino and NEMLEC or anyone including his boss, who won't want

Benton around, but that won't stop him. Gail Shipton was suing Double S and she's dead and now people at Double S are dead. Benton will be thinking about the Capital Murderer while what I continue to see is the hologram of an octopus on plastic bags over the heads of those women in D.C.

I envision powerful tentacles shimmering in rainbow hues, a sea creature known as a bottom dweller, with rubbery flexibility and grace, and a master of camouflage, squeezing into impossible spaces, four pairs of arms leading to an intelligent beaked head. The invertebrate has been used as a symbol for evil empires that abuse power and take over. Fascist governments, conspiracists, imperialists, Wall Street. Dr. Seuss depicted the Nazis as an octopus.

The metaphor may be a coincidence or maybe it's not. The killer may view himself as a far-reaching superhuman with a stranglehold on whatever he decides to dominate, but I'm seeing him as something far more banal and poorly designed, like multiple devices hooked up to a single electrical source that leads to an overload, to sparks, to fire and an explosion.

An octopus connection, a dangerous way to plug too many cords into one outlet, and a circuit blows, which is what I think has happened. I feel the rage and arrogance of someone silent and swift as I'm reminded of the railroad tracks and the killer who fled along them in running gloves, leaping from tie to tie in the slippery dark, a Nijinsky from hell who's a prima donna but not necessarily as masterfully

348

balanced as he believes, not emotionally, not mentally.

'Supposedly the suspect showed up at the office building,' I continue relaying to Lucy what Marino summarized for me. 'It's believed the door was unlocked and he slipped in and killed the first three people he saw.'

'Who are they?' Lucy asks as we follow Massachusetts Avenue, a Christian Science church on one side, the dark brick buildings of Harvard Law School on the other.

I'm noticing a lot of police cars.

'So far they're unidentified.' I check my e-mail for emergency-response-system alerts.

'If they're Double S employees, how can we not have names?'

'Marino says the bodies don't have any form of identification on them, that apparently the killer stole their wallets. The police may have an idea but nothing's verified.'

'But other people work there.' Lucy says it as if she knows and she would.

She's a witness in the lawsuit against Double S. She's been deposed and as recently as this past Sunday spent hours going over the case with Gail Shipton and Carin Hegel. Lucy has a grasp of the details. She probably knows more about Double S than most. She would make sure of it.

'Three people is what I've been told unless there are other bodies they've not found yet,' I reply. 'And Public Safety's alerting area police departments and schools that there's a man-hunt.'

'Great,' Lucy says. 'Everyone will think it's a

damn terrorist attack.'

'At least three dead in what appear to be planned executions,' I read what's been publicized so far.

'Where the hell did that come from? Who's handing out press releases? Let me guess.'

'Harvard, MIT, BU, and all grad schools are shutting down. Essential personnel only at McLean Hospital.' I scan through alerts landing in my e-mail. 'The FBI — '

'Here we go,' Lucy cuts me off in disgust. 'They're not wasting any time, meaning pretty soon they'll be crawling all over everything.'

'Special Agent in Charge of the Boston Division, Ed Granby — '

'More of his propaganda,' Lucy interrupts.

'He's asking the public for information about the young male seen fleeing Minute Man Park and to review any photos or video anyone might have taken,' I relate.

'Good luck. Concord people aren't exactly into community policing unless you're driving your ATV over wetlands or stepping on protected plantings.' She makes a typical acerbic snipe about where she lives.

'The victims are a man and two women. That's all Marino had,' I add. 'We're going to have to dig into whatever information Carin Hegel's got. Her client Gail Shipton's dead and now people from the firm she was suing are dead.'

'Carin's not going to have anything that will help,' Lucy says.

We roar through Porter Square, its shopping

center off to our right, and then the post office, churches, and a funeral home.

'She was working a straightforward case that's anything but,' Lucy adds.

More police cars pass us with no flashing lights or sirens. Cambridge, Somerville, Quincy. NEMLEC, I think.

'If she wasn't scared before, now she's got to be,' Lucy says.

I mention I ran into Hegel at Boston's federal courthouse last month. She told me she was sequestered in an undisclosed location until the trial was over and she referred to Double S as a gang of thugs.

'Do you know where she is?' I catch a glint of a smile playing across Lucy's face as if what I've been saying is somehow amusing.

Maybe it's shifts of light in an afternoon that's turned volatile, gray clouds, churning and flat on top like anvils, far off over the ocean and outer harbor. It's stopped raining along the South Shore and South Boston and I look up at the clouds closest to us, the wind continuing to shift around crazily like a compass in a store selling magnets. Building storm cells are ragged underneath, trailing down like ripped gauze, more heavy rains coming. Thank God the scene we're headed to is indoors.

'Is it possible she's in danger?' I push my point.

'Her case isn't safe but she is,' Lucy says and it occurs to me where Carin Hegel may be staying.

'She's at your place.'

'She's safe,' Lucy repeats with the same grim

351

smile playing on her lips, her face in profile, angular and strong, her short rose-gold hair tucked behind her ears. 'She's at the house with Janet. If anybody unwelcome shows up, you'll be even busier than you are.'

Lucy is openly in touch with the part of her that can kill and has before. It's not even a deep or unhappy place for her or difficult to reach, and at times I envy her being comfortable with who she is. I follow the firm shape of her right leg down to her booted foot on the accelerator, looking for an ankle holster and not seeing one. She wears a black flight jacket over her black flight suit, lots of pockets for whatever she needs. I have no doubt she's armed.

★   ★   ★

In North Cambridge now traffic is typically heavy, eighteen-wheelers and buses in the opposite lane headed toward Boston, where the sky is misty and overcast but not ominous like it is to the west. Directly overhead building white clouds are carried along by patchy gray ones, and where blue shows through it's glaring, the light strange, the way it gets before violent thunderstorms and hurricanes, what I remember from growing up in Miami.

Nobody gives Lucy's handcrafted, military-looking SUV a thumbs-up or the finger. They stare at it with an expression that is a mixture of fascinated and puzzled, awed and baffled. Nobody tailgates or tries to cut in front of her. Only oblivious people texting or talking on their phones come anywhere near the big black machine that growls like a jungle cat on paws as huge as a dinosaur's. She's careful not to speed. Given an excuse, cops would pull her over because they're curious.

'The door wouldn't have been unlocked.' Lucy states this as if there can be no disputing it. 'Every exterior door on the property has dead bolt locks and the front door of the office building has a biometric one for fingerprint scans like we have at the CFC. Some stranger didn't just walk in and kill people at their desks.'

I consider whether I should ask how she knows about the locks at Double S. As usual, I have to weigh my options. They're always the same. Is my need to know greater than the conflict it could create if Lucy has done something she shouldn't?

'We'll see what it looks like when we get there' is what I say.

'Someone let him in. Someone opened the door for him and, if so, it means nobody at Double S was worried about whoever it is.'

'Maybe it's someone who works there,' I suggest.

'That doesn't fit with a young guy in a hoodie running through a park with an envelope of cash. It's not a regular member of the staff and the description isn't right. Nobody who works at Double S is under the age of forty. Did Marino mention that? Is anybody unaccounted for?'

'He said the partners are out of town for the holidays.'

'There are four. Accountants, investors,

lawyers, thieves one and all,' Lucy says. 'And they don't exactly keep regular hours and are hardly ever here. It wouldn't be unusual if they're out of town in Grand Cayman, the Virgin Islands, greased up like pigs in the sun, spending their hard-earned money,' she adds as if she despises them.

'Marino didn't mention anybody missing. And running through a public park with an envelope of cash strikes me as desperate. It strikes me as panicked and unplanned.'

'Ten grand in hundred-dollar bills feels like a payment of some sort.' Lucy tries to figure out the problem of where the money came from and what it was for. 'A circumscribed amount that was intended for some purpose.'

On Alewife Brook Parkway we curve through hardwood trees that this time of year are bare. An empty bike path cuts starkly through them like a scar.

'They have an alarm system and cameras everywhere,' Lucy then says. 'They could see anybody on the grounds on monitors, tablets, smartphones, whatever was handy. He didn't worry anyone and that's why he was able to pull it off. But there's not going to be a recording of what the cameras picked up.'

'Why do you say that?'

'They'd already know who it is if the DVR recorded it and is still on-site and I'm betting it's not. Multiple cameras, an IP based surveillance system, and it's worthless if there's no recording. Whoever we're talking about may be desperate or deranged at this point but he isn't stupid.'

'Have you been there?' I go ahead and ask.

'I've never been invited.'

'If you've done anything that can be traced,' I say to her, 'now might be a good time to think about it. You don't want to become an issue if there are security camera recordings and you're on them. Especially with the FBI involved.' I think of Granby and wonder what else this day holds.

What has been unleashed around here and how much of it is his fault even indirectly? He'll show up at some point and I'd better think fast about appropriating what evidence is mine and making sure he can't touch it.

'I wouldn't be on any recordings,' Lucy says. 'And if the DVR hasn't been removed, it would be me looking at it unless the Feebs get there first.' Her snide slang for the FBI that ran her off the job when she was in her twenties, for all practical purposes firing her.

'Good God, Lucy. It's not a phone you can scrub.'

'The phone is mine. It's a different situation.'

Her ethics again, I think.

'There's nothing to worry about,' she says. 'But when you look at the way Double S has set things up it will tell you quite a lot about them, a consciousness of dishonesty, of big crime, of huge business where hardly anybody works regular hours, if at all, because their commerce isn't on the surface. The rumors aren't new but it's never been proven. The FBI has dropped the ball repeatedly over the years and I wonder why. Now that people are dead, you wait and see what comes out. And not just about the victims.'

'Who else, then?'

'I feel sorry for Carin,' Lucy says. 'It's not her fault but she'll have some explaining to do.'

'I don't want you implicated in anything.' I look at her.

'I'm not the one who will be implicated and all I've done is do a high recon or two. The same thing I'd do from the air.' She doesn't sound the least bit concerned but determined.

'Did you do a flyover?'

'It wouldn't have been helpful and it would have been too obvious. My helicopter isn't exactly quiet,' she says. 'What I can tell you is if you show up uninvited you'll never get past the main barn with its perimeter of cameras, supposedly to safeguard extremely valuable Churchill Thoroughbreds with racing pedigrees. The killer didn't sneak in. And with the people who do keep regular hours at Double S? The housekeeper, ranch hands, a groundskeeper, the full-time chef? Somebody knows damn well who it is and isn't saying anything.'

'Marino thinks it's Gail's friend Haley Swanson, a close friend apparently.'

'The person who posted information about her on Channel Five's website. I got an alert and saw the name but I don't know who Haley Swanson is and I'm not aware of Gail having any close friends.' Lucy scans her mirrors, cutting in and out of lanes skillfully, effortlessly, the way she walks along a sidewalk, always in front and aware of what's around her.

'It seems to me Gail didn't tell you

everything,' I reply pointedly.

'She didn't have to and I don't know everything. But I know plenty.'

'He works for the PR firm Lambant and Associates. Maybe Haley Swanson was doing crisis management for Gail.'

'Why would she need that? She wasn't a public figure and had no public business or even a reputation to lose. Although she was about to,' Lucy adds.

'She was at the Psi Bar last night,' I reply. 'Who might she have been with?'

'She didn't say when I talked to her. I didn't ask because I didn't care. If she was with this PR person, she wouldn't have mentioned it anyway, not if she felt it was something she needed to hide, like most everything about her conniving, dishonest life. People are stupid thinking you'll never find out. I don't know why people are so fucking stupid,' she says and I can't tell if she's more angry or hurt or if she feels embarrassed that Gail might have fooled her about anything at all.

'I'm calling Swanson a he because that's what's on his driver's license, although there seems to be some question about his gender. An officer who confronted him early this morning described him as having breasts.'

'If Gail knew him, she didn't mention it to me for good reason. Maybe this Swanson person is someone she met through a mutual acquaintance,' Lucy adds and it seems an allusion to something else, something unpleasant and bad.

'He also called nine-one-one to say Gail was

missing and when he was told he'd have to come to the department to fill out the report he posted the information on Channel Five's website instead. Then he called the police again and asked to speak to Marino,' I let her know as the first drops of rain begin to fall. 'All of these actions might make sense if Haley Swanson was with Gail in the bar and she went outside to take your call and never came back.'

'Lambant and Associates may have been doing PR for someone else and that's how they met.' Lucy seems to be working it out in her head more than anything else.

I continue to be struck by how dead the relationship is to her. It's as dead as Gail Shipton and that's the dark art of Lucy's emotional sleight of hand. She can love one minute and feel nothing the next, not even anger or pain, because after a while those, too, will pass and what she's left with is what I called her *magic friendship hat* when she was a little girl who spent most of her time alone. *Where's so and so?* I would ask and she'd shrug and reach into her imagined hat and come up empty-handed. *Poof,* she'd say and then she'd cry and then it would go away, as far away as her mother who has never loved her.

33

Distant thunder rolls in waves of reverberating drumming and a slow starting rain hits the windshield in drops the size of quarters. I tell Lucy that someone may have been spying on me since I came home from Connecticut.

'He was behind the house at around five-thirty this morning when I took Sock out,' I explain. 'It's believed it might have been Haley Swanson.'

'Believed by who?'

'The police. Marino certainly is convinced.'

'Why?'

'Where Swanson's SUV was spotted and the early hour certainly makes it appear it could have been him,' I reply. 'The officer who talked to him believes it was.'

'Did Swanson admit to it when he was questioned? Did he say he knows who you or Benton are and was near your property at five-thirty this morning?'

'No. But I don't think he was asked that directly and one might expect him not to admit it if he was stalking me or casing our property. Especially if this is someone who has a lot to hide.'

'You mean if he's the Capital Murderer.'

'I have no real basis to know any such thing but I don't believe it.'

'What about the description of the hooded sweatshirt with a face on it, what supposedly looks like Warhol's Marilyn Monroe?' Lucy asks.

'I didn't notice the person had on something like that. He also was bareheaded but it could be he didn't have his hood up.'

'Was it raining?'

'My impression was he wasn't dressed for the weather or at least wasn't wearing rain gear.'

'Somebody revved up and overheated, excited and in overdrive. He might not have cared that it was raining and he probably wasn't Haley Swanson,' Lucy says.

'When he was questioned by the police he didn't look like he'd been out in the rain. It probably wasn't him behind the wall but I don't think the person intended to hurt me.'

'Not yet and that's always your default,' Lucy says. 'You don't want to think that what you do might draw dangerous people to you.'

'He'd had opportunity if that's what he wanted.'

'It's more likely he wasn't ready and you had your Sig, let me guess.'

'All he had to do was shoot me with a stun gun if that's who we're talking about. It wouldn't have mattered if I had a gun. I would have been on the ground.'

'You don't know who it was,' Lucy says flatly. 'Just because Haley Swanson was in your neighborhood doesn't mean it was him and it probably wasn't. And just because Marino's decided Swanson is the man spotted running through Minute Man Park doesn't mean anything either. I'm not jumping to conclusions.'

'None of us should.'

'Marino's basing it on a sweatshirt, deciding

Swanson's the killer because of a hoodie.'

'That's not the only reason but we need to be careful,' I reply.

'Do you have any idea where Swanson lives?'

'Near Conway Park. Apparently he'd stopped at the Dunkin' Donuts on Somerville Ave first,' I repeat what Officer Rooney said.

'If he left the Dunkin' Donuts and headed to the projects on Windsor it would make sense for him to have passed right behind the Academy of Arts and Sciences and within blocks of your house. He probably was taking Park to Beacon.'

'And I assume his name hasn't come up in case discussions with Carin Hegel.'

'No, but I'm not surprised. If I've never heard of him, she probably hasn't either.'

'When he called nine-one-one he asked to speak to Marino. I've assumed Gail might have mentioned him because you might have mentioned him,' I add what I know she won't like to hear.

'I never talked about Marino with her' is her emphatic answer and then I remember Benton's remarks to him this morning at MIT.

He infuriated Marino by reminding him that his pickup truck with the design flaw cost him a lot of money after a failed class action suit. Lambant and Associates represented the dealership and spun stories that blamed the owners for being bad drivers and causing the damage. This was all very recent and it's possible Haley Swanson might have known who and what Marino is because of that. I suggest the scenario to Lucy.

'What it doesn't explain,' I add, 'is why Haley Swanson would call nine-one-one and think to ask for him specifically.'

'If he was desperate it would explain it,' Lucy says. 'If he talked to a nine-one-one operator and got nowhere? Next he calls back and asks for a detective by name.'

'Did you ever discuss Marino with Carin Hegel?'

'I didn't discuss him or any of us but it's not exactly a secret where I work and who my friends and family are,' Lucy says. 'All of us are law enforcement or former law enforcement or criminal justice, and Gail sure as hell had reason to be aware that I'm surrounded by people she needed to worry about. She'd wandered into a really bad airspace and she's probably better off dead. She had nothing to look forward to except what I was going to have to do about it and it's a shame she put me in that position. But she did.'

I look at her and she seems unbothered and sure of herself and her convictions as she drives with one hand on the wheel, the other on the four-wheel-drive gearshift, resting on it, her fingers curled around the carbon-fiber knob inside her carbon-fiber cockpit with instruments and joysticks worthy of an aircraft.

'What was it you felt you were going to have to do exactly?' I inquire.

'I was about to tell Carin the truth.' Wipers sweep the glass and more thunder sounds in a guttural rumble that ends with a sharp crack. 'She would have fired Gail as a client but that wasn't good enough.'

'After what you've told me, I don't blame you for being angry.'

'I was building a case and needed to prove it and I waited because nothing was enough,' Lucy says. 'I was stupid. That's why you can't hate anyone. That's why even when I feel it I put a stop to it. I try really hard to put a stop to it but I didn't with her and that was a mistake. Hate makes you stupid.'

★   ★   ★

Wind blows across the surface of a gray body of water beyond Lucy's window. On my side are rows of small houses that bring to mind Monopoly's Baltic Avenue or regimented developments I associate with military bases.

'The two of you met her at the Psi, had a few drinks, and, next thing, you're working on a project together,' I point out. 'You may not have heard of Gail Shipton some eight months ago but maybe she'd heard of you. Maybe she was aware the Psi is a place you frequent.'

'I probably shouldn't frequent any place. It's not smart.'

'Maybe it wasn't chance she sent drinks to your table last spring.'

'It wasn't chance but it didn't turn into what it became until later,' Lucy says. 'She was running out of what money she had left and then by summer Double S was doing everything it could to escalate her legal fees. She was going under and was too proud to tell anyone. But Double S knew. They knew exactly how much money she had left and how quickly they could go through it. Then they had her where they wanted her.'

I feel the deep rumbling thunder and smell rain in the fresh moist air blowing through the open vents. Lucy doesn't like recirculating air and she doesn't like being hot and I smell expensive new leather and the clean grapefruit scent of the cologne she wears, the same cologne I bought her for Christmas and have yet to wrap.

'Who was there when you were deposed?' I ask. 'Did you meet anyone from Double S?'

'Just their dirtbag lawyers.'

Light shimmers in rolling clouds and shines on wet pavement, the eerie light of storms, and I ask nothing more. The rain's not as heavy as we drive farther west and the view opens up to a huge spread of shallow water, sandbars, and conservation land.

'What about Gail?' I ask. 'Where was she when you were being deposed?'

'She was sitting at the table the entire time.'

'What was her demeanor?' My suspicions are gathering.

'Something I didn't trust,' Lucy says and she should have distrusted her sooner but I don't say it. 'She wasn't a good actor. She wasn't a good anything anymore.'

As we get closer to Concord, woods are interspersed with clearings, pastureland and dormant plowed fields that look like faded corduroy. Homes and barns are tucked back from the turnpike in this old-moneyed part of the world where people keep a few chickens or goats or designate land for preservation to get another tax write-off. Peace and conservation foundations and famous cemeteries flourish and cutting down a tree is close to a felony. Single-serving bottled water has been banned because plastic is a sin and Lucy's fuel-guzzling vehicle must be appallingly offensive to her Concord neighbors. Knowing her, that might be why she got it.

In minutes we're crossing Main Street in the center of a town where Ralph Waldo Emerson and Louisa May Alcott's homes can be toured and their graves and those of Thoreau and Hawthorne can be visited. Shops and restaurants are small and quaint and at every corner there are monuments, historic markers, and battle-fields.

Through pastures and over a river we follow Lowell Road, bearing right onto Liberty Street, where we pass Minute Man National Park. I notice people out sightseeing and staff in Colonial period dress as if nothing happened earlier. They seem oblivious to unmarked cars and plainclothes law enforcement prowling the grounds. They pay no attention to a television crew. Channel 5 again. I recognize Barbara Fairbanks talking into a microphone on a wooden footbridge, maybe the one the killer raced across and into a group of children he scared and scattered.

The road we're on bends to the left and the woods get impenetrably dense, the typical forests of New England, with thick canopies and no undergrowth. In about a mile and past an open field, electric gates are frozen in the open position and SS is posted on a stone pillar with no street address. Lucy slows and turns in. She rolls her window down as we stop next to a Concord cruiser parked just inside. I retrieve my credentials from my bag, handing the thin black wallet to her as she digs into a pocket for her CFC badge.

'Cambridge Forensic Center. Lucy Farinelli. I have Dr. Scarpetta with me.' She displays our IDs and badges to the officer, who could pass for twenty. 'How are you doing?'

'You mind if I ask what you're driving?' He bends down, his admiring face in her open window.

'It's just an SUV.' She returns my creds to me.

'Yeah, right. And I'm driving the space shuttle. Care if I look?'

'Follow me up.'

'Can't do that.' The officer is equally enthralled with the SUV's driver. 'I've got to make sure nobody comes in who's not supposed to and have already turned away half a dozen reporters. It's a good thing the weather's crappy or they'd have news choppers up. My name's Ryan.'

'Have you been inside?'

'It's pretty unbelievable. I'm thinking someone crazy who escaped from MCI.' He refers to the nearby medium security men's prison. 'How fast can this thing go?'

'Tell you what, Ryan, come by when you're not busy and I'll let you test-pilot,' Lucy says as I try to get Marino on the phone.

She shoves her beast of a vehicle back into gear and we begin to follow a paved driveway that's more like a road. Ahead are acres of manicured paddocks, maintenance sheds, small barns, and the big red one Lucy mentioned. On either side of us are straight rows of peeling birch trees, a scattering of dead leaves clinging to their branches and stuck to the wet blacktop. Marino answers my call and I tell him we're two minutes out.

'Park in front and I'll meet you at the door,' he says. 'I've got your scene case. Make sure you cover up good, Doc. It looks like someone spilled a vat of borscht in here.'

34

Past outbuildings and a small natural pond, the two-story timbered headquarters is set on the highest point of immaculate grounds. It fronts paddocks and pastureland and is connected by covered walkways to the rest of a compound that's not visible from the long paved drive unless one follows it to the end where it bends around. Lucy explains the layout to me. I no longer ask her how she knows.

The steeply pitched roof is copper tarnished like an old penny and there are thick stone columns on either side of the veranda. Beveled leaded transom windows are over the heavy front door, with big windows across both floors and I imagine a clear view of rolling fields, sheds, barns, and people on the grounds if the shades aren't drawn like they are right now. I think of security cameras that would detect an uninvited guest.

It's no longer raining, as if Double S can buy its own weather, and I tilt my head back and feel the chilled moist air on my cheeks and pushing through my hair. I can see my breath just barely. The sky is turgid and dark as if it's dusk instead of almost two p.m., and I imagine what Benton is doing and what he knows. He'll be here soon. There's no way he won't be and already I'm looking for him.

I follow the rows of silvery birch trees that in

warmer months meet in a canopy over the long black driveway, my eyes moving past the quiet muddy-green pond, then the empty brown paddocks behind gray split-rail palings. Horses will be in the main barn because of the weather, an angry colliding of warm and cold fronts that could hammer down sleet or hail. Beyond the fencing and a meadow fringed in switchgrass are heavy woods that lead to the park where a fleeing man in a hoodie frightened children and teachers hours earlier. I estimate it's not even a mile as a crow flies. Already I suspect that Double S's intruder wasn't one.

A half dozen Concord police cruisers and unmarked cars are parked on a spacious tarmac and I notice an expensive white Lincoln Navigator and a white Land Rover that I suspect belong to Double S. Marino's SUV has the windows cracked, his rowdy German shepherd crated in back whining and pawing frantically like a jailbreak because he knows it's us.

'Marino lets him sleep in his bed, too,' Lucy says. 'The dog's totally worthless.'

'Not to him,' I reply. 'And you're one to talk. You and Janet cook fresh fish for Jet Ranger and dehydrate vegetables for his treats, the most spoiled bulldog on the planet.'

'We won't get into who spoils her dog.'

We walk around to the tailgate of Lucy's SUV, backed in close to a glass and stone sunporch that's detached from the main building and set alone in the midst of evergreens like a palaver hut. Through its open blinds I see modern leather furniture, a sofa and two side chairs, and a slate table with magazines loosely stacked. There are two coffee mugs and one small plate with three or four brown cupcake liners and a crumpled blue paper napkin on top. I notice what look like chocolate crumbs on the table near the plate and it doesn't appear the other person drinking coffee was eating. The housekeeper didn't clean up after whoever it was.

Lucy continues to describe the ranch to me, telling me the detached sunporch isn't original to the property.

'The office building is red oak,' she explains, 'and this is new pine lumber painted to match it, built in the spring, coincidentally about the time the murders in Washington, D.C., began. There are cameras everywhere but not here.'

'Coincidentally?' I repeat.

I scan the roof, the entrance, the single glass-paned door leading inside the small outbuilding and see no sign of a security system. There's no alarm keypad visible inside a small space with a sitting area and what looks like a half bath.

'I'm simply pointing out the timing.' Lucy opens up the back and we collect coveralls, safety glasses, sleeve guards, and nitrile gloves with extended cuffs.

Then she checks her phone again as I pull out personal protection kits that include HEPA respirators, antimicrobial towelettes, and bio-hazard trash bags because I have no idea exactly what to expect.

'It's on Twitter.' She scrolls with her thumb. 'A massacre in Concord.'

'I hope that word didn't come from Bryce, for

God's sake.' I worry about reporters calling him and he blurts out to them what he did to me.

'I suspect he came up with the word because he got it from the Internet. Let's see, rumors and misinformation posted as news feeds.' Lucy continues to scroll. 'It's all over and has been for the better part of an hour, *USA Today*, *Piers Morgan*, Reuters, and everybody and their brother retweeting. Multiple fatalities at international financial company, at least three homicides, possibly robbery related. Now, I wonder who released that. Well, it gets worse. FBI denies link to MIT death from earlier today, Gail Shipton, who was suing Double S. No evidence there's any connection, Boston Division Chief Ed Granby states, and hello? Who's suggested a connection? 'At this point her cause of death is unknown and hasn't been ruled a homicide,' Granby says.'

'I don't know what it is he thinks he can deny since he knows nothing about her case,' I reply as my bad feeling returns like a muscle spasm. 'Benton wouldn't have passed on something he shouldn't when he knows I've not officially released anything about Gail Shipton and won't until certain test results are in.'

'It's not Benton,' Lucy says. 'It's his douchebag boss who's scripting what he wants people to think.'

CODIS has been tampered with and Granby threatened the chief medical examiner of Maryland and now he's manipulating the media about my cases here. I feel a flare of anger and a growing sense of alarm.

'He's basically speaking for you and our office. So why do you think that is?' She looks at me and I know what she overheard in the bay when I was talking to Dr. Venter, and Benton has given her information, too.

We lean against the bumper to pull on latex boot covers with a heavy-duty tread, what I prefer when a scene is extremely bloody.

'To manipulate,' Lucy then says. 'It's got to do with the DNA screwup, doesn't it?'

'I'm afraid it may be more than a screwup.'

'Granby's got a special interest. Maybe he's protecting people with money so he can make sure he doesn't sail off into the sunset with nothing but a government pension.'

'Be very careful what you say, Lucy.'

'He came up with Martin Lagos for a reason,' she says. 'If you're going to tamper with DNA and need a profile to swap, why this kid who disappeared seventeen years ago? Why would Granby think of him?'

'We don't know for a fact who thought of him.'

'Saying it was Granby, why would he? Let me answer for you. He probably knows Lagos is dead, which is why he's never shown up and why I can't find him in any database. If you're going to steal someone's identity, it's helpful if that person never shows up to complain about it.'

'Granby was with the Washington field office at the time,' I reply. 'He may remember Gabriela Lagos. It was a sensational case.'

'No kidding he'd remember it. The question is, was he involved in some way? Is there a reason it would suit his purposes to make people think her missing son is the Capital Murderer?'

'What I know for a fact is something is profoundly wrong with the DNA analysis in Dr. Venter's case, Julianne Goulet. The stain on the panties she was wearing couldn't have been left by a man. Martin Lagos didn't deposit vaginal fluid and menstrual blood and what this suggests to me is someone tampered with the DNA in CODIS and didn't bother to check what the stain was comprised of or it would have been apparent the profile wasn't going to work for a male.'

'That sounds like the stupid mistake a macho FBI dick like Granby would make. You'll know for sure he's got a special interest if he shows up here. A division chief doesn't bother with a crime scene or get his hands dirty,' Lucy says. 'And he'll be here, you watch. I'm sure he considers it his turf and he needs to control it because he's got an agenda, a rotten one.'

'At the moment it's my turf.'

Lucy stares at the outbuilding with the coffee cups inside where somebody was having a private conversation before three people died.

'A handy little place to chat.' She peers through a window. 'If you want to come out here and talk about incriminating activities, criminal activities' — she moves to another window, cupping her hands around her eyes — 'there's no telephone inside to bug. And it looks like we have commercial-grade sound masking. See the small white speakers in the ceilings? They're probably in the ductwork, too. Similar systems are installed in courtrooms these days so when lawyers approach the bench no one can hear what's being said.'

She begins pointing out cameras on the roof, over the mahogany front door of the office building, and on copper lampposts along the sidewalk and the driveway.

'Weatherproof, infrared high-res that automatically switch from color to black-and-white in low light like what we've got now,' she says. 'Not wireless though. See the cables? You know what the problem with cables is? They can be cut. What's interesting though is it doesn't look like they were.'

'You'd have to know where they are to cut them,' I reply. 'You'd have to think of it first, from the moment you decide to step foot on the property.'

'He didn't,' she says as the front door opens. 'Score one point for unpremeditated.'

Then Marino fills the doorway, his foot propping open the storm door behind him. His face is stubbly and keyed-up, his big hands gloved in latex that I can see the dark hair of his wrists through.

★   ★   ★

Behind him through the space in the door he wedges open, I notice crime scene investigators in BDUs, one of them taking photographs, another working a laser-mapping station.

One woman, one man — NEMLEC, I suspect. I don't know them at a glance. A

374

number of the small neighboring jurisdictions have experts and special equipment, the training and purchases funded by grant money, but there's little violent crime. Some police in the area have never been to my headquarters.

'All ready and waiting for you, Doc.' Marino slides a pack of cigarettes from a pocket and shakes one out. "Two Concord detectives plus a crime scene guy from Watertown and me. Everybody else I ran out. It's not a spectator sport.'

'It will be,' Lucy says. 'The FBI is on its way.'

'I said no to calling them yet, not when the Doc hadn't even gotten here.' He flips open a lighter and a flame spurts up. 'They'll just make things worse right now and my main interest has been to protect the scene.'

'They don't need you to call and they don't need your permission. Granby's already making statements to the press and there may have been a couple Feebs at Minute Man Park when we drove past. They'll be closing in whether you've invited them or not.' Lucy checks to make sure her SUV is locked. 'I give it a couple hours before they're here taking over.'

'The kind of money and suspicious shit we're already seeing is going to hand this to them on a silver platter anyway.' He sucks in as much smoke as he can. 'The murders will be small potatoes to them.'

The tip of the cigarette glows bright orange as he holds it the way he always has, midway, with the lit end tucked in toward his palm. Downwind of him I pick up the acrid toasted smell of burning tobacco. It's a ritual hard for me to watch.

'I think we're talking about some really serious white-collar crime.' He flicks the filtered butt with his thumb to knock free the ash. 'And that's without seeing the half of it yet. Some areas are locked up behind steel doors like a friggin' bank vault.'

'So you've not gotten into those,' Lucy says.

'Some things I wasn't going to disturb until the Doc got here. Anything to do with the bodies we haven't touched.' He's starting to show his irritation with her, what was already there and it's rapidly breaking the surface. 'But you'll see when you get inside. The place looks like a front for something.'

'Since when are we smoking?' I ask him. 'I thought you quit for good after the last time you quit for good.'

'Don't start.'

'That's what I should be saying to you.'

'A couple drags and I put it out.' He talks as he blows smoke sideways out of his mouth.

Like the old days, I can't help but think. Smoking at a crime scene, holding a cigarette with gloves on, bloody gloves, it didn't matter back then. What I wouldn't give for a lungful of my favorite poison and if I knew I had only an hour left to live I'd light up. I'd sit on the steps with Marino and drink beer and smoke the way we did during tough times and tragedies.

'How many?' I ask him. 'You told me three. Have you found any others?'

Lucy and I step up on the stone veranda,

where I notice small rustic tables and rocking chairs, a place to relax with no evidence anybody does. The furniture is neatly arranged and glazed with rainwater and I have a feeling that private discussions don't occur at Double S unless they're behind closed doors and thick glass with sound masking. I can't shake what Lucy implied about the sun-porch being built as recently as last spring about the time the D.C. murders began, serial crimes that now involve DNA tampering and an FBI division chief who may have directed it and has threatened at least one colleague of mine.

'We're going to hang for a minute so I can fill you in. One male, two females.' The cigarette wags as Marino talks and he plucks it out, squinting as he exhales a stream of smoke. 'We were worried at first there might be more victims in other parts of the building or on other areas of the property since we haven't been able to search some of the locked-up spaces. Plus it's a huge place, with all these walkways connecting everything like spokes on a wagon wheel. Friggin' unbelievable. If you put them end to end, they're probably a mile long. And there's golf carts so a fat load like Dominic Lombardi never had to walk,' he adds and I notice he uses the past tense.

'Nobody has keys?' Lucy asks.

'Yeah, and I wasn't going to touch them until you do your thing since they're in a puddle of blood under a dead body.' He says this to me, not her. 'But based on conversations with a couple of the ranch hands, it's three fatalities total. Everybody else is accounted for except the asshole who did it.'

'And nobody saw anything,' I suppose.

'That's what they're saying. Of course it's bullshit.'

'IDs?' I notice Marino is in the same clothes he had on before dawn this morning when he showed up at my house in the pouring rain.

I can smell his excitement and stress, his musky male odor that turns rancid if he goes without sleeping or bathing and works nonstop. In another eight or twelve more hours he'll stink so strongly of sour sweat and stale cigarettes, one will pick him up at ten paces.

'Dominic Lombardi. Or Dom, as he goes by, like the champagne. I guess this will be a bad year for Dom,' Marino says. 'And hold on about the other one.'

He digs into a pocket, the latex glove resistant against the fabric, the cigarette clamped in the corner of his mouth, one eye screwed shut. He flips pages in a notepad, holds it some distance from his face because he doesn't have reading glasses on.

'I can't pronounce this worth shit. *Jadwiga Caminska*. They call her Ika. His administrative assistant. That's their expensive white SUVs here in the lot. Dom and Ika were visually identified preliminarily by the investigators from Concord PD, who you'll meet,' he says to me. 'They've been here before, this past Friday night late when Lombardi reported a possible intruder.'

'Was there one?' Lucy asks.

'Maybe.' He looks at her. 'They searched every

nook and cranny, spotted a shadow on a video recording picked up by a security camera at the main barn. Like somebody careful about the cameras because he knew what to look for and then cut the wires. Those quadrants on the video displays went black while Lombardi was at his desk at around midnight.' Marino doesn't take his eyes off her. 'He was so appreciative he promised to donate ten grand to the Concord PD Christmas fund, cash withdrawn from his bank two days ago, the withdrawal slip in his desk drawer but no sign of the money and Concord PD never got it.'

'The same amount found in the envelope under the footbridge,' Lucy says.

'You'd make a good cop.'

'Been there, done that.' Lucy stares back at him as if they're in a standoff.

'So the killer probably stole it and any other cash he could grab.'

'Sounds like a reasonable deduction.' Lucy crosses her arms staring at him, goading him into confronting her about what I suspect she did.

Marino crushes the cigarette against a stone column and sparks go out as ashes drift down. He tucks the butt in a pocket, blowing one last stream of smoke off to the side away from us. Maybe Lucy was never invited to visit Double S but that doesn't mean she's never been here.

'I guess they didn't catch the intruder,' Lucy then says and Marino glares at her.

'If you did what I think, just tell me why,' he says loudly.

'I can suggest why someone would,' she replies. 'If you want to walk around and to see what's going on, you have to take out those cameras. The ones along the driveway you can dodge but not until you've gotten past the barn unless you want to swim across the pond.'

'Two detectives show up and this intruder's still walking around?' Marino is getting louder, almost yelling at her.

'They'd be looking in the barn where all the expensive horses are. Then they'd check the locks of everything else to make sure there wasn't a problem. Then they'd call it a night.'

'Why would someone want to see what's here?' Marino's demeanor has gone from cocky and angry to incredulous.

'Maybe not to see what but who. Who he was sleeping with.'

'And was that determined?' Marino's look turns to disbelief.

'You could ask the two detectives who showed up.' Lucy gestures toward the house. 'But by the time they got here twenty-three minutes after Lombardi called nine-one-one Gail was long gone,' she says.

'Jesus Christ, it would have been nice if you'd fucking told me that earlier!' Marino's frustration erupts. 'Gail Shipton's here Friday night and now she's been murdered and you just mention it as a by the way?'

'I've known for a while she's in collusion with the enemy, probably involved in insurance fraud and who knows what else,' Lucy says. 'I've been trying to find an answer that's provable.'

'Sleeping with the guy she's suing,' Marino exclaims in disgust.

'Not because she wanted to,' Lucy says. 'She needed money.'

35

'You said there are three,' I prompt Marino because I have a job to do.

I don't have time to question Lucy further and maybe I don't want to hear another word about what Gail Shipton had gotten into and what Carin Hegel will do when she finally finds out. Her case is over anyway. Lucy's right. There isn't one. It turned into a lie, a ruse. Double S made Gail desperate for money and what could be greater leverage than to wound someone and then offer to make the person whole again. And she was weak, maybe flawed beyond repair in more ways than one. Not just her heart with its leaky valve but all of her.

'Got no idea about the third victim,' Marino tells me. 'She was in the kitchen when he attacked her, maybe opening the refrigerator or getting something out of a cupboard. You'll see when you get there.'

'The staff doesn't know who it is?' It's hard for me to believe.

'They said Lombardi picked up somebody at the commuter rail station in downtown Concord this morning. They don't know who, just that Lombardi left in his white Navigator and came back and had someone with him who obviously ended up being in the wrong place at the wrong time. That's all they know but they're probably lying.'

'Why would they lie?' Lucy asks.

'Because they're probably used to lying about everything that goes on here,' Marino says. 'Unlike the other two, she didn't go down like a shot. I'm thinking the first slice didn't get her right because she turned her head, maybe heard him coming up behind her. And then he finished her.' He makes a slashing motion with an imagined knife. 'She walked a couple steps and collapsed where her body is behind a counter.'

'Have you found a weapon?' Lucy walks the length of the veranda, looking up at cameras and out at trees.

'Nope.' The way he stares at her is different now.

'And the guy in the hoodie wasn't spotted with a weapon when he was running through the park,' she says.

'Nope. Haley Swanson wasn't noted to have a weapon. That's who we're talking about.'

'Just because he was wearing a sweatshirt with Marilyn Monroe on it? You know for a fact who it is?' Lucy says.

'It's unusual and that's what Swanson had on this morning when he was questioned by police after being spotted near your aunt's house. Two plus two, right?'

'As long as it doesn't equal twenty-two,' Lucy says.

'Maybe Swanson was doing PR for them.'

'And part of doing PR was to kill Gail and spy on my aunt?' Lucy says. 'I assume you think Swanson's responsible for all of it.'

Marino doesn't say anything. I can tell by the

way he's looking at her he has a begrudging respect and he's gone from wanting Lucy out of his way to trying to figure out how he can use her.

'Has anybody touched the body in the kitchen or the other two?' I ask.

'Video and photographs and that's it. I made sure everybody knows to give them a wide berth. But we won't be able to keep the Feds out of here for long.'

'You won't be able to keep them out of here at all,' Lucy says.

'You'd better make hay while the sun shines,' Marino says to me.

'And no one has so much as a clue who the dead lady in the kitchen might be.' It's hard for me to believe no one does.

'We've not let anybody in here to take a look. Only essential personnel — in other words, cops.' Marino leans his shoulder against the doorframe.

He absently stares at his gloved hand, a yellowish nicotine stain on it that he rubs with his thumb. He's been smoking up a storm and I wonder how many butts he has in his pocket. At least he knows better than to drop them at a crime scene.

'We can't exactly have an open house,' he says. 'A ranch hand or the housekeeper comes in and leaves DNA everywhere or starts touching things or puking.'

'Their DNA would be in here anyway,' Lucy says.

'I also don't intend to walk around showing the staff photographs of dead people with their necks sawed through,' Marino retorts.

'But you've checked with them to see who should have been inside the house,' Lucy says.

'Jesus. Now I've got two of you on my ass.'

'I know who works here,' Lucy states in a way that conveys she's not being difficult or even personal with him. 'Names, ages, addresses. I know a lot more than I wish I did about these assholes. Describe the unidentified victim.'

'About your size, about your age,' he says. 'Early thirties, I'm guessing as best I can because she doesn't look so hot with her head practically cut off. Short dark hair. White. Scrawny and bony. Looks like she worked out a lot and might have had an attitude and wasn't into men.'

Lucy ignores him. 'There's no one here who fits that description or is that young. The three ranch hands and groundskeeper are forty-four, fifty-two, and one just turned sixty, originally from Texas, Arizona, and Nevada. The chef is French. He's forty-nine. The housekeeper's South American, forty-three, and claims to speak very little English. The partners in the business are two Americans and two Brits, men over forty, and then there was Lombardi and Caminska, who are rumored to have had more than a professional relationship. And, yes, they called her Ika, as in *Eeeka*, not *Icka*.' She mocks the way Marino pronounces it.

'Assailant entered the house the way you are, past the stone columns, on this porch, and he opened this door,' Marino says and he's backing away from assuming it's Haley Swanson we're looking for.

'What about the lock?' Lucy indicates the brushed-nickel biometric lock as she pulls on gloves.

'It was blue skies until a couple hours ago and it's possible when the weather was decent they'd leave the front door open with just this one shut.' He opens the inner storm door, a push-button lock all that separated the people of Double S from someone who cut their throats.

'Who says they kept the front door open?' Lucy doesn't believe it and as I watch her I'm reminded of what it used to be like when she did this for a living.

When she was with the FBI and later with ATF she was so amazing they got rid of her. Maybe it's in the Scarpetta DNA that we can't work for anyone. We're Lone Rangers and have to be in charge and walk right into trouble.

'I was told it could be an explanation,' Marino says. 'A ranch hand I talked to said he's seen it like that when it's decent weather and a lot of people are in and out.'

'They're lying,' Lucy says. 'They know who it is.'

'It's a good thing you got here. Now I can go home and forget about it.'

'The four partners are out of town so who was around to be in and out?' Lucy asks. 'And it wasn't toasty warm this morning even with the sun out.'

'There's a back door and a basement door, both of them locked and dead-bolted. This is the way he came in, just like you are,' Marino says. 'Maybe he had access because his fingerprint is scanned into the lock and he got in that way. In other words, it's someone they knew.'

'That would be good if we have his fingerprint. You're right,' Lucy says. 'You can go home and forget about it.'

Marino tries not to smile. He works so hard to look severe he looks ridiculous.

'As security minded as they seem to be it's hard for me to believe they'd leave the front doors open and unlocked,' I agree with Lucy.

'No way,' she says. 'Have you checked what was picked up by the cameras?'

'Hell no. I'm stupid,' Marino says.

★   ★   ★

The open room has four offices in a row that are horseshoe-shaped consoles with built-in desks and drawers.

Each work area has a multilined phone and several video displays as if one is supposed to imagine financial experts constantly monitoring stock markets and investment accounts. I don't notice a scrap of paper, not a single pencil or pen or hint that whoever works here has hobbies or family. The appearance is of a business that's transparent, with partners engaged in open communication and camaraderie, yet there's an empty, fake feeling as if I'm walking into a design showroom or a movie set. I don't sense that anybody lived here even before people were dead.

On the far right side is a floating staircase with cables and plate-steel treads, the wall next to it old brick hung with modern art prints and across from it is a wall of light ash cabinetry. It's a masculine space lacking warmth or creativity and at least four thousand square feet, I estimate. It adjoins a room that I can't see into but I hear voices through the open door, a steel door with no window that's been propped open with a magnetic stop. The two Concord detectives are inside what must be another office, the CEO's private suite on the left wing of the building where Lombardi and his assistant are dead.

In the front office, at the back of it, is an open kitchen with exotic deep red wooden cabinetry, what looks like the Bois de Rose used to make musical instruments. From where I stand I can see the blood-streaked dark trousers, the white pockets turned inside out, and the bloody sneakers of the victim who remains unidentified. Her coagulating blood is spread over the wide-plank flooring behind a dramatic sculpture in zebrawood folded around a corner of a whitewashed wall to the left of the granite counter that blocks most of my view. I ask Marino about the pockets.

'Did the police go into them looking for identification?' I want to know.

'They were already inside out. Remember, he took their wallets, IDs, cash.'

'Cleaned out the cash and whatever else he wanted and probably threw the wallets into the pond on his way out of here.' Lucy starts walking around. 'A perfect place to dump stuff, across from the barn, you'd go right past it if you're heading into the woods on foot, getting the hell out of here.'

I scan work areas with their ergonomic chairs, all exactly arranged with no sign of violence, and again I'm struck by the vacant feeling. During office hours on a Wednesday morning and only three people were inside except for their killer.

'The DVR's gone,' Marino then tells Lucy — reluctantly, it seems, as if he hates to admit she's right about something.

'Check off a second point for unpremeditated,' she replies.

'You'd have to know where to look and what for.' Marino hunches a shoulder, wiping his sweaty face on his shirt. He tends to overheat anyway and now his blood pressure is up because he's a cop again who smokes again.

'How hard would that be?' Lucy asks.

We're having this discussion in the entryway near the officer at his laser-mapping station, where black hard cases are open on the floor. A yellow power cord connected to a charging station is plugged into a wall, and the officer and his scanner are in sleep mode, waiting. He doesn't look at us. He doesn't want to appear he's listening to people who aren't talking to him.

'There's a closet in the other room with all the components for surround sound, the server and wireless networks, their phone system and security stuff.' Marino walks over to my scene case near the stairs and picks it up.

'The server.' Lucy's like a snake spying a lizard and she strikes. 'Double S's server. Now we're talking.'

She walks over to the desks against a wall, four of them in a row. Nudging a chair with her knees, she rolls it out of the way and picks up the phone.

'But you'd have to know what a DVR is.' Marino hands my field case to me. 'Most people wouldn't think of it unless they're familiar with security cameras.'

'It's not rocket science and it may be someone who's been here before. We need to get the server to my lab.' Lucy looks at the display on the desk phone and pushes a key. 'Concord PD can receipt it here and I can take it in.'

She walks to each desk and does the same thing, checking the phones. Then she returns to the first one and picks it up again.

'You might want to write this down,' she says to Marino. 'None of these phones have made any outgoing calls since last Friday as if nobody's been working in the front office. With the exception of this one.' She indicates the phone she's holding and she gives him a number. 'Lambant and Associates,' she reads the display.

'What?' Marino walks over and looks. 'Well, big surprise. So I'm right. Haley Swanson was here and he called his office.'

'Someone did,' Lucy says. 'Someone made an outgoing call from here to that number at nine fifty-six this morning and was on the phone for twenty-seven minutes. If the guy running through the park was spotted around eleven then whoever was on the phone here probably hung up right about the time everybody got killed.'

'We know who that guy is, the one in the

hoodie with Marilyn Monroe on it and now we know he was in here using the phone.' Marino has it all figured out again. 'Haley Swanson.' He's latched on to that conviction all over again. 'Lambant's the crisis management firm where Gail Shipton's gender-bender friend works,' Marino says and Lucy just looks at him.

'One might conclude they've been handling Double S's PR,' I suggest. 'Possibly Swanson is who Lombardi picked up at the train station this morning.'

'Exactly,' Marino says.

'I guess we know how Gail met him, at any rate, both of them in thick with Double S,' Lucy says with nothing in her tone. 'Did you confirm who she was with at the Psi last night?'

'She was there talking to someone who wasn't a regular. It could have been Swanson and that would make sense since he's the one who reported her missing. It was really crowded and Gail was jammed at the bar with a lot of other people. That's what witnesses have said and it's as good as we're going to get.'

'Why would someone take the commuter train here instead of driving?' I point out. 'Why would a PR person do that?'

'Haley Swanson,' Lucy says dubiously. 'And I guess we're to conclude that about an hour, an hour and a half later, he killed everyone and fled.'

'It's not for you to conclude, anything,' Marino says rudely.

'Earlier today we were told he was driving an Audi SUV,' I remind him.

391

'We're looking for it. It's not at his apartment in Somerville and not at his business in Boston,' Marino says. 'The people who work at his PR firm haven't seen him or his SUV today but he called them.'

'The call made from here,' Lucy says. 'Someone made it.'

'Why wouldn't Swanson drive himself?' I ask.

'When we find him he's got a hell of a lot of explaining to do, but my answer is he didn't want his car spotted at Double S because he was planning to commit murder,' Marino says. 'That's a good reason not to drive your own damn car.'

'I'm guessing that isn't it at all,' Lucy disagrees. 'These murders don't appear to be planned.'

'Nobody's asking you to guess,' Marino says just as rudely.

Lucy isn't slowed down by Marino's attitude. It doesn't even seem to register.

'Has anybody checked with his uncle in the projects?' I ask.

'I got Machado doing that and haven't heard back.'

Lucy unzips her white coveralls halfway and pulls her gloves off as if she's hot and has her own idea about what needs to be done.

'I have to get the server out of here,' she says to him, 'before it's not possible.'

'I hear you.' Marino knows what she's thinking and he's conflicted, the way he is about Gail Shipton's phone.

He wants Lucy's help but he's afraid of it. He

knows if the FBI gets its hands on the server before we do that will be the last we hear of it. Granby will hold a press conference and talk decisively about joining forces with local agencies and a joint effort but the reality is when evidence goes to the national labs in Quantico and the prosecutor is the U.S. attorney there's no such thing as a joint anything.

That's under the best of circumstances. Marino doesn't know about evidence tampering. He doesn't know about Gabriela Lagos or her missing son Martin who supposedly left a stain on a pair of panties in the most recent Washington, D.C., case. Marino has no idea just how impossible it will be for us to work these murders here unless we're proactive now, ruthlessly so. I decide to blame it on the media, something that Marino will accept as an inevitable obstacle to avoid.

'It depends on how big this gets. A huge case and it's similar to what I just faced in Connecticut. TV trucks everywhere and those of us trying to do our jobs are stepped on.' I look at him and he understands.

'No shit,' he says.

'Have you talked to Benton?'

'Briefly.'

'Then you know what's going to happen,' I pile it on. 'He had to pass along certain information to Granby, who's already releasing statements to the press.'

'Bogus ones,' Lucy says. 'The Feebs already have taken over and they're coming.'

'Yeah, Santa Claus is coming to town,' Marino

393

says angrily. 'I can hear him on his sleigh heading this way. He's going to land on the roof any minute, dammit. This is fucking bullshit. Whatever happened to just taking care of things and protecting the public like we're supposedly paid to do?'

'You used to say that twenty years ago,' I reply.

'People still suck.'

'We don't have much time before we have no control over anything,' I bring up again.

'The DVR is where you'd go in the aftermath unless you're not very bright.' Lucy is back to that. 'You show up here and you're on camera and you don't care because at that time whatever your reason for showing up is normal. You didn't drop by to commit a crime. Then something goes wrong and now you've got to fix it after the fact. So you find the closet because it's too damn late to cut the cables to the cameras.'

'It could be how it went down.' Marino is getting prickly with her. 'But you'd have to know what a DVR is to look for one,' he repeats.

'He must have pitched it. I doubt he ran through the park with a video recorder tucked under his arm. He wouldn't have tossed it in the woods, not anywhere it would be found. You might want to get some divers to search the pond.'

'It wouldn't still work if it's been in the water.' Marino wants to at least appear he's fighting with her but he's not.

It's just the three of us in this together, no different from how it's always been.

'I'm not sure what you'd be able to recover,'

394

she says. 'It depends on the brand and model and how protected the recorded data is on the digital storage device. My bigger question is whether video and audio might have been transferred over a network for remote monitoring on a computer, maybe on some other area of the property. If other people were looking, they could have seen at least some of what was going on.'

'I haven't had a chance to check everywhere.' Marino doesn't look at Lucy now.

He hates what he feels about her and thinks he can hide it. He can't, not about either of us.

'The barn and the outbuildings, the bedrooms,' Lucy says. 'Wherever there might be workstations or even laptops and iPads, someone might have seen something they didn't think to mention to you.' She's diplomatic about it. 'You mind if I check?'

'Don't touch nothing,' Marino says.

'And I've got to take the server in.'

'Stay out of that closet in the other room and don't touch nothing.'

'Then who's going to make sure data's not being deleted remotely, maybe from New York or Grand Cayman or anywhere even as we speak?' she says to him.

'You should know all about deleting things remotely.'

'Who's going to get through the layers of security? I guess you could ask around for the system admin password. Maybe somebody will hand it over.'

'I didn't ask for your help.'

'Well, Merry Christmas, Marino. The FBI will

be here landing on the roof before you know it,' Lucy says. 'I guess you can turn the server over to them. Maybe before you retire they'll tell you what's on it. But probably not.'

She walks back out the front door, her retreating footsteps light on the veranda and the steps, and then I can't hear her anymore.

'You should get it out of here and you know it,' I tell him quietly. 'I have a feeling even Benton would suggest that.' I'm careful what else I say with other people around but the way I look at Marino he understands there's a problem that's much bigger than he imagines.

'Jesus.' His face is deep red and he stares at the cop with the laser station on the other side of the room.

If he hears us, he makes no indication of it, but no cop with NEMLEC would snitch to the FBI anyway.

'She knows what she's doing. And so do I. And you're about to know a lot.' I hold Marino's stare and he doesn't know what I'm talking about but he gets that it's a severe problem.

'What the fuck.' He enters a number on his phone. 'Do it,' he says when Lucy answers. 'Don't disturb nothing or talk to anyone. Pack it up and get it to the CFC, get it the hell out of here and you'd better not screw anything up. I'm trusting you.'

He ends the call and turns his attention to me. 'I'm going to walk you through it. Show you exactly what I think he did.'

'Not now.' I move deeper inside in my latex boots. 'I'll let his victims tell me what he did.'

36

I want to be alone with the dead and alone with my thoughts.

I walk over to the officer in charge of the mapping station set up on a sturdy bright yellow tripod. He's packing a laptop computer and an Ethernet cable, the system on pause, its oscillating mirror and rapidly pulsing laser beam quiet and still.

'Have you got this?' I indicate the kitchen I'm heading toward, assuming he's already captured its images and measurements.

'How you doing, Dr. Scarpetta? Randall Taylor with Watertown.'

He's got a wide, tired face with thinning hair that's mottled gray and combed back, a pair of reading glasses perched low on his nose. In the battle dress of faded blue cargo pants and a matching shirt with the sleeves rolled up, he reminds me of an old warrior who has learned new ways of doing his job but isn't eager anymore. Cops, even feisty ones, get worn down like a river stone and he has a smooth and easy way about him, unlike Marino who is a product of nature protecting itself like a sea urchin or a briar patch.

'We met last year at the dinner when the chief retired,' Randall Taylor says. 'I wouldn't expect you to remember.'

'I hope your former chief is enjoying a little peace and quiet.'

'They've moved to Florida.'

'What part? I grew up in Miami.'

'A little north of West Palm, Vero Beach. I'm angling for him to invite me down. Come January, I'll be begging.'

'What's been done?' I ask.

'I've gotten multiple scans that I'll stitch together with point to surface, line of sight measurements and blood trajectory analysis,' Taylor explains. 'So you've basically got each entire scene in volumized 3-D, which I'll get to you as soon as I'm back at my office.'

'That would be helpful.'

'I worked the other room first, just finishing up in here.'

'Am I going to be in your way?' I ask.

'I'm all set but I wanted to make sure you didn't need anything else.'

'What about stringing?'

I want to know if he's going to use the tried-and-true method of attaching strings to blood drops and spatter to determine points of convergence. It's a reliable mathematical way to reconstruct where the assailant and victim were in relation to each other when the blows or injuries were inflicted.

'Not yet. You don't really need to with this.' He pats the scanner with a gloved hand.

It's a matter of opinion but I'm not going to tell him that.

'Obvious arterial spatter patterns, fairly obvious point of origin,' he says. 'The victim here in the kitchen was standing, the other two sitting, not complicated scenes except you wonder how someone took out three people like that. They must have happened really fast. But still, nobody heard anything?'

'If you cut through someone's trachea, he can't scream. He can't speak.'

'The two in there' — he indicates the open steel door — 'dead at their desks like that.' He snaps his blue-gloved fingers and the sound is dull and rubbery. 'I've been careful not to touch the bodies or get too close, waiting until you got here. They're exactly like we found them.'

'Do you know what time?'

'I wasn't first, but from what I gather?' Randall Taylor lifts his left arm and looks at his watch. 'Maybe two hours ago when Concord first arrived, following up on the envelope full of cash they found in the park, which in my opinion was in Lombardi's desk drawer. You'll see when you get in there that everything was rummaged through and in one of the drawers was a withdrawal slip for ten grand from two days ago, Monday. Maybe robbery's the motive but I agree with what I overheard you talking about. Whoever it is didn't come here to kill everyone. Something went haywire.'

'And no one else on the property knows what might have happened.' It's a point I can't get past.

'You and me are on the same wavelength.' He selects a menu on the touch screen to power off the system. 'I'm guessing nobody wants to be involved. Each person was waiting for the other to be the one who found them.'

'What makes you say that?'

'Everywhere I look I'm seeing computer screens and cameras.' He walks over to a wall socket and unplugs the battery-charging station. 'You telling me nobody saw the guy running? You telling me nobody at least tried calling here to see what was going on? Like hello, is everything all right over there? That's just strange as hell. And then Concord made it easy by rolling up and finding the bodies. What if they hadn't? Who was going to call nine-one-one?'

'It seems inconsistent with human nature to look the other way if you spot someone fleeing the property, I agree.' I'm noncommittal about it.

I've learned the hard way to be careful about my opinions, which tend to get circulated like the gospel truth.

'This whole place gives me a bad feeling.' He loosens screws and lifts the scanner off the tripod and carries it over to a large foamlined transport container. 'Like it's way too quiet and empty and nobody sees or hears a thing, what I associate with businesses that are fronts and neighborhoods where everybody's guilty of something.'

I pull up my synthetic white hood to cover my hair and find a safe spot to set down my field case near the kitchen, then I move inside, careful where I step. Dark red dried blood is streaked, dripped, and spurted in waves on appliances, cabinets, and the floor, and the dead woman is between the refrigerator and the counter in a dark, stagnant puddle that's thick in the middle and separating at the edges. I smell blood breaking down and overcooked coffee.

She's flat on her back. Her legs are straight, her arms folded at her waist, and I know right away she didn't die like that.

★   ★   ★

I look at her for a long, careful moment, pushing thoughts out of my head, letting her body tell me the true story it knows.

I'm conscious of the ripe smell of blood. Where it's dried and coagulating it's dark red turning rusty brown, viscous and sticky, and the message I'm getting isn't right for someone stumbling as she hemorrhages, finally collapsing on the floor. The killer turned her pockets inside out and he did something more. I open my field case and get out a Sharpie. I find the sheet of labels and fill in one with the date and my initials. I stick it on a plastic ruler I'll use as a scale, and I get my camera.

She's tall, approximately five-foot-eight, with fine features, high cheekbones, and a strong jaw, and her dark hair is cropped short and she has multiple piercings in her ears. Her eyes are barely open, dark blue and getting dull. The irises will fade and cloud as death continues its destructive changes, coldly stiffening, what seems an indignant resistance at first. Then an escalation of breaking down that always strikes me as the flesh forlornly giving up.

The injuries to her neck gape widely, and her navy blue khaki slacks and white leather sneakers are streaked with drops of blood, some elongated, some round because they fell at different angles. I'm not surprised that her palms are bloody. It's what I expect with a severed carotid, and the top of her left index finger is cut at the first knuckle, almost through the joint. I envision her grabbing her neck to stop the bleeding, which wasn't possible, and while her hands were there, her attacker slashed again, almost cutting off her fingertip.

What's completely wrong is blood has soaked into the back of her kelly green button-up fleece, especially into the back of her collar. There's no blood in front, not a single drop that bled from the deep wounds in her neck. But I notice smudges, most of them around the buttons, and the inner cuff of the right sleeve is saturated almost up to the elbow, and this isn't what I should see if she was wearing the fleece when she was standing up and someone cut her throat.

As I study the coagulating puddle that reaches from under her back to some five feet away I easily deduce that this is where she was on the floor when she bled out. But originally she wasn't in this position. Somebody moved her after she was dead and I take photographs to capture the exact position she's in. Next I lift her arms and check her hands, strong ones, large ones, a gothic silver ring with an amethyst on the right middle finger, a plaited black leather bracelet on her right wrist. Rigor has begun in the small muscles and her temperature is tepid on the way to cool because she has very little body fat and has lost most of her blood.

There are two incisions to her throat. One begins on the left side of her neck below her ear, terminating in approximately three inches, slicing through her jaw, and the bone shows white against red tissue that is drying. I notice a peculiar wide, shallow cut with abraded edges, the skin peeled in places like a wood shaving, and it's not something I've seen before. It parallels the deep incision from its beginning to where it terminates like a ragged path running along a road. I have no idea what made it. The weapon is an unusual shape or perhaps the tip of the blade is bent.

The second wound ended her life swiftly, an incision with the same strange peeled shallow cut running parallel to it, both beginning at the right side of her throat. This second fatal wound is deepest where a sharp sturdy blade first went in below the right jaw, then moved horizontally across the throat in a neat, forceful slice, severing her carotid artery, her strap muscles, and airway, cutting all the way through to her spine. I stand up.

I take in every inch of the open kitchen, getting a perspective of the two granite countertops across from each other, the one closest to the front door and the other on either side of the stovetop and the refrigerator. I note a white bakery box and inside it are two cupcakes that look fresh and smell like rich mocha and chocolate, from a food shop on Main Street in downtown Concord, based on the logo. Maybe Lombardi bought them on his way to the commuter rail station when he was picking up his visitor and I think of the three or four cupcake wrappers on one plate and the one used napkin on the sunporch. I wonder if one person ate that many cupcakes. If so, it was a lot of sugar.

Near the bakery box is a stainless-steel coffeemaker, the type that has a tank instead of a carafe. I open the lid, feeling the heat of coffee that smells strongly bitter. The gold filter is full of grounds and I check the gauge in back. There are four cups remaining, and I think of the two mugs on the table inside a space where people could have a private conversation that couldn't be spied on or overheard.

I look across the room and don't see coffee cups on the other desks, and there are none in the sink. I open the dishwasher and there's nothing inside but a spoon. I try drawers and discover several are faux. Others are empty. In one are folded dishcloths that look new and unused, and in another are four place settings of silverware. I look for sharp knives but don't find any. I pull out the trash compactor and there's not even a bag inside.

In glass door cabinets above the dishwasher are stacks of dishes, simple white china, four place settings each, and more mugs like the ones on the sunporch. Moving to one side of the refrigerator, staying clear of blood near the handle and on the floor, I open the door. I find blood on the inner edge of it that's also smeared on the gasket.

Coffee cream, soymilk, bottles of water, both sparkling and flat, and a take-out foam container, and I push open the lid. Inside is a leftover gyro wrapped in deli paper. It doesn't look fresh, possibly from many days ago. Condiments and low-fat salad dressings are in the door, and inside the freezer I find ice cubes that look old and a container of grocery-store chili that's dated October 10.

She came into the kitchen for a reason, possibly for coffee or a bottle of water, and I retrieve the UV light from my scene case. I find the switch for the kitchen lights and turn them off, then I squat by the body. I rest my weight on the back of my heels, looking again at the blood and the spread open wounds of her neck, and I turn on the UV light and the lens glows purple as I direct the black light at her head and move down, checking for trace evidence and instantly the same neon colors fluoresce. Bloodred, emerald green, and bluish purple.

The fleece she has on shimmers and then turns kelly green again when I switch off the UV light. A dusting of the same residue I saw this morning and it's only on the fleece, and my misgivings grow about who this person is and how it's possible she's dressed this way. I collect samples with adhesive stubs. Then I take off my gloves. I reach Lucy on my cell phone and hear a TV in the background, Spanish, what sounds like the Dish Latino Network.

'Where are you?' I ask.

'Checking out the barn. There are monitors in here and cameras, nanny-cams for the horses.' She's suggesting that the killer would have been picked up by security cameras if anybody was watching.

'Are you alone?'

'The housekeeper's in here sitting by herself, watching TV. *Gracias por su ayuda. Hasta luego,*' Lucy calls out. 'And I'm on my way to get the server before the Feds show up. Benton just drove by so they're probably not far behind.'

'I need you to drop off evidence to Ernie and tell him I want it looked at right away.'

'Something good?' Lucy asks and she's outside the barn. I can hear her breathing as she jogs.

'There's nothing good about any of this' is what I say as I hear the familiar throaty rumble of a powerful sports car in the parking area.

The engine stops and silence returns and I imagine Benton getting out of his Porsche. He'll walk around for a while before he comes inside.

★   ★   ★

Marino's footsteps are heavy and widely spaced, never fast but with purpose like a steady train coming. Then he's on the other side of the counter holding a fingerprint dusting kit.

'He came up behind her and inflicted this injury first.' I point to the incision on the left side of her neck and jaw.

'I've not dusted in here or the back offices,' he says. 'I didn't want to do that before you were done.'

He knows the routine. We've been doing this for more than twenty years.

'So far I'm not seeing any patent prints. No bloody ones and no footprints,' I let him know.

'He had to have stepped in blood. Benton just got here and is looking around outside.'

'I'm not seeing any indication the killer stepped in blood. The two cuts to her throat were in rapid succession and then he may have gotten out of the way and let her hemorrhage to death. Within minutes she would have been unconscious and gone into shock.' I continue glancing at the windows on the other side of the room as if I can see through the drawn shades and I think of what Lucy predicted.

Ed Granby will show up and if he does we'll know his special interest. To protect people with money, she said while we were driving here.

'In scenes this bloody usually they step in it.' Marino has his flashlight out, shining it obliquely over the floor, and thick blood glows deep red. 'It's hard not to.'

'There's no sign he did and no sign anything was cleaned up. There's a partial tread pattern here.' I point it out. 'But that's from her stepping in her own blood, possibly after she was cut the first time.'

'Haley Swanson's SUV is still parked in the projects where his uncle lives,' Marino says. 'All four of his tires are flat. Maybe the same assholes doing car breaks and vandalism around there. His expensive Audi SUV is parked there often, the uncle told Machado, about a sixty-thousand-dollar SUV if Swanson got it new. I have a feeling he was doing more than visiting his uncle several times a week. Maybe mixed up with shitbags dealing drugs over there, some of the really bad designer drugs killing people around here.'

'The uncle doesn't know where Swanson is?'

'He said he doesn't.' Marino clips the flashlight to his belt. 'But Swanson headed out around eight this morning on foot, said he needed to be somewhere and he was going to take the train. I guess we know for sure who Lombardi picked up at the commuter rail station here in Concord.'

'If you could get two thermometers from my field case?' I ask. 'You can help me take photographs and there's a notepad in there, too. She was standing upright, facing the refrigerator, holding the door open, when he attacked her from behind.'

'How can you tell about the refrigerator?' He bends over my field case on the floor. 'How do you know she had the door open?'

'The blood here.' I indicate drips near the handle. 'This area is in line with her neck and chin if she was standing with the door open when the left side of her neck was cut. Blood caught the edge of the door, which wouldn't have been possible if it was shut, and then the blood was transferred to the gasket when someone closed the door.'

'Who did that?'

'I can't tell you who.'

'You think maybe she shut the door after he cut her the first time?' Marino moves next to me, holding his camera, handing me the thermometers.

'She might have. I just know that someone did.'

The storm door in the entryway opens and Lucy is here. I give her the package with the adhesive stubs in it and she stuffs it into a big pocket on the leg of her flight suit.

'Benton's walking around and the others can't be far behind,' I say to her.

'I'll be out of here in ten minutes max.'

'He didn't come with them. He came alone. That's my point,' I add.

"To get here first,' she says and she knows what it means.

Then she's gone through the open steel door, jogging toward the back offices where what she wants is in a closet. It's past three now and I'm listening for cars pulling up. I'm looking for Benton and I'm waiting for the arrival of the rest of them. He isn't acting as if he's part of them and I'm reminded of the way he was talking when we were following the railroad tracks. He talked about the FBI as if he wasn't FBI and right now he's not. Benton is here to solve these homicides and Granby is coming with a very different agenda in mind, one I certainly don't trust.

I unbutton the top of the dark green fleece and tuck a thermometer under the arm. I set the second thermometer on top of a counter.

'It could have been a reflex when she was ambushed by the attack.' I measure the wound on the left side of her neck. 'It may be as you suggested, that he came up behind her and she turned at the same time he sliced, missing major vessels, and the blade went through her jaw. Maybe she pushed the refrigerator door shut or fell against it. That incision is three and a half inches long, from left to right and upward.'

Marino squints as he scribbles on the notepad. He pats himself down for his glasses as if he can't remember which pocket. He finds them, cleans the lenses on his shirt, and he puts them on.

'There are shallow incisions that run parallel, strange ones with abraded edges and some of the skin is peeled back.' I give him the measurements. 'I have no idea unless the tip of the blade is bent.'

He looks up from his notes, his eyes magnified. 'Why would he use a knife with a bent blade?'

'Maybe it got that way because of something he did with it. I've seen acutely bent blade tips in stabbings when the blade tip strikes bone.'

'Was anybody stabbed?'

'She wasn't.'

'Didn't look to me the other two were,' Marino says.

'I haven't gotten there yet.'

'There's no blood on their backs, no indication they have other injuries. I think he cut their throats and that was it,' he says.

'That was enough.'

'Yeah, no kidding.'

'This second incision is five inches and one-quarter and I'm thinking it was inflicted from in front. He was facing her.'

I show him the deep cut on her left index finger, across the first knuckle.

'Like this.' I get up to show him. 'The first incision is when my back's to him and I'm turning around.'

I act it out.

'I hate it when you treat yourself like an anatomical doll. It gives me the creeps,' Marino says.

'Then I'm going to grab the left side of my neck while drops of blood are falling straight down, perpendicular to the floor.' I show him. 'Those drops are perfectly round like the ones close to the refrigerator door and on the tops of her shoes. Now I'm facing my attacker and he cuts again, cutting my left index finger. I'm still upright but moving this way.'

I step to the right of the refrigerator.

'Then I'm facing forward, toward the counter, possibly leaning against it, my hands on my neck.'

'Maybe he held her there.' Marino looks at the waves of arterial blood on the cabinets. 'Maybe he had his hand on her back until she started getting too weak to run or struggle. I'm thinking he might have held the other two down. They're bleeding to death at their desks and he pushes his hand against their backs so they can't get up. It would only take a few minutes. It would explain why there's blood only on their desks and under them. Most people would try to get up but they didn't.'

'We'll see when I look at them,' I reply. 'Here's the arterial pattern on the cupboard, and a mist of it on the glass from her strangling on her blood, forcibly exhaling it because her trachea is severed. She's aspirating blood. It's accumulating in her airway and lungs and now she's going down and here's the pattern on the cabinets beneath the stove and the sink.'

I point out waves of blood drips, the crests and troughs from blood spurting in rhythm to the beating of her heart. Large drops of dried blood with long tails trickle down, across a cabinet, up and down and up, getting weaker and lower.

'She's on her knees,' I continue, 'explaining the spatter here on the floor from blood dripping into blood and the blood soaked into the knees and lower area of her pants legs. And this puddle indicates where she died but not in this position.'

I look up as Lucy walks swiftly through the front office, carrying a tower server through the entryway, pushing through the doors with her foot. Marino moves the plastic ruler, using it as a scale in photographs he takes, and I show him smeared areas of blood on the floor that tell me the most important part of the story as I hear the loud rumble of Lucy's SUV and then she's driving away fast.

'Blood already had begun to clot when she was moved.' I point out a red outlined circle and a smear, a distinctive pattern shaped like a big tadpole. 'What you're seeing is a drop of blood that was coagulating when something was dragged over it and that happened after some time had passed. There are more of these smeared clots. Here and here and here.'

He begins taking photographs of them, placing the labeled scale next to each one.

'I wonder if you're picking up on the same thing I am,' he says. 'The way her arms are resting on her belly like she's sleeping. It reminds me of Gail Shipton.'

'It's similar.'

'Someone posing the body in a peaceful position. Almost like he felt bad about it.'

'He looked her in the face when he cut her throat a second time. He didn't feel bad about it,' I reply. 'I think you're going to find this isn't her fleece.' I remove the thermometer from under her arm, noting her black padded push-up bra.

Her chest has a wide circumference but her breasts are small.

'Eighty-point-six.' I pick up the thermometer from the counter. 'It's a seventy-one degrees in here. She's been dead at least three hours, probably closer to four.'

'What do you mean it's not her fleece?' Marino frowns.

'I think she was dressed in it after she was dead. It has what appears to be the same residue that fluoresces in UV. It's all over the fleece, and the blood pattern on it is inconsistent with her injuries and the way she would have bled out.'

I unbutton the fleece all the way and turn her partially on her side, her body leaning heavily against my Tyvek-covered thigh. Livor has begun to form on her back but is far from set. When I press my finger into her flesh it easily blanches, the same way it does when someone is alive. I notice her well-defined muscularity. And when I rest her on her back again I unbutton her pants and unzip the fly. Underneath are women's black panties. And then I touch her face with my finger and makeup is transferred to my glove. I ask Marino to open one of the kits I brought with me.

'There should be some towelettes in there,' I say to him, and he hands me one.

I wipe her cheeks and upper lip and the stubble wouldn't have been noticeable because her face is close shaven and covered with layers of foundation and powder. Her chest and lower abdomen have been waxed, I suspect, and when I pull down her panties the answer is there.

'You got to be shitting me.' Marino stares.

'A male taking female hormones and the killer dressed him in his own bloody fleece.'

'What the hell?'

'Switching clothes because he needed to disguise himself as best he could in case he was seen somewhere. The suspect running through the park at around eleven . . .' I begin to remind him. 'And you wouldn't do that if you came here intending to murder people. He came here for another reason and something went terribly wrong and now he's got to escape.'

'Shit. The black hoodie with Marilyn Monroe on it, which is what Rooney said Haley Swanson had on this morning when he talked to him in the projects. Shit!' Marino exclaims in astonishment. 'He kills Swanson and then puts his damn hoodie on? It would have been bloody as hell. What kind of fucking lunatic would do something like that?'

'Locate a photograph of Haley Swanson as quickly as you possibly can,' I tell him as the storm door in the entryway opens. 'We need to see if that's who this is.'

'Hell yeah, that's who it is,' Marino says and he's already stepping away to make a call,

414

probably to Machado.

Benton is walking across the room, heading toward me, as I hear the distant noise of another vehicle or maybe more than one along the driveway.

'They're here,' he says simply.

'Do they know you are?' I ask as he reaches us and looks at the body and the blood.

'They're about to,' Benton says.

37

It's after six p.m. and as dark as a moonless night
when I begin packing up.

I've done what can be done, which is very little
in the final scheme of things when I examine
ruined biology, when I smell its foulness and
touch what feels unnatural after life has given up.
I know what killed the people at Double S and
am faced with a much bigger problem that can't
be resolved by CT scans or autopsies. The
victims have said what they need to say and now
I'm after their killer and the FBI official
protecting him.

I take off my coveralls, booties, and gloves and
stuff them into a bright red biohazard trash bag
on the floor inside the entranceway where
Benton waits with a stony resolve about what we
intend to do. It's important I look for the type of
weapon that was used and I don't believe the
killer found it in the office kitchen or inside this
building and I seriously doubt he brought it with
him when he showed up at Double S and
murdered three people this morning.

The bodies and any evidence relating to them
are my jurisdiction and that certainly includes
any weapon used. This is my argument but it's
far from the whole truth about why I refuse to
leave the scene even as I'm about to give the
appearance that I have. While I'm exerting my
authority as a chief medical examiner, what I'm

feeling like is an intruder or a spy as I plot, plan, and sneak around. Granby and his agents would never allow me inside Dominic Lombardi's house, not in a million years no matter what I argue, but that's where I'm headed.

Benton is going to take me and in the process blatantly counter a direct order because he's not motivated by politics or personal advancement or dishonesty. It's never about anything like that with him and he's incensed by the situation he finds himself in, which isn't entirely new but so much worse it's shocking. Respecting me professionally and doing what I've asked would get him fired if he still had a job he could be fired from. Granby stripped him of his power and dignity and he did it in front of everyone. No crystal balls are needed here, Granby had the nerve to say. Have a drink or two or three and he told us to have a very merry Christmas and a happy New Year. By the time that happens Granby will be ruined. I will make sure of it.

I will see whatever there is to see before it has been tampered with. I'll take photographs to preserve the truth before Granby can continue to distort and manipulate it in whatever fashion suits his pathological ambition and need to cover up lies he's told and whatever crimes he's committed. He's not going to get away with it. We won't let him and it's all in the execution. We can't do anything we would have to misrepresent later, Benton and I strategized as we stood outside a little while ago, our voices quiet beneath the diesel rumble of my boxy white office truck parked in front, the tailgate open and a hydraulic ramp lowered.

We agreed that if we get caught in even one deception or are accused of fabricating anything at all it would discredit everything else. So we'll document our every move and protect what we can in a way we can prove, and Benton won't need to verbalize a single detail he shouldn't share with his lover, his wife. I was here because I had a right to be. I'll be asked in court about the weapon and I'm expected to have an answer. And as for the confidential information that Lucy is sending wirelessly to Benton, it's too damn bad if I happen to see it for myself as text messages land on his phone.

He doesn't need to tell me classified details about the Russian or Israeli mafia or money laundering or other massive crimes that possibly include murder for hire. I can't help what I overhear or see with my own eyes that might explain why Granby continues to shield a spectacle murderer who has rapidly spun out of control. And I can almost conjure him up, his pale skin and dark hair, compactly built and wearing size-eight running gloves that look like rubber bare feet. By now there can be no doubt it was the killer behind my wall this morning and I envision him in the rainy dark in a kelly green button-up fleece and bareheaded, oblivious to the wet and cold.

I imagine his wide eyes and dilated pupils, his limbic system roaring like an inferno as he witnessed my bedroom light blink on at a few minutes past four a.m. Then the light in my bathroom was next, and after that the stained glass was illuminated over the landings on the stairs as he witnessed my response to the evil thing he'd done.

I can imagine the intensity of his excitement as he watched me emerge from the back door and heard me talking to my skittish old dog, the lady doctor getting ready to respond to a murder scene choreographed by a profoundly disturbed human being who fancies himself more powerful and professional than any of us. I see him as a crazed cruel monster and maybe it's true that he went into overdrive after the massacre in Connecticut. Maybe he got curious about me. And then I wonder how he felt when I opened my door and yelled at him like a nagging next-door neighbor.

I doubt he was frightened. He might have been amused or more excited and aroused, and I imagine him running nimbly back to the MIT campus along the railroad tracks to watch me show up with Marino, to watch Lucy land her helicopter and Benton climb out. What fanfare and reward for a sadistic narcissist and I feel certain he'd been watching me for days as he premeditated Gail Shipton's murder, gathering intelligence about her, stalking, fantasizing what a superhero he would be when he created more terror and drama and in the process eliminated what he wrongly rationalized was a problem for Double S, assuming he rationalizes or reasons or has any logic at all.

The killer didn't need to be asked to murder Gail Shipton nor would he have been, Benton has said repeatedly over recent hours. On his own this deluded, violent individual took care of someone who in his mind was a thorn in Lombardi's side. When this rogue killer showed up or was summoned to Double S this morning, it's possible he expected to get praised and rewarded as he devoured cupcakes on the soundproof sunporch. But that's not how it worked out for him or for any of them, Benton theorized not long before Granby wrapped his arm around him and told him condescendingly to go home and enjoy the rest of his life.

The killer is rapidly decompensating. He may have become psychotic, Benton explained as the bodies were pouched and carried like black cocoons out to my truck. Lombardi was the intended target but his murder wasn't planned. His assistant Caminska was personal but not as much. And the third victim, who we believe is Haley Swanson, was in the wrong place at the wrong time.

Swanson took the commuter train to Concord to meet with Lombardi because suddenly there was, to say the least, an unexpected PR dilemma, Benton did his best to impress upon his FBI colleagues. The killer is someone Lombardi knew but murdering Gail Shipton wasn't in Double S's plans or best interest. It wasn't necessary and would only bring unwanted attention and public scrutiny, which is the last thing organized criminals want or need. In fact, Lombardi may have been enraged when he found out the news.

Crisis management is what Benton called what may have gone on early this morning. It's likely the killer was castigated and berated for the reckless thing he'd done, and Benton could well imagine this person driving off stung and belittled and then returning on foot to slaughter Lombardi and whoever else was inside this building. But Granby hasn't listened and not because he doesn't care. He cares, all right, because he can't possibly solve the cases honestly.

He damn well knows what he assumes we don't, the falsified DNA, the tampering in CODIS. He has to be frantically aware that DNA recovered in the cases here in Massachusetts or some place else won't come back to Martin Lagos who isn't leaving biological evidence anywhere. He's nothing but a string of numbers in a database, a stain that couldn't have been left by him on a pair of Sally Carson's cotton panties.

'The blood card from her autopsy in Virginia will have to be reanalyzed but we can't mention this to anyone right now. It will have to wait until it's safe to address,' I say to Benton as I go through my scene case, doing a last-minute inventory.

I pick up envelopes and containers I've labeled and sealed, evidence from three people savagely killed, each of their tracheas cut all the way through like a vacuum cleaner hose.

'That's how we undo the tampering and show Sally Carson's profile was changed to Martin Lagos's,' I explain. 'We can straighten this out but the timing is imperative and right now we really don't know who to trust but absolutely not the head of your labs in Quantico. I worry she's in thick with Granby.'

'Someone is,' Benton says.

'Maybe that's how she got the job, a big step up to go from the director of the Virginia labs to the director of the national ones. She took over last summer about the same time Granby took over the Boston division and some months and two murders later a DNA profile is corrupted in CODIS. It had to be someone who has access and knows how to alter data.'

'The Bureau will blame it on lab contamination or a computer entry error.' Benton stands near the front door, his eyes on me, the two of us alone and ignored inside the front office. 'But it won't even get that far publicly. It will go away silently.'

'We'll see about that.' I continue checking evidence, making sure what I collected is accounted for as we head out into the night. 'I suspect your boss knew back in April who murdered Klara Hembree, that her killer is someone in thick with Double S and that's why Granby ended up here so he could be in Lombardi's backyard.'

'Klara Hembree is key to figuring it out. In her case there may have been a motive,' Benton says. 'But obviously doing something as drastic as tampering with CODIS didn't become necessary until Sally Carson and Julianne Goulet were murdered.'

'Because they weren't supposed to be,' I say angrily. 'Because the person doing it is worse than a loose cannon. He's a contagion on its way to causing a plague. I'm surprised someone didn't take him out by now.'

'It may have been too late for that. I suspect

what we're dealing with has very deep roots.'

'As deep as deep gets.' I can't disguise the outrage I feel.

'You might want to put this on.'

Benton holds out my coat and I see the love he has for me. I see it in his eyes, and I see the shadow of disgust and indignation that feel like sickness. Granby may as well have kicked him in the gut, and I saw it happen and it bothers Benton that I did. It bothers him terribly as if I will think less of him and that only makes me hellbent and angrier.

'The fresh air is what I need.' I want to breathe clean air, pleasant-smelling, bracing air, and I need to think clearly. 'The cold will feel good right about now.' I don't put my coat on yet.

Adrenaline has banished fatigue and I've gone from being hungry to not feeling it anymore, and I send a text message to Bryce. I tell him Dr. Adams needs to return to the CFC immediately to confirm identifications.

'Already on his way,' he answers before I've finished typing that I'm going to be tied up for a while.

'Gavin's only called about ten million times,' my chief of staff fires back about the *Boston Globe* reporter who's a close friend of his and therefore gets preferential treatment that I've given up quibbling about.

Gavin Connors is a fine journalist who goes to concerts and sporting events with Bryce and Ethan, they cook together, and when needed he takes care of their Scottish Fold cat named Shaw.

I will have quite the story for Gavin Connors but it needs to wait until I'm sure what it is and am ready to hand it off in a way that won't be traceable, and I have no doubt Barbara Fairbanks will blast it everywhere next. The news will be too sensational for the government to bury, and I let Bryce know that when I'm back we'll deal with the media, and I'll want to hear all about the interview with Marino's possible replacement.

'I rescheduled. Are U surprised?'

'Good thinking. Don't want visitors at CFC right now. Nobody comes in without my permission, including FBI.' I type with my thumbs, standing near the kitchen where blood has dried from bright red to a dark unpolished ruby like lights dimming before they burn out.

I sense Benton's tension and preoccupation as he waits for me, checking his phone, rolling through messages and going back and forth with Lucy who is rocketing through the cyberspace and databases of Double S's tower server.

She has very little time and I give it but a few hours before she's backed up every byte of information. When the FBI arrives at the CFC and demands the computer there will be no sign we so much as plugged it in. My labs are jammed with a huge backlog of cases, I'll suggest if necessary. We didn't get around to it yet will be the implication. This is what the likes of Granby has reduced us to. Working against the FBI, working against our own people because we don't know who our people are anymore.

Bryce's next text lands with a chime and I let

424

him know that all cases need to be done tonight.

'Do U want us to save U one?' he writes back as if an autopsy is a slice of cake or a sandwich.

'No. But make sure Luke is the one doing post of victim tentatively ID'd as Haley Swanson.'

'10-4 & btw. Ernie has results. Gonzo for the day but U can call him at home. He's always up late.' As usual, Bryce is in a mood to chat.

'Thanks.' I turn around at the sound of footsteps.

★ ★ ★

An FBI agent in a polo shirt and khaki cargo pants passes through in tactical boots, wearing a Glock on his belt and carrying an M4 carbine, the short barrel pointed down, the black nylon strap hanging to his hip.

He pauses to look at us with a smile that flashes brightly without a trace of warmth, and he opens the steel door and shuts it behind him, returning to the rooms where the others have been busy for hours digging through documents.

'We should head out.' Benton stares toward the back offices, fully aware of what's going on without him.

While I was examining Caminska's body, slumped over her bloody desk, I overheard a mention of the Bureau's Eurasian Organized Crime Squad. It primarily targets criminals with ties to the Soviet Union and Central Europe and I'm aware the entire compound is now a crime scene that's been taken over by the FBI.

The entrance to the driveway is barricaded

and guarded and soon it won't be possible to walk anywhere without running into agents armed with assault rifles and sub-submachine guns. Benton and I will be noticed by someone before we're done. But I have my reason, an unusual murder weapon and my right to look for it or something like it.

'What about keys?' I ask.

I saw Marino hand over the big set of them to the agent who just walked through. This was after Marino and Benton returned from searching the grounds without permission or telling anyone. The agent took the keys from Marino with an inquisitive look, wondering how he got them or where they were from. I remembered seeing them in blood on Lombardi's desk, partially under his nearly decapitated body, and later the keys weren't there anymore. Benton offered no explanation to his young FBI colleague while Marino disappeared into the night with his dog, loudly mentioning something about teaching Quincy to be friends with horses without being kicked or stepped on.

He emphasized the words *kicked* and *stepped on* and that's when I knew he understood what was going on and being done. In the blink of an eye Marino has gone from trying to push Benton around to being his biggest ally.

'We don't need keys,' Benton says to me.

I don't ask him how he expects to get back into the locked-up private places he and Marino explored, Lombardi's secret rooms, his massive garage. I will see what's there for myself in this very brief window of time. Benton and I need to be done in an hour, not much more than that, without risking an interference that we can't afford.

'Everything will be fine.' I retrieve gloves and a small camera from my field case and tuck them into a pocket. 'There are steps that can be taken and we're taking them.'

Benton doesn't answer. He continues to stare in the direction of the offices where the FBI has busied itself after instructing NEMLEC officers to clear the scene and telling him to go home and not return to work until he's called, which will be never, he says. Only one Concord detective remains with them. I can't imagine he's saying much, hanging around and ignored like a cigar store wooden Indian, there for appearances, the FBI cooperating in a joint operation, as joint as it gets with an unscrupulous bastard like Ed Granby in charge.

'We're okay. We're way ahead, Benton.'

He looks at me with no expression. 'We shouldn't have to be,' he says.

'It doesn't matter whether we should or shouldn't. We're ahead of them and will stay ahead of them.' I glance back toward the offices where Granby and his team are investigating *the mother of cases*, as Marino put it after he and Benton had gone building to building, room to room. 'They're so busy with whatever's locked in filing cabinets and drawers and all the bankers boxes in that back storage area I saw that they aren't focused on the computer yet,' I add.

'I don't think they know it's gone,' Benton says. 'They're still wondering what happened to the DVR or if there was one.'

'They'll get nothing from us. Not one glimmer of enlightenment.' I snap shut the oversized clasps of my field case, grateful Lucy left with the server before Granby and his agents showed up.

I've said nothing about any evidence that's at my labs or en route to them and the FBI can't just roll in and take everything. There's such a thing as chain of custody and they'll have to work it out with the Concord and Cambridge police. And if trace or DNA evidence is in my possession already, then they'll have to work it out with me. I can make the process as slow and weighed down by bureaucracy as they've ever seen. There's no right reason for evidence from my cases in Massachusetts to go to the national labs in Quantico, only the wrong reason that has to do with what Ed Granby decides to alter, destroy, or simply hide. I won't give him anything until I don't need it anymore.

Meanwhile, every minute that passes Lucy is at her keyboards surrounded by flat screens, mining for truths, and she's already causing Granby the most trouble he's ever had in his life. It couldn't be more deserved. He can go to hell and he will before I'm done.

'Ready,' I say to Benton.

I carry my gear through the front door and onto the veranda and I'm delighted Granby isn't the sort to take me seriously. He never has even when he's acted like it. As many times as he's been in my presence at his office and mine, out to dinner and over to the house, he doesn't know me, only what he projects from his self-image and filters through his self-absorption. He doesn't know Benton any better.

I don't yet have an idea how far Granby has stepped over the line but anyone who would tamper with evidence is capable of anything and what I can't get out of my mind is his career trajectory. I saw the press release when he was named the special agent in charge of Boston. I've heard him talk ad nauseam about all of the important things he's done.

When I was the chief medical examiner of Virginia he was the assistant special agent in charge, the ASAC, of the Washington, D.C., field office, where he worked public corruption and violent crime, among other lofty responsibilities that included the White House. For a long time after that he was a Hoover Building bureaucrat at headquarters, overseeing field office inspections and national security investigations, and then last summer he came to Boston.

I remember Benton telling me it was a lateral move Granby requested because he's originally from here but now I'm convinced there's another reason, a filthy one. His transfer occurred last summer, not long after Klara Hembree left Cambridge in the midst of an acrimonious divorce. She moved to Washington, D.C., to be near her family because she didn't feel safe and already Lucy has discovered that her estranged husband has an extensive business relationship with Double S.

She's found purchase and sale contracts for pricey real estate and evidence of all sorts of payments and monies moved in and out of different bank and investment accounts. She's texting bullet summaries to Benton almost in real time and I happen to hear them land and see them glowing bright green on his phone as I did a few minutes ago.

'I feel sure about this. It's going to be fine,' I say to him in an upbeat way that blankets my slow-burning indignation and fury.

38

We load my gear and the red bag of soiled protective clothing into the trunk of Benton's powerful turbo sports car as if we're leaving.

He shuts the lid and locks it with a chirp. On foot we divert away from the parking lot, pushing through a barrier of pines with low-hanging branches, veering away from the driveway toward more trees, a meadow and acres of yard in a precise direction that he determined earlier. I notice him check tall lamps glowing dull yellow, their security cameras pointed like periscopes to pick up any movement along the blacktop we avoid as we make our way carefully through the foggy dark toward the house where Lombardi lived alone.

His grounds are deliberately planned, with the office building about a mile into the winding paved drive. Then a glass-enclosed walkway connects that building to a larger one, what Benton tells me is a spa, gym, and indoor pool, that in turn is connected by another enclosed walkway to a generous guest quarters. From there an additional walkway leads to the house painted dark green with dark brown shutters and a dark green metal roof, tucked in pines and not easily spotted from the air. Benton describes the dead billionaire's lair as architecturally camouflaged.

Doors leading into Lombardi's personal

spaces are secured with anti-drill dead bolt lever locks, each with a key that can't be duplicated, and every area of the compound, with the exception of barns, maintenance sheds, and the sunporch, is connected by these glass and stone walkways that remind me of covered bridges, unusually long ones. As we skirt the soggy perimeter in the inky dark and Benton explains the layout and security to me, I can't help but think of an octopus reaching out its tentacles across the property, beyond a dark horizon obscured by black clouds and into other cities, states, countries, and continents.

'You'll judge it for yourself,' Benton says. 'You'd never imagine this is going on around here but it shouldn't be the priority. It can wait, goddamn it. He's going to kill someone else. And nobody's looking for him.'

'We are. But he'll never be caught if we don't catch Granby first. I believe he knows damn well who this guy is.'

'You have to wonder why he'd help protect him if he has no idea,' Benton replies. 'It's not just about clearing cases in D.C. that are bad for politics and tourism. Granby wants them blamed on someone else for a reason, possibly because Lombardi wanted it. Hang three murders around the neck of a missing man who's probably dead and no harm done unless the Capital Murderer kills again somewhere else where the DNA can't be tampered with. And he did and here we are and Granby must be secretly panicking.'

He doesn't say it as if he's happy about it. Benton isn't heavy-handed or vindictive and maybe I can be both. He steers me around low-hanging branches I can barely see and when my shoulder grazes them cold rainwater showers me. I put my coat on and button it up.

'If we walked on the driveway, who's going to see us and what would happen?' I comb my fingers through my damp hair.

'The cameras would pick us up and we'd show up on monitors. They'd be here in two seconds and Granby would have us escorted off the property immediately.'

'You really think so?'

'It wouldn't be pretty,' he says.

'That's assuming they aren't too busy to notice.'

'They probably are at the moment. When more backup arrives we'll be out of luck and out of time. I'm surprised they aren't here already.'

'What happens when we get to the house?' I ask.

'The door near the garage has an alarm but the system's off. The chef disarmed it earlier and didn't reset it. There's no camera at that entrance probably because Lombardi wanted to come and go with various acquaintances, colleagues, mobsters, or his women, and not be seen or recorded.'

'Colleagues such as friends in high places,' I suggest.

'I think that's the picture we're getting.'

'And his women like Gail Shipton.'

'To control her. To overpower. To bend her to his will.'

'It wasn't just about sex.'

'Power,' Benton says. 'He made her do it

because she didn't want it. And to put her in her place. Carin Hegel thought she was a match for these people at first because she had no idea. She thought it was just a lawsuit. And Lombardi was putting her in her place, too.'

'She doesn't think it's just a lawsuit now as she hides out at Lucy's house. And I wonder how many other former clients Lombardi did this to. Took everything they had in a way that couldn't be proven, then settled with insurance money that he got a cut of — the biggest cut, I'm sure. Or maybe he simply got them to bend to his will because they felt they had no choice or might be killed.'

'What he did with Gail would have been a small transaction for him,' Benton says.

'A hundred million is small?'

'Whatever the settlement would have been, a payout from insurance companies, pocket change to him but an amusement because a big trial lawyer like Hegel dared to sue him. Gail was weak and got desperate and then he owned her and any technology she might help him with.' Every other minute he's looking at his phone, getting information from Lucy. 'If she wasn't dead, she'd be charged with fraud. She'd be out of MIT and life would be over for her.'

'Does Granby know about that part of it? That she was in collusion?'

'I don't know what he knows on his own but you heard what I told him.' Benton's voice is as hard as iron. 'I laid out what was important and I'm not telling him another damn thing. I'm home for the holidays, remember? And we're not here unless they've noticed my car.'

'Some investigators they are if they haven't.'

'They're not noticing anything except what's in the documents they're rooting through,' Benton replies. 'They've probably gotten the safe open by now and no telling what's in it — I'm guessing millions in cash, gold, foreign currency, and account numbers for offshore banks — and he's on the phone with headquarters every other minute, plotting, planning, cracking another big case. He's predictable and he's got it all figured out and the person we should worry about isn't on their radar. No one's looking for a reason. Granby's diverted them.'

'He cheated the DNA. He solved a case that isn't solved and now what's he going to do about it?' We walk through bunchgrass that would be bright with wildflowers in warmer months. 'He'll clear the D.C. cases, blame the murders on Martin Lagos, and make what's happened here a separate investigation into organized crime and professional hits,' I suppose.

'Which is totally illogical and someone will point that out eventually. Not everybody in the FBI is incompetent and corrupt,' Benton says. But what he's really saying is he doesn't want to believe anybody is.

'We don't have the luxury for what will happen eventually.'

'A contract killer brings his own weapon to a job,' Benton says. 'He doesn't leave clothing at the scene, take a blood-soaked hooded sweatshirt from one of his victims so he can disguise himself as he runs like hell through a crowd of schoolchildren on his way back to wherever he left his car. He doesn't grab an envelope full of cash and then accidentally drop it in a public park, an envelope with blood and a return address on it.'

Benton watches where he steps, his borrowed sneakers drenched. The wind is more frigid than I thought and everything we brush against is waterlogged.

'This is someone out of control who didn't kill the people of Double S for money,' he says. 'Maybe he wanted a reward and the ego gratification of being thanked for getting rid of Gail Shipton but the others were personal. They had it coming. Maybe not in Swanson's case. He may have been in the way and that's it.'

'The killer is someone they knew and underestimated or ignored.' The legs of my pants are soaked and my hands are cold. 'People like this don't unlock a door or turn their back on someone they have even the slightest hesitation about.'

'Rage,' Benton says. 'Lombardi hit this person where it hurts. He insulted and humiliated him and I have a feeling Lombardi had done it before. We're going to find there's a history. He knew him and I maintain no one at Double S asked him to murder Gail and wouldn't have because of the scam she was involved in, and that's not why he killed her anyway.'

'He may believe that's why. He may believe that's why he's killed all of them.'

'He believes what drives him is rational but it's all about what arouses him,' Benton says. 'And maybe he's gotten crazy because what he just did was dangerously foolish and it surprises me that someone as ruthless as Lombardi missed every cue until his blood was gushing all over his desk.'

'Arrogance. A bully above the law who thought he was untouchable. Or maybe there's another reason he took this person for granted.'

'Granby's looking for a Russian gangster to arrest and I'm sure he'll find one somewhere,' Benton says bleakly.

I envision Ed Granby, trim and dapper, with glittery small eyes and a long nose as pointed as a pencil, his hair combed straight back and gray only at the temples. His hair is so perfect I'm sure he dyes it like that and I feel my indignation swell and rise and I walk close to Benton, feeling him against me, and I feel calmer as the house looms nearer but still about a quarter of a mile off, a light on at ground level, the rest of it dark.

I check messages, my phone display glaringly bright in a darkness moiling with fog. Lamps in the distance illuminate little as they barely push through as if we're out on a ship approaching a socked-in shore. I have another reminder from Ernie Koppel that he's home if I want to talk and I try his number as we walk.

'I'm outside and it's windy,' I apologize when he answers.

'I imagine you're still in Concord and we're eating dinner glued to the TV. It's on every news channel.'

'What have you got for me?'

'An early Christmas present, a lot of things.'

'That makes me happy.'

'A tool-mark match, yes, and you're not surprised because you suspected it. And you're right about the Maryland case,' he says. 'The same mineral fingerprint as this one here at MIT and also from the residue you just collected at the Concord scene.'

'From the stubs Lucy dropped off.'

'Yes,' he says. 'The same mineral fingerprint on the dead person's fleece. Halite is basically rock salt and under SEM it's obvious it was artificially grown by saturating salt water and allowing it to evaporate, which makes me suspect the residue that's turning up is from something manufactured for a specific commercial use.'

'Do you have any idea what?'

'Calcite and aragonite are common in construction, found in cement and sand, for example. And I know that halite's used in glassmaking and ceramics and also to melt ice on the roads. But the three of these minerals together with the same elemental fingerprint as in the Maryland case and now this one and basically every sample I tested? It could be some sort of art supply for pottery or sculpture, maybe some type of mineral pigments in tempera paint or special effects. Under black light it sure as hell would be iridescent.'

'Anything about the fibers?'

'From Gail Shipton, Lycra from the blue fibers you collected and also what she was wrapped in. The white cloth is also Lycra. And that's also consistent with the fibers found in the Washington, D.C., cases, maybe the same fabrics in all of the cases but different runs of it. One thing that surprised me is the vapor rub. I can't pinpoint the brand but the spectral fragmentation pattern made for a relatively easy identification that's the surprise in the Cracker Jacks. Apparently someone was looking to do more than clear his sinuses. MDPV,' he says.

'You're kidding.'

'I'm definitely not kidding. DNA handed off a sample to me late afternoon and I gave it a whirl with FTIR and that's what I got but I'm not a toxicologist. If you're not opposed to using up some of the sample, I suggest liquid chromatography — tandem mass spec just to confirm. And by the way the tox lab tells me it's the same methcathinone analog as that suicide from last week, the lady who jumped off her building. A really dangerous designer drug someone's selling on our streets, the same one that's been wreaking havoc this past year I'm afraid.'

'Thank you, Ernie.'

'I know it's not for me to offer but I'm going to anyway. I think it's the same guy. He's doing something weird to them, maybe wrapping them in stretchy fabric and then using some sort of artistic medium, maybe painting portraits of them after they're dead, who the hell knows. You be careful, Kay.'

'Racehorses and bath salts,' I say to Benton when I get off the phone. 'I guess if you want to focus keenly and experience superhuman energy and euphoria and wreak havoc on your neurotransmitters, mix a little monkey dust in your vapor rub and keep swiping it up your nose.'

'That helps explain what he just did. It might explain a lot of things. Increasing paranoia, agitation, aggression, and violence.'

'His system's going to be roaring, hot and sweating, his blood pressure through the roof.' I think of the bareheaded young man with no coat on in the rainy cold. 'He may be getting psychotic.'

I imagine him watching me in the dark behind my house and I wonder who and what he thought I was, and who is Benton? Who are any of us or his victims to him?

'The horror of this drug is that you can't escape from it and you never know what dose you're getting in a package,' I explain. 'So the reaction can go from mild to insanity and brain damage. Eventually it will kill him.'

'Not soon enough,' Benton says.

★　★　★

Through fragrant evergreens that smell like cedar we near the lighted windows on the first floor, careful about cameras, making sure no one is around as I continue looking back like a fugitive.

I see no headlights or flashlights, just the darkness of the wet foggy night and our foggy breath, and I hear the wet sounds of Benton's borrowed shoes. I estimate that from the entrance of the property to where the driveway curves past the outbuildings and the office and around to Lombardi's house the distance is almost two miles. We trudge through a vegetable garden that's dormant and dead and then spreading out before us are a tennis court with no net, a barbecue pit, and a lap pool that's covered for the winter.

There's another tarmac, this one round and made of pavers that I suspect are heated, and beyond it are four bay doors that are heavy metal like hurricane shutters. Inside are cars, Benton says, rare Ferraris, Maseratis, Lamborghinis, McLarens, a Bugatti, all with Miami plates, the baubles of the super-rich and super-thieves, and like yachts, business jets, and penthouses, they're a way to launder illegal money. The cars probably were destined for the Port of Boston and headed to places like Southeast Asia and the Middle East, Benton suspects.

A solid-wood door opens onto the long, glass-enclosed stone walkway that up close I can see has a golf cart inside and is stacked with split firewood. This leads from the outbuilding that's a spa to the house that includes the private kitchen and living area, the master suite on the top floor and the garage on the lower level. Benton opens another door that he left unlocked when he was here earlier with Marino and we enter Lombardi's private kitchen, an open space with a deep fireplace near a breakfast table and zinc counters and big windows overlooking the grounds.

A wine cellar is visible beneath plate glass in the hardwood floor and when I walk across it I have the fleeting sensation of vertigo, a fear of falling, that flutters in my stomach. I step to one side of it and don't look down at the hundreds of bottles in circular wooden racks and decorative wooden casks and a table for tasting.

Copper cookware as bright as rose gold hangs from a wrought-iron rack above a butcher block with a maple top where plastic bags of groceries are spilled open, hastily set down by the chef when he returned from shopping late today. Milk and fine cheeses and cuts of meat have been left out and I can see evidence of his panic after he discovered police cars in the driveway.

He would have driven right past my big white truck with *MA Office of Chief Medical Examiner* and our crest painted in blue on the sides and there are few sights less welcome than my staff and machinery showing up. It's heart-stopping. It causes instant visceral terror and I tend to forget the god-awful effect I have especially when I'm unexpected, which is almost always. I resist the impulse to tuck perishables into the refrigerator. It seems such a waste. I photograph them instead.

I pause by the commercial French cooktop to look at fine carving sets with green beechwood handles. Paring, boning, tomato, bread, and chef's knives, wide and narrow and up to twelve inches long, and also sharpening steels, are all in the proper slots of two cutlery blocks. I take more pictures, documenting every place I look and whatever I touch, as Benton continues to check messages landing from Lucy in a rapid succession of alert tones that he's set to sound like an irritating bicycle bell so he doesn't miss a single one.

39

'All the phones here are on software like a PBX.' Benton talks more freely now, showing me what Lucy just sent.

'A good way for Lombardi to keep tabs on what everyone was doing,' he elaborates but not happily or with the gratification that I feel as the facts are made plain, 'and apparently he got a call at four fifty-seven this morning from a number that has blocked caller ID. None of Double S's sixteen phone lines including the ones here in the house accept blocked calls.'

Inside drawers I find wooden boxes of steak knives and a variety of cooking tools, potholders, and dishcloths. There are takeout menus for local pizza and Chinese but I doubt anybody delivered up here.

'So this particular caller had to enter star eighty-two like every other poor schmuck on the planet or his call wouldn't have gone through,' Benton says. 'Lucy's asking if I recognize the number and I do. It's Granby's mobile and it's not the only time he's called here. She says this same number has shown up a lot. The question is when.'

He types his answer to her, and he's no longer careful about what he tells me out loud. We have evidence of Granby's criminal involvement. Double S's computer is proving to be a treasure trove and it's no longer our word against anybody else's. It's not a suspicion or circumstantial evidence, and it's impossible we can be accused of misrepresenting the ugly truth. The data are irrefutable and safely backed up at my office. And Benton's boss has no idea what's about to happen to him.

'Marino arrived at my house around five this morning,' I point out. 'By then news of the body at MIT and who it might be was already on the Internet. So it appears Granby's call to Lombardi was probably about that.'

Another irritating bicycle ring and Benton reads, and then he says, 'A lot of calls back and forth between the two of them, clusters of calls back in March, April, during the time when Granby was relocating here, and dozens of them last month, some on the very days that Sally Carson's and Julianne Goulet's bodies were found. Christ.' Benton leans the small of his back against a counter. 'This is fucking awful.'

'We knew it would be.'

'What else would Granby have been calling about if it wasn't Gail Shipton?'

'I think you know the answer.'

'A simple one,' Benton verifies what he already believed. 'She wasn't supposed to be murdered. Nobody asked this psycho to do it and Lombardi was ballistic and he'd been there before with whoever this person is only now there's even worse trouble because Gail is directly connected to Double S. It's like asking a drunk to run your bar.'

'You don't ask a drunk to run your bar unless you don't know he's a drunk or have something personal with him.' I slide out a knife with a nine-inch carbon-steel blade that's curved to carve around bone.

'Get your rogue killer here, get your PR person here, serve cupcakes and straighten it out,' Benton says.

'Good luck when the rogue killer is on stimulants and craving sugar, swinging out of balance and about to explode.' I hold the knife in my gloved hand, feeling its balance and the smooth, hard shape of its elegant wooden handle.

It wouldn't be good for killing someone. I return it to its cutlery block and it makes a quiet steely hiss as it slides into its slot.

'Of course the chef would have to confirm if something's missing.' I don't need to look at any other knives in Dominic Lombardi's kitchen. 'Any one of these could inflict lethal damage.'

'But it's not what was used,' Benton says and I shake my head.

The weapon is nothing like any of these. It's an oddity, whatever it is, and as I continue taking photographs I explain that the blade we're looking for is short and narrow, single-edged, with a beveled angle, and possibly the tip is rounded and badly bent.

'I'm basing this on the shallow incisions with peeled skin and abraded edges that parallel the deeper ones,' I add. 'And the pattern on a towel he used to wipe off the knife also gives us a clue about its shape and that it might have burrs that snagged threads when he wiped it off. Knives generally don't get burrs unless you sharpen them.'

Another bicycle bell, a long text from Lucy, and she informs Benton that Lombardi's second wife spends much of her time in the Virgin Islands where he has a number of companies registered. Shell companies, Lucy suspects, including art galleries, high-end spas, stores, hotels, construction, real estate development.

'Businesses convenient for money laundering and probably drugs,' Benton suggests. 'Maybe labs where the designer drugs are coming from, here or abroad.'

He opens a door near a half bath, with a toilet and sink, and a windowsill overflowing with gourmet magazines. *Bon Appétit, Gourmande!, Yam.* The leisurely reading of a French chef who suddenly has no job anymore. And people like him would be a dime a dozen if he went back to Paris, where his wife is with someone else and his children have no use for him. *Tout est perdu. Je suis foutu*, he said to Benton when he and Marino were making their clandestine tour.

We climb carpeted steps, four of them, and then a landing with prism crystal sconces spilling from faux-stucco walls. I imagine Lombardi climbing and pausing to rest or catch his breath with thick, stubby-fingered hands on the polished brass railings, the diamond ring on his right pinky and the bracelet of his solid gold watch clicking against metal as he moved his heavy body along. Getting around his compound and up to the master floor couldn't have been easy, as big as he was.

Benton opens another door that isn't locked because he left it that way and on the other side is a vast space overwhelmed by antique Italian furniture in rare woods, and the elaborate crown molding and decorative relief on the walls and ceiling are gold. A multicolored, two-tiered Murano fruit chandelier hangs from a faux Michelangelo mural of God creating Adam, and there's a circular conversation settee upholstered in gold satin near the foot of a bed fit for a king. The headboard is more than five feet high and a brilliant red with gilt acanthus.

A Renaissance desk with a Florentine throne chair would never have handled Lombardi's considerable girth, and the Venetian mirrored chests of drawers would have reflected his discontent and glutted boredom every time he opened a drawer. Drapes across the floor-to-ceiling windows are crimson velvet with intricate gold and silver embroidery, and when I push a panel to one side the lining is gold silk, heavy and lush against my hand. I look out at the view of his bloated world where everything had a price and probably meant nothing, paid for with the blood and suffering of whoever he could squeeze the smallest commodity from, whether it was sex, murder, or money for designer drugs that will make you insane and dead.

The unlit connected walkways are barely etched in the foggy dark early night and there are no lights on in the spa building, and I notice for the first time that the back of the office building has no windows. Lamps along the winding drive are smudges of yellow light and beyond are the voids of the paddock and the pond, and then the gambrel barn. It hulks against a black

447

horizon, a hint of light seeping through spaces in the wide sliding door and shuttered windows that are barred, and I wonder who's in there besides the horses. The staff who heard and saw nothing have made their exodus, and Marino would be waiting for us but I doubt he can. He's NEMLEC, he's nothing, and Granby's henchmen will have told him he's nonessential and to leave. I continue to glance at windows and doors and to look for lights and listen for sounds, wondering when the same thing will happen to us.

I walk over to the bed stand, with its alabaster lamp, a cut-crystal carafe, and water tumbler, and I slide open the drawer. Inside are a pistol with a satin nickel finish, a .50 caliber Desert Eagle with enough rounds to wipe out everyone on the property and on neighboring farms and then some. Lombardi didn't bother to arm himself when he picked up Haley Swanson at the commuter rail station and sat down with some drugged, sugar-craving acquaintance or connection who might have fancied himself an assassin or a hero.

I close the drawer and move to a mirrored bookcase to the right of the bed, its reflective shelves arranged with framed photographs of Lombardi during different eras of his violently ended life. A young boy sitting on the front steps of a row house in what appears to be a rough neighborhood, probably in the fifties based on the cars lining the city street, and he was sandy-haired and cute but already hard looking. There are plenty of pictures of him with women,

448

a few of them famous, in nightclubs and bars, and then sitting at a wrought-iron table with a handsome dark woman who I suspect is his wife, surrounded by a lush tropical garden on the edge of a magnificent stone pool.

Then another photo of the two of them and in the background is a magnificent villa that looks very old and reminds me of Sicily. And there are photographs of the couple and possibly their three children, a boy and two girls in their late teens or early twenties, on a white yacht, cruising turquoise waters near dark green mountains and red-roofed villages that could be the Ionian Islands, and Lombardi is older now and grossly overweight. His puffy face and small, squinting eyes look discontented and bored as he poses on the teak deck in the midst of beauty and luxury that should have seemed beyond the wildest dreams of the boy sitting on the steps in a poor neighborhood, assuming Lombardi remembered that boy. But I doubt he thought of him anymore or dreamed.

A photograph that doesn't fit with any of them is the one I pick up and look at carefully, a big gray elephant that dwarfs the young man giving him a bath, holding a running hose and a scrub brush. I move the photo in the lamplight and study the small but strong-looking shirtless figure in baggy camouflage shorts, tightly muscled with dark hair and an empty, icy stare as he grins boldly into the camera.

I feel the hair prickle on my scalp as I notice his shoes, black running gloves, his powerful tan legs ending in what look like black rubber feet.

The photograph was taken in a grassy area with coconut palms surrounded by a chain-link fence and beyond are deep blue waters, a speedboat going by, and beyond it white cruise ships are moored at what I recognize as the Port of Miami.

'Who is this?' I ask Benton.

He steps close to look, and then he steps away to give me space as I continue seeing what there is to see for myself.

'I don't know,' he says, 'but we should try to find out.'

'The Cirque d'Orleans is based in South Florida.' I return the photograph to its mirrored shelf. 'And at the first of this month it was in this area and the train was parked at Grand Junction for several days. Right in the middle of MIT.'

'I suppose it's possible Lombardi owns a circus, too. That would be a good venue for distributing drugs, also a way to launder money, faking ticket sales, and who knows what. Maybe he dealt with the black market selling of exotic animals. Who the hell knows?'

I take several photographs, angling the camera to avoid reflection and glare as best I can, and I ask Benton about Dominic Lombardi's family.

'He has the second wife in the Virgin Islands, according to Lucy, possibly the woman in a number of these photographs,' I say. 'What about children? Has Lucy mentioned anything about that?'

'I'll ask her.' He types a text on his phone.

★ ★ ★

Benton waits in front of a standing cheval mirror carved with cherubs playing music and I see him front and back, facing me and reflected in the glass.

I look at a Luca Giordano painting of blacksmiths and next to it an André Derain seated woman before an abstract background of reds and greens. Pierre Bonnard, Cézanne, and Picasso are arranged unimaginatively on one wall and I ask right off if they might be expert forgeries.

'I'm sure that's what he told anybody who might have seen them,' Benton says. 'What do you think?'

'I feel like I'm in an art gallery or a vulgar palace, I'm not sure which. I guess the answer is both. I don't know if they're real or not but they're magical and he probably didn't even notice them beyond what they're worth.'

'The Maurice de Vlaminck you're standing in front of, stolen in Geneva in the 1960s. Valued at around twenty million.' Benton's eyes follow me.

'And the others?'

'The Picasso was last in a private collection here in Boston in the 1950s. It would go at auction for around fifteen million except for the minor problem that it's hard to sell stolen art unless the buyer doesn't mind and there are plenty who don't. Masterpieces like these end up in private homes. They hang in yachts and Boeing business jets. They make the rounds until they surface like these will now. Someone dies. Someone gets caught. Someone realizes what he's looking at is genuine. In this case all of the above.'

'You know this off the top of your head.'

'When I was growing up we had a Miró in the living room and one day it was replaced by a Modigliani, and after that a Renoir, and at some point there was a Pissarro, a snow scene with a man on a road.'

Benton moves away from the mirror to look at the Vlaminck, a painting of the Seine in intense colors that are mesmerizing.

'We had the Pissarro the longest and I was very unhappy when I came home from college and it was gone. There was this space above the fireplace where the art rotated. My father bought and sold it often, never really got attached to it. To me each one was like a cat or a dog I grew to love, or not love, but I missed every one of them when they were gone the same way you miss your friend or most boring teacher or even the bully in school. It's hard to explain.'

I know about his father's love of fine art and how much money he made from it but it's the first time I've heard about the space above the fireplace and the Pissarro that Benton missed.

'It took five minutes to find out about these. I e-mailed photographs to my office before Granby sent me home.' Benton holds up his phone, which has become our most trusted link to truth and justice. 'The small bronze on the bedside table is a Rodin. You can see his signature at the base of the left foot, stolen from a private collection in Paris in 1942 and off the radar ever since.'

There are scraps of paper and what look like receipts under it. Lombardi was using it as a paperweight, and the loathing I shouldn't feel

452

because no crime scene should be personal only gets more acute when I look inside his dressing room crammed with racks of hand-tailored suits and shirts and rows of handmade shoes and what must be hundreds of Italian silk ties. In the master bath is a countertop made of tiger's-eye with a gold-plated sink and a shaving set made of mammoth ivory.

The back wall beyond the shower and the tub is filled with an opulent trompe l'oeil mural of Lombardi in a suit and tie posed with a magnificent Arabian horse inside an English barn, and, behind it, a stone arch that opens to what looks more like a Tuscan landscape than the Concord countryside. His plump hand rests possessively on the horse's sleek neck as a farrier in a leather apron and chaps bends over the hind leg he holds in his leather-gloved hands, trimming the hoof. Lombardi's jowly face with its small cold eyes seems to stare at me as I lean closer to get a better look.

The workbench is mounted with a vise and arranged with many picks, rasps, nippers, and sharpening files and a leather strop, but it's what the farrier grips securely in his right hand that transports me to a place I never thought I'd be while inside the private spaces of Lombardi's house. Suddenly I find myself inside the gambrel barn without going there, staring at a knife with a long wooden handle and a short, chisel-shaped blade, one side beveled, the other flat, with a hooked tip that curls in on itself to trim away a horse's loose and dried-out sole.

'When you were in the barn with Marino was

this what it looked like?' I point to the work-bench inside a large stall with hay on the floor and dark wooden exposed beams overhead.

'Not quite as nice and tidy and no stone arch opening onto vineyards,' Benton says wryly. 'There are a lot of tools. The horse's name is Magnum.'

40

'A hoof knife.' I touch the painted one the farrier holds in the mural on the wall.

'The sharp curled tip would explain the wider, shallow abraded cut that peeled the flesh in places and runs parallel to the deep incision made by the straight edge of the blade,' I describe to Benton. 'The killer may have gone into the barn because he knew what was easy to grab and how it would function as a weapon. It's impossible to imagine he's not familiar with the grounds and that nobody saw him.'

I run my finger along the brown wooden handle gripped by the farrier and along the narrow short silvery blade to where it curls in on itself at the tip. I feel the thick layers of paint on cool tumbled marble and I imagine Lombardi in his shower or bath looking at the very tool that one day would almost sever his head from his neck.

'It's not what you would think of unless you know about it.' I envision getting my hands on a hoof knife and trying it on ballistic gelatin to see precisely what it does. 'If you saw one on a workbench, you might not realize how effective it is, sharp enough to trim a hoof but not so sharp as to cut too deeply into the sole, not straight-razor sharp, which is difficult to control if you're frenzied or bloody. It's quite an art how farriers sharpen their tools — not too sharp, not too dull — so you can do the job without injuring the horse or yourself.'

'An eccentric choice that on the surface seems illogical.' Benton walks behind the long, deep stone tub to study the mural. 'But I didn't see any regular knives in there and maybe that's why he grabbed what he did and it could be related to the drugs he's on. If he's watched horses being taken care of and shod and seen farriers get tired and sweaty and the horses not stay still the same way people don't stay still if you're cutting their throats, he might have been present when someone cut himself or he might have watched the knives being sharpened.'

He looks at the hoof knife clamped in a vise on the workbench in the painting.

'And in his increasingly disordered thinking it means something to him.' Benton works his way around the edges of the killer's mind. 'He envisions himself a horse, just another one of Lombardi's possessions he controlled and kept in a stall and treated with disrespect and indifference, and maybe this morning was reprimanded, verbally whipped. There could be symbolism like with the vapor rub, like the tools under rocks. Power. I win, you lose. It's all about that but also at this stage a by-product of his delusions.'

'What I can say with some degree of confidence,' I reply, 'is whoever did this didn't wander into the barn randomly and happen to see an unusual tool with a long wooden grip and stubby blade that's hooked on the end and figure it would work just fine for killing people.'

456

'He knows horses, this barn and this place,' Benton states. 'And he's become so preoccupied with his delusions they're completely disrupting his life.'

'Why wouldn't the staff want to say who it is? For fear he'd find them and hurt them if he's not caught first?'

'Maybe the opposite. They might not fear him because he doesn't fear them. Especially if he was in the barn with them earlier and was friendly and has been here before.'

'Now they're accessories to murder after the fact, participants by concealment.'

'If it can be proven, yes.'

'It's probably not a new way of life for them,' I decide as I photograph Lombardi and the farrier with his knife. And then the bicycle bell rings again, another message from Lucy landing in Benton's phone.

'He has three children with the second wife,' he informs me. 'A son who is a financial planner in Tel Aviv and two daughters who are in school in Paris and London.'

'Sounds like a lovely family,' I reply as I decide the photograph of the young man and the elephant needs to go to Lucy because I have a feeling about him, not a good one.

Then Benton and I leave the house as we found it and the night seems more raw and cold. The heavy pines we walk through seem more sodden than they were before and their wet branches grab at us as the wind shoves and shakes them. In the parking lot we find more unmarked cars and light fills the shades in every window on both floors of the office building where the dead are gone, by now autopsied and safely in my coolers.

It seems later than it is and the powerful rumble of Benton's turbo Porsche seems louder than I remember as we follow the driveway, passing the huge red barn, stopping at the barricades where a black FBI van with dark-tinted windows is parked. A surveillance vehicle, and I know where there's one there will be others, monitoring Concord and the roads leading in and out of it and intersections along any route the target might take. I'd find it reassuring if they were looking for the right target but they're not.

Benton shifts the Porsche into neutral and pulls up the brake. He opens his window and waits, knowing exactly how the FBI thinks and the importance of doing nothing suddenly or nervously that might be misinterpreted. Maybe the agents inside the van are aware of his car and that it's been parked on the property for a while but Benton is of no concern to them as they've held their post at the entrance of the driveway, out of sight inside their van with all of its equipment. I imagine them tracking every car, truck, or motorcycle that passes on the street, communicating with other agents in vehicles and on foot, waiting to use diversions or decoys to mobilize into what Benton calls a floating box that invisibly surrounds whoever they're after.

Benton touches a button in the center console and my window hums down, and I look out into the foggy night, watching an agent materialize in black tactical clothes, his carbine across his waist, his index finger ready above the trigger guard. If he didn't know whose car this is, he will have run the tag while we've been sitting here. He's not aggressive but he's not relaxed.

His unsmiling face is in my open window, young, with a buzz cut, nice-looking and lean like all of them, what Lucy calls Stepford Cops, automatons identically programmed and physically crafted, and she would know since she used to be one of them. Federal agents whose polish, power, and camera-ready presence make America look great, she says.

It's all too easy to hero-worship and emulate and my niece couldn't have been more enamored when she started out with them as an intern while still in college. There's nothing more impressive and sexier than the FBI, she'll tell you now, until you run head-on into their lack of practical experience and absence of checks and balances. Until you are confronted by an Ed Granby, who answers to Washington, I think, and I'm no friendlier than the agent when I inform him who I am and that I'm clearing the scene.

I don't offer my credentials with its shield. I'll make him ask and he looks past me at Benton, who says nothing and ignores him, and all of it has the intended effect. Uncertainty twitches on the agent's face as he recognizes an impatient authority that has no fear of him and then something else is there. The agent smiles and I sense his aggression just before he puts Benton in his place.

'How you doing tonight, Mr. Wesley?' He rests an arm along the length of the carbine strapped around his shoulder, crouching down lower. 'Nobody said you were still here but I figured you wouldn't just leave a car like this and catch a ride with someone.'

'I wouldn't,' Benton says with complete indifference to what the agent is implying.

His expensive sports car was noticed and maybe it was a given that we were still on the grounds and looking around but we're inconsequential. We aren't part of the huge machinery and nobody cares. We aren't a threat and maybe even Granby doesn't think we are and then a second agent appears from around the side of the van I can't see from where I am, a pretty woman in fatigues with her hair in a ponytail pulled through the back of her baseball cap. She moves close to her colleague and smiles at me.

'How's everybody doing?' she says as if it's a fine evening.

'The weapon you're looking for may have come from the big barn.' I look back in the direction of it but from here it's out of sight around a bend in the driveway. 'A knife used on horse hooves, a long wooden handle with a very sharp blade that's hooked at the end.'

'The murder weapon might be in the barn?' The male agent doesn't take his eyes off us.

'One would think he didn't run into the barn after killing three people and return the knife.' I say it blandly. 'But I would expect you'd find other hoof knives and it's quite possible he was in there earlier. That's the important point. You might want to pass that on to your evidence response team.'

'What are you basing this on?' the female agent asks, more curious than concerned.

'The injuries to the victims' necks are consistent with the knife I described and unless he brought one with him to the scene he got it from the property. I don't know what else could have caused the incisions I saw.'

'You're sure it's a certain type of knife?' she asks as if it matters to her and I can tell it doesn't.

'I am.'

'So we shouldn't be looking for a variety of knives like kitchen knives.'

'It would be a waste of your time and unnecessarily burden the labs.'

'I'll make sure we take a look.' The male agent removes his hand from the window frame and backs away from the car. 'You folks have a nice Christmas.'

The two of them move sawhorses to the side and we drive through, in first gear, then second, and Benton guns the powerful engine before shifting into third, his way of saying fuck you. It's as close as he can get to saying it and it occurs to me that Granby may have said it first. He may be saying it to us right now.

* * *

As I reach Lucy on my cell phone I'm already uneasy about what Ed Granby may have put into place. I feel a spike of paranoia and my thoughts begin to race.

It's more than possible if not a certainty he

461

knows we've been here unauthorized for the past hour and he did nothing about it because he's secretive and calculating. He's a consummate politician and wouldn't want to give the appearance that he escorted the chief medical examiner of Massachusetts from the scene of a triple homicide that's all over the news.

He would look dirty and as if he's hiding something. He would look exactly like what he is. And while he wouldn't have hesitated to have Benton escorted off the grounds, Granby isn't stupid. He'd be sneakier than that with me. He'd hold off having his evidence response team or any other agents swarm Double S until Benton and I were gone and suddenly my electronic communications don't seem safe. Nothing does.

'We're just leaving and I'll make this succinct.' It's my way of letting Lucy know I intend to be careful about what I say.

'Sure,' she answers.

'I don't know when we'll be home and I'm worried about Sock.' She knows I'm getting to something else because Janet picked up my dog around five when our housekeeper Rosa left and Lucy's already assured me of that.

'He's fine and by the way Rosa said if you're not going to put up a tree, she will. That's assuming Bryce doesn't barge in and do it first.'

'I'm going to take care of it,' I reply.

'And Sock can't go home tonight.'

What she's saying is I can't and Benton shouldn't either. The killer has been on our property before and we can't predict how deranged he is but he's deranged enough. Right now Sock is probably napping at Lucy's house, which isn't far from here, and I wish there were time to drop by. I wish life were settled and safe enough to have a nice late supper with my family and my dog.

'Who's still at the office?' I ask.

'Bryce, security, me. Marino's out with Machado. The docs are done and have left.'

'Anne's gone home?'

'She and Luke went to get something to eat and I don't know where she'll go after that but both of them said they'll come back in if you need them.'

I've had my suspicions Anne might be sleeping with the handsome, womanizing Luke Zenner. I don't care but it won't last and that's fine as long as she doesn't care either.

'It won't be necessary,' I reply, 'but let them know they need to be very careful. There's reason to be concerned about the stability of the person the FBI is looking for.'

'I guess so since he murdered four people in a twelve-hour period and no telling what's next.'

'Are you okay?' I'm asking about what she's doing, which is going through Double S's server. 'Any inquiries about location or status?'

'Roger that.'

The FBI knows we have the server and the CFC has been contacted.

'The usual paperwork that will take a little while,' Lucy adds.

She's stalled them.

'But I couldn't be better.' She continues to follow my cue, saying nothing obvious or direct.

'When I get there I'll go straight into the PIT if it's been set up.'

'Waiting and ready. I replaced the bad projector. Tell him to see me upstairs right away.' She doesn't mention Benton by name. 'I've this really cool new search engine to show him.'

She's found more incriminating information about Ed Granby. No matter what he's calculating, he's not calculating this, but he's calculating something and we need to be careful.

Most of all we need to be cunning and smart. 'Will do,' I reply.

I end the call and place my phone in my lap, looking out my window at the dark night, passing Minute Man Park, a foggy emptiness now with vague silhouettes of statues and the bowed wooden footbridge the killer fled across this morning. Through the shapes of trees the distant lights of Double S seem to flicker as we move along the deserted street.

'What you're implying would be illegal wiretapping,' Benton says.

'I don't recall implying anything.' He's going to stick up for them, it occurs to me sadly, a deeply aggravated sadness that creates a space between us whenever I feel it.

'I know the way you talk, Kay.'

'And you know why I would worry, Benton.'

I'm not sure he'll ever believe how bad it's gotten and I feel what I've felt before, dismally and outrageously it gnaws at my soul. Benton idealizes the Bureau he began with in his early optimistic life when he started out a street agent, working his way up to his eventual zenith as the chief of what was then the Behavioral Science Unit at Quantico.

I understand his dilemma. Even Lucy does. For him to accept what the FBI and the Department of Justice that owns it are now capable of would be like my believing that when I do an autopsy it's nothing more than a callous science project on a par with dissecting a frog.

'Whatever they can justify they will, whether it's secretly intruding upon everyday people or journalists or even a medical examiner, and it's not new, just worse.' It's a truth I repeat all too often these days. 'Once that gate has opened it's a hell of a lot easier for someone like Granby to step legally out of bounds with impunity.'

'There's no probable cause for him to spy on us. I don't want you getting paranoid.'

'Don't be so damn decent, Benton, because he's not. He can violate whatever he wants and what recourse do we have? We sue the government?'

'We need to stay calm.'

'I'm quite calm, I couldn't be calmer, and I know the cases out there and so do you, and for every one of them we hear about there are countless others we don't. You know it better than I do. It's your damn agency, Benton. You know what goes on. The DOJ, the FBI, decides to spy without a court order and who's going to stop them?'

'Granby's not the FBI I know. He's not the FBI either of us know.'

'The FBI we used to know, yes. That's for damn sure.' I don't say it unkindly or with the

465

vehemence I feel because it will only make Benton more defensive.

I don't use the phrase *police state* that's on the tip of my tongue because what neither of us need right now when we're stressed and tired is to turn on each other. Benton and I have had our fights about the Department of Defense and the Department of Justice, each of us taking different sides, and during normal times we have a peaceful understanding.

But now isn't a normal time and it's inevitable he's going to have to take down his boss Ed Granby. It has to be Benton who does it and he knows it and is principled enough to regret it would come to this and the problem is he'll insist on doing it discreetly and with dignity. That will never work, considering the snake we're dealing with. Lucy and I need to find a way to help Benton be a little shrewder and less honorable and it's coming to me.

'The Bureau's far from perfect but what the hell isn't?' Benton doesn't look at me as he drives. 'He'll get what he deserves.'

'I intend to make sure of that.' I have an idea that's beginning to form.

'This isn't your battle.' He downshifts and the throaty rumble of engine drops an octave as he slows at an intersection surrounded by dense trees.

'Your office wants us to turn over Double S's server,' I pass along what Lucy just implied. 'And I'm willing to do so tonight but Granby needs to sign for it. Otherwise I'll make sure the process is mired down and the FBI won't get it for days. I doubt they'll raid the CFC.'

'Of course not.' Benton glances over at me and I sense his resolve, which is tainted by the deep disappointment he feels. 'What you're suggesting is a good idea. He needs to show up in person.'

My phone glows brightly in my lap as if waiting for what I'll do next and I know what it is. *Witnesses*, I think. Ones who aren't law enforcement but are well connected to people who are powerful, lawyers who don't give a damn about the Feds and consider them fodder as a matter of fact. Lucy's partner used to be FBI and now is a prominent environmentalist attorney, and then there's Carin Hegel, who's friends with the governor and the attorney general, to name a few.

Benton turns left onto Lowell Road, rolling slowly through a pedestrian crossing, and the two-lane road crosses a dark ribbon of river, moving us back toward the center of town, where we'll pick up Main Street and then the turnpike. I place my hand on his arm and feel the small muscles move as he moves the titanium shifter in its leather boot. Then I get Lucy on the phone again.

'If you could let the party that contacted you know we're happy to cooperate fully as long as the chain of evidence is intact in a way that satisfies all of my protocols,' I tell her, 'meaning I will personally receipt it to the head of their division, otherwise the process will be encumbered and slow. They can pick up this evidence as late as midnight because I'm headed in now. And on a different subject, I'd like Sock brought to the office right away.'

My niece is silent as she tries to figure it out.

'As skittish as he is and with a killer on the loose, I've decided the office is the safest place for all of us until the FBI finds who they're looking for or gives us reassurance he's no longer in the area,' I say for the benefit of whoever might be monitoring my call.

Maybe no one is but I'm going to act as if it's true.

'No problem,' Lucy replies. 'I'll pass on the messages and we'll take it to the next level.'

'That's exactly what I have in mind. I don't think there's a choice in light of the circumstances.'

'I'll get it worked out. I'll have some food brought in.' She'll have Janet and Carin Hegel do it, and she'll make it clear that if the FBI wants the server, then Ed Granby will have to show up at the CFC and get it from me personally.

'I have stew and a nice minestrone in the freezer. And lasagna and a Bolognese sauce that turned out very well.' I try to think what else. 'And bring a can of Sock's food, his pills, and also one of his beds.'

41

I'm alone inside the PIT, where I'm known for my sardonic, cutting quips, because to resort to such extreme technology is to admit how utterly and completely it has failed us.

It's moments like this when I'm keenly aware that if the world wasn't flawed and people weren't limited, I wouldn't need a Progressive Immersion Theater equipped with multi-touch tables, tactile interfaces, projection mapping, and data tunnels to discover what bad or sad thing resulted in tragedies that might be better understood but not undone.

As my father used to say when he was dying and could no longer get out of bed or eat on his own, *If my wish was my reality, Kay, I'd be sitting in the backyard in the sun, peeling an orange.* The dead Dr. Schoenberg wished he could stop his dead patient Sakura Yamagata from wishing she could fly to Paris on wings she didn't have and the dead Gail Shipton wished to break through what had blocked her since she was too young to be blocked, but given a choice none of them wished to be drug-addicted, dishonest, weak, depressed, and no longer here.

People fail, everything fails, the magic we're born believing in and working for and then doubting and finally fearing eventually rusts, rots, fades, breaks down, withers, dies, and turns to dust, and for me the response is always the same. I clean up. It's what I do and I'm doing it now as I stand at a long glass interactive table with data projectors under it that display computer images of documents and photographs I lightly touch with my bare hands to slide out of virtual files and move and flip through as if they're pages of paper, to zoom in and out, as I review Gabriela Lagos's autopsy, lab, and investigative reports.

Nearby on a curved wall her virtual image glows hugely and grotesquely in 3-D, and I've been going back and forth from the glass table to a smaller one where a wireless keyboard and mouse are set up. It's as if I'm in that room with the tub and its scummy water and bloated body and I can see every vein and artery etched greenish-black beneath translucent skin that's slipping and underneath where it's blistered and red from full-thickness burns. I move images in a way that gives the sensation I'm walking around and looking as if I'm there, as if it's up to me to work the scene instead of my former deputy chief Dr. Geist, in his late seventies now and comfortably ensconced in an upscale northern Virginia retirement home.

When I call him he's cordial enough at first, saying it's a nice surprise to hear from me after all these years and how much he loves retirement, consulting on a case here and there, not as many as he used to, just enough to keep his feet in it because it's important to keep the brain young. He gets more condescending and gruffer as the conversation goes on and then he's combative when I push him on the details of Gabriela Lagos, the same details he and I argued about in 1996. But now I know what I didn't then.

On the third of August, he responded to her home at one-eleven p.m. and quickly determined her death was an accident because he'd already determined it. He knew what he was going to find and how he would interpret it, and that's the part I didn't put together until tonight.

'I remember her body in the tub and there was water in it, maybe filled up halfway,' he says to me over the phone and it's about half past ten and I can tell he's been drinking. 'An obvious drowning that wasn't suspicious. I seem to recall you and I had a professional difference of opinion.'

'In hindsight are you sure there was nothing staged about what you saw?' I wonder if the years might have covered his lies until he can't make out the reason for them anymore or maybe he'd like the chance to finish up his existence on earth as an honest man.

But unsurprisingly I find him the same as I left him. He says he remembers how hot and airless it was inside her house and that flies blackened the bathroom windows, the droning of them infernally loud as they batted between the drawn shades and the glass. The stench was so terrible a cop threw up and then two others began to gag and had to escape into the yard. Gabriela Lagos had been drinking vodka before taking a hot bath and this increased her risk for an arrhythmia, which rendered her unconscious, and she drowned,

Dr. Geist recites to me.

There was nothing unusual about the scene; he says what he's said before, his story not changing because nothing has happened over the past seventeen years to cause him to revisit or revise or cover his ass. Before I called he probably hadn't thought about the case in almost that long.

'And nobody straightened up the bathroom in your presence or perhaps before you got there,' I suggest.

'I can't imagine it.'

'You're absolutely sure of that.'

'I don't appreciate the insinuation.'

'The kitchen door that led outside was unlocked and you must have noticed the air-conditioning had been turned off, Dr. Geist. And it wouldn't have been turned off by her while she was still alive. It was late July and in the high eighties.'

I go through photographs on the data table as I talk with him. The thermostat with its turned-off switch. The unlocked door and through its windowpanes a large, densely wooded backyard where it would have been easy for someone to access her house after dark and tamper with the crime scene. Someone who knew what investigators would look for, someone well informed and comfortable with conspiracies, with created perceptions and outright lies, and not even Dr. Geist would have been so brazen as to commit a criminal act. But he would have overlooked certain details if persuaded by a government official that it was in the best interest of everyone.

'Her blood alcohol level of point-oh-four very

472

likely was due to decomposition.' I move that report in front of me next. 'There's no toxicological evidence that she consumed any alcohol.'

'I seem to remember the police found an empty vodka bottle, an orange juice carton in the kitchen trash.' His nasty tone and arrogant argument are like a recording he's played many times before.

'We don't know who was drinking vodka. It might have been her son or someone else — '

'At the time I knew nothing about the son and what he eventually was accused of, accused of largely because of your insistence to turn the case into a sensation and create a damn uproar,' he interrupts me rudely and that is nothing new with him. 'It's not the job of a forensic pathologist to make deductions and I've always said you'd be better served if you wouldn't get so damn involved. I might have thought you would have learned that after you resigned, which of course was a dark day for all of us.'

'Yes, and I have no doubt that my position in this very case had a little something to do with that dark day and its resulting in your having a few good years with no chief second-guessing you and creating uproars before you retired and made a very good living consulting on cases, mostly federal ones. I apologize for calling so late but I wouldn't if it wasn't important.'

'I was always respectful in my assessments of you as hardworking and competent,' he says and I can only imagine what spiteful reviews he gave about me to whoever might have weighed in about my staying on as chief. 'But you've always gone too damn far. The body is what you're responsible for and not who did it or didn't do it or why or why not. We're not even supposed to care about that or the outcome in court.'

He lectures me the same way he used to and my dislike of him is as fresh as it was the last time I saw his stooped gait at a meeting after I'd left Virginia for good. He greeted me with his hawkish face and yellow teeth as he pumped my hand, sorry to hear the news, but at least I was young enough to start over or maybe I could teach at a medical school.

'I have a copy of the entire file, including call sheets,' I say to him and by now he's openly belligerent. 'And I've noted that the FBI called you about a matter that must have related to the Gabriela Lagos case since it's in her file and marked with her accession number.'

'She was of interest because she had a security clearance to work at the White House. Something to do with art exhibits and she used to be married to an ambassador or something. I need to go.'

'The Assistant Special Agent in charge of the Washington field office, Ed Granby, called you at three minutes past ten a.m. on August second, 1996, to be exact.'

'I fail to see what you're getting at and it's getting very late.'

'Gabriela's body wasn't found until the next day, August third.'

Before he can butt in or get off the phone I go on to remind him it was believed she died on the early evening of July thirty-first and on August

474

third a concerned neighbor noticed her news-papers on the driveway and windows swarming with flies and called the police.

'So I'm curious why Ed Granby would have contacted you about this case a day before the body was found.' I get to a point he never thought I'd make. 'How would he have known about something that hadn't happened yet?'

'I think there was concern because the boys were missing.'

'Boys? As in more than one?'

'I don't remember except there was a concern.' He raises his voice like a weapon he might strike me with.

'I suspect the reason Granby chatted with you was to make sure there would be no concern if and when something unfortunate was discovered. And it was about to be,' I reply bluntly. 'Coincidentally, the very next day.'

'I would appreciate your not calling me again about this!'

'It won't be me who calls you next, Dr. Geist.'

★   ★   ★

In 3-D and high-resolution my former colleague's deliberate deception couldn't be more apparent. I'm looking inside the bathroom, with its tradi-tional old-style décor, at the open doorway now, peering in, getting the perspective from the out-side in as if I've just arrived and haven't been here before. Then I move inside again.

The black lid of the white toilet is down, as if someone might have been sitting on it, and on the black-and-white tile floor in front of it a plush white mat is indented by large sneakers that were approximately an eleven or twelve in a men's size. I imagine a male, probably a young one, perched on the toilet lid with his big sneakered feet resting on the mat while Gabriela was taking her ritualistic bath, and that's consistent with the diary Benton went through on fifteen-year-old Martin Lagos's computer disk, pages of it displayed on the data table.

She smears that gross chalky white shit all over her face & calls me over & over again. 'Martin! MARTIN!' Until I come in & find her staring at me the fucking scary way she stares when she's in her sick mood, don't know how to describe it & I shouldn't have to & I don't know why I'd go in there. I hate myself so bad for going in there but she'd yell & so I'd go. I hate it, hate it!

HATE! I feel hate & I don't want to. But that's what human nature of people does to you after you start out relatively okay & then people do things to bring you down. I know for the rest of my life I'm going to see her white face as white as a clown face or the Joker surrounded by flames & steam that smells like the shit she rubs all over me when I have a cold & I remember it started like that when I was six & in bed & she'd come in & I'd want to die. It's what I think of each time I walk in & she's screaming at me. 'Martin, come here! Come sit down & talk to your mother!'

The small flames were votive candles that after Gabriela's death were arranged on the edge of the tub and it couldn't have escaped Dr. Geist's attention they were streaked with spilled wax, two of them chipped and cracked, and a spatter of pinpoint waxy droplets were on the floor and floating on top of the water. I'm seeing them clearly in the photographs Lucy stitched together and projected onto the curved wall and it's obvious that at some point the candles were knocked over. They fell on tile and into the tub and the liquid wax hardened unevenly, and then someone rearranged the candles, spacing them just right like everything else.

I observe big white towels perfectly folded on racks and small, elaborately framed paintings perfectly straight on a gray stone wall, a robe hanging neatly from a hook next to the glass shower stall. On a washcloth spread open on the counter by the sink are a jar of white-tea face mask with a price tag from the spa store called Octopus, and next to it a bottle of eucalyptus body oil that would have permeated the humid air with the sharp, pungent aroma of a vapor rub. Items were tidied up to set the scene, to tell the story that Dr. Geist wanted told, which was of Gabriela applying her mask and pouring aromatic oil into her bath before having the misfortune of suffering some episode that caused her to lose consciousness and drown.

While my former deputy chief was clever and competent, he wasn't flawless in his execution. Thank God most amoral people aren't, especially ones with no personal investment in what they're lying about. He didn't care what happened to Gabriela Lagos. As far as he was concerned he had nothing to do with it and in his lofty learned way he could argue the case a number of ways and almost believe his conclusions.

Dr. Geist cared only about himself and probably assumed ASAC Granby's interest was to avoid creating a sensation about her death because people over him in the Department of Justice, the attorney general's office, and who knows how far up it went were worried about any political fallout. The presidential election was three months off and no point in casting a smutty shadow on the White House, where Gabriela Lagos was well known for pulling together exhibits and acquiring fine art for the First Family. It didn't matter. Dr. Geist would have been more than happy to comply if in his mind it did no real harm and there was some benefit for him.

What I couldn't see in printed-out photographs I reviewed at the time were the perspectives of the two people who might have been together in that bathroom before everything went so horribly wrong. I need the PIT for that. Had Martin been sitting on the closed toilet lid with his large feet resting solidly on the mat he would have been looking directly at his mother's stark-white face while she looked directly at herself in the large mirror on the wall next to him. He mentions it in his diary, an electronic document that Benton believes is genuine in what it implies.

She looks at both of us in a mirror & no matter how much I don't want to I watch her watching both of us & I want both of us dead. How did everything get this fucked up? It's so bad for me right now (not that it's ever good) . . . but I finally told Daniel, my best friend ever.

I'm tortured by thinking I shouldn't have but I told him the entire fucking story going back as far as I remember. We were drinking beer in his basement & I was upset because of what the shit at home is causing with my grades & everybody hates me. I don't know what the hell's happened, it's like I was okay & then I hit this wall. SLAM! I feel people looking at me like I'm a freak & I've finally figured out existence is nothing but a punishment & what the hell do I have to look forward to?

At least he didn't call me sick cuz he says it's her fucking fault & if I keep putting up with it he won't have anything to do with me anymore. He says I need to record it cuz he needs 'evidence' or he won't believe me. So that's what I have to do, hook up the spy camera & after he's convinced he'll fix 'the bitch' & I felt nothing when he said it. I HATE her & that's the truth & if he leaves I'll be so lonely w/o a friend. I plan to go to Radio Shack tomorrow & get one of those spy video recorders & I need to get money out of the safe w/o her knowing . . .

42

I move pages of the diary, spreading them with my index fingers to make them bigger, sliding them closer to Benton, who has just walked in after spending the past few hours in Lucy's lab. He seats himself nearby in a black mesh chair and I give him the gist of my conversation with Dr. Geist. Then I summarize.

'Martin Lagos didn't leave the shoe glove prints along the railroad tracks. He couldn't have killed his mother and you might be right that he's dead and has been since he disappeared and supposedly jumped from the Fourteenth Street Bridge.'

'Reported anonymously from a pay phone,' Benton says. 'It didn't happen.'

'He certainly sounds suicidal and extremely vulnerable.'

'I believe he was murdered and that certain people know it, which is why it was safe to steal his genetic identity.' He peruses the introspective writings of Martin Lagos, idly moving pages on the table the way one does when something has been read many times.

'What could be better?' *Ed Granby needs to go to prison*, I think angrily, and maybe no punishment is bad enough for him. 'Someone missing who's wanted and you have inside knowledge that he's dead. The problem with taking a step like that is only a very limited number of people would have the information.'

'Granby had to know it to instigate the DNA being altered. He had to feel it was a sure thing to take a chance like that.'

'He's behind all of this. He's why at least seven more people are dead.' I check my emotions, which have moved well beyond a visceral response to raw vengeance.

I ask about the friend named Daniel and if Martin ever made those secret video recordings he mentions in his diary.

'We don't have them if he did,' Benton says. 'But he references them several times up until about a week before her murder. I suspect her sexually provocative bathing was recorded and would have fueled a budding killer's violent fantasies.'

I want to know if we have a physical description of Daniel and if we know where he is.

'Dark hair and eyes, white, don't know what he'd weigh now,' Benton says.

'Thin if he's hooked on MDPV.'

'He's probably about five-six or -seven, based on pictures from his high school and college yearbooks.'

'Can you give them to Lucy?'

'I just did.'

'Small and dark like the young man giving the elephant the bath,' I remind him of the photograph we found in Lombardi's bedroom.

'Let's see what Lucy can do with it. Why do you say Martin couldn't have killed his mother? Not that I doubt it but I need everything solid I can get.'

I move a photograph close, Martin puffing out

481

fifteen candles on a chocolate birthday cake, July 27, 1996, four days before he vanished and his mother was drowned.

'This is why,' I reply.

A boy who's grown too fast for his bodyweight to catch up with his limbs, he's rawboned and awkward, with big feet and hands, in a tank top and baggy shorts, his ears cupped out from his closely shorn head, his upper lip dirty with facial hair. I zoom in on his right arm encased in its clean white plaster cast that only one person has written on: 'Remember not to do what I say, bro. HA! HA! HA!' His friend Daniel wrote it boldly in red Magic Marker, and next to his flamboyant signature is a bright blue cartoon figure that looks like a fat Gumby doing a cartwheel.

'Martin didn't drown his mother.' I'm sure of that. 'He couldn't have gripped both of her ankles with only one good arm.'

'He looks reasonably strong. And when his adrenaline kicked in? You don't think he could do it with one arm?'

'He didn't. Two hands were used.' I hold up both of mine as if I'm gripping something hard. 'Her injuries make that patently clear. He didn't kill her but that doesn't mean he didn't agree to it and witness her murder from the best seat in the house.'

As I study Martin's forced smile and eyes that look haunted, I imagine someone taking the photograph of him on his birthday. Based on the way he's looking at the camera as if he's been ordered to, I suspect his mother did.

'Do we know how he broke his arm?' I ask.

482

'I know he liked to skateboard. That's as much as I can tell you without calling his mother back, which I don't want to do right now.'

'Maybe skateboarding with his friend Daniel. His only friend,' I reply.

'Daniel Mersa. He mentions him throughout his diary and that bothered me then but not nearly as much as it started bothering me a few weeks ago when I heard about the DNA results that we now know were tampered with.'

'He must have been interviewed after she was murdered.'

'The police couldn't find him at first,' Benton says and I think of Dr. Geist's comment about *the boys*. 'When they finally did, his mother gave some convenient excuse that he'd been visiting her sister in Baltimore and the sister corroborated this of course. When Daniel eventually was questioned he claimed he had no idea what happened to Martin's mother. He said Martin wasn't doing well in school, the girls didn't like him, he was depressed, getting into alcohol, and that was as far as the questioning went seventeen years ago.'

'It went as far as somebody wanted it to go,' I reply.

'Granby,' Benton says.

'I strongly suspect some relatively competent and self-assured person visited the scene before her body was found and turned off the air-conditioning, filled the tub with scalding water, rearranged the bathroom, removing the hidden video camera, possibly taking Martin's computer hard drive, not realizing there was a backup hidden in his bedroom. Kids wouldn't think of so many details, although it wasn't a perfect job. It's pretty obvious.'

'Granby's pretty obvious,' Benton says.

'I don't know how you'd prove it at this stage.'

'I probably can't prove he did the tampering at the scene. But it probably was him especially if it was amateurish.'

'You have the call sheet at least,' I reply. 'He called Dr. Geist about Gabriela Lagos the day before anyone except those involved should have known she was dead.'

'Let's print a hard copy of that.'

I text the document identification number to Lucy and ask her to print it. I don't say what it is or give a reason and I ask her to bring it downstairs. She texts me back that we have company coming and I have an idea why Benton wants the hard copy. I have a feeling I know what he'll do with it and while some people would enjoy it, Benton won't.

'After Gabriela was murdered and before her body was found somebody alerted Granby that there was a problem,' Benton then says. 'Otherwise I don't see how he could have known in advance. Someone who knew what Daniel had done, someone powerful who Granby would want to help.'

'Then Daniel must have told whoever it is.'

'Of course,' Benton says. 'He's a kid who's just killed his best friend's mother, a prominent Washington woman who collected art for the White House.' Benton continues to run information through his mental database while I run it

484

through my own. 'Daniel made a call because he would have needed help to get away with it.'

'The person at the center of this, all roads leading to the same source.' I think of an octopus again. 'How old was Daniel then?'

'Thirteen.'

'That surprises me. I would have assumed he was the older of the two.'

'He was the dominant one in the relationship,' Benton says, 'overly controlling and organized, a risk taker and show-off with an excessive need for stimulating his senses and a very high threshold for pain. He doesn't feel pain or fear the way other people do.'

I can well imagine Daniel coercing Martin into extreme feats with the skateboard that may have resulted in a broken arm and other injuries and humiliations.

'Martin was two years older and two grades ahead of him but had very poor self-esteem, very bright but not particularly gifted athletically,' Benton explains. 'He was a loner.'

'Had they been friends for a long time?'

'Apparently their mothers were very close.'

'How convenient that Martin's mother was an art expert who put together exhibits and acquired masterpieces for the First Family.' I envision the stolen works in Lombardi's bedroom.

'I'm thinking the same thing you are.'

I ask him who and what Daniel Mersa is today and where he is and Benton says he started gathering information when Granby told the BAU that DNA had identified the Capital Murderer as

485

Martin Lagos. Benton talked to Daniel's mother and told her it was crucial to know if anyone had heard from his childhood friend Martin, who might be in danger or he might be dangerous to others.

She claimed she wouldn't know because she hadn't heard from her son Daniel since he dropped out of a college summer program in Lacoste, France, when he was twenty-one. He'd been in and out of trouble, she admitted, and in and out of different schools and sent abroad, and he never graduated and had nothing to do with her anymore.

'Do you believe she was telling you the truth?' I ask.

'About that, yes.' Benton moves the projected image of a file closer. 'I honestly think she's worried now.'

'Because of the Capital Murderer cases.'

'I didn't mention them.'

He slides documents out of the virtual file and begins turning virtual pages and they make a papery sound.

'But I had a feeling she knew what I was talking about when I brought up Martin and that we need to find him,' he says. 'Something about her demeanor caused me to suspect she knew damn well we weren't going to find him because he's dead. But that doesn't mean Daniel isn't out there somewhere killing people and she knows it.'

He lines up pages of a student disciplinary record with the Savannah College of Art and Design in the headers.

'One of many places Daniel was in and out of and his academic records are telling.' Benton taps the glass with his index finger and a page gets small and he enlarges it again. 'Breaking into another student's locker, sneaking into a girl's dorm and stealing lingerie from the laundry room, setting fire to a guidance counselor's garbage cans, drowning a dog and bragging about it, disruptive in class, vandalism. It's a long list that includes his high school years.'

'Were the police ever involved?'

'They were never called. The matters were handled privately, typical of schools, and maybe there's another reason.'

'What else did his mother say?'

'She did everything she could for him, sparing no expense on counseling and therapy. As a child, Daniel was diagnosed with Sensory Processing Disorder, and I gathered from what she said that in his case SPD manifests not in his overresponding to sensation but not being able to get enough of it. Originally it was confused with ADHD because of his sensory-seeking behavior, his inability to sit still and obsession with touching things, his thrill seeking and high-risk activities, walking on stilts, climbing up telephone poles and water towers and out windows and down drainpipes, showing off to other kids, who would try to imitate him and hurt themselves. She said she couldn't control him no matter what she tried.'

'Sounds like she was making excuses for him because she suspects the worst,' I comment.

'She wanted me to know she was a good

mother, availing him of the typical home therapies for SPD. Backyard swings, obstacle courses, monkey bars, trampolines, gymnastic balls, sensory body socks, personally supervising tactile art like finger painting and working with clay.'

'Clay,' I repeat. 'What Ernie's found.'

'It's entered my mind.'

★   ★   ★

'A mineral fingerprint that might be from an art supply like paint or sculpting clay,' I think out loud to Benton.

Lycra fibers from a stretchy material like a body sock, and I move the photograph of Martin so I can look at it closely again. I study what Daniel drew on the white plaster cast, a bright blue Gumby-like cartoon that could depict a boy zipped up head to toe in what looks like a body bag sewn of a colorful thin but sturdy fabric that can be stretched into different creative shapes in the mirror or in shadows on the wall. A therapeutic body sock is see-through, impossible to tear, and if the zipper were locked, one couldn't escape. It's breathable but that doesn't mean you couldn't suffocate someone with it if you wrapped it tightly around that person's face.

It would be a good way to restrain someone, the soft, silky fabric causing very little injury, and I imagine Gail Shipton paralyzed by a stun gun and zipped up inside such a thing. It would explain the blue Lycra fibers all over her body and under her nails and in her teeth. And then I see her struggling inside this stretchy bag-like prison while she's in the killer's car, clawing, maybe biting at the material as she panics, her damaged heart hammering against her chest.

I hope she died quickly before he could do the rest of it and I suspect I know what the rest of it was, as if I'm watching what the bastard did, perhaps spreading open what's no different from a body bag on the car seat and the minute he's got her inside he's zipping her in, assuring her that he won't hurt her as long as she behaves, and she doesn't want to be shocked again, does she?

I can see him driving her somewhere in the dark, perhaps talking to her while she doesn't resist, and then he gets her to a place he's picked in advance and he tightens the stretchy material around her face and suffocates her. It would require about as much time as it takes to drown someone unless he was cruel enough to do it slowly and he could have, tightening and relaxing, letting her come to and doing it again, as long as he wanted, as long as her body could sustain such torture before it quit.

Then he poses his victim, adorning her as it gratifies his sick fantasies, tightly securing a plastic bag around her neck with designer duct tape that left a faint furrow and mark postmortem and adding a decorative duct tape bow under her chin and then another victim's panties. All symbolic. All part of his incredibly twisted mind and soul, the choreography of his evil imagination, his evil art, a deviant inspiration that goes back to the beginning of his blighted time on this earth and possibly fueled by deviant home movies of Gabriela Lagos bathing and seducing her son.

I envision Daniel Mersa dragging the body on some type of sled or litter, displaying it by a lake near a golf course. An arm outstretched, the wrist cocked very much the way Gabriela's left arm was positioned as it floated on the surface of the water in the tub, languidly stretched out, the wrist drooping, her other arm floating across her waist.

Such an image would be indelibly imprinted in Daniel's violent mind after he drowned her, watching her naked body go completely still, then limp, settling lower in the water, her arms drifting up as if she's relaxing in her steamy, sharply fragrant bath surrounded by candles and huge plush white bath sheets. He may have recorded her murder and repeatedly watching what he did to her would have fueled what drives him and made him sicker.

'You don't necessarily outgrow SPD,' Benton is explaining and I look at him and try not to see what I just did. 'And the worst thing someone with that disorder could do is to take designer drugs, stimulants like MDPV.'

'And none of what you're telling me about Daniel Mersa was taken seriously by the BAU.' I feel exhausted and chilled and I try to will my mind to clear.

'No one's been listening to me because they're listening to the DNA. It's not Daniel Mersa's profile that got a hit in CODIS. In fact, he's never been in CODIS or arrested and for a good reason.'

The images of women dying are stubborn in my mind. I see their terror and suffering as they were suffocating. *'HA! HA! HA!'* Daniel Mersa wrote with a flourish on Martin's cast.

'A lot of people have disturbing backgrounds and they don't end up becoming serial killers,' Benton is saying. 'And Granby's discredited me with the BAU.' He repeats the depressing story I know so well. 'I don't know exactly how or when it started but it's not a hard thing to do when people worry about their jobs and are competitive.'

'Daniel Mersa's father. There's been no mention of him.' I sense the direction the roads are moving in, all headed to the same source at the center of such cruelty.

'Sperm bank,' Benton says. 'His mother's always claimed she doesn't know who the biological father is and you have to ask how she afforded therapy, college, studying abroad. Veronica Mersa is a former beauty queen, never married, was a secretary for a New Hampshire congressman who only recently retired from politics. She wasn't paid a lot and had no other income. She has never seemed to hurt for money.'

'I'm not uploading anything to CODIS or any other database until I know it's safe.' I'm adamant about that. 'We'll do any comparisons in my labs and I'm going to ask for a familial search to look for first-order relatives, siblings or parent-child relationships. If Daniel's related to someone and we've got that individual's DNA, we're going to figure it out.'

'It would explain it,' Benton says. 'It would

491

explain a lot of things. And Granby might have pulled it off if you'd let Geist have his way and decide Gabriela Lagos's death was an accident.'

'There's no question it wasn't. There should never have been a question.'

'Show me how you know the killer used both hands. I need to see it for myself. I've got to be able to say it in no uncertain terms.'

I touch the glass tabletop where her autopsy report and photographs are side by side.

43

'Medical history: none.' I read what Dr. Geist reported about Gabriela Lagos on his autopsy protocol. He included some facts and omitted other ones.

'No history of seizures, fainting, cardiac problems, nothing, and suddenly she takes a bath and dies at age thirty-seven. Negative for drugs that were screened for, and the alcohol present in her blood was due to decomposition.' I show Benton what's on the four-page document, going over the displayed image of it projected on the table. 'White froth in her nose, mouth, and airway because it wasn't possible to disguise the fact that she was a drowning.'

Benton gets up from his chair and walks into the PIT, where Gabriela's bathroom and her decomposing body are all around him, their projected light and dark shapes reflected on his face as he seats himself at the small table, what Lucy calls the cockpit. The wireless keyboard and mouse allow him to reorient whatever he wants, moving the scene as if he's moving through it, and the tub with the body, roll to the right and in closer, a little jerky at first until he gets warmed up.

I can see her long brown hair splayed over the stagnant surface of the cloudy water, and drifting nearby is a black elastic band with a shiny black bow that held her hair up and out of the way before she was drowned. A white mask smears the outer layer of skin that has slipped, her frog-like face bright red from the chin down because that's how she was submerged after the tub was drained and refilled with hot tap water. Dr. Geist omitted that important fact, too. He failed to record the pale areas of exposed flesh above the surface of the water, the upper face, the tops of the wrists, while the rest of the body was scalded red.

'Had the water been scalding hot when she was being drowned,' I explain to Benton, 'every inch of her upper body and head would have had full-thickness burns. And that's a critical piece of information because it indicates the water got hotter after she was dead, and that alone tells me homicide.'

'I've never understood froth.' Benton clicks the mouse and Gabriela's face suddenly looms larger, blown up by the gases of decomposition, her eyes bulging as if in horror. 'People are underwater and the froth is still there. Why doesn't it wash away?' He moves an arrow to the white foam between her protruding lips, pointing it out.

'It seems stubborn because it's not really just between her lips,' I reply. 'When someone is drowning and gasping violently froth builds up like dense soap suds in the lungs, the trachea. That's where most of it is and what you're seeing is leaking out of her mouth. It doesn't wash away because there's a lot of it and Dr. Geist knew he couldn't say she didn't drown. He knew her body wouldn't let him get away with that lie. The best he could do was decide it was an accident.'

I walk over to where Benton is standing and as I look at her again I'm reminded why I felt the way I did at the time and drove to the funeral home in northern Virginia. While the contusions aren't easy to discern because of the condition she's in, they are there, dark red areas, some slightly abraded, on her right cheek and jaw, her right hip, and on both hands and elbows. Small fingertip bruises are scattered over both ankles and lower legs, with wider, more indistinct bruises behind her knees.

'It would take two hands to leave those bruises on her ankles, and two hands were used, not big hands like Martin's hands, and that's the other thing,' I tell Benton. 'These circular bruises from fingertips pressing into the tissue of her lower legs and ankles are small.' I hold up my hands. 'Not much bigger than mine. Someone held her firmly, grabbing her ankles with his hands and yanking up, hooking her lower legs in the bend of his arms, causing the bruises behind her knees.'

I show him.

'Now she's held by her lower legs tightly against his chest and her upper body is completely underwater. The other bruises on her hip, hands, elbows, and face are from her thrashing and striking the sides of the tub. It would have been violent, with water splashing everywhere, knocking candles onto the floor and in the water, and then in minutes it was over.'

'I can see how that wouldn't work if one arm was in a cast,' Benton says.

'Martin couldn't have done it but I think he

495

watched. Sitting on the closed toilet lid, his big feet on the white mat, where he'd probably sat for most of his life through every hellish episode of her forcing him to be an audience to her seductive bathing,' I explain. 'You can't blame him for wanting her dead, wanting to be free of her, but he wouldn't have anticipated what it was like to actually witness such a thing.'

I imagine him wide-eyed, paralyzed and shocked as he watched his mother cruelly and horribly die before his eyes. Once it started he couldn't have stopped it and he may have wanted it but he didn't.

'It would have been appallingly awful,' I say to Benton. 'I can promise you her son couldn't have imagined how awful it would be.'

'He wouldn't have enjoyed it,' Benton says. 'Martin Lagos wasn't a sociopath and he wasn't a sadist. And he didn't need to constantly over-load his senses with the next huge thrill, in this case a kill thrill.'

'I wonder what size shoe Daniel Mersa wears.' And I envision the young man and the elephant in the photograph.

I feel a change in the air as the door behind us opens and light from the corridor makes the room brighter. Lucy walks in holding a sheet of paper and she looks really happy, the kind of happy she gets when she's about to nail someone or pay them back in a way that's lasting.

'Granby and his troops are here,' she says. 'By the security desk. I said they had to wait and you'd be right out. The computer is wrapped up and ready to go. Ron has it and I've signed off on

496

the paperwork, all set for you to do the honors of receipting it. There's a lot more to go through but we've got everything backed up and they don't know that. Carin and Janet are upstairs.'

'Good,' I reply.

Lucy glances at her phone and when she looks at me she smiles, then she hands the sheet of paper to Benton. 'Well?' she asks him.

'I was getting to it,' he says.

'He has bad news that's good news,' Lucy tells me cheerfully.

I spot Bryce in the corridor heading toward us and at this late hour he looks a bit rumpled and scruffy but has that wide-eyed nervousness that we see around here when we're in the throes of the latest tragic drama.

'The *Globe* is here . . .' Bryce starts to announce as he walks through the door. 'Oh God!' he exclaims. 'She's so awful to look at. Can't we take that picture down yet?' He averts his face from what's displayed in the PIT. 'I've said it before and I'll say it again. If I die, please don't let me look like that. Find me instantly or never. Sock's upstairs in your office in his bed and I gave him a treat, there's food in the break room, and Gavin's in the parking lot with his lights turned off and he just saw the FBI roll up and in a minute I'll bring him inside as if he works here. This is going to be the most amazing story. I want him to hear it for himself when they demand the computer and everything else.'

'Bryce, you're talking too much,' I warn him.

'Payments of ten grand a month, supposedly for the lease of Washington, D.C., office space,'

Lucy starts to tell me what Benton hasn't gotten to yet. 'Wires to a bank in New York City and from there they are broken up into different sums and wired out to another bank, broken up again and wired out again, and on and on like clockwork for the past seventeen years, literally from August of 1996, and that sure as hell can't be a coincidence. It might never have led to Granby being the recipient of funds that clearly are laundered but he did one really stupid thing. An e-mail.' Lucy gets really happy again. 'About six months ago he had lunch with an investor who mentioned it in an e-mail to Lombardi.'

She shows it to me on her phone:

From: JP
To: DLombardi
RE: 'Gran Gusto'

Thx for hooking me up, great lunch with such a grand guy (nothing small about his FBI ego & didn't realize the pun when I picked my favorite Italian spot!). Am recommending his account be moved to Boston now that he's taken the job there. Modest amount in cash, rest in stocks, bonds, etc. He knows someone who can help with my irritating audit problem, f'ing IRS. Cheers.

Bending around my curved corridor that leads to the receiving area, I walk briskly, my lab coat over field clothes I'm scarcely aware of anymore. I've reached a zone of fatigue that broaches an out-of-body state, hyper-awake and also in slow motion.

'I don't guess you or Marino could arrest him on the spot,' I say to Benton.

'He'll deny everything.'

'Of course he will.'

'By daylight he'll be lawyered up.'

'I don't care. He's done, Benton.' I've made sure Granby's defeat will be a public one.

Benton looks at me and he's single-minded in what he needs to do. And while it should give him pleasure, it doesn't.

'No lawyer is going to save him and none of his usual powerbrokers in Washington are going to touch him with a ten-foot pole,' I add and then I get quiet as we reach the receiving area.

Ron is inside his office with the window open, and for an instant I'm knocked off guard by Granby and his entourage of agents. He looks exhausted but polite as if he knows he's on my turf and is most appreciative of my having him here, the three agents in cargo pants and jackets standing some distance behind him. It occurs to me Ed Granby is scared and I wasn't expecting that.

I wonder if he's suspicious Lucy has been inside Double S's server and then I decide he knows what's about to happen. He's not naïve about who she is and what she's capable of. And whether or not he's cognizant of any incriminating information she might find, he has to be expecting the worst. That's the way it works with people who are guilty of as much as he is. For every one sin uncovered they know of at least a hundred more.

'I apologize for the inconvenience,' he says to

499

me while he doesn't look at Benton and has no idea about Bryce or the young bearded man next to him who is dressed in a plaid shirt, sweater-vest, and jeans and sneakers.

Lucy walks past us and toward the elevator and I hear the door slide open.

'Obviously this is a significant white-collar criminal investigation we've got going here and thank you for respecting, uh, for appreciating our need to get Double S's computer to our labs,' Granby says to me. 'Your cooperation is so appreciated,' he stumbles nervously, too polite and smiling too much.

'Of course,' I reply and I'm not smiling at all or remotely friendly. 'We have it ready for you.' I meet Ron's eyes and he nods at me through his open window.

'Yes, ma'am — Chief,' he says and maybe I'm sleep deprived but I catch a trace of a grin. 'I've got it right here and all the paperwork's in order.'

'And then there are the homicides.' I look Granby in the eye as he uses both hands to smooth his perfect hair at his perfectly graying temples. 'We'll continue working those up and get the FBI any information needed.'

'As always, much appreciated.' He continues smoothing his hair as he watches Ron open his door and push out a cart that has the computer server on it, upright and shrouded in plastic. As if to make a point, Lucy has overwrapped it with bright red tape that boldly warns in black: *SEALED EVIDENCE — Do Not Tamper.*

I pull a Sharpie out of a pocket of my lab coat and slide the evidence submission form out of its transparent plastic window that's taped to the computer. I initial and date it in front of everyone and then I hand it to Granby, doing things the proper way, officially receipting evidence to the FBI for analysis that we sure as hell don't need. I wonder when the last time was that the head of a division actually received evidence or bothered to show up at a medical examiner's facility. I wouldn't be surprised if Granby's never seen an autopsy.

'I'm surprised to see you here,' he says to Benton. 'And why are you here?' he asks as he touches his hair again.

'Enjoying time off. Probably more than you will.'

Granby's eyes seem to get smaller when he's nakedly aggressive but he smiles again. 'Not me. Too much to do.'

'I think you're about to have a lot of time on your hands, Ed.'

I hear energetic footsteps from the direction of the elevator and then Lucy, Janet, and Carin Hegel appear. They stand next to Bryce and Gavin Connors, a crowd of witnesses gathered according to plan.

'What's this?' Granby's attention fixes on Hegel like the darts from a stun gun, his eyes seem to anchor right into her skin.

He would know who she is for every reason imaginable. She's often in the news because of high-profile trials and is almost as recognizable around here as a professional athlete. But more to the point she was Gail Shipton's lawyer and pitted against a firm that as it turns out has been paying off Granby for years. Enough monthly cash and who knows what other favors and he must have assumed he had little to worry about as long as he didn't get ensnared by his own deceptions. And he has. The life he's enjoyed is about to be over.

'If you know who this is really about, Ed, now's a good time to say something.' Benton hasn't taken his eyes off him. 'It's not Martin Lagos we're looking for. I know what you've done. All of us know.'

'I don't have any idea what you're talking about but I take umbrage at the implication.'

'You're about to pin the Capital Murderer cases on a kid who disappeared seventeen years ago based on DNA that to put it diplomatically must be a mistake. A lab error, I'm sure you'll say.'

'This isn't the time or the place!' Granby fires back at him. 'We'll discuss this in private.'

'You won't,' Carin Hegel says and I just now noticed she must have taken time to dress in power clothes at this hour.

A small, fiery woman with short chestnut hair and an attractive face that doesn't look remotely threatening until she talks, she bothered to put on a dark cashmere jacket with a dramatic collar and large silver buttons and black slacks and boots.

'Everything said is going to be said right here in front of all of us.' She sounds more like a judge than a lawyer.

'This is a joke.' But Granby doesn't think it's funny and his nervousness transitions to fear that's palpable.

I watch him get wound tighter like a spring about to snap and it occurs to me he might run.

'I thought you might like to see this.' Benton hands him the printout of the call sheet. 'I know it was a long time ago but you might remember giving Dr. Geist a telephone call. He was the medical examiner in Gabriela Lagos's drowning, a homicide that you wanted him to decide was an accident.'

Granby stares at the sheet of paper he holds, staring at it as if he doesn't know how to read.

'We have evidence her crime scene was tampered with,' Benton says and he illustrates what he means, mentioning the air conditioner turned off, the scalding-hot water in the tub, the spilled wax, the tidying up.

'And her son Martin had a broken arm so it wasn't him gripping both of her ankles to drown her,' Benton adds. 'I can show you the contusions on her lower legs, the two sets of fingertip bruises, if you'd like to see them.'

Granby is so dumbfounded he doesn't notice that the young bearded man in the plaid shirt and sweater-vest is furiously taking notes and that the very pretty blond young woman next to Lucy is holding a digital recorder that she makes a point to say is running. Janet has made this point several times by announcing that she's recording our conversation and if any party present refuses consent, speak up now or consent is implied. Granby doesn't speak up but I do. I tell Ed Granby who Janet and Carin are, that both of them are lawyers, and then I make it clear why they're here right now.

'Forensic evidence links the murders of Gail Shipton, Haley Swanson, Dominic Lombardi, and Jadwiga Caminska with those in D.C., despite your protestations to the contrary,' I say, to his visible shock. 'Fibers, a mineral fingerprint, and we've only just begun, and I happen to know for a fact that a DNA profile in CODIS was tampered with. The sample you got a profile from and then changed to Martin Lagos came from a female, from a mixture of fluids including menstrual blood.'

'This will be dealt with through the proper channels, my channels. I certainly don't trust your channels or anything about you, for that matter.' Carin Hegel looks at him and the agents standing behind him. 'I've already left a message for the attorney general,' she starts to say and this is when Granby runs.

The call sheet he was holding flutters to the floor as he bolts through the door leading into the open bay, flinging it open so hard it bangs against the wall, and he gets as far as the parking lot, where Marino is climbing out of his SUV. When he sees all of us emerging from the building he does what he used to do when he was a Richmond cop.

'Whoa! Where are we going in such a hurry?' Marino says loudly as Granby runs toward his car.

In several big strides Marino intercepts him, grabbing him by the back of his belt and lifting him off the asphalt so that only his toes touch. Granby flails powerlessly as Marino uses his other hand to pat him down for a weapon, a pistol he finds in a shoulder holster under Granby's suit jacket. Marino hands the gun to Benton.

'I'll put you down when you quit tussling,' Marino lets Granby know sweetly.

'Get your fucking hands off me!' he screams, and his agents do nothing to intercede.

They stand back watching their boss's humiliation with blank expressions on their faces, smart enough to know which side to take, which isn't his anymore.

'Tell us who and where he is, Ed.' Benton gets close to him in my well-lit parking lot filled with white crime scene trucks. 'It's not Martin Lagos or you wouldn't be trying to get him indicted for murder and I suspect he's not around to defend himself and hasn't been since he disappeared. Did you help get rid of him or did his friend Daniel Mersa do it?'

Granby stares mutely at him from his tiptoe position. His arms and legs go completely still as if he's wilted and Marino sets him down squarely on his feet but keeps a grip on the back of his belt.

'Where is he?' Benton asks. 'Do you want him to murder someone else?'

Granby stares at him with dead eyes.

'You really don't give a shit, do you,' Benton says and I hear his disappointment again.

'Go to hell,' Granby says quietly, dully.

'You have a chance to make this right,' Benton says what I already know won't move any part of Ed Granby.

I know about desperation that turns hard and empty, then as cold as outer space. I know where it leads and I know where it ends.

44

A train whistle makes a mournful sound, disso-
nance in a minor key, somewhere to the west of
me.

It's a different train I hear on a distant rail
line, not the candy-apple-red circus train with
gold lettering that bakes brightly in a wintry
Florida sun on a switch of railroad tracks
flanking parking lots that as recently as last night
were crowded with people eager to be thrilled
and entertained by aerialists, acrobats, clowns,
animal trainers, and of course the lions, tigers,
camels, and most of all the elephants, smaller
than African ones but big, gray, and sad.

A homeless man named Jake who parks
himself behind the arena most days tells Lucy
and me the reason elephants sway from side to
side is they're trying to touch each other because
they're lonely and when granted wide-open
spaces they bark, growl, rumble, and trumpet as
they bump and nudge each other playfully like
children. They are good to their mothers and
take care of one another and can signal members
of their pack from great distances with vibrations
and odors that humans can't hear or smell.
Elephants are very intelligent and sensitive and
he's seen them cry.

If we allowed them to live freely the way Jake lives freely, our new friend says, we could utilize them to find water in the desert and detect sinkholes, earthquakes, tsunamis, and all sorts of danger, including evil people, and by following the example of the elephant we'd do better dealing with death. I've commented that it would be a very good thing if humans were more respectful of death and less afraid of it but I haven't mentioned to Jake what I do for a living or that I have good reason to know what I'm talking about.

I have yet to hint that my niece and I are loitering behind the arena near the circus train because we're waiting for a detective friend and my FBI profiler husband to clear a rather ghastly scene, a killer's lair, which like the elephant's is a train car only elephants don't hurt anyone. Jake hasn't a clue that his two new snowbird acquaintances aren't in Miami simply to spend the holidays with family but are involved in the very homicide investigation that relates to the very circus he's had his eye on since he was born, according to him. I've said nothing and I won't.

I'd rather chat about elephants and he considers himself the keeper of them, claiming he's studied them when the circus is in town for as long as he's been disabled, which was 1985, when his charter boat was hit by a tanker in the middle of the night, breaking almost every bone in his body and requiring countless surgeries. The arena wasn't here in 1985 so I don't know if the story is true or if any of his stories are. But I believe what he says about elephants and the cold-blooded young man who performed acrobatic tricks on the backs of them until just yesterday when he was led away in handcuffs, escorted from the bright red train by a plainclothes posse that included Benton and Marino, whose pictures were in *The Boston Globe* and all over television this morning.

Quite small, almost as small as a child, and you'd think Daniel Mersa was one from the back until he turns around and you see his hard, narrow face and cruel gray eyes, as Jake has described the demented spectacle killer whose name he didn't know until Lucy showed him the *Globe* story that she displayed on her phone. Gavin Connors was honorable and didn't run his big scoop until Mersa was arrested and it's a stunning story, I have to say, and it's 'everywhere on the planet,' to quote Bryce, who has decided his reporter pal will 'win a Pulitzer' and Santa will bring Ed Granby 'an orange jumpsuit for Christmas' and Daniel Mersa 'will be extradited to Virginia so he can get the needle.'

'Never did like him,' Jake has continued to mutter with a shake of his head since we first started talking this morning. 'So that's his name, Mersa, like the staph infection. How'd they find him?'

'Computer software,' Lucy replies as if she had nothing to do with it while she hands out café con leches with extra shots. 'They have programs that can recognize people by their facial features. For example, if there's a photo in a college yearbook and the same person has recent ones out there because he's a performer with a circus. And then of course you can confirm with DNA and other evidence.'

'I don't use a computer. Never have.'

'It doesn't look like you need one.'

'I'm telling you I hated the little bastard the first time I laid eyes on him.' Jake says what he's said at least half a dozen times, sitting on the seawall where his old bicycle is parked. 'I'd see him out there with the elephant hook grabbing a back leg just right to get the tendon so it hurts like hell. And for no reason he'd slap them like this.' He slaps the air with a leathery hand. 'And squirt them right in the face with the hose, making the pressure really hard, and laughing.' He imitates that, too, spraying an imaginary hose.

'I wish I'd seen it,' Lucy says.

'I'd want to go right over the damn fence,' he points at the fenced-in area beyond us at the edge of the water, 'and go after him with the hook and see how he liked being gaffed in the back of the leg.'

'I would have helped you but I would have used more than the hook,' Lucy says and Jake is very pleased with her. And if it's possible to keep in touch with a man whose home is his bicycle and all that he carries on it, I suspect she will.

My niece and I need to be here right now for a lot of reasons, and as I wait for Benton this is the view I'm most comfortable with, shiny red train cars stretching for a mile between parking lots and the white pavement of Northeast 6th Street as it curves from the mainland and over the water to Watson Island and beyond. The red train I've seen so many times some fifteen hundred miles north of here in Cambridge is quiet for now with wide, sturdy metal ramps extended from open doors as workers finish loading up the Cirque d'Orleans.

All of its people and exotic creatures are headed out of Miami to the next stop in Orlando, then Atlanta, making their way back north again as if nothing has happened, as if there's nothing unusual about an FBI profiler and a Cambridge detective helping local law enforcement collect evidence inside the eighth train car from the end and from the big black SUV on a flatbed, which is how a lot of circus performers and staff haul their vehicles around from city to city, living on the rails.

Daniel Mersa's arrest was without his usual drama and that seemed poetic justice for a spectacle killer who most recently starred in a horror show in the Massachusetts countryside, slashing the throats of three people, including his biological father Dominic Lombardi. There was no need for the FBI agents from the Miami field office, no need for the Dade County cops in tactical gear who surrounded Daniel Mersa's train car. Benton and Marino would have been fine on their own.

I didn't see it happen. I heard the details later when Benton called me from the Federal Detention Center at the corner of Northeast 4th Street and North Miami Avenue just a few blocks from here. He said that Mersa was dazed and disoriented, rambling that he didn't want to be kidnapped by aliens before the Apocalypse. He wished to be left in peace to make his

510

pilgrimage to the Pyrenean village of Bugarach in southern France, known for its upside-down mountain and wooden tools and hats. His father had died suddenly several days before the world would end, bled to death by these same aliens who can't survive on earth if they don't steal blood, and Daniel had plenty of money to take anybody to Bugarach who wanted to go before it was too late.

And Marino, mixing up the Mayan end of the world with the Christian Rapture, said to him, 'Guess what, you fucking little piece of shit, it's already too late. December twenty-first was three days ago and you've been left behind.' He said he was turning Daniel over to these same aliens, who were waiting for him, hovering over Miami and ready to steal his blood and do even worse things to him, or words to that effect.

Benton cautioned Marino about making such statements to someone delusional — at least this was what Benton reported to me over the phone while Lucy and I dealt with my mother and my sister Dorothy in Coral Gables, where we stayed last night. Benton and I talked on and off while I did what I've always done in the land of my birth. I cooked and cleaned, decorated for the holidays, and made sure everyone was all right, and I slept alone in the second bedroom while Lucy took the couch. I will see Benton soon enough. All of us will be together and we'll work our way through the awful things that have happened, all of them beginning with Connecticut and ending here, as much as anything ends.

★　★　★

Lucy and I wait by the seawall behind the arena, what's been called the American Airlines Arena for as long as I can recall. But it wasn't here when I was growing up and the Cirque d'Orleans would pitch a huge tent in the same spot near the switch of tracks where the long red train would park.

Behind us is the Bongos Cuban Café, with its glass dome on top that's shaped like a pineapple, and at close to three p.m. we've just now feasted on stuffed green plantains, roasted pork, and vegetarian rice while Jake was happy with a grilled fish sandwich. To our left the variegated blue water of the Biscayne Bay surrounds the Miami port, where cruise ships are lined up like small white cities, and directly in front of us on the other side of a fence is the circus's tent city, which really isn't a tent city but that's what it's called because it was called that in the old days when there really was a tent.

I calculate it's about ten acres of grass and coconut palms, and white trailers and trucks are arranged like a city of sorts whenever the circus sets up camp here for a few days and then moves on. There is a penned-in area for the elephants to be 'let out,' Jake has explained, but I can't see them now and I find myself looking even though I know I won't see them anymore.

When we first got here early this morning we watched police close off Biscayne Boulevard in front of the arena, completely blocking off traffic between Northeast 6th and 8th Streets, so the

512

elephants could walk their methodical walk, tail to trunk, from the fenced-in area through an empty parking lot and onto NE 6th, where they were slowly herded toward the train tracks and one by one up ramps and into awaiting cars.

Lucy and I were transfixed by the great pachyderms on a public promenade that they may have been indifferent to or not minded or hated. No one really knows because any signals they might have sent to one another we couldn't hear or smell. In awed silence we stood off to one side of the small cheering crowd and for some reason the sight of the huge lumbering land animals brought tears to my eyes that I discreetly dabbed away and blamed on the glare of the subtropical sun low over the bay.

I found myself having to blink often and breathe deeply as I watched them move heavily past until I couldn't see them anymore, and then I wandered back to the seawall where Lucy and I sit with Jake, who I find a pleasant comfort as we chat in the breeze off the water, the sun warm on my hair and the thin long-sleeved shirt and pants I wear. We've been happily resurrecting a past both of us remember well since we're close to the same age. And while I've not lived outdoors most of my adult life, we have much in common, both of us children in Miami once, both of us feeling a bit like elephants in an overbuilt world that doesn't understand much.

When I was growing up here and the circus came to town, the elephants would make a longer, more drawn out parade on the boulevard for the benefit of a massive crowd, and the entire world would stop, or so I thought. I've described things like this to Lucy because I want her to hear more about the past she's from even if she didn't live it. Before my father was too sick he took me to watch the elephants, I've explained, and I can still see their measured gait as they slowly plodded along, these massive gray creatures with patchy brown hair and crinkly small eyes and round, drooping ears carried on pillar-like feet, each elephant curling its trunk around the tail of the one in front as if they were holding hands to cross the street.

Today there was but a small straggle of spectators along the short segment of the boulevard closed to traffic, a few police cars and traffic cops in vests, and I doubt anyone had any idea at all why a young athletic-looking woman and with an older, less athletic-looking one were standing silently alone in poignant wonder. Then we retreated without a word to the seawall where the homeless man we hadn't met yet was stripping palm fronds into wire thin ribbons that by now he's fashioned into a lizard, a fish, a grasshopper, and a bird. I gave him twenty dollars for the grasshopper and that's when I found out his name is Jake — not the grasshopper but the man who created it.

He has trash bags filled with his belongings in the baskets of his dented blue bicycle leaning against the railing of the seawall and just now he points out a dolphin charging after a fish, a streak of silvery gray underwater that ripples on top, and then I see the gray rolling curves before the bottlenose breaks the surface and it seems he's laughing at his good fortune of having the small fish he holds in his mouth, throwing it back as if he's going to toss it like a ball, and I smile at such a happy mammal.

Jake has watched the dolphins and the elephants for many years, as many years as he's lived outdoors in a Florida sun that has weathered his skin to the texture of old brown leather, his graying blond hair tied back in a ponytail, scars and tattoos all over his sinewy arms. His eyes are almost the same blue as the shallow water in the bay, a light greenish blue that turns a deeper aqua when he turns philosophical and digs into his memories and offers his opinions.

'What are you doing for Christmas?' I ask him as I look at the latest photographs Benton has texted me, those of Daniel Mersa's train car, where he's lived for his past eight years on the road with the circus.

'I don't do much.' Jake reaches for a bundle of coconut palm strips upright in a basket of his bicycle. 'Every day's the same. It's all about the weather.'

'Why don't you eat with us?'

'I could make an angel because that's what both of you are,' Jake says. 'But I think they're boring.'

'I'm not an angel,' Lucy says and truer words were never spoken.

'What about a hibiscus flower?'

'My aunt's a pretty good cook,' Lucy says.

'*Pretty* good?' I don't look up from my phone, cupping my hand over it so the sun doesn't white out the display.

45

The train car looks like a one-bedroom trailer, and the photographs Benton texts show a single bed, a couch, a coffee table, several lamps, a TV and a kitchenette, very tidy and clean and unremarkable except for the masks.

'You should have Christmas dinner with us,' Lucy encourages Jake as he weaves palm strips together, the long, narrow green ribbons shiny side up and flashing as they whip in the bright sun.

The ceramic masks are displayed on stationary stands attached to a shelf high up on the wall, seven faces that in the spectral bandwidth of the nonvisible black light mounted over them shimmer iridescently. Bloodred, emerald green, bluish purple. Seven faces of seven women, only four Benton recognizes, he writes to me. The Washington, D.C., victims and, most recently, Gail Shipton.

'He's killed before,' Benton's next text lands.

'In Coral Gables,' Lucy says to Jake.

'I used to go to the Venetian Pool when I was a kid,' he replies as the hibiscus flower takes shape in his quick fingers. 'The Gables are so expensive, nobody can live there anymore.'

'Where my grandmother used to live?' Lucy says. 'A neighborhood off Seventy-ninth.'

'The worst street in Miami. I never go there.'

'It didn't used to be. We had to move her.'

'To the Gables,' Jake considers. 'I never go there. Too much money but that was a nice thing to do. Nobody's grandmother should be a victim of crime.'

'I'd worry about the other guy,' Lucy says and Jake guffaws.

'Maybe Lucy can try facial recognition on 3 masks you don't recognize,' I type to Benton. 'Are there women missing & presumed murdered from cities where circus performs? If so compare masks to them?'

'Or victims could be women DL wanted out of the way,' Benton answers. 'Could go back years.'

DL is Dominic Lombardi and the theory is that while he may have asked his troublesome sociopathic biological son to get rid of an occasional inconvenient human being like Klara Hembree, he never intended for Daniel Mersa to kill people for fun. But you get what you get, I always say. Benton believes Daniel was helping distribute the drugs that have been his downfall. Methylenedioxypyrovalerone. MDPV. Bath salts the organized criminals of Double S were getting from Chinese laboratories and distributing in cities across America including Cambridge.

'He would have had his car up north recently,' Benton continues to inform me of what's going on. 'Circus was in Boston early December then Brooklyn before going back south. SUV travels on flatbed & he has it wherever circus stops.'

Daniel Mersa's Suburban would seat nine if he hadn't taken out all of the seats except the two up front and I saw those pictures yesterday.

A partition covered in black carpet is between the front and back and behind it is his studio, an empty plyboard space painted black and lined with soundproofing insulation where he suffocated his victims and made death masks of air-drying clay before posing the bodies in just the right position. One arm stretched out and cocked at the wrist, the way Gabriela Lagos's right arm looked after he drowned her in her tub, and then he draped the body in a long white cloth reminiscent of a big white bath sheet.

The clay would set as rigor mortis did and he'd dress his latest victim in the panties of a previous one. And when he arrived at the location he picked he'd drag his morbid cargo on a bamboo stretcher that he kept in the back of his murdermobile, as Marino calls it. He and Benton have recovered colorful Lycra body socks, plastic bags from the Octopus spa shop, the designer duct tape, and several stun guns and dozens of cartridges, and white aerial silks, which also are made of Lycra. The long special fabrics are the stock-in-trade of performers like Daniel who fall, swing and suspend themselves from these silks and use them to fly through the air as they strike daring poses that thrill and amaze their audiences.

Also recovered from Daniel's possession are hundreds of violent pornographic recordings, including ones of Gabriela Lagos bathing lewdly while her son Martin watched with his broken arm from the closed lid of the toilet, and there are also several recorded minutes of her being drowned by Daniel Mersa. Over the years he transferred his film library to DVDs, and more recently his iPad, and he had quite a collection of stories and recordings about notorious violent offenders, including ones Benton has written about.

There can be no question who the Capital Murderer is and exactly what he's done but it continues to perplex me that his circus associates never questioned the strange reconfiguring of his SUV or the gaudy, shimmering ceramic masks inside the train car he's lived in for years. But then the world he inhabits isn't exactly a normal one, as he dresses in costumes, sometimes painting his face, before stepping into the ring to somersault onto horses or do backflips off elephants or hang and spin perilously from silks, ropes, and hoops or roll inside a human-sized hamster ball.

'I can come pick you up if you tell me where.' Lucy is still trying to talk Jake into eating Christmas dinner with us. 'You won't have much fun with Grans and would be best served to totally ignore my mother.'

'Well, that's quite an enticement,' I remark as I look toward the red train where Benton and Marino are finishing up.

'Okay,' Jake says and he presents Lucy with his green woven flower, which is as close to looking like a hibiscus as something is going to get if it's crafted from strips of a coconut palm frond. 'You can pick me up here any time as long as you can fit my bike.'

'I can fit it. But I need a time.'

'I mostly tell it from the sun.'

'What time are we eating Christmas dinner, Aunt Kay?'

'It depends on my mother.'

'Everything depends on Grans,' Lucy says as an eye-rolling aside.

'I'm here most of the time so it doesn't matter to me.' Jake has something on his mind he won't say. 'Tomorrow's Christmas, I guess. I wouldn't have thought about it. Everything for me is the weather. It's all about where I go if it's raining hard and I don't like lightning.'

'They're coming.' I get up from the seawall.

'The Red Coats?' Jake jokes but it's as if a cloud has passed across the sun, his face shadowed by a wistfulness I can't interpret.

'Marino wants baby back ribs.' I read the message from him that just landed. 'He wants to know where to go. I recommend Shorty's on South Dixie Highway.' I type my response as I talk.

'Janet can pick it up,' Lucy says.

'Marino will want to. Lighted beer signs, wagon wheels, cow skulls, and saddles everywhere. It's his kind of place. We may never see him again.'

'I know where you can get the freshest fish you've ever put in your mouth,' Jake says and then I understand what's happening with him.

'I'm in the mood for conch but it has to be just out of the shell and in cold salt water.' I see Benton and Marino walking away from the long red train, heading toward us. 'And yellowtail on the grill with a simple Japanese marinade, very light is all that's needed if the fish is fresh,' I say to Jake as if I'm giving him my order.

'You just follow Sixth Street to the Miami River. Not even ten minutes from here.'

'Can you show me?' I ask even though I know my way around.

'Sure I can,' he says.

★   ★   ★

My mother's house is a twenty-minute drive from downtown when traffic is reasonable as it is right now.

Benton and Marino will meet us after they've picked up ribs, slaw, corn on the cob, and whatever else Marino decides to order at Shorty's, a famous Texas-style barbecue restaurant with a big chimney in back that may have been the only thing left standing when the place burnt to the ground in the early seventies. I'd been to the original a few times when I was growing up, usually on my birthday, when my father's health was good and he was still making a living at his small grocery store.

I follow Granada Boulevard deeper into Coral Gables where the foliage is old and lush, with ivy draping coral walls that go back to the 1920s and tall privacy hedges of lady palm and dense barriers of natal plum, with its fragrant white pinwheel flowers and sharp, spiny branches. The names of the narrow, quiet streets are painted in black on white curbstones and the white pavement is shaded by huge pin oaks with dense canopies and ficus trees with thick, ropy roots that crack roads, sidewalks, swimming pools, and penetrate plumbing.

Homes here range from small gems to villas and columned mansions, and the small rich city of some fifty thousand is where we used to sightsee at this very time of year when my father was well enough to drive us around to look at Christmas decorations that used to be far more outrageous than I've seen so far. I remember winterland scenes of snowmen and life-sized Santas in sleighs with reindeer on rooftops and so many lights that the illumination could be seen for miles away. My father's car was a 1950 Chevrolet, white, with bumper wings and fender skirts, and I remember the smell of the fabric upholstery when it got hot in the sun while riding with my window cranked down.

My mother's house wouldn't be on any Christmas tour, with its electric candles in the windows and the small potted lemon cedar I found at a Whole Foods grocery store. Left to her own devices she doesn't lift a finger to decorate or cook, and my sister usually hires somebody to do such things, depending on the financial status of her *hombre del dia*, as Lucy and I refer to whoever she's dating on any given day. At least my mother won't bat an eye when we show up with a homeless man we've invited for dinner — or maybe several dinners. She's never forgotten what it is to be poor while Dorothy has no memory of it and is to the manner born, if you have the misfortune of witnessing the experience of her, which I don't wish on anyone.

I take a left on Milan Avenue and my mother's

house is on the corner, built of white stucco, with a red barrel tile roof and a one-car garage that conceals the Honda sedan I wish she'd no longer drive. I see the slatted wooden blinds move in a front window, which is my mother's hallmark way of checking who's arrived, even though I've told her countless times that once she's made it obvious she's home it's a little more difficult not to answer the door. Of course Lucy and I made sure she has a peephole and an alarm system that includes front and back cameras, but she doesn't check. She'd rather part slats in the blinds and peer out the same way she's done all of her long, hard life.

I pull into a driveway that's just long enough to tuck one car off the street and Lucy, Jake, and I get out.

'Who did you bring?' my mother's voice precedes her as the front door opens a quarter of the way, another old habit. 'It's not that awful man everybody's after!'

'No, Mother,' I reply. 'He's been caught and is in jail.'

I open the door the rest of the way and my mother is in the same housedress she had on yesterday, white with big colorful flowers on it, and the big floral design makes her look wider and shorter and white makes her hair not as white and her skin more sallow. It does no good at all to say a word and I never do unless there's a question of hygiene and there rarely is, maybe a food stain she can't see or an odor her sense of smell won't pick up anymore.

'Why is Lucy dressed like that?' My mother

looks Lucy up and down as we file in with an ice chest full of fish.

'It's the same thing I had on this morning, Grans. Cargo shorts and a sweatshirt.'

'I don't know why you need all those pockets.'

'To shoplift just like you taught me. What happened to Janet and the dogs?'

'Doing potty in the backyard and she better pick it up. Three dogs? My house isn't big enough. And Quincy won't stop chewing things. Why would anyone name a dog after that silly TV show?'

'Where's Mom?'

'Getting her nails done. Maybe it's her hair. Who can keep up with her?'

'I doubt what's-his-name can keep it up with her,' Lucy says, 'he's so old and still eats like he's fat, won't be pretty when he pops that rubber band around his gullet. But he's rich, I guess. She's not bringing him over, is she?'

'This is Jake.' I introduce him inside the living room and take the ice chest from him.

'How do you do, ma'am?' He hands my mother a flower he made.

'Well, isn't that something. What is it?'

'It's a hibiscus like all those you've got growing in front of your house.'

'They aren't green. Do I need to put it in water?'

I carry the ice chest into my mother's small kitchen with its terrazzo floor and painting of Jesus praying in the garden next to the refrigerator, and for the next half hour I rinse tuna filets and mix a marinade of soy sauce, fresh chopped ginger, Japanese sweet cooking wine, sake, and canola oil. Placing the fish inside the refrigerator, I take out a cold bottle of a very nice Sancerre and when I pull out the cork I smell grapefruit and flowers, and I pour a glass and get started on the fritters.

'Can I help?' Janet is in the doorway, very blond with bright eyes and a touch of sun, Sock and Jet Ranger at her heels, and then Quincy barges in, banging me with his swinging tail.

'There's room for only one.' I smile at her. 'How about a glass of wine?'

'Not yet.'

'If you could take our friends with you, please.'

'Come on, Quincy. Let's go, gang.' She whistles at them and claps, and off they go.

I chop the tough conch meat, green pepper, celery, and garlic while I overhear voices in the living room of Lucy, Janet, my mother, and our guest chatting as if they've been friends for many years, and my mother's voice is louder the more deaf she gets. The hearing aids I bought for her usually stay on top of the bathroom counter near all of the various cleaning pastes and brushes she needs for her dentures. And when she's alone, which is most of the time, she wears the same housedress and doesn't care if she can hear or has teeth.

I squeeze Meyer's lemons and find the deep fryer in a cupboard when I hear the front door open again, and then I smell the baby back ribs Marino carries in, huge white bags with *Shorty's Bar-B-Q* on them in red with their logo of a cartoon cowboy wearing a ten-gallon hat that has a big bullet hole in it.

'Out, out, out.' I take the bags from Marino and shoo him out of a kitchen that can't possibly hold both of us. 'I don't think you bought enough.'

'I need a beer,' he says and that's when I catch the look on his face, and then a different look on Benton's face as he appears in the doorway.

'When you get to a stopping place,' Benton says to me and something has happened.

I dry my hands on a towel as I look at both of them in jeans and button-up shirts, their nondescript windbreakers hiding the pistols they carry. Marino's face is stubbly and pink from long days and the sun while Benton's looks the way it always does when something is wrong.

'What is it?'

'I'm surprised your office hasn't called,' Benton says.

I check my phone and there's an e-mail from Luke Zenner I didn't notice while I was buying fish and driving and then distracted by my mother. Luke writes that everything is under control and not to worry, he won't get started on the autopsy until later tonight when the Armed Forces chief medical examiner General Briggs is there. He's flying in from Dover Air Force Base to assist and act as a witness, and what a shitty thing to happen Christmas Eve. They'll take care of it and hopefully everyone can have tomorrow off. Have a nice holiday, Luke wishes me.

'It's better you're out of town anyway,' Benton informs me, and then he tells me what little he knows and there isn't much to know, really.

There rarely is when someone makes the simple decision to end life and end it easily.

Ed Granby waited until his wife had gone out to her spinning class today at around four p.m. and he locked all of the doors of their Brookline house, using the key on dead bolts that could be opened only from the inside so she couldn't get back in and find him first. Then he sent an e-mail to the assistant special agent in charge, a close friend, telling him to drive to the house right away and let himself in by breaking out a window in the basement.

Granby's e-mail has been forwarded to Benton and he shows it to me inside my mother's kitchen as oil heats in the deep fryer.

'Thanks, buddy,' Granby wrote. 'I'm done.'

He went down into the basement, looped a rope over the chin-up bar of a cable machine, wrapped a towel around his neck, sat on the floor, and hanged himself.

'Come on.' I turn off the deep fryer and grab the Sancerre and two glasses, and Benton and I walk out of the kitchen, past everyone in the living room, where piles of presents from my compulsive shopping are around the small tree.

My sister Dorothy has just arrived, wearing skintight faux-lizard designer pants, a low-cut leotard, and heavy makeup that make her look exactly the way she doesn't want to look, which is older, flabbier, with oversized augmented breasts as rigid and round as rubber balls.

'I believe I will.' She eyes the wine and I shake my head *Not now.* 'Well, excuse me, I guess I'll have to serve myself.'

'We only came down so we could wait on you,' Lucy says.

'As you should. I'm your mother.'

Lucy doesn't go after her the way she usually would, her eyes on Benton and me as I open the back door and feel the pleasantness of the late afternoon and see the long shadows in my mother's small yard, not the yard from my childhood, and I always remind myself of that when I come here and don't recognize anything, not the plantings or the house or the furniture, everything new or redone and soulless.

The grass is thick and springy beneath my feet, and the air is cool as it blows through old grapefruit and orange trees still heavy with fruit. We sit in webbed lawn chairs near the rock garden, with its palms and small statues — an angel, the Blessed Mother, a lamb — amid sunflowers and firecracker plants.

'So that's what he does to his family the day before Christmas.' I pour wine and give Benton a glass. 'I'm not sorry for him. I'm sorry for them.'

I lean back and close my eyes, and for an instant I see the key lime tree my mother had in her backyard when I was growing up. The citrus canker got it and it's not the same part of town and not the same yard, and Benton reaches for my hand and laces his fingers through mine. The sun smolders a fiery orange over the low, flat roof of a neighbor's house and we don't talk. There's nothing to say and nothing that's happened is a surprise, and so we are quiet as we drink and hold hands.

When most of the wine is gone and the yard is

in the shade, the sun too low to see, only a tangerine hint in the lower part of the darkening sky, he tells me he knew Granby was going to kill himself.

'I figured he might,' I reply.

'I knew it when Marino lifted him off the pavement by the back of his belt,' he says. 'I could see it in Granby's eyes that something important was gone that was never coming back.'

'Nothing was ever there to come back.'

'But I saw it and I didn't do anything.'

'What would you have done?' I look at his sharp profile in the early dusk.

'Nothing,' he decides.

We get up to go inside because it's getting chilly and if I drink much more, I won't be safe with the deep fryer or the grill or anything.

Benton puts his arm around me and I wrap mine around his waist and the thick grass makes a dry sound as we walk on it. The grapefruit this year are huge and pale yellow and the oranges are big and pebbly and the wind rocks the trees as we move through a yard I pay to keep up but rarely sit in.

'Let's get Dorothy to talk about herself so we won't have to talk about anything at all,' I suggest as we climb the three steps that lead to the door.

'That will be the easiest thing we've ever done,' Benton says.

We do hope that you have enjoyed reading
this large print book.

Did you know that all of our titles
are available for purchase?

We publish a wide range of high quality
large print books including:
Romances, Mysteries, Classics
General Fiction
Non Fiction and Westerns

Special interest titles available in
large print are:
The Little Oxford Dictionary
Music Book
Song Book
Hymn Book
Service Book

Also available from us courtesy of
Oxford University Press:
Young Readers' Dictionary
(large print edition)
Young Readers' Thesaurus
(large print edition)

For further information or a free
brochure, please contact us at:
Ulverscroft Large Print Books Ltd.,
The Green, Bradgate Road, Anstey,
Leicester, LE7 7FU, England.
Tel: (00 44) **0116 236 4325**
Fax: (00 44) **0116 234 0205**

Other titles published by
The House of Ulverscroft:

ALL THAT REMAINS

Patricia Cornwell

When the bodies of young courting couples start turning up in remote woodland areas, Dr Kay Scarpetta's task as Chief Medical Examiner is made more difficult by the effects of the elements. Eight times she must write that the cause of death is undetermined. However, when the daughter of one of the most powerful women in America goes missing, Kay becomes prey to political pressure and press harassment. She finds that vital evidence is being withheld from her — or even faked — and all the time a sadistic killer is still at large . . .

BODY OF EVIDENCE

Patricia Cornwell

Someone is stalking reclusive writer Beryl Madison, spying on her and making threatening, obscene 'phone calls. Terrified, Beryl flees to Key West, but eventually returns to her Richmond home. The very night she arrives, Beryl inexplicably invites her killer in . . . Thus begins for Chief Medical Examiner Dr. Kay Scarpetta the investigation of a crime as convoluted as it is bizarre. Beginning in the laboratory with microscopes and lasers, Scarpetta is led deep into a nightmare that soon becomes her own.

POSTMORTEM

Patricia Cornwell

A serial killer is on the loose in Richmond, Virginia; three women have died, brutalised and strangled in their own bedrooms. The killer always strikes early on Saturday mornings, so when Chief Medical Examiner, Dr. Kay Scarpetta, is awakened in the early hours, she knows the news is that there is a fourth victim. She realises she must dig up new forensic evidence, but not everyone is pleased to see a woman in this powerful job, and someone may even want to ruin her career and reputation.

UNTIL YOU'RE MINE

Samantha Hayes

Claudia seems to have the perfect life. Heavily pregnant with a much-wanted first baby, she has a ready-made family in the form of two small step-sons, a loving husband and a beautiful home. But she is also committed to her full-time job as a social worker. So when Zoe arrives to help her, it seems like the answer to a prayer. Except that, despite Zoe's recommendations as a nanny, there's something about her that Claudia does not trust. And when she finds Zoe in her bedroom, going through her clothes and reading her papers, Claudia's initial anxiety turns to fear. Meanwhile, vicious attacks on pregnant women are taking place, and Claudia becomes acutely aware of just how vulnerable she is . . .